Julia Stephenson was born and raised in Surrey. After leaving the Lucie Clayton College she had stints as a professional cook, a chalet girl and a housewife. She is now a full-time writer. When she is not working she enjoys travelling and moving house, and is a student of Buddhism and *feng shui*. PANDORA'S DIAMOND is her first novel.

PANDORA'S DIAMOND

Julia Stephenson

HEADLINE

First published in 1997 by
HEADLINE BOOK PUBLISHING

First published in paperback in 1997 by
HEADLINE BOOK PUBLISHING

10 9 8 7 6 5 4 3 2 1

ISBN 0 7472 5444 3

Typeset by Palimpsest Book Production Limited,
Polmont, Stirlingshire
Printed and bound in Great Britain by
Caledonian International Book Manufacturing Ltd, Glasgow

HEADLINE BOOK PUBLISHING
A division of Hodder Headline PLC
338 Euston Road
London NW1 3BH

For my parents

Acknowledgements

Many people and places have helped and inspired me to write this novel. My thanks to everyone at Headline, especially Diane Rowley, my *shoten zenjin*! My editor, Jane Morpeth, for her excellent advice and enthusiasm. Nigel Pendrigh, of Pendrigh Computers, for his patience and genius and for saving Pandora from certain destruction in the labyrinth of my wilful computer which has never quite recovered from being dropped from a great height at Zurich Station. For heavenly Switzerland, whose soaring mountains and soothing valleys gave me the space to write when the fleshpots of London became too distracting . . . To Jan Cisek, for his excellent *feng shui* advice – the red towels really worked! To Bisley Office Furniture for all its help and for furnishing my 'office'. And of course to the Soka Gakkai, the lay organization of Nichiren Daishonin's Buddhism through which I found the determination, grit and courage to turn my dream into reality and for showing me that the diamond was inside all the time . . . Nam Myoho Renge Kyo!

More valuable than treasures in a storehouse are the treasures of the body, and the treasures of the heart are the most valuable of all. From the time you read this letter on, strive to accumulate the treasures of the heart!

From 'The Three Kinds of Treasure'
The Major Writings of Nichiren Daishonin, volume 2.

Prologue

The Wedding

The white helicopter circled the steep hill, hovering over the ancient church. Pandora pulled down her veil and glanced at her father who was sitting, ashen-faced and tight-lipped beside her.

'Is everything OK?' He was speaking into a mobile phone to the chief usher, presumably located within the church porch. 'Right, we're *going in*.'

'Really, Daddy, you make us sound like the SAS or something.'

'I should think the Gulf War was a piece of cake to organize compared to this wedding,' grumbled James, 'and probably a lot cheaper.'

'Well, at least no one's going to die today,' smiled Pandora happily as the helicopter landed on a small patch of wasteland behind the church, narrowly avoiding a Portaloo that had been specially erected for the occasion.

'Don't speak too soon!' said James grimly.

Pandora slid out of the helicopter, straight into a pool

of mud despite the attentive ministrations of the chief usher. It was raining steadily now and freezing cold, but she felt marvellously happy. Annabel, her bridesmaid, came rushing out of the church to greet her, shivering. 'Pandora, you look gorgeous!' she yelled over the roar of the helicopter. 'It's such a shame about the weather. *Oh no!*' The girls watched in disbelief as Annabel's headdress blew clean off her head, resting for a moment on the Portaloo before being whisked into the trees.

'Hurry up!' yelled James. 'We'll look for it later.' And the small mud-spattered group hastily made their way to the porch, composing themselves as the Bridal March echoed around the church.

'We're *going in*!' whispered Pandora to Annabel who was running her fingers anxiously through her sodden blonde hair.

'Good luck!' she replied.

And they were off, James staring grimly ahead as if he was about to face his execution, Pandora wreathed in smiles and displaced foliage, greeting all her friends.

'Pretty gel, shame she's got a hedge growing out of her head,' mumbled an elderly person, whom no one was quite able to place, in a deceptively hushed voice that carried around the church.

Coriander Angelica, London's leading florist, famous for her avant-garde headdresses, frowned irritably.

'Slow down, slow down!' hissed Pandora, longing for her fifteen seconds of fame to last for ever. 'Hi, Mummy!' Georgina was sitting in the front pew, looking tanned and glamorous in a Jasper Conran creation. Beside her sat Davina, Pandora's godmother, her glossy dark hair swept up beneath an elegant Frederick Fox hat. Pandora glanced around. Ah, there was Daniel. Gosh, he looked handsome.

Within seconds father and daughter had reached the altar where John was waiting patiently for his bride. Pandora grinned at him through her gauzy veil. 'How're you?' she whispered, trying hard not to giggle with nerves.

Half an hour later, rings exchanged, troth plighted and love declared, the guests surged out into the drizzle, congratulating Pandora and John who stood shivering in the rain having their photographs taken. Duty done, everyone dived with relief into the Range Rovers, arranged with military precision outside the church, that were to whisk them away to the grand stately home where the reception was to be held.

'Such a shame about the rain,' said one, climbing into the car.

'All that money and they can't fix the weather,' laughed someone else.

'Bad omen,' grumbled another, glancing at his mud-splattered shoes.

'What an *unusual* wedding,' said a friend to Georgina as the family lined up to receive their guests. 'And what *interesting* music.'

'Yes, it was my daughter's idea to have "Fool on the Hill". She's a great Beatles fan.'

'I wonder who the fool was?' asked Daniel, shaking Georgina's hand.

'You'll have to ask Pandora,' laughed Georgina.

'It was probably me,' said James. 'I should never have allowed Pandora to choose the church, but she's wilful, like her mother.' Georgina smiled icily and turned to greet the next guest.

'Who *are* all these people in brown suits?' muttered Lord Henry Verney to Georgina, his daughter, frowning at a group of men chatting in unintelligible Cumbrian accents. 'And beards too! I don't know what your mother will say.'

Georgina smiled, he had said exactly the same at her own wedding to James thirty years ago. Except that James's relatives had spoken in South London accents, not Cumbrian. But James had stood out from the rest of his relatives; even then there was something that set him apart. A sort of charisma, a presence. She fumbled for a cigarette, glancing around the huge banqueting hall. They were being summoned into dinner now but Davina and James were sitting in a corner smoking, laughing at something. It was obvious from their body language that they were old friends. James was leaning towards her, Georgie could see the silver Dunhill lighter flash in the candlelight as he lit Davina's cigarette. Georgie had given it to him on their first wedding anniversary. She wondered if he remembered. She turned away, a lump in her throat. If only things had worked out differently.

There was a discreet cough behind her. It was John. 'Mrs Peronista? Shall we go and sit down?'

Georgina smiled at him. 'Do call me Georgina. Mr Peronista disappeared a long time ago.' She laughed,

John smiled. He could never think of anything to say to Pandora's mother. She was very attractive but she reminded him a bit of Patsy in *Absolutely Fabulous*. Although Pandora took after her physically, that was where the resemblance ended, thank goodness.

'Look at your father and Davina,' Annabel was saying to Pandora. 'Talk about chemistry. Even their smoking is synchronized. Are you sure they're not bonking?'

'Not now, but they used to years ago,' said Pandora. She smiled at John and Georgina as they found their places at the top table. 'How are your parents enjoying it?' she asked John, peering anxiously at her father who was reluctantly taking his place next to John's mother, radiant in red crimplene and wreathed in smiles. James caught her eye and grimaced. John intercepted the look and winced. 'Your father seems to be getting on well with Mummy,' said Pandora, sipping her champagne cheerfully. Her face was flushed with excitement and tendrils of blonde hair kept falling out of her complex hair arrangement. John's heart swelled with pride.

'You look stunning,' he said quietly. 'I'm the proudest man in this room.'

But his voice was drowned out by the toast master crying, 'Ladies and gentlemen! Please be seated,' and Pandora didn't hear him. She was busy trying to place the elderly lady who had been so loud in church about her headdress. She was sure she had spotted her the day before in Maidenhead going through a rubbish skip.

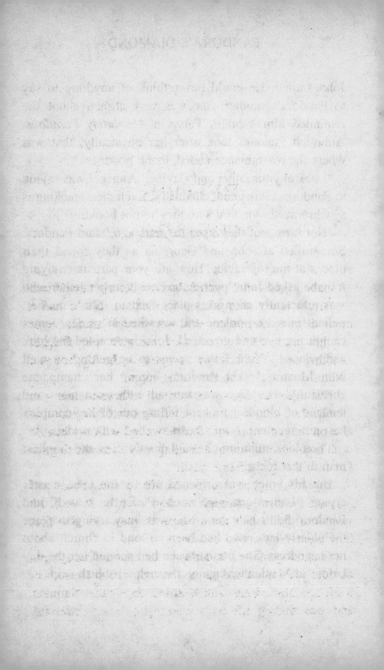

BEFORE

Chapter One

'Annabel, I'm home!' called Pandora, letting herself into the small house they shared in Chelsea. She'd had a tiring day and there were shadows beneath her blue eyes and her pretty heart-shaped face was pale with fatigue. She dropped three bags of shopping in the kitchen and collapsed on a chair in the sitting room.

'I've been arranging flowers all afternoon and I'm absolutely exhausted,' murmured Annabel lying immobile on the sofa opposite. She was a tall willowy blonde with high cheekbones and slanting grey eyes which gave her face a slightly feline quality.

'So am I,' sighed Pandora, kicking off her shoes and running her hands through her hair wearily. It needed a wash but she hadn't the strength to blow dry it before they were due out that evening.

'Tough day in the lift, darling?' asked Annabel sympathetically. Pandora had taken a summer job at Harrods as a lift operator, along with Beatrice, their other flatmate, and was finding life as a working girl very stressful.

Annabel had recently been sacked from the same position for spending more time in Way In, gossiping to old school friends, than in her lift, leaving Pandora and Beatrice to sweat it out alone.

'Any interesting punters today?' asked Annabel, drawing up her legs beneath her in anticipation of a juicy chat.

Pandora grimaced. 'A man wearing a poncho tried to get in this morning, can you believe it!'

'What did you do?'

'I cut him in half of course and told him to go away and try another lift.' Pandora insisted on a strict dress code. 'Sophie wouldn't let him into hers either so he had to use the stairs.'

'Quite right too,' agreed Annabel firmly.

'I thought being a lift operator might be quite glamorous,' said Pandora, 'sort of like Shirley Maclaine in that movie where she falls in love with Jack Lemmon. I thought we'd wear white gloves and snappy suits, not horrible old green overalls with Horrids blazoned all over them. It's so degrading.'

A key sounded in the lock and Beatrice staggered in, looking shattered. She shrugged off her dark green cashmere coat and undid a green, gold and black Hermès scarf that set off her shiny chestnut hair and greenish hazel eyes beautifully. Today she was wearing a smart black suit that was a fraction too tight around her full hips and bust but which showed off her slim waist to perfection. Beatrice waged an unreliable battle with her weight and frequently complained she only had to look at a yogurt to jump from a C to a D cup. Her curves were a source of great envy to Annabel and Pandora, who, as a result of the confused state of their love lives, were whippet thin.

'Tough day, old thing?' asked Annabel. 'Really, you two should pack it in. It's not doing your looks any good. And remember, we've all been asked to dinner at the urchins tonight, they're having a party for their new flatmate. Wonder what he's like.' The urchins were a group of old Etonians who shared a house in Notting Hill and whose impeccable social origins didn't prevent them living in total squalor.

'I hadn't forgotten,' said Beatrice. 'I remembered to buy some Ajax for them.' Beatrice was Swiss-German and took cleanliness very seriously. Annabel and Pandora had grown up in large houses where cleaning was thankfully someone else's responsibility and Beatrice's cleaning rotas were a source of great amusement.

'I know they said bring a bottle, but they meant a bottle of plonk, not a bottle of cleaning fluid,' said Pandora, getting up. It was time to get changed.

The house belonged to Pandora so she had the largest and sunniest bedroom at the top. Clothes, make-up and old magazines lay scattered all over it. Annabel followed her in. 'Would you like an opportunity to reveal your generosity, Pandora?'

'Not particularly,' said Pandora. 'I suppose you want to borrow my red dress.' She rummaged around underneath the bed.

'Gosh, have you been tidying up in here?' asked Annabel. 'You put me to shame, my room looks ten times worse. I keep going in and expecting someone to have cleaned it up for me but no one ever has.' She gazed with interest at the heaving contents of a three-month-old cup of coffee which Pandora had just discovered beneath her bed.

'Here it is,' said Pandora, reappearing with a skimpy piece of red material. 'I'm afraid I haven't had time to wash it for a while.'

'Oh, don't worry, I'll spray lots of scent on it.'

'Isn't it a bit dressy for the urchins?'

'Yes, but I've got a hot date with Rufus after dinner.' Rufus was the lead singer of the Funky Donuts and he and Annabel had been conducting a passionate affair for the last two months, despite the fact that Annabel was unofficially engaged to Hugo Wolvaston, heir to the Earl of Wolvaston, who stood to inherit a vast estate and the most valuable privately owned art collection in England.

'Would Hugo kill you if he found out?' asked Pandora.

'Probably not. He's more interested in his beagles than in me. Besides, he's living in Cumbria, I'm in London, Rufus is in London – and when the cat's away the mouse will play.'

Both girls giggled. 'Maybe I should find a lover,' said Pandora. 'I can't *believe* I'm twenty-one and still a virgin.'

'Neither can I,' replied Annabel who had lost her virginity at fifteen and had never looked back. 'I don't know what's wrong with Joshua. Are you sure he's not gay or something?'

'No, I don't think so. He just says he respects me too much.'

'Huh!' Annabel flicked back her hair derisively. 'I'll just slip this slinky number on and then we ought to leave.'

'The flat's looking *interesting*,' said Pandora, gazing round the urchins' sitting room.

'Glad you like it,' said Rupert who was training to be a lawyer. His T-shirt read 'SEX IS EVIL/EVIL IS SIN/SIN IS FORGIVEN/ SO GET STUCK IN'. All the pictures in the room had been taken down and replaced by rows of dead grouse hanging off the walls in varying stages of decomposition. 'Felix went shooting last weekend,' explained Rupert. 'We're cooking some of them tonight.'

Beatrice wrinkled her nose dubiously.

'Girls, girls, how lovely to see you all!' Felix emerged from the kitchen followed by Harry and John, and a dense cloud of smoke. 'You haven't met John yet, have you? He was at Bristol too. You'll all be very impressed to know he was the captain of the university rugby team.' Through the smoke a tall sandy-haired figure grinned broadly at them. The three girls tossed back their hair and smiled encouragingly.

'I'm afraid there's been a bit of a setback with dinner. The recipe basically didn't deliver.'

'He means we burnt it, basically,' said John.

'Third degree burns, I'm afraid. But John has kindly agreed to share his speciality with us instead.'

'What's that?' smiled Annabel.

'Um, cheese on toast with peanuts sprinkled on top.'

'But you don't have a grill,' Pandora pointed out.

'John's a very ingenious cook,' said Harry. 'He's going to make it in the toaster. Come into the kitchen and help if you like.'

'All right,' said Beatrice, 'but we're not washing up. I brought you this, by the way.' She handed Felix the Ajax scouring powder.

'Thank you *so* much,' he said, kissing her hand extravagantly.

They trooped into the kitchen where John was tearing foil off packets of Dairy Lea processed cheese and smearing them on sliced white bread. 'You put the toaster on its side like this and just slide the bread in. It makes a bit of a mess in the toaster but it tastes really nice.' As he handed round slices, he explained he had just started working for a merchant bank.

'So where were you living before you moved in, John?' Pandora asked, pouring ketchup on her dinner.

'I was in Cumbria, studying for my exams.'

'That's where his people live,' explained Harry.

'Oh, then you must know my boyfriend, Hugo – Hugo Wolvaston?' said Annabel.

John looked blank. 'No, I don't think I do.'

'But if you live in Cumbria you must be neighbours. I mean, hardly anyone lives there.' In Annabel's world everyone of a certain class knew one another within a radius of at least fifty miles.

''Fraid not,' said John. 'Anyone fancy seconds?'

'No thanks. I've got to go to work in a minute,' said Rupert, slinging on his jacket.

'Rupert's on the game,' said John drily. 'On second thoughts, who'd pay to have sex with him?'

'Oh, don't be mean,' laughed Beatrice, loosening her skirt and helping herself to some more wine. 'What are you really up to, Rupert?'

'I'm supplementing my meagre income as a barrister by cabbing in South London. It's a real bore. By the way, I've just discovered an amusing little restaurant off the Portobello Road. If you get there before eight in the evening they give you three courses for a fiver. I'm meeting some friends there tomorrow if anyone wants to come along.'

'Sounds horrible,' said Pandora, covertly removing a hair from her toasted cheese and peanut sandwich. 'I don't know how you can live in Notting Hill.'

'Well, you're welcome to live in Chelsea. As far as I'm concerned it's a rich man's ghetto,' retorted Rupert bitterly. Happily, the dwindling remains of his trust fund made this impossible.

'Anyone seen my tuck box?' Rupert peered in the fridge.

Everybody groaned. Rupert was famous for trawling wedding receptions for leftover hors d'oeuvres – pineapple chunks, breaded prawns, smoked salmon roulade – which he would compress into a large ice-cream container to make a terrine. Slices of this mixture kept him going for weeks.

'Some thieving rascal's pinched it!' accused Rupert. He snapped open his briefcase. 'Ah, here it is.'

Annabel glanced at her watch. 'Rupert, can you give

me a lift to Clapham? Rufus is playing tonight and I'm meeting him when he finishes.' She sighed happily. 'Don't wait up for me,' she called to Pandora and Beatrice as she followed Rupert out to his car.

'We'd better make a move too.' Beatrice was starting to get terrible indigestion.

'Yes, we must,' agreed Pandora readily. She was feeling very queasy indeed. 'It was a lovely supper. Very original!' She and Beatrice gathered up their things hurriedly. 'Let's meet up again next week. Annabel says the Funky Donuts are playing in Fulham and she'll get us all tickets, if you like.'

'Yes, count us in, we'd like to check out the famous Rufus.'

'*Vita lurga.*'

'What?' said John.

'*Vita lurga*. It's Swiss-German for see you soon,' explained Beatrice, smiling up at John and running a hand flirtatiously through her glossy chestnut hair.

'He's a bit of a dish, isn't he?' she said as they drove home.

'Who?'

'John of course.'

'He was very friendly but I wouldn't describe him as dishy. I felt a bit sorry for him when Annabel starting banging on about Cumbria. Henry told me he went to the local grammar so he obviously doesn't know anyone. He had a great sense of humour though.'

'Your trouble is that you've only got eyes for Joshua,' said Beatrice.

''Fraid so, although I wish I knew how to incite his animal passions. Maybe some slinky black underwear would help, or d'you think that might frighten him off altogether?'

'That's a tough one,' replied Beatrice rubbing her stomach carefully. 'I don't know about you, but my stomach feels *dreadful*.'

Pandora's summer job soon ended and she was finally able to leave the dark troglodytic confines of her lift which the supervisor had nicknamed the Bermuda Triangle, because it had a mysterious tendency to disappear into the black nothingness of the lift shaft for hours on end. Eventually it would reappear ejecting crowds of young people who would sneak out into Perfumery clutching empty bottles and the occasional picnic hamper when the supervisor was looking the other way.

On her last day Pandora celebrated by inviting all her friends to a leaving party, purposefully stopping the lift between the third and fourth floors to drink champagne and eat chocolate truffles bought with her employee discount voucher.

'It was rather dreadful because the manager kept banging on the lift with his wooden leg – he lost his own in the war – because he thought we'd got stuck,' explained Pandora to Joshua's father several weeks later. 'He eventually called the fire brigade and the whole of Horrids ended up being evacuated.'

'I remember. It made headlines in the *Evening Standard*,' laughed the General. 'I said to my friend

Uri, I said to him, she may not be Jewish, but for a goyisher she's got a hell of a lot of bottle.'

'Dad, you must stop calling everyone a goyisher, it's not polite,' said Joshua coming into the room.

'What else am I meant to call them?'

'Why do you have to call them anything? After all, you married one.'

'Married a what?'

'A goyisher.' Joshua's mother was the ex-Miss Norway, a fact that she didn't allow anyone to forget, omitting to mention that she'd won the title in 1959.

'Gotcha! "You shouldn't use words like that",' said the General, imitating his son. 'Political correctness! I'd like to string up the jerk who invented *that*.'

'Probably an idiot goy,' laughed Pandora. She loved coming to the Paddington Palace, the General's six-storey mansion in Paddington. Various intriguing characters were always coming and going, champagne flowed and its inhabitants lived in a Bohemian world of their own. Pandora had never found out what the General actually did, but he was obviously very wealthy. She had asked him once and he had replied, 'Import export,' and then changed the subject. Judging by the swarthy Israelis wearing dark glasses who were frequently to be found within, making long telephone calls in guttural Hebrew, business was very lively indeed.

The phone rang in the hall and the General went out to answer it. Joshua sighed and Pandora looked at him longingly. He had inherited his mother's Aryan looks and when he took Pandora out people often asked them if they

16

were brother and sister. That was about the extent of their relationship – brother and sister with a miniscule amount of incest thrown in. The trouble was that Joshua's mind was on higher things. He had been working on an exacting translation of the works of Elias Lönnrot, Finland's most famous playwright, into Hungarian for the past two years. The project gripped him totally and whilst he was fond of Pandora, his heart really belonged to Lönnrot. However, tonight he was feeling unusually affectionate and stroked her hair.

'It's so nice when you're here, Pandora. The old man really loves having you about the place. You're fresh blood, you see, someone new to bore with all his old stories about Israel.'

'Oh, but I'm really fascinated,' said Pandora. 'It seems such a beautiful, romantic country.'

'You probably wouldn't think so if you'd been there,' smiled Joshua. 'You know, I could understand it if he ever visited, but he hasn't seen the place for twenty years.' There was a crescendo of guttural Hebrew from the hall as the General's conversation came to an end.

He returned to the drawing room. 'That was Yonathon. His father and I grew up together and we were in the same unit thirty years ago. We're doing a bit of business together so I've asked him to come and stay when he's next in London. I think we'll have a party for him, he'll like that. I'll get Peregrine downstairs to invite some pretty girls. You better watch out, my boy, he'll love Pandora!' The General stomped out of the room to make more telephone calls.

'Is poor Perry still in his bad books?' asked Pandora. Peregrine was an impoverished old Etonian baronet who was renting a room in the basement. A month ago he had broken a chandelier under mysterious circumstances (Pandora suspected that he had probably been trying to swing on it) and had been forbidden to come upstairs ever since.

'Peregrine knows too many pretty girls for my father to be cross with him for long,' said Joshua wisely. 'Now, where would you like to go for dinner? There's a very amusing Finnish restaurant that's just opened in Shepherd's Bush that we could try, if you like. Then we could go on to Annabel's. The General will be there with some of his cronies, and Peregrine will probably be looking in – it should be fun.'

'Sounds wonderful,' said Pandora enthusiastically, re-applying some lipstick. Life at the Paddington Palace was such a treat. Wait till she told the girls that she had been dancing at Annabel's. They would be *green* with envy.

'It was a *blissful* evening,' said Pandora the next day, flicking idly through *Vogue*. 'Joshua is such a great dancer.'

'That's all very well,' said Annabel, 'but what about afterwards? Are you sure he isn't a hermaphrodite?'

'Of course he's not,' said Pandora, who wasn't quite sure what a hermaphrodite was but thought it might have something to do with snails. She carried on flicking through the magazine. 'There's a really interesting article here about something called *feng shui*. Apparently if your furniture is in the right place you'll have unbelievable amounts of good fortune and romantic happiness. Hmm, it says there are courses you can take. Perhaps I should go on one.'

'Sounds like another one of your crackpot ideas to me,' said Annabel, slipping on her coat over a pair of sleek jodhpurs. 'I'm off to Richmond to see Merlin now. *Vita lurga!*' Merlin was Annabel's horse and her one true love. But Pandora was so engrossed in learning about *feng shui* that she barely heard her leave.

When Beatrice struggled in from Swiss Bank International, where she had recently begun working, she found Pandora busy shifting furniture.

'Good day at the office, darling?' asked Pandora. She had been watching *Bewitched* and was in Stepford wife mode. *Neighbours* was about to begin.

'Exhausting,' said Beatrice. 'I'm so busy I don't even have time for lunch at the moment. I think I've lost weight. What d'you think?' She held her stomach in optimistically but Pandora was busy shifting furniture and didn't hear her. 'By the way, why are all the chairs upside down, and where are all the pictures? Hang on, I want to watch that.'

Pandora was struggling to heave the television into an obscure position but succeeded in disconnecting the aerial instead.

'It's very bad *feng shui* to have it there,' she insisted. 'I've just enrolled myself on a course to find out more about the ancient science of object placement.'

'Oh, I've heard about that,' said Beatrice, picking

up *Vogue* and glancing at the article. 'It says here that the right-hand corner of the room as you enter is the relationship area.' She glanced up. 'That's where the television was.'

'Precisely. We've got to put an aquarium there. I went round to Fishy Fun on the Fulham Road and they can put in as many as we like.'

'Fishy Fun,' said Annabel coming up the stairs. 'Sounds like a porn shop. I should think your relationship corner is quite good, Pandora, judging from the way John was looking at you the other night.' Annabel pulled off her jacket and glanced around the room. 'I like this *feng shui* idea though. Which is the equestrienne part of the room? I was thinking of entering Merlin for the dressage at Badminton.'

'I'm not sure,' said Pandora, flattered at the thought of John's apparent interest but dismissing it immediately as a picture of the multilingual Joshua sprang into her mind, 'but I think it might help if we knocked down the front door and painted the front of the house black.'

The *feng shui* course began the following week and Pandora soon became an industrious student. Wind chimes, mirrors, goldfish and potted plants began to sprout all over the house.

'There's no alternative, I'm afraid,' she said one evening after they had all finished watching *EastEnders*, 'the magnolia walls will *have* to go. Mr Fook says that as we are all Water Tigers it's the worst possible thing. I've decided to call in the decorators and get the place sorted out.'

'But not black walls, darling. Anything but black. Pleeeeese?' begged Annabel.

'Mr Fook says that a very, very dark purple would be nearly as good.' Pandora loved winding Annabel up.

'Fuck Mr Fook. Bet he doesn't have purple walls.'

'No, he lives in Belgravia and has white walls and parquet floors.'

'Getting the decorators in wouldn't be such a bad idea,' mused Beatrice, taking in the chipped skirting boards and peeling wallpaper.

'Exactly. I've been meaning to do something about this place for ages. It'll only take a few weeks and it might change our lives for ever. Joshua says we can all stay at the Paddington Palace while the work's going on.'

'Ugh, and witness your deflowering first hand? No thanks! Beatrice and I can stay with my father. He won't mind. What you and Joshua need is quality time together.'

Pandora doubted it. Sadly the *feng shui* alterations had not improved things in that department, but Mr Fook had stressed the importance of dark red walls in the bedroom. Pandora had been busy checking paint samples on her bedroom wall all afternoon.

Chapter Two

Pandora's stay at the Paddington Palace was proving to be a great success. After her *feng shui* course finished, she embarked on a kosher cookery course which involved a long and grimy trip on the Tube to Golders Green three times a week. It was worth it though. Joshua and the General had adored her first attempt at gefilte fish, though it hadn't agreed with her. Still, though she admitted it herself, her felafels were fabulous and would add a little variety to her, Beatrice and Annabel's diet which normally consisted of bowls of grapenuts and low-fat yogurts.

It was while returning from Golders Green one day that she had bumped into John. He seemed delighted to see her, and sheepishly explained that he had been visiting his sister in Burnt Oak. 'She must be very, um, adventurous to be living out here,' said Pandora brightly, but John changed the subject quickly. Pandora had noticed that he loathed talking about his family and wondered if there was something wrong with them. But they had got on so well that she had invited him back to the Paddington Palace to meet the General and Joshua, but the visit hadn't been a great success. 'Draft dodger,' the General had barked between phone calls. 'I know the sort, blows in the wind and has no opinions. Clever though.'

'Oh, come on, Dad, he's one of Pandora's friends. I quite liked him,' said Joshua kindly. Pandora looked at him fondly. He didn't have a jealous bone in his body. Still, she thought, lying in the bath later, she would have preferred it if he had threatened John to a duel or at least with some sort of mild physical violence for daring to look at her. Beatrice and Annabel insisted that John had a humdinger of a crush on her, and she was beginning to think they might be right. The decorators were busy painting her bedroom dark red this week; the *feng shui* was working, but on the wrong man!

Pandora had been staying for two weeks when the General decided to throw his party.

'Yonathon just rang, he's coming to stay. It's great timing, we can throw a party for him to coincide with Sukkoth!'

'What's suckit?' asked Pandora, trying not to blush.

'It's a sort of Jewish festival,' explained Joshua vaguely, his eyes never leaving a precious copy of the *Finnish Times*.

'Now, Pandora, as the temporary chatelaine I would like you to ring the caterers and the florist. I shall supervise the decor. Aah, it'll be just like old times. You would love Israel, Pandora. To me it will always be the land of flowers and sun. I remember one summer on the kibbutz,' Joshua rolled his eyes, 'I must have been about fourteen, and my job was to patrol the orchards to stop the local Arab children from stealing the fruit. It was the first time I had ever held a gun and I was so proud. I used to practise shooting every day. The apples were my targets at first, then at night I would lie in wait and shoot the jackals that came sniffing around.'

'Was the kibbutz totally self-sufficient then?' asked Pandora, who loved hearing about the General's past. The world he described seemed as far away as another planet.

'Oh yes. Our cows were famous for having the richest milk yields in the whole of the country. We grew bananas, apples, all our own vegetables, we kept chickens, there was even a rose garden.' He ruffled Joshua's hair fondly. 'Oh my boy, you don't know you're born.'

'And was it terrifically hard work?' asked Pandora.

'I got up at four a.m. every morning, but it wasn't too hard. Our kibbutz was so high we could see for miles.' The General refilled his glass with Jack Daniel's; he was well in his stride now and becoming very misty-eyed. 'On one side you could see the Sea of Galilee, and on the other the River Jordan winding through the banana groves in the valley. Sometimes you could even see Mount Hermon covered in snow.'

'Could you ski on it?'

'No!' laughed the General, getting up to answer the telephone.

'I'm sorry he bangs on so much, darling,' said Joshua,

25

putting down his newspaper. Pandora smiled at him adoringly, she loved the way he called her darling.

'Oh, he doesn't. I think it's *riveting*. It's a whole new world to me. But if he loves it so much why doesn't he ever go back?'

'His sister was shot at the nineteen seventy-two Olympic Games and he lost it for a bit. I think going back would remind him too much of her. Besides, his business is here now.'

'But what exactly is his business?'

'Import export,' said Joshua, returning to his newspaper.

'But what does he im—'

The General returned to the room, his weathered face wreathed in smiles. 'Aah, Pandora, you are lucky for me, business is going very well indeed.'

Pandora smiled back. She didn't quite dare ask any more questions. Beatrice said she thought that the General sounded like a gun-runner. Could it be true?

A few days before the party, Joshua's mother, Eva, returned from Norway and dropped in to the Paddington Palace. She was a curious combination of Joan Collins, Zsa-Zsa Gabor and Lady Penelope from *Thunderbirds*, and Pandora found her a little intimidating.

'Your parents seem to have a very, um, volatile relationship,' said Pandora. 'It's funny, sometimes they seem to get on really well, and sometimes . . .' she trailed off. From the top of the house came deafening sounds of crockery being smashed and Eva yelling. Ten minutes later she stormed downstairs, preceded by a waft of Chanel Number Five. Pandora had never seen her looking so well.

'You look m-marvellous, Eva, your new v-vitamins must really be working wonders,' she said nervously.

'I like this girl,' said Eva to Joshua. 'No, it is not the vitamins, it is the fighting. It makes me glow. I like fighting. That is why I married an Israeli. Your father is an animal!' She flounced out of the room dramatically, stopping beneath the stairs and yelling up, 'You're like the sodding Israeli prime minister. He's like a wall, you know it's there for a reason but you don't try talking to it!' She returned to the sitting room cheerfully. '*Ciao* for now, my darlings!'

'Bye,' said Joshua, barely looking up from his *Daily Telegraph*. 'You'll have to excuse Mummy, she gets a bit emotional about things.'

'She's very witty. I know your parents are divorced and that they're always fighting, but there is still this *passion* between them, isn't there?' said Pandora hopefully.

'They can't live with or without one another,' said Joshua, kissing her. Pandora snuggled up to him optimistically. He had been much more affectionate lately, she was hoping that the party would unleash some dormant sexual instinct in him; she had even splashed out on some new underwear to help things along.

'I've been discussing our relationship with my therapist, and she says that I have a fear of intimacy.'

Pandora drew herself away stiffly. 'Would it help

27

perhaps if I put a bag over my head when you kissed me? That might make it a lot less intimate for you.'

'Darling, please don't be cross, I know you want to take our relationship, um, further and quite frankly it puts me under a lot of pressure.'

'I'm not cross,' said Pandora crossly. 'It's just that I hate the thought of you discussing me with your therapist. It's just so *new age*. Look, we can't discuss it now, we're meeting Annabel in ten minutes.' She stomped off to get her coat.

The day before the party Pandora was balancing precariously on a stepladder, arranging flowers in the drawing room, when she heard the front door crash shut and the sound of heavy footsteps echoing on the marble floor. It was probably yet another delivery, hopefully the party planners who were to transform the Paddington Palace into what sounded like a stable. The whole of the first floor was to be turned into a huge straw room to represent the thirty days the Jews had spent in the wilderness. Eva would have a fit. The General had told her that he was going to turn the place into a Norwegian summer garden.

It was a real attraction of opposites, thought Pandora. Eva was a tall, exquisitely well-preserved Nordic blonde while the General was short and stocky with iron-grey curly hair and twinkling brown eyes that masked a shrewd intelligence. She was still working out what he and his cronies got up to all day.

'Hello.'

Pandora turned round, startled to see a tall heavy-set man standing in front of her. She hadn't even heard the drawing-room door open.

'You must be Pandora. The General has told me all about you.'

'Gosh. Has he?' She blushed, not knowing what to say. From where he was standing he could look right up her skirt. She was uncomfortably aware that she wasn't wearing any knickers as the three pairs she had brought with her were being washed and she was saving her new pair for the party.

She edged her skirt down and smiled at him. 'You must be Yonathon, we were expecting you later.' She tried to tug down her skirt and continued, 'You're so light on your feet I didn't even hear you come into the room. It must be your training in the secret service.' She was longing to climb down but was loath to make any movement that might reveal even more of her bottom. Yonathon was standing staring at her, a smile playing around his lips.

'I thought Pandora was meant to open a box, not stand on one. Let me help you down from your pedestal.' As their hands touched she felt a volt of electricity surge down her arm.

'Good,' said Yonathon matter-of-factly. 'Now you're down you can go fix me some breakfast. I haven't had anything since I left New York.'

'You must be starving.' Pandora wondered if she should be offended at being treated like a maid but found to her surprise that she rather enjoyed the novelty of being told what to do. 'Unfortunately Eva came round the other day and did one of her fridge clean-outs. There really isn't very much left and the caterers aren't coming till later.' She thought for a moment. 'How about a nice bowl of grapenuts? They're American.'

'I am not American,' said Yonathon firmly, following her to the kitchen with his bulging suitcase. Pandora smiled to herself. Of course he wasn't American, he was Israeli!

'Have you got guns in your case, Yonathon?' she asked innocently.

'No, I haven't. I am a businessman not a spy.'

'Oh.' Pandora was disappointed. 'The General said you used to be in the Mossad.'

Yonathon grinned. 'Did he?' He helped himself to a massive bowl of grapenuts which he finished in six huge mouthfuls.

'It must have been tremendously exciting going on secret missions and fighting for Zionism. The General has been telling me all about the kibbutz where your families grew up and about his expeditions into the Negev Desert. He says he saw a snow leopard once.'

'I lived in the desert for two years.'

'Did you?' Pandora was riveted. 'What did you eat?'

'Very little.' He was leaning against the fridge and smoking a cigarette and watching her with dark, amused eyes.

'I suppose you were given army rations and things.' She had a thousand questions and didn't want to waste a moment.

'No, not really. Our unit was dumped in the desert for two weeks with nothing as part of our training. Some people ate snakes and insects but I couldn't face that so I used to eat the roots of a small bush that grew everywhere. It tasted a bit like garlic. The Bedouin say that it improves virility.'

Pandora blushed. 'Gosh! It sounds revolting. After two weeks of that you must have been as skinny as a reed.'

'Here you both are. Pandora, I've been looking for you everywhere.' It was Joshua, looking even more cerebral than usual, fresh from the London Library. 'Hi, Yonathon. We weren't expecting you till later.'

'Pandora has been looking after me very well,' smiled Yonathon. 'You didn't tell me that you had such a sexy girlfriend.'

Pandora blushed again. 'Yonathon was telling me about surviving in the desert,' she said with sparkling eyes. 'It sounds absolutely dreadful. How's the research going?'

'Extremely well. I'm translating the entire works of Elias Lönnrot into Hungarian,' he explained to Yonathon.

'Why?' asked Yonathon, lighting another cigarette. Joshua coughed, he was very sensitive to smoke.

'Lönnrot is one of Finland's greatest playwrights,' Pandora said loyally; she had asked herself the same question many times.

'How interesting.' Yonathon was saved from further explanations by the ringing of the doorbell.

'I'll get it.' Pandora was eager to escape the atmosphere

in the kitchen which had suddenly got a little oppressive. 'It'll probably be the florist.'

She spent a pleasant hour showing the confused florist around the house and trying to explain the Middle East meets Norwegian flower garden look that the General was aiming for. There was no point in upsetting Eva unnecessarily. Then the General burst through the heavy swing doors talking Hebrew excitedly into his mobile phone. He interrupted his conversation to smile at Pandora. 'Is Yonathon here yet?' he asked.

'Yes, he's having breakfast in the kitchen.'

The General shouted something into the phone. 'Good girl. We will all meet for a cocktail at seven o'clock in the drawing room.'

It was a bit like Cluedo, thought Pandora as she dashed into her bedroom that evening to change into something more alluring. The General, the playwright, the spy and . . . Who could she be? She rummaged through her clothes and selected her red dress. Of course, she was Miss Scarlett! The murder weapon could be a mobile phone. She sighed with pleasure as she poured quantities of Floris into the bath, dipping her hand absently into the water to check the temperature. Life at the Paddington Palace was bound to get even more exciting now that Yonathon had appeared. Really, having her house *feng shui*-ed was the best decision she had ever made.

At seven o'clock Pandora slipped downstairs in a state of contained excitement. The constant adrenaline rush of life in the Paddington Palace had resulted in her losing five pounds and she was feeling very svelte.

Yonathon and Joshua were already downstairs. Joshua jumped up when she came into the room. 'Hi, darling, let me pour you some champagne.'

'Oh, you've lit all the candles, it looks wonderful in here.' The room was bathed in soft, flickering light. The telephone rang and Joshua disappeared to answer it. Yonathon patted the seat next to him on the sofa invitingly and Pandora willingly obliged. She couldn't help responding to his charm.

'I was just thinking that living in this house is a bit like a game called Cluedo.'

Yonathon smiled. 'Yes, I know it.'

'You see, the General is always ordering us to meet at strictly appointed times in various parts of the house, often for no reason at all.' They both laughed. 'Tonight we have the Secret Agent masquerading as a businessman – that's you, the General, the Intellectual – that's Josh, and me.'

'And you are, let me think. Of course! Mata Hari.'

'Gosh!' She wasn't quite sure who Mata Hari was but doubted that she had still been a virgin at the age of twenty-one.

Yonathon edged a little closer. 'You have very alluring eyes, Pandora.' He stroked her thigh with light fingers. Pandora felt herself melt into the candlelight, shocked and also flattered by his attention. He leant over her suddenly and kissed her, forcing his tongue into her mouth so that she was unable to breathe. No one had ever kissed her like that before and she pulled herself away quickly, her cheeks flushed, repulsed yet attracted in equal measure.

'Yonathon, be careful. Josh is only next door!'

'I'm taking you to lunch tomorrow. Then we will come back and make love all afternoon. Joshua and the General will be out all day. I have already checked their schedules.'

'Have you?' Like a leaf she felt herself blown around by the force of his determination. 'But I don't do that sort of thing really. I've only had one lover in my life.' She couldn't face telling him that she was a virgin, it might put him off.

'Well, soon you will have number two,' said Yonathon, grabbing her with such force that her earring fell off.

She pulled herself reluctantly away from him. 'Hold on, I've lost my earring.' She patted herself gingerly. 'Ah, here it is.' She put her hand down her dress but dislodged it and felt it drop into her knickers. 'Damn.'

'Here, let me help,' said Yonathon slipping his big hand up her dress and into her knickers. 'God, you're really wet.'

Was she? How embarrassing! 'Have you found it?' she laughed as he lunged on top of her, kissing her passionately.

'Ah, Pandora, I have been fantasizing about you *all* day.'

'Have you?' she breathed.

The door burst open and they sprang apart. It was the General. 'If you're ready, Yonathon, we'll make a move,' he said casually, pouring himself a whisky while scanning the *International Herald Tribune*.

'I'll just go and see what Josh is up to,' said Pandora hurriedly. The General would think she was a right old slapper. But she didn't care, Yonathon was the most exciting man she had ever met. How could she possibly have thought Josh was the man for her? He didn't want a girlfriend, he wanted a sister.

She eventually found him upstairs absorbed in computer literature.

'Josh, I can't find my earring. I think I've lost it in my knickers.'

'We'll look for it in a minute,' said Joshua indifferently, picking up another leaflet.

'What are you doing tomorrow?' she asked innocently.

'Oh, I'll probably spend the whole day at the London Library. Why d'you ask?'

'No reason. I'll probably stay in and help the caterer or something . . .'

'That sounds like a good idea.'

Pandora wandered disconsolately out of the room, aware that Joshua had not even noticed her leave.

The next morning Pandora applied her make-up carefully, topping it up with several coats of lip gloss, and went into the kitchen to make tea. She didn't normally bother about what she looked like first thing, but it would be too awful to bump into Yonathon looking less than her best. She had been looking forward to her lunch date all night. At last, someone was interested in her for her body not her mind. It was an intoxicating thought.

'Pandora.' The guttural voice calling her from the hall could not belong to anyone but Yonathon.

'Good morning, Yonathon. I'm in the kitchen. Would you like a cup of tea?'

'Yes. And then I would like to make love to you.' He grinned boyishly at her as he crossed the room and her heart melted.

'Ssssshhhh, Joshua is upstairs!' But she wasn't too worried, he wouldn't be awake for another hour at least.

'So why don't you sleep in the same bedroom as Joshua?' asked Yonathon.

'Because he respects me too much,' said Pandora a little defensively.

'Hah! I respect you but I want to fuck you too.'

'Well, I guess Josh is old-fashioned. He wants to wait until we're married.'

'You won't marry him, you're going to marry me and have my baby.'

'Yonathon, you're quite mad. You'll say anything to get me into bed.'

He stroked her face and looked into her eyes. 'That's true. Pandora, I've waited a long time to meet a girl like you.' He kissed her. 'Come with me to Amsterdam tonight.'

'How can I? I promised to help clear up after the party.' Really, he was unfair to tease her like this. She would have given her left arm to go to Amsterdam with him.

'I don't care about that.' He coughed. 'My throat is so sore, can you make me chicken soup?'

She laughed. 'I could, but it would take days. How about some hot lemon and honey?'

'Whatever. Bring it to me in my bedroom.' He winked at her and left the kitchen.

She took the brew up to him a few minutes later. 'Now, drink this.'

Yonathon looked at it doubtfully.

'Really, I insist you drink it,' said Pandora firmly.

'Do you now. Interesting. Sit down.' He patted the bed.

She knew it wasn't a very good idea but sat down anyway. 'It's probably the flying that has given you a bad throat,' she said conversationally.

'Why won't you come with me to Amsterdam? You will love it there.' He sipped the lemon and honey, slipping his hand beneath her jersey and stroking her breast persuasively.

'Pandora, where are you?'

She froze. It was Joshua, he must be on the stairs. There was no way she could leave Yonathon's room without him spotting her. She scurried into the adjoining bathroom and hid in the shower.

'Have you seen Pandora anywhere?' asked Joshua, peering into Yonathon's bedroom.

'No. Perhaps she is in the kitchen? I heard some noise in there earlier.'

'I'll go and have a look.'

She heard the door shut behind Josh and climbed out of the shower carefully. She peered round the door. 'Is the coast clear?' she whispered dramatically, enjoying every moment of the intrigue.

'Come to bed.' Yonathon stretched out an inviting arm in her direction. Instinctively Pandora made towards the bed and then changed her mind.

'Not on your life. Josh will have my guts for garters if he finds me here. I'm off.' She scampered out of the room before he could catch her.

'I'll be back at one o'clock to take you to lunch. Don't be late,' he called after her.

She went to find Joshua. She had promised last night to drive him to the London Library then she had to run some errands for the party tonight. She grinned to herself. Roll on one o'clock!

At one fifteen she let herself into the silent house wondering if Yonathon had arrived back yet. Her footsteps echoed on the polished parquet floor and the air was heavy with the scent of lilies that the florist had been busy arranging all morning. The house felt empty and her heart sank with disappointment. He had obviously changed his mind about taking her to lunch. She decided to make a nuisance call to Annabel, they hadn't spoken for a few days and there was loads to catch up on.

'Yes, I'm really well,' said Pandora, once she had got through. 'Life at the Paddington Palace is full of intrigue.' She lowered her voice. 'A Mossad secret agent has come to stay and he's asked me to run away with him to Amsterdam after the party tonight. D'you think I should go?'

'Does the Pope pray?' said Annabel cheerfully. 'I'd be off like a shot. If you hang around with Joshua any longer you'll be the world's oldest virgin.'

Pandora caught her breath. Yonathon had just come into the room. He was wearing a dark suit and a white shirt, but despite the conventional clothes he still looked exotic and dangerous. Ignoring the fact that she was on the telephone he slipped his hands beneath her dress and pulled down her knickers, caressing her with gentle hands before getting down on his hands and knees and licking her between her legs. This must be what an ice cream feels like, thought Pandora, shutting her eyes in ecstasy. 'Something's come up, Annabel, I have to go.' She put down the receiver and gave in to the waves of pleasure that were engulfing her.

'Now, will you come to Amsterdam with me?' demanded Yonathon, surfacing for air.

'Yes, oh yes, please,' sighed Pandora before pulling herself together. 'Yonathon, we must be careful, the caterers will be arriving soon.' Wordlessly he picked her up and threw her over his shoulder, climbing the stairs two at a time until he reached his bedroom. He threw her on the bed then locked the door.

'Joshua took me to Amsterdam once,' she mused, 'but he didn't lay a finger on me all weekend. It was very odd really.'

'He is a very strange man,' said Yonathon. 'If I took you away and you refused to make love with me I would throw you from the hotel window!'

Defenestration! How dramatic! thought Pandora, her eyes sparkling. 'But you'd have to catch me first!' She bounced off the bed and made towards the door. 'Come on, you're meant to be taking me out to lunch.' She'd never felt less like eating but thought she ought to make a pretence of resisting him. But Yonathon was too fast and caught her arm, reeling her in towards him; some things in life were just impossible to resist and Yonathon was one of them. Sweeping her extravagantly into his arms he kissed her passionately, peeling off her clothes with such practised hands that she was barely aware that he was doing so. Suddenly a picture of Mother Superior from St Mary's appeared unbidden in her mind's eye. 'He won't respect you, you'll lose your reputation, he's only interested in one thing . . .' But wasn't she? Desire evaporated and was replaced by guilt. Shouldn't they at least have a conversation together before they made love? She pushed him away firmly. 'The General said that you fought in Lebanon. Is that true?'

'Yes.' He was obviously not in the mood for talking but Pandora persevered.

'I think that's tremendously brave.' She was very impressed. She was in bed with a real war hero. Annabel would be green with envy.

Yonathon grunted and continued peeling off her clothes.

'Wouldn't you like us to talk for a bit?'

'I don't want to talk to you, I want to fuck you,' said Yonathon decisively, smoothing back her hair and kissing the nape of her neck.

'Oh, all right then,' said Pandora, arching her back and abandoning herself to the sheer pleasure of being touched by him. After all, nothing that felt this good could possibly be *that* sinful. She had a sudden vision of Rupert's T-shirt, sex is evil/evil is sin/sin is forgiven/so get stuck in. She wondered if that had been written by a Catholic trying to make sense of life and thought that it probably had.

'Oh, darling, that feels sooooo good,' sighed Yonathon pulling her on top of him and gasping with pleasure as she caressed his balls tentatively. Pandora smiled with relief; her pleasure had been tinged with some doubt – was she doing it right? She hadn't had very much practice, after all, but discussing sex endlessly with her girlfriends had yielded a great deal of useful information. Eventually Yonathon came in great juddering spasms, yelling something in Hebrew and holding on to her with the intensity of a drowning man clinging to a raft. Pandora felt a surge of power. This strong, powerful man now lay as soft as a child in her arms. She cradled his head and stroked his hair.

'Pandora, you are like a little tiger in bed,' said Yonathon admiringly.

'Am I?' A tiger in bed. Her? Extraordinary. Yonathon said the nicest things, sometimes phrased rather crudely, admittedly. 'Actually, I was born in the Year of the Tiger, but I've always felt that I was something a bit more quiet and passive, like a sheep or a squirrel or something.'

'In-terest-ing,' said Yonathon.

Pandora shivered, she loved the way he said in-teresting in that deep, slightly sinister way of his. She wondered if he really had killed hundreds of people like Joshua said he had. It was a dreadful thought!

'We will have a great time in Amsterdam,' he said softly in her ear. 'I have booked us on to the last flight

41

tonight, so you will have plenty of time to say goodbye to Joshua. Then I shall whisk you away.'

'It sounds wonderful,' murmured Pandora, trying not to think about what she was going to say to Josh. 'Won't the General be cross with you if you whisk his potential daughter-in-law away in the middle of the night?'

'Just leave the General to me. We are old, old friends.' Presumably this sort of thing happened all the time in Tel Aviv.

'Yes, he said that your father and he had both grown up together on the same kibbutz. He talks very poetically about Israel.'

'It's easy to be poetic about a country you haven't visited for twenty years,' said Yonathon.

'Josh says going back reminds him too much of his sister.'

Yonathon sighed. 'Oh, Pandora, you are so lucky.'

'Why?'

'Because you will never have to go to war. Nothing is worse. Nothing.'

'But at least you were fighting for Zionism – for Israel,' said Pandora, who had been well primed by the General.

'I have seen enough death to know that nothing is worth dying for. When I was a boy, all I wanted to do was be a soldier. I would have been proud to die for my country and I used to despise artists and businessmen and poets. But after a few years in the army I began to envy them. I wanted to be anything but a soldier.'

'But you were in the army for a long time. Why

didn't you leave?' asked Pandora carefully, feeling that her earlier comments had been horribly naive.

'Oh, some of it was fun.' He smiled distantly. 'Coming home on leave, all of us were national heroes. Aaah, the women, they fell at our feet like, how do you call them, moths.'

'You probably mean flies. Yes, I can imagine that must have been wonderful,' said Pandora, rather worried that she, too, was just another fly to be swatted, a moth to Yonathon's flame. The conversation was interrupted by Yonathon's mobile phone.

'No, I'm afraid something has come up. It will not be possible. Yes, I'll call you when I get to Tel Aviv.' He sighed to himself.

'Anything interesting?'

'A girl. She was meant to be coming to Amsterdam with me, but then I met you.' He stroked her hair. 'You are much nicer.'

Pandora didn't know whether to be shocked or flattered, he had spoken so coldly to the poor girl. She got up and started to pull on her clothes. 'Yonathon, you've probably broken her heart.'

'Perhaps. Now I must get up. I have to go to a meeting. Ah, Pandora, you have made my throat much better.'

'Yes, lemon and honey is a life saver,' said Pandora briskly. 'It's the English version of chicken soup.'

He smiled. 'I will always remember you and your goyisher soup, it is a miracle cure.' His phone rang again and she took the opportunity to escape.

She tripped into the kitchen feeling a little sore but

wreathed in smiles. She'd done it! She'd lost her virginity at last! Not only that but she was going on a real dirty weekend to Amsterdam as well. Thank goodness, now Annabel would stop threatening to notify the *Guinness Book of Records* that she was the oldest virgin in England.

She went into the drawing room. The party planners were busy with bales of straw. Yonathon put his head round the door, stared at the straw in disbelief and muttered something in Hebrew to himself. 'What the hell is going on? The Sukkoth is not for *months*. I tell you, the General is really losing it.' He had showered and changed into a clean white shirt and suit. 'Now tell me, which tie shall I wear for my meeting?' He produced two, one flashy and red, the other dark and muted. Pandora selected the dark tie, flattered that he had asked for her opinion.

He kissed her. 'Now I go to my meeting and then I shall buy you a little present.'

The heavy front door crashed shut behind him.

44

Chapter Three

The General's parties were famous and most of the guests poured in punctually at eight o'clock, unwilling to miss a moment. Pandora had never felt so well, her eyes sparkled and she had a new confidence that attracted the admiring glances of all the men present. All the men except Yonathon, who had barely glanced at her all evening. Still, it was good to see Peregrine, who had been allowed upstairs for the evening.

'It's such a relief to escape from my troglodytic existence in the basement,' he said, patting a well-padded knee for Pandora to sit on. 'Honestly, it's not my fault I broke the General's beastly chandelier, it was about to drop off anyway.'

'Oh, he'll forget about it soon, I'm sure,' said Pandora soothingly. 'Now, Peregrine. I need your advice. Yonathon has asked me to Amsterdam tonight, he's bought me a ticket and everything. But he's hardly said a word to me all evening.' They both looked at Yonathon who was chatting up a heavily peroxided blonde in the corner.

'God, I don't believe it! He's taking her telephone number!'

'The General says he's been so brutalized by his experiences in the Israeli army that he's completely fucked up,' said Peregrine helpfully, smoothing back his unruly fair hair.

'Really? Poor Yonathon. What he must have gone through for his country.' Pandora was suddenly full of sympathy. Yonathon's flagrant promiscuity obviously had deep psychological roots. Maybe she could help him. The champagne was beginning to make her feel very misty-eyed and overly optimistic. Their conversation was brought to a sudden halt as Eva stormed into the drawing room looking unspeakably glamorous in a diaphanous white dress. 'Where is that useless man?' She stormed up to Pandora and Peregrine. 'He said he was going to turn the house into a Norwegian summer garden, instead I find straw everywhere, on the roof, on the floor. What is this? A stable, for Christ's sake? And my son. Where is he?'

'He hasn't come back from the London Library yet,' said Pandora. Joshua was so vague that he was likely to have forgotten the party completely. With a bit of luck he wouldn't even notice if she did disappear. Eva stormed off in a cloud of white silk and perfume while the guests went into the dining room to help themselves to felafels and gefilte fish. Pandora found herself cornered by a pantheon of admiring Israelis, eager to share their early experiences of kibbutz life with her. Yonathon was chatting up Eva, who had calmed down considerably and was looking up at him admiringly through heavily blackened eyelashes.

46

Right, that's it, thought Pandora. He can jolly well take someone else to Amsterdam. I'm not going.

The champagne cocktails were inciting all sorts of *louche* behaviour amongst the General's guests and the evening spun by. At ten thirty Yonathon appeared at her side. 'Pandora. Come to my room, please.' It was an order and Pandora followed him meekly upstairs. Joshua still hadn't come back and she wondered vaguely where he was. Perhaps he had been locked inside the London Library. It wouldn't be the first time.

'Ah, Pandora. I am so looking forward to having you all to myself in Amsterdam.' He shut the door and held out his arms towards her.

'I think that might be a bit difficult,' she said firmly. 'I don't think I'll be able to make it after all. Perhaps you could take one of those other blondes instead.'

Yonathon looked crestfallen. 'What do you mean?'

'Peregrine told me that you took seven telephone numbers this evening. I mean, I was too busy to notice but he told me. I mean, *seven*. And you didn't talk to me all night. And I don't want to hurt Joshua's feelings.' This was a bit of an exaggeration as she had hardly thought about Joshua all day.

'I tried to talk to you but you were surrounded by men all night.' He took a step towards her.

She decided to make him sweat a little longer. 'I'm not coming with you.'

'We'll see about that,' and with a deft movement he picked her up and carried her to her room. 'Pack your things, we leave in ten minutes.'

'No!' squealed Pandora, who was beginning to feel a bit queasy. 'I'm not going anywhere with a man of your reputation!'

Yonathon walked over to the window, loving the feel of Pandora as she wriggled against him. 'In that case I shall throw you out of the window.'

'All right. I'll come, I'll come, just please put me down before I'm sick.'

'I bought you a present this afternoon. Do you want to open it now?' He proffered an expensive, slim orange box tied with brown ribbon.

'Oh, yes please,' said Pandora. She untied the brown ribbon and opened the box, shaking out the heavy silk scarf within, sighing with pleasure. 'Oh, Yonathon, a Hermès scarf. It's quite, quite lovely. And it's got a tiger on it!'

'Because you were born in the Year of the Tiger. See, I remembered.'

'Yes. It's so thoughtful.' She pointed at her small overnight bag. 'I'm all packed up and ready to go.' She tied the scarf round her neck, enjoying the feel of the heavy silk against her skin. 'Red, black and gold. My favourite colours, it'll go with everything.'

'Yes, I know,' said Yonathon quietly, picking up her bag and leading the way downstairs.

'Let's go down the back stairs,' suggested Pandora. 'There's less chance of running into anyone. I'm dreading seeing Josh, I haven't had a chance to say I'm off for the weekend yet. Mind you, if I don't tell him, he probably won't even notice I've gone. Whoops.' She narrowly avoided a couple glued together in a passionate embrace; in the gloom she could just about make out Eva and one of the ageing kibbutzniks she had met earlier. 'I'm just showing Yonathon where the broom cuboard is,' said Pandora, edging past carefully.

'Good idea. You can both sweep up some of that ridiculous straw from the drawing room,' said Eva who was obviously a little the worse for wear.

'I'm not surprised Joshua has disappeared,' said Pandora as Yonathon put their bags into the boot of her Mini. 'Life at the Paddington Palace is terribly confusing. His father fills the house with straw for a well-known event in the Jewish calendar when it's the wrong date, his mother is conducting a clandestine relationship with a Mossad officer outside the broom cupboard, and to cap it all, his fiancée is being spirited away by an Israeli secret agent in the middle of the night. No wonder he gets obsessed by depressive Finnish playwrights, it must be a form of escape. Poor Joshua.' She opened the car door.

'Hold on, I'm not being driven by a woman!' said Yonathon, taking the car keys from her.

'Oh, all right then,' said Pandora, handing him the keys willingly. He was so deliciously masterful.

'Poor Joshua? What that boy needs is more sex,' said Yonathon, adjusting the seat. 'He is a great disappointment to his father.'

'I don't know about more sex – he doesn't have any at the moment.'

Yonathon snorted.

'D'you need to go to Amsterdam for a particular

reason?' asked Pandora as Yonathon pulled out into Westbourne Terrace.

'Just to sign some papers,' he said evasively. 'Perhaps on Sunday I will take you with me to Tel Aviv so I can make love to you for hours and hours on the beach. Did you know that Tel Aviv means Hill of Spring?' He sighed happily, slipping his hand up her skirt and beneath her pants, stroking her softly and rhythmically with practised fingers. She shut her eyes, inhaled his aftershave and let herself be swept away by a tidal wave of sheer animal attraction. 'Does that feel good?' asked Yonathon smiling at her in the darkness.

'Ummmmm,' she murmured, a slave to his relentless fingers and unable to speak. She was overwhelmed by delicious waves of pleasure that were getting bigger and bigger. Even when Yonathon crashed into a bollard she wasn't distracted. The danger only served to heighten the excitement and she felt herself explode like a firework inside. She sagged into the seat and sighed blissfully. Her first orgasm. Now she could die happy. She yawned and quite suddenly fell into a deep, satiated sleep, not waking up until they had reached the short stay car park at Heathrow. As they passed through customs, she felt people looking at her and Yonathon curiously and wondered if they made an odd looking pair, she small and blonde, him so tall and dark and, well, Middle Eastern looking.

'I wonder if someone at the Paddington Palace has reported our absence,' mused Pandora as they settled into their airplane seats. 'It's a bit like Bonnie and Clyde really.'

'Life with me is never boring,' said Yonathon, reaching over and kissing her.

'You can say that again,' agreed Pandora. 'But what about the other girl you were going to take?' Yonathon's casual attitude to women intrigued and repelled her.

'What about her?' said Yonathon without interest.

'Well, does she have a job?'

'Yes, she's a model.'

'Gosh.' Pandora was very impressed. 'She must be very attractive.'

'Yes, she is. And also verrrry boring.'

Phew, thought Pandora.

Yonathon went on, 'You know, eating a strawberry for the first time is lovely, but when you've had sixteen strawberries you start to get a little sick of strawberries.'

Pandora wilted a little inside. What was she? An apple?

'You wanna come with me to the lavatory?'

'I've just been, thanks.' She'd read about the Mile High Club but was in no great rush to join it. After the episode in the car she thought it might be better to practise being a little restrained for a while. After all, she didn't want to suffer the same fate as the strawberry.

Two hours later they were taxiing through the silent streets of Amsterdam, past dark, glistening canals until they reached the Excelsior. They checked in and Yonathon was handed a clutch of faxes. 'We're on the top floor,' he whispered in the lift, crushing her against the velvet-lined walls and kissing her. The lift doors opened directly on to the penthouse suite, but neither he nor Pandora noticed for over a minute; each was far more interested in what was inside the lift than what was outside it. Yonathon scooped her up wordlessly with one hand and carried her into the bedroom, where they fell entwined on to the soft, kingsize bed, oblivious of the tactful cough of the bellboy who arrived ten minutes later with their luggage.

Pandora slept until midday, only waking when Yonathon appeared fully dressed and sat on the bed, ruffling her hair with a big hand.

'Oh, are you going out?' she said, taking a while to come to. She had been dreaming of a punnet of strawberries that had suddenly turned into a pumpkin. It hadn't been a very pleasant dream at all.

'I have just come back from a verrrry successful meeting. Have you been sleeping all this time?' She nodded. 'Amazing,' he said.

'I sleep rather a lot,' she explained. 'Joshua used to say that I should go on *Mastermind* and make my special subject sleep.' Yonathon smiled at her uncomprehendingly and she realized that they probably didn't have *Mastermind* on Israeli television.

'Oh Yonathon!' she laughed, leaping out of bed and going into the bathroom. She simply had to wash before he grabbed her again. 'We're from different planets. It's a miracle we get on at all really.'

'No, it is not. You are a very sexy girl and I am a very sexy man, so of course we get on. Now hurry up and I will take you for lunch.'

Pandora smiled to herself under the shower. Peregrine

had been right about Yonathon having an ego the size of a house. She rubbed herself down with a big fluffy towel and stepped into a luxurious bathrobe. If this was what life was like as a fallen woman, she wished she'd fallen years ago. Humming happily to herself she rummaged through her small but exquisitely formed overnight bag. God! All she had brought with her was a huge bag of make-up, three changes of underwear, some unsuitable shoes and a challenging tome she had borrowed from the Paddington Palace called *The Making of Modern Israel* which she had been going to discuss with Yonathon if they ever got around to having a serious conversation. She wandered back into the bedroom.

'Um, I don't seem to have any clothes with me. It's quite extraordinary.' She had always been a bad packer, but this was ridiculous.

'So? What's the problem. Wear what you came in,' said Yonathon, smiling at his *double entendre* which was lost on Pandora, who was burrowing inside the bed looking for the slither of red silk she had worn last night.

'Found it! Thank goodness. Won't be a sec.' She slipped on the dress self-consciously, aware of his dark, glittering eyes fixed on her.

'I have a better idea,' he said. 'Let's stay here and order room service.' He came over and put his arms round her, burying his mouth in her hair. 'How about I order us champagne and caviar?'

'Ummm, that sounds wonderful,' said Pandora, 'but are you sure you don't want to see Anne Frank's House?'

'Quite sure,' said Yonathon smoothly, peeling off her red dress.

'Or the Rijksmuseum?'

'I have never felt less like visiting the Rijksmuseum.'

Pandora sighed happily. Who needed culture anyway?

Several hours later they sat up in bed and spooned caviar on to small triangles of toast. Both had temporarily eschewed the Chrystal champagne cooling at the bottom of the bed and Pandora was restoring herself with a pot of strong tea while Yonathon was drinking beer.

'I've never drunk tea with caviar before, they go together really well. Not that I'm an expert on caviar or anything.'

'But you are becoming an expert in love,' said Yonathon, licking his knife unselfconsciously. Pandora's nanny had always told her that licking one's knife was a social catastrophe and she found Yonathon's insouciance terribly attractive. This lack of self-consciousness was reflected in his attitude to sex. Making love with Yonathon was a revelation.

'I certainly needed some lessons,' said Pandora, pouring herself another cup of tea.

'You have a natural talent,' said Yonathon flatteringly.

'Huh, you should try telling Josh that. I don't think he fancies me at all.'

'I told the General it was a mistake to send him to one of those strange English schools.'

'But Westminster is a wonderful school, you have to be terribly clever to go there.'

'Huh, if he was that clever he would be fucking you himself and would not have allowed me to steal you from him.'

'Yes, you've got a point there,' agreed Pandora. 'Yonathon,' she turned towards him, resting her face on her elbow, 'when you were fighting in Lebanon, what went through your mind? You must have been really scared sometimes.'

'No, just excited. I was younger then, and when you are young you think you will live for ever. I remember before one battle, everyone was sleeping and I was writing a poem to my girlfriend.'

'How romantic. What happened to her?'

'She married someone else while I was away. I didn't look at another woman for a year. Girls used to come to my bedroom but I wasn't interested. My heart was broken. But then one day I woke up and I was completely cured.'

'And you've been making up for it ever since,' said Pandora, burying her face in his chest and kissing it. So he did have a heart after all. There was so much she wanted to ask him, she hardly knew where to start. For this fleeting afternoon he belonged to her; after that, who knew. She longed to believe his promise about taking her with him to Israel, he had sounded so sincere. Yet she was probably only kidding herself.

Yonathon stroked her hair and gazed unseeingly at the ceiling. 'I remember once a friend was shot right in front of me by a young boy, he was no more than eleven years old. I ran after him and when I caught him he just looked at me with these big brown eyes. He didn't say anything.' He was silent for a moment then continued softly, 'What would you have done?'

'I don't know. What did you do?'

'I let him go. And you know what happened? He killed six more of my soldiers. And he's probably still killing, if he hasn't been killed himself.'

'Those that live by the sword die by the sword,' murmured Pandora.

'And the parents of those soldiers he killed? They now hate me. They say I murdered their sons. Whatever you do, it is wrong.'

Pandora remained silent. Nothing she had experienced in her twenty-one years compared with the things Yonathon must have seen and done. Imagine if Annabel or Beatrice were killed right in front of her, how would one ever get over something like that? No one she had ever known had even died; Yonathon was the closest she had ever come to death. She nudged his hand tenderly with her nose and kissed his palm.

'Ouch! You are lying on my balls. Could you just edge over a bit? I need to make a telephone call.' He dialled a number and started talking loudly in Hebrew. Pandora eased herself out of bed, shrugged on her bathrobe and opened the French windows that led on to the balcony. The canal glistened in the early evening sunshine and reflections of the tall, sixteenth-century houses that lined it swayed in the water as it lapped beneath her. She glanced at her watch. It was six o'clock already. Where had the day gone? A breeze was blowing in from the canal and she shivered suddenly and returned to the room. Yonathon now lay fast asleep, his face as smooth and innocent as a child's.

Pandora wasn't remotely sleepy and quietly slipped on her dress, flinging her coat over it. Once she was out on the street, she breathed deeply, and started to walk, emptying her mind of everything except the feel of her legs skimming the cobbles and the canal shuddering in the faint breeze beside her. She stopped at a cafe and had a coffee then, propelled by the thought of Yonathon waking up and thinking she had disappeared, she dashed back to the hotel. He was sitting up in bed eating a hamburger, watching CNN, flicking through the *New York Times* and talking on the telephone. He waved his hamburger at her then broke into English.

'Ahh, Pandora! She has returned, I thought she had abandoned me!' He laughed loudly at the impossibility of the very idea. He put the telephone down and reached out to her. 'My darling, this deal is going soooo well. I shall have to buy you another present.'

Pandora smiled and thought of all the diamond shops she had passed on her walk. Such a pity they were all closed now. 'What do you actually do, Yonathon?' she asked.

'Oh, import export,' he replied, spreading some mustard on his hamburger and licking the knife. 'Tomorrow morning verrry early I have to return to Tel Aviv, but I shall ring you as soon as I arrive. I would so like to have stayed for another night but I am too busy at the moment. I am in Tel Aviv, then I must be in New York – I never stop.' He sighed cheerfully, slipping his hand beneath her dress. Not knowing when they would next be meeting brought a lump to Pandora's throat and she responded passionately. But while her lips were warm, the thought of their parting was like an icy wind and her heart froze.

Time stood still as they kissed, explored and talked until eventually in the early hours they drifted into sleep. As she slept, Pandora dreamt of hot nights laced with the scent of orange blossom, the rustle of tamarisk branches and cypresses swaying in the wind, but somewhere in the distance she could hear jackals howling. They were getting closer and closer, their baying was getting louder, and she woke with a start, bathed in sweat. Yonathon was shouting something in his sleep, he was obviously having a nightmare. 'Shhhh, darling, it's OK.' She hugged him tightly, trying to squeeze the demons inside his head away, until suddenly he was quiet, his head between her breasts, a tame wild animal in her arms.

Pandora lay awake for a long time, wondering what horrors had prompted his nightmare and thinking how strange it was that two people from such different worlds could share so much and yet share so little. She thought of the cultural chasm that gaped between them. She, a product of comfort, money and the Home Counties, he a product of a hot, dusty world that she could only dream about, a world of sun, red earth, sweat and death. And yet here they were lying in one another's arms . . .

She woke up with the sun streaming through the French windows, deliciously warm on her face. She was alone. She glanced around the room. Perhaps Yonathon had gone down to breakfast. She looked at her watch and sat up in horror. It was midday! His flight was at ten, he had gone without saying goodbye!

She quickly dialled reception. 'Could you tell me if Mr Dayan has left?'

'Yes, he left a few hours ago,' confirmed the receptionist.

Pandora replaced the receiver numbly. The room was as if he had never been there. Had she dreamt everything? But she could still smell his scent on her body and remember the way he had put the fingers that had explored her so intimately into her mouth. A bottle of Evian water stood on the bedside table and she put it to her lips. It tasted of him.

The telephone rang and she leapt to answer it. It was the concierge.

'Is that Miss Simpson? Mr Dayan has left a small box for you. Would you like someone to bring it up?'

'Yes, please,' said Pandora hopefully. Perhaps there would be a message attached.

A few minutes later there was a discreet knock on the door. A bellboy handed over a package, inside which lay an exquisite small diamond tiger. She held it up to the light, watching it dance and sparkle in the sunshine spilling through the window. There was no message. She threw herself on to the bed, burying herself in his pillow. Inhaling Yonathon's pungent aftershave – a curious mixture of overripe Sharon fruit and pure sexuality – she burst into tears.

*　　*　　*

Pandora flew home and took a taxi straight to her house. The builders had finished work now and Beatrice and Annabel had moved back that weekend. She hoped to God they would be in – she'd left her front door keys at the Paddington Palace and hadn't the strength to face Joshua and the General.

She screamed as her front door opened and a black, glistening face peered out.

'Pandora! Thank *God* you're home. No one knew where you'd gone, we were thinking of calling Interpol!'

Pandora burst into tears as Annabel ushered her inside. 'I'm sorry, I'm feeling a little over-emotional. What on earth have you got on your face?'

'It's mud from the Dead Sea, it's terribly good for the skin.'

Pandora started sobbing again. It was no good, there were reminders of Yonathon everywhere.

'I don't know how long it's been dead for but it smells terrible,' complained Beatrice, coming downstairs. 'Pandora, where on earth have you been?'

'He's left me, he just disappeared. I've just flown back from Amsterdam.'

'I take it we're talking about Yasser Bond, the Israeli Secret Agent,' said Annabel grimly. 'I knew he was trouble. Peregrine rang us yesterday to say that he had whisked you away to an unknown destination.'

'But he's not trouble, he's lovely. I've fallen in love with him!' sobbed Pandora.

'Well, the *feng shui* is obviously working,' said Beatrice optimistically.

'How can it be if he didn't even take my telephone number?' wailed Pandora.

'Let's look on the bright side. At least you're not a virgin any more,' Annabel pointed out.

'No, I mean yes.'

'In that case I'll have to tear up that letter I was just about to send to the *Guinness Book of Records*. And as our landlady has obviously joined the ranks of the fallen women, perhaps Beatrice and I could have a rent reduction.'

Pandora managed a watery smile.

'That's better,' said Annabel. 'You look done in. Why don't you have a nice hot bath and I'll make you a cup of Horlicks. Then we can have a good long chat about your weekend and decide what to do about Yasser.'

'You can't call him Yasser if he's Israeli,' said Beatrice. 'Yasser's a Palestinian name.'

Annabel's grasp of Middle Eastern politics had always been a bit sketchy. 'Well, whatever his name is, he sounds like a complete nightmare.' She went into the kitchen and switched on the kettle.

Chapter Four

During the days that followed, Pandora felt herself sinking into a pit of depression which she couldn't climb out of. Yonathon's sudden disappearance was a catalyst that reactivated the pain she had felt when her father had suddenly left home twelve years earlier. Then, without the resources of maturity to help her cope, she had retreated into an inner world, rejecting the friendship of children her own age and finding solace in solitude and school work. But after a while the gnawing pain had become less raw and she had learnt to live with the day-to-day anxiety and loneliness that replaced it. Her mother had consoled herself with a succession of boyfriends and frequent holidays abroad, but her search for contentment proved just as elusive. By the time Pandora was eighteen and had left home, her natural gregariousness had come to the fore, though it wasn't until a year later, when she began sharing her house with Beatrice and Annabel, that the shadow of the past finally began to retreat. But the episode with Yonathon tore the scab off the old and painful wound. At least this time she had Beatrice and Annabel around. How she would have got through those weeks without them to cheer her up she couldn't begin to imagine.

Joshua hadn't been in the least bit jealous about the Yonathon episode. He had taken her out to dinner soon after she had returned but all she had done was cry. The evening hadn't been a great success and though they had spoken occasionally on the telephone they hadn't been out since. A friend of Annabel's cousin's step-sister – a usually faultless source of information – had heard that he was seeing a Hungarian librarian who worked at the London Library. That would have explained a lot, she thought sadly.

One night she arrived back from late-night shopping to find Beatrice and Annabel screaming with laughter on the sofa.

'Beatrice has just made another one of her lists,' explained Annabel.

'Not *another* cleaning rota?' sighed Pandora wearily, stocking her shelf in the fridge with low-fat yogurts.

'No, we're composing an advert to put in *Country Landowner Magazine*. Beatrice wants to get laid.'

'How can you say that?' said Beatrice indignantly. 'I just said that I wouldn't mind being taken out to dinner by someone who doesn't have spots on the back of his neck for a change.'

'Listen to this,' said Annabel. '"Foxy equestrienne seeks master to tame her wild excesses. Please send picture of house".' The three girls burst out laughing.

Pandora realized that it was the first time she had really laughed for weeks; maybe she was getting better. Maybe.

'Were there any phone calls?' she asked hopefully.

'John rang,' said Annabel sympathetically, noticing Pandora's face fall. 'Perhaps we should put in an advert for you, Pandora. It might help take your mind off Yasser Bond.'

'How about, "Occasional skier and *feng shui* enthusiast seeks Israeli explosives expert, must have access to a telephone",' smiled Pandora.

'Maybe that's why he hasn't rung. Perhaps there aren't any telephones in Israel.'

'Yes, and perhaps all his fingers have dropped off so he can't dial. Come on, Israel is hardly a banana republic,' said Pandora sadly. 'No, I'm giving up men for good.'

'Never say never,' said Annabel cheerfully. 'You've got to keep your hand in.'

Beatrice opened the fridge door. 'Anyone want a yogurt?'

'Oooh, can we have one of your coffee ones?' asked Annabel.

'Of course.' She handed round the small glass pots.

'Happiness is a Swiss yogurt.' Annabel licked her spoon enthusiastically. 'If only men were as reliable. Now, let's get back to business. Beatrice – where's your list?'

Beatrice picked up a neatly typed list of names, headed 'Men That Fancy Me'.

'Robert, small, dark and boring. Henry, red hair, hairy nostrils. Rupert, possible Oedipus complex, spotty and a bit stingy. Now, here's my other list, "Men I wished fancied me and possible difficulties". J.F. Kennedy – dead. John Black – problem, he fancies Pandora.'

'God, I wish he didn't,' said Pandora. 'I mean I really *like* him but . . .'

'He's too available.'

'He might make you happy.'

'He has access to a telephone.'

'I just don't really fancy him very much. It's a shame because we're really good friends and he's great fun but . . .'

'Quite. You can't fall in love with a man who wears white socks,' said Annabel briskly. 'I'd better make a move now, Daddy's taking me to the Savoy Grill tonight. We're going to discuss putting my trust fund into Lloyd's of London. It's incredible, they pay you huge amounts of money for doing nothing.'

'But it's quite dangerous, my father won't touch Lloyd's,' said Pandora. 'They have the right to take all your money and everything if things go wrong, you know.'

'But nothing ever does. It's safe as houses.' Annabel put on her coat and skipped downstairs. '*Vita lurga!*'

The phone rang. Pandora leapt to answer it. It was John and her heart sank.

'Hi, Pandora, I was wondering if you wanted to come and see a film tonight?'

Why not? she thought. Anything was better than staying in with the silent telephone. 'I'd love to,' she said. 'Could we go and see the new Mel Gibson movie?'

'*Mad Max*? I haven't seen that yet, it's meant to be brilliant. Let me just check where it's on – great, it starts at the Chelsea in twenty minutes. I'll come round and pick you up.'

'D'you want to come out with us, Beatrice?' asked Pandora, replacing the receiver.

'I'd love to but I've simply got to stay in and study. My banking exams are only two weeks away now.' Beatrice gathered up her books and retreated to her room with another yogurt. 'Have a great evening. *Vita lurga!*'

Fifteen minutes later a horn sounded outside and Pandora ran downstairs and slipped into John's car. 'Hey, I like the new car,' she said admiringly. 'It's a Golf GTI, isn't it?'

'Yup,' said John, pulling expertly into the Brompton Road. 'The bank said I could have a new one.'

'Gosh, you must be doing very well.' Pandora was full of admiration for anyone who earned their own living. 'I wish someone would give *me* a brand new car. But there's not much chance of that.'

'Couldn't you just ask your father?' John had checked James out at work and knew that Simpson Rubber Industries was worth well over eighty million pounds.

'Not really,' said Pandora cagily. She hated discussing her family with men in case they pretended to be interested in her for her money, not herself. Thank goodness John didn't have a clue about all that. 'Things are a bit difficult for him at the moment,' she lied, knowing full well that business was booming.

They both loved the film, Pandora primarily because it was set in the desert and the Neanderthal hero reminded her of Yonathon. It was comforting sitting next to John but her heart ached painfully for Yonathon. When it ended she longed to go home and burst into tears but John persuaded her to have a drink with him in the pub opposite the cinema.

'I'm sorry I'm such rotten company at the moment,' she said, blowing her nose. 'I just don't know what's got into me. I mean I hardly knew the man really.' John was fully up to date with the Yasser Bond saga and had been ready and willingly available as a shoulder to cry on. If he was bored of hearing her banging on about another man every time they met, he never said so. Pandora was beginning to wonder what she would do without him.

'It's funny, but I just feel that life has blown a great big hole through me. D'you ever feel like that?'

'Not very often, no,' replied John, smiling. 'It's a great line though – it sounds like a lyric from a song.'

'It is,' she laughed, soothed by his practicality. 'By the way, I'm so grateful for the way you sorted out my car the other night. I'd probably still be there now if you hadn't rescued me.' Her ancient Mini had ground to a mysterious halt two miles from her house at midnight, and knowing that John was good with cars, she had rung him. He had appeared five minutes later with a pair of jump leads and got her car going first time. She had been very impressed. 'I'm having a dinner party next Saturday, it would be great if you could come along.'

'Count me in,' said John eagerly. 'I'm playing rugby that day but I'm definitely free in the evening. It'll be a relief to eat something decent. Our oven has collapsed and we've been living off my cheese surpreese all week. The only surpreese about it is that we're still alive the morning after eating it. Harry said he'd cook us a West Indian groundnut stew last night. I don't know what recipe he used but this old boiled chicken materialized at ten o'clock perched on top of a tub of peanut butter.'

Pandora burst out laughing. 'Enough, enough! I promise there'll be no cheese surpreese, and no – this I can guarantee – no ge—'

'—filte fish!' finished John. 'Thank *God* for that.'

As the weeks passed, Pandora found herself thinking about Yonathon less and less. The heart was amazingly resilient. A few months ago she had cried herself to sleep every night and had been unable to pass a Sharon fruit in the supermarket without breaking down; even a packet of dried dates had upset her dreadfully. Now all she really felt was a pang of melancholy whenever she glanced at the diamond tiger displayed on her dressing table, or wore the beautiful Hermès scarf that he had given her. Josh had told her that he had heard that Yonathon was dating a string of Swedish models in New York and rather going to seed. This cheered her up immensely. One of these days he would probably catch a horrible sexually transmitted disease. She was well out of it.

Besides, things were becoming rather interesting with John. After a party he had insisted on walking her back to her house and more out of gratitude than anything else she had offered no resistance when he kissed her. She had had so much to drink that in the morning she couldn't remember whether she'd imagined it or not. She rather hoped she had. Quite a few new men had recently appeared on the scene and she had no great wish to become embroiled in a relationship. But the next morning he rang, and Beatrice answered.

'It's John,' she whispered.

'Say I'm not in!' Pandora whispered back, wrapping her dressing gown round her and collapsing on the sofa. She was feeling a little hung over and confused.

Once Beatrice had put the phone down, Pandora explained what had happened last night. 'It's all coming back to me now. He was showing me how to do a rugby tackle in Cadogan Square, then he offered to walk me home. I hate walking around in the middle of the night, it's so scary, so I let him snog me because I was grateful.'

'Was he *snogtastic*?' Beatrice's grasp of English idioms was most impressive. No detail of the girls' sex life was considered private, every crumb was examined in microscopic detail for days afterwards. They reckoned that such frankness would give them three times as much sexual experience and possible expertise.

'I can't really remember. I think it was quite nice, but not as nice as with Yonathon,' sighed Pandora, allowing a delicious wave of *tristesse* to sweep over her. 'I'll probably never meet anyone who snogs as well as he did ever again. He has ruined me for all other men!' she declared dramatically. 'Still, it's nice to have someone to see films and have dinner with.'

'Yes, you both seem to sort of sparkle when you're together,' said Beatrice. 'God, I'd go out with him, I think he's very sexy.'

Annabel came downstairs, yawning blearily, and walked into a brace of pheasants that were hanging from a lightbulb. She had forgotten to put in her contact lenses. 'It was only a matter of time before you two got together. It's been on the cards for ages.' She sniffed disapprovingly. For some reason she felt suspicious about John, but she couldn't quite put her finger on why. She dumped a pile of estate agent details on a coffee table and went into the kitchen.

'Annabel, you're not serious about buying your own place, are you?' asked Pandora.

'Daddy thinks it's a good idea to buy something while the market's reasonably low. I'd quite like to put some of my money into something safe like a house. There's a little mews cottage just round the corner I've got my eye on. Don't worry, I'm not going to be adventurous and live somewhere like Fulham.'

'Chelsea's for chicks, Fulham's for families!' they chorused in unison.

'But I'll miss you both dreadfully,' said Pandora sadly. 'Who else will put up with maroon walls and the racket those wind chimes make?' Beatrice was also leaving, having decided to return to Switzerland to work in her father's bank.

'Oh, don't worry, I'll only be round the corner. You can come and stay with me if you get lonely,' said Annabel, plonking down three cups of tea on the coffee table and settling down on the sofa.

'And I'm sure John would be only too happy to keep you company,' said Beatrice enviously.

Pandora missed her friends even more than she thought she would. The four-bedroom house echoed without them. Annabel had decided against the mews house and had bought a luxurious penthouse in Chiswick overlooking the Thames, which meant she could spend more time with Merlin in Richmond whom she was busy training up for dressage competitions.

'I've put "equestrienne" in my passport under career,' said Annabel, one crisp January morning when the two of them were hacking around Richmond Park together.

'I don't know what I should put,' mused Pandora. '"Dilettante" maybe. You know, while you were away' – Annabel had just returned from a three-week Christmas cruise around the Caribbean with her parents – 'someone tried to break into the house one night.'

'God! Were you there?'

'Yes. It was about two a.m. and I was fast asleep. I was woken up by the sound of men's voices on the roof, they were trying to open the skylight. I was absolutely petrified. I managed to call the police but by the time they came round the men had disappeared. I didn't get a wink of sleep that night and I've been terrified ever since. But John's been wonderful, he's been staying over every night since it happened. He's practically moved in!'

'But are you quite sure that's what you want?' asked Annabel doubtfully. 'I mean, why don't you just come and stay with me till you get your nerve back?'

'No, I'm fine. To be honest, I'm really glad that John enjoys staying. We get on amazingly well. It's great having a boyfriend who's your best friend as well. He's so secure and having him around makes me feel safe, not just physically, but emotionally too. I suppose we're officially living together now. This weekend he's going to bring the rest of his stuff over and move in. I'm so grateful, and he says it'll save him a fortune in rent.'

'I hope he's offering to pay you something.'

'Oh no. But I expect he'll take me out for a nice dinner every now and then.'

'Do you want to bring him to Hugo's shoot next month?' asked Annabel unenthusiastically.

'He'd like that. You and Hugo seem to be very close these days. I take it Fergus is taking a bit of a back seat.'

'Well, yes and no,' said Annabel evasively. They giggled. 'But you know Hugo's the man for me. He's asked me up to stay for the whole of next month. I'm driving up in the horse box with Merlin and we're all going to go on long romantic treks on the moors. It'll be like *Wuthering Heights*. And we're both mad about hunting. It'll be tremendous.'

'But if you marry Hugo you won't be able to marry my father,' said Pandora. 'I saw him recently at work and he seemed so depressed. The trouble is that he has no romance in his life, all he ever does is work. So I've decided to start auditioning potential stepmothers. Just think, if you were my stepmother we could go shopping together and take cruises – wouldn't that be fun?'

'Couldn't very well take Merlin on the QE2, could I?' said Annabel. 'Come on, race you to the pond!'

'Harry says I can borrow his gun for Hugo's shoot,' said John, taking a break from attaching a safety lock to the skylight one weekend. Pandora handed him a cup of tea and a homemade flapjack. She loved watching him do things around the house – he was blissfully handy.

'Oh good,' she replied, making herself comfortable on the stairs. 'D'you know how it works and everything?'

'Of course. I've been shooting with Harry and my father used to take me with him.'

'To shoot pheasants and things?'

'Yeah, pheasants and rabbits and the odd stray cat!' They laughed. Pandora wondered what his family was like, he so rarely mentioned them.

'Perhaps we should go and see your parents one weekend. If they live in Cumbria they can't be too far away from Hugo. We could drop in and see them after the shoot.'

'I'll have to ring them, I've got a feeling they might be going away that weekend.' John didn't feel in the mood to reveal that his parents were leading members of the local caravanning club and spent most weekends trundling around the countryside in considerable discomfort. He banged the skylight shut. 'Done. You'd have to be Houdini to get through that.'

Pandora glanced at a postcard she had brought up with her. It was from her mother, Georgina. 'A missive from the Bolter,' she explained. 'She says she's left her third husband, you know, the Argentinian polo player I was telling you about. It's such a shame, I really liked him.' She sighed bleakly. 'Oh dear, she's terrible between husbands. Are your parents still happy together, John?'

'Think so, yes. I mean they never argue.'

'Your father doesn't have affairs and your mother doesn't elope with Argentinian polo players?'

'There aren't any Argentinian polo players in Cumbria,' he smiled. 'No, they lead a pretty boring life really.'

'God, you are lucky. Fancy doing a swap?'

Chapter Five

John hated trains so they decided to drive up to Cumbria on Friday afternoon. Pandora enjoyed every moment of the drive, filling John in about Hugo's extraordinary house and eccentric family. 'According to Annabel, it's like going back two centuries!' It was nice being driven, she thought, gazing out of the window at the grey northern scenery whizzing past. John drove very fast and very well, which was a relief after Josh who seemed to have no spatial ability whatsoever.

John ate the smoked salmon sandwich Pandora proffered him absently. He was enjoying living at Pandora's house very much; after the squalor of life with the urchins the home comforts she provided were a revelation. The thought of returning to bachelor life again filled him with horror. He was intrigued by the shooting invitation, but a little apprehensive too. Fortunately he had stayed with Henry several times and knew the form, but this world wasn't his natural *milieu*. He had been raised in a small semi-detached house on the outskirts of Lake

Windermere where his parents ran the local post office. Determined and ambitious, he had worked hard and got a place at Bristol University where he had found himself sharing a room with Harry. A fast learner and a talented sportsman, he had quickly learnt to fit in and though he never exactly lied about his background, he preferred to skate optimistically over it.

Thanks to John's sense of direction rather than Pandora's map reading, they eventually found themselves motoring up a long curved drive and pulling to a halt in front of an enormous red brick mausoleum of a house. A member of staff immediately materialized and ushered them into a great hall. Pandora looked up in awe at the Titians and Stubbs lining the walls then smiled as Annabel clattered down the elegant staircase to greet them.

'Everyone has arrived and is having baths. I'll show you where you're sleeping.'

John picked up their suitcases.

'Oh, don't worry about them, someone will bring them up in a minute,' said Annabel, smiling at him sweetly. John didn't like Annabel very much, she was so brittle and a crashing snob. He couldn't understand why she and Pandora got on so well.

'I've saved you both the best two rooms,' Annabel was saying as they followed her down an endless twisting corridor lined with gloomy pictures of Hugo's ancestors before flinging open a heavy door.

Pandora gasped as she walked in. It was the largest bedroom she had ever seen. The soft, low lighting shone on walls hung with pink silk, glinted on matching curtains threaded with the palest green and warmed the lace-strewn four-poster. Through the window she could just about make out the lake glittering in the late-afternoon sunshine, beyond which undulating farmland stretched as far as the eye could see. An interconnecting door opened on to a more masculine room decorated in deep reds and greens.

'By the way,' Annabel laughed, 'I'd better warn you now about the Galloping Major. He's quite insufferable. He invited himself to stay this weekend and because he's Hugo's godfather we couldn't tell him where to go, worse luck. You know, he actually described me as a racy piece, can you *imagine*. I mean, chance would be a fine thing – I haven't seen Fergus for *months*!'

'What time is Beatrice coming?' asked Pandora.

'I'm picking her up from the station after lunch tomorrow. Then we'll both drive over and meet up with the guns. I've invited the gorgeous Daniel Snog-Option for her. He's tall, dark and incredibly dishy – he works at Dougall and Douglas with Hugo. I do hope they hit it off.'

'Snog-Option?' laughed Pandora. 'What's his real name?'

'It's not much better – Snodstein. Dreadful, isn't it? But he isn't. Wait till you meet him,' she said with a sidelong glance at John. And with that she left them.

'Mine!' shouted John, firing at the small speck above him. It fluttered to the ground a few feet away, where it

lay, still twitching, a beautiful *mélange* of gold, brown and coppery red glinting in the cold February sunshine. Pandora didn't know whether to say well done or bad luck for being responsible for killing something so beautiful.

'John's a great shot,' said Hugo admiringly. Pandora's heart swelled with pride.

'Do you shoot, Pandora?' Daniel asked. He really was as gorgeous as Annabel had said. Pandora had hardly been able to keep her eyes off him over dinner last night. When they had all piled into the Land Rover after lunch today she had been delighted to find herself squeezed into the back beside him.

'Gosh, no,' she said. 'I'll do some loading and picking up, but not actual shooting.' She couldn't justify the sport but there was something irresistible and primeval about standing in the freezing air, listening to the beaters rustling through the woods and the crack of gunfire, smelling the singed flesh of the small birds as they hit fields of sugar beet as if they were falling into feather down. At least they stood a better chance than the average battery chicken or shackled sow whose excruciating lives ended in agonizing anticipation and pain at an abattoir.

She looked up and caught sight of Beatrice who had just arrived; her face was frozen in an expression of pure horror as she watched the birds come raining down from the sky. She turned to say something to Annabel, but her voice was lost in the crack of gunfire, and instead she raised her hands in an expression of defeat and shut her eyes.

At tea, Beatrice was unusually subdued.

'I can understand that people want to eat meat,' she was saying, 'but to actually *enjoy* killing things, well, it just seems a bit sick.'

'But you love pheasant, Beatrice,' said Pandora, 'except when Harry cooks it, of course.'

'I know, but I think it's just horrible watching anything die. I don't know, maybe it's something to do with Switzerland being neutral.'

'Yes, nobody's seen any blood for so long they've forgotten what it looks like.'

'Oh God, here comes the Major,' said Annabel. '*Scatter!*' she hissed. But it was too late.

'Ah, ladies. You've been talking together for so long I thought I'd come and rescue you. You must be running out of things to talk about.'

The three girls looked at one another blankly. Run out of conversation? What an extraordinary idea.

'Can I top anyone up?' he asked.

'No, thank you,' said Annabel. 'I'm quite topped up for the moment.'

'I wouldn't mind a refill,' said Pandora.

'China, I presume, weak with a little milk?' smiled the Major, eyeing up her slight figure and delicate face with interest. There was a fragility about her that was most appealing.

'Actually, I'd prefer Indian, very strong with lots of milk and two sugars, please,' replied Pandora.

The girls took advantage of the Major's slow progression to the tea trolley to disperse. Pandora went to sit by John.

'Don't you think the Major's a bit odd?' she asked him quietly. 'He's got a sort of squint.'

'He's got an Aryan fixation as well,' whispered John. 'I've been watching him carefully and he only talks to blonde people. I'd watch out if I was you. He's coming back with your tea now.'

The Major was indeed making his careful way back holding two cups of tea aloft.

'You're a lucky man, John, ensnaring this lovely creature. Let's hope your children inherit her looks and your brains, and if they shoot half as well they won't be doing too badly either, eh?'

Pandora blushed. Really, the man was presumptuous. Glancing up she caught Daniel staring at her; he winked and looked away. Her blush deepened.

After the physical exertions of the day, everybody was taking it easy. The large room buzzed with the sound of children playing, the clink of fine china and the rustle of newspapers. There was an occasional discreet explosion as Great Uncle Herbert farted in the corner, but this was tactfully ignored by the assembled company. John was absorbed in the *Financial Times* while Pandora read a gripping article in a ten-year-old copy of *Tatler* entitled 'Does Class Still Exist in England?'. The Major, stimulated by five cups of China tea in quick succession, was on his way to the lavatory. He peered over Pandora's shoulder to see what she was reading.

'Ridiculous question, of course it does. Don't know who writes this pinko rubbish.'

Pandora yawned. 'I'm feeling a bit sleepy, darling,'

she said to John. 'I think I'll have a bit of a snooze before dinner.'

'I'll catch you up, I just want to finish reading this,' John replied, watching Daniel watching her leave. He smiled to himself as he returned to his newspaper. Pandora was the best looking girl there and he was the best shot. They made a great couple.

Pandora walked down the long, twisting corridor that led to her room, stopping outside it to glance at a picture of Hugo's great-grandfather, the tenth Earl of Wolvaston, painted in 1916, presumably during leave from the trenches. A pinched, tragic face stared back at her; the weight of that terrible time bearing down on his slim khaki shoulders. What horrors had those dark pain-filled eyes seen? She thought of Yonathon's dark eyes and the way he had yelled out in his sleep, she remembered the way Beatrice had shut her eyes in horror during the shoot and she smelt her own fingers on which the scent of charred feathers still lingered.

There was another picture of the same Earl in her bedroom painted in 1913. The face was barely recognizable – the eyes were laughing, the mouth was smiling. He stood in a field, perhaps the very one she had stood in that day, carrying a gun in one hand and a dead bird in the other, master of all he surveyed. She couldn't believe they were one and the same man. Funny how men celebrated carnage even in times of peace, for wasn't a shoot a ritual carnage? Hadn't someone said, 'There will never be peace because men love war'? She yawned and climbed into bed.

She didn't know how long she had been asleep when she became aware of John, the smell of the shoot still on him, climbing into bed beside her. She sighed with sleepy anticipation, arching her back pleasurably as he drew her towards him, grasping her tightly and kissing her with a passion that took her breath away. Raising himself on his elbows, he caressed her breasts, sighing as they became plump and full beneath his urgent fingers before slipping his hand between her legs, touching her gently and rhythmically until she thought she would explode with the need to feel him inside her. And then he entered her, forcing himself into her urgently, as if his life depended on it. She heard him gasp as he climaxed, the sound reminded her of the crack of gunfire and the small birds falling like splinters of gold from the sky and how John had killed again and again. She came immediately, with an intensity that made stars explode behind her eyes. It was as if death had created an instinct to create life, giving their lovemaking a ferocious intensity.

They lay silently, entwined and exhausted, in the damp sheets. Pandora opened her eyes and found herself looking at the portrait of Lord Wolvaston. The smiling eyes stared right back at her and she shivered, burying herself in John's expansive chest.

'Someone walk over your grave?' he asked, wrapping his arms protectively round her as if she was a small, frightened bird.

'It's just that picture of Hugo's great-grandfather. It's so sad. Hugo says he was bayoneted in 1916 leading his men across no-man's land in the Somme. He has such a lovely face.' The sexual release opened the floodgates and she burst into wracking sobs. She cried despairingly not just for her pain, but for her parents, for war, for love, for Yonathon . . . She felt that her heart was so swollen with tears that she could cry for the whole world and still have some tears left over. She clung to John as if he was a raft in stormy seas, fearing that if she let go she might drown. He continued to hold her, not understanding her pain but aware that his presence, his solidity was at that moment the only rock she could cling to.

Eventually her tears subsided, and her mind was calm again. She kissed him gratefully, her face wet with tears. 'I do love you, John, I love you so much,' she whispered. 'Don't ever leave me.'

'I'll never leave you. I love you, I've loved you for ages.' He dried her face with a corner of the sheet and kissed her. 'I want to marry you. Will you marry me, Pandora?'

Pandora's eyes filled with tears again and she felt quite dizzy. 'Yes, yes, please!' and they hugged one another tightly.

'We'd better get up if we're going to make dinner,' she said softly, easing herself out of bed and splashing her eyes happily with cold water. She always felt wonderfully relaxed after a paroxysm of weeping. Not many men could put up with her emotional intensity, she was sure, but John was so calm and unemotional that he seemed able to absorb it like a sponge. And now they were secretly engaged! It was such an adventure!

John slipped next door to get changed, returning ten

minutes later to say he was going downstairs for a drink before dinner. Relishing the stillness, she carefully made up her face in an age-speckled mirror, into which countless other women had probably looked and played with brushes and boxes of powder. Slipping on her favourite gold evening dress, she felt somehow disembodied from the present, almost as if she were a character in a novel.

Ready at last, she ran down the corridor, past the ghosts of Hugo's ancestors, and joined the guests in the drawing room. Daniel was hovering by the well-stocked drinks tray and bowed chivalrously as she entered, her eyes sparkling and her cheeks flushed. She felt wonderful. 'Has anyone told you yet that you're the prettiest girl here?' he murmured, touching her hand as he passed her a glass of well-chilled champagne.

'No,' she laughed, gazing up at him with a flirtatious smile.

Dinner was announced. 'I hope I'm sitting next to you, Pandora,' Daniel whispered, before he was commandeered by Annabel who was anxious to introduce him to Beatrice before they went in.

The dining room looked stunning, the polished mahogany table gleamed in the candlelight, and silver and glass glistened at every place setting. As luck, or rather Annabel, would have it, Daniel was seated between Pandora and Beatrice. Pandora glanced round the table, noticing several new faces and a minor member of the royal family seated next to Hugo. Annabel was in her element. Tonight she wore a simple silk sheath dress in emerald green which gave her coltish figure a natural grace. She had swept her hair up into an elegant arrangement on the top of her head and her slim neck was set off with a gorgeous emerald necklace which she had persuaded Beatrice to lend her.

Pandora was fascinated to see her and Hugo playing host and hostess. Privately she and John thought Hugo was a total Hooray Henry. He seemed to adore Annabel, but in a rather oblique way, showing her the reverence one might show a valuable Ming vase. Pandora glanced at John fondly. He always looked uncomfortable wearing his dinner jacket, it seemed to restrict his large frame and its blackness drained his pale face of colour. Catching his eye she smiled and then looked away, turning her attention to the German prince on her left, who was discussing his servant problem. 'You have to give them enough to do otherwise they go mad,' he was advising in careful Teutonic tones.

'You mean like polar bears in zoos?' said Pandora helpfully.

He burst out laughing. 'I suppose that's one way of looking at it, yes.'

Hugo was a relaxed and generous host. Champagne and wine flowed, everyone was soon intoxicated by the alcohol, the exquisite food and the dreamlike setting. The women sparkled in chic evening dresses, the men shone in their black dinner jackets and starched white shirts.

During the main course Daniel turned his attention to Pandora, who soon had him and Prince Heini eating out of her hand. 'I've got two ambitions in life,' she confided to them both, adjusting a dress strap that kept falling down her arm. 'To write a novel and to jump out of a cake covered in cream.' The topic kept all three hilariously occupied until Annabel led the ladies into the drawing room after pudding and Pandora unaccountably found herself discussing nanny horror stories with a group of county wives. When the men rejoined them, Daniel and Prince Heini gravitated towards Pandora where they continued to discuss her ambitions.

'It'll have to be soon,' said Pandora, swaying slightly, 'because I've only got a few good years left. Mummy says that after a certain age women become invisible.' John was across the room, chatting rather earnestly to Beatrice.

'Pandora!' cried Beatrice suddenly. 'Congratulations! John tells me you've got engaged!'

'Gosh,' said Pandora. She suddenly felt rather disappointed, she was getting on so well with Daniel. Now she was engaged he would probably lose interest and go and talk to someone else. 'Yes, isn't it thrilling?' she added rather half-heartedly.

'I'm disappointed,' said Daniel, echoing her thoughts, 'and we were getting on so well.'

Pandora smiled rather blankly as everyone raised their glasses and toasted them both. John joined her and put his arm round her shoulders. She clung to him; the room was beginning to spin most alarmingly and if he hadn't been there she would probably have lost her balance completely.

Lunch the next day was a slightly more subdued affair,

several guests were wearing dark glasses and no one could quite face Cook's famous apple crumble. Everyone was thrilled to have witnessed the engagement announcement and as the Golf GTI pulled away down the curved drive, John and Pandora laughed at the clanking of old tins that someone had attached to the underside of the car.

It was fun being engaged, thought Pandora. Everyone had been so enthusiastic, and several nice couples had already asked them to dinner in London. Daniel and John had exchanged cards and planned to meet up for lunch the following week.

'I'm glad you got on well with Daniel. I thought he'd be a very useful single man to invite to dinner parties.'

'Yes, I really liked him,' said John. 'He's a hell of a flirt though.'

'I know. He's having dinner with Beatrice next week, in Zurich. Apparently he's got to go there for business so they're going to meet up.' Pandora was slightly envious but consoled herself with the thought that Daniel was the sort of man who picked up women and dropped them just as quickly. He seemed impressively high-powered, and had mentioned that he had met her father recently at a business meeting. It was such a small world.

'He seemed pretty keen on Beatrice.'

'I know, glamorous types like that always go for her,' said Pandora. 'Did you know she speaks five languages?'

'Well, she'll have something in common with Daniel then. He speaks four, including Mandarin Chinese.'

'Gosh.' Pandora wanted to go on gossiping about

Daniel and Beatrice but John seemed preoccupied. She had persuaded him to visit his parents for tea on the way home and he had reluctantly agreed, making her promise not to mention the engagement just yet.

'They live quite near here,' he said as they passed a sign saying 'The North'. Pandora tried to think of something complimentary to say about the grey suburbs through which they were driving and failed. She had never felt entirely comfortable in The North. Eventually they pulled to a halt outside a pleasant semi-detached house in a quiet tree-lined road.

'Bit of a culture shock after the weekend, I'm afraid,' said John.

'No, it's not. It's bigger than my house,' said Pandora, trying to make him feel at ease. John had once told her that his family were descended from a local squire. Fortunes must have taken a turn for the worse in the last few years, she thought sympathetically. Before she had time to speculate any further, the front door was flung open and a small, plump woman came rushing out with a baby in her arms. Pandora's heart sank. A baby!

'John, here you are at last. We'd nearly given up on you. Hello, Pandora, I'm so pleased to meet you. I'm Eileen, John's mother.' She extricated a hand from beneath the infant and shook Pandora's warmly.

'What a lovely baby,' said Pandora politely.

'Thank you, she is, isn't she? This is little Christine, John's niece.'

'Gosh, I didn't know you had a niece,' whispered

Pandora, following his mother into the house. The small sitting room was full of people, and the swirly patterned carpet and intricate floral wallpaper made the room appear even smaller. John's father sprang to his feet and pumped her hand enthusiastically.

'It's a pleasure to meet you at last, Pandora. As soon as we heard you were coming, the whole family insisted on being here. Now this is John's brother Darren, Julie—'

'I'm married to Darren,' Julie explained, smiling.

'And Christine is our daughter,' added Darren.

'This is Kevin,' went on John's father happily, 'and Wendy, and their little girl Norelle, and Jackie, Jim and Ted, and some more of us might be dropping in later.'

'Gosh,' exclaimed Pandora, feeling immediately at home and sinking into a flowery sofa, 'you're so lucky having such a big family. I'm an only child.'

Eileen patted her hand cheerfully and Pandora smiled at her. When she was younger she had always longed for a mother like this. 'Now, everybody sit down for tea,' and Eileen bustled off to the kitchen, returning with a huge steak and kidney pie which was attacked with great enthusiasm by the assembled company.

John ate very little, visibly embarrassed at having to eat dinner at five thirty in the afternoon.

'We've only just had lunch,' he pleaded, refusing the garishly coloured slice of Battenburg cake that followed.

'But steak and kidney is your favourite,' said his

mother, 'and you love a nice slice of Battenburg. Anyone fancy another cup of tea?'

'Yes, please,' said Pandora, thinking that steak and kidney pie washed down with strong tea was an unbeatable combination. Perhaps she could try it at a dinner party. 'The pie was delicious. Where did you get the recipe?'

'In my head, I'm afraid, but I can write it down for you if you like,' said Eileen, flattered and patting Pandora's slim shoulder on the way to the kitchen. 'There's nothing of you, dear!' she laughed.

As soon as he decently could, John got up. 'Better make a move. We've got a long drive.'

Pandora noticed a sudden flicker of pain in Eileen's eyes but she smiled cheerfully. 'Next time you come, make a night of it. We never see you now you've moved to London.'

'Yes, definitely,' said John, backing out of the room in his impatience to leave. 'It's been great to see you all. No, don't see us out.' Escaping into the car, he took a deep breath and switched on the ignition. 'Thank *God* that's over for another six months.'

Pandora started crying softly. It had been a long weekend and she was feeling over-emotional. 'You're so lucky having such a nice family. They're so . . .' she blew her nose, 'so *normal*. I bet your mother used to make cakes and listen to Radio Four while she was waiting for you to come home from school.'

'Radio Two actually.' He smiled and squeezed her hand. 'Wasn't your mother much of a cook then?'

'The nanny did most of the everyday things. Mummy travelled a lot when I was younger. She was good at making club sandwiches though.'

John had seen pictures of Georgina dotted around Pandora's house, revealing a slim, bronzed and glamorous woman chain-smoking her way around the Caribbean. He compared his chic future mother-in-law with his own mother and winced.

Pandora gazed into the impenetrable blackness beyond the car window and remembered Georgina at the wheel of her purple Lotus Elan. ''Bye, darling,' she would call as the screeching wheels threw dust into the air in their impatience to leave the suburbs for the sunshine. Various boyfriends would accompany her to Acapulco, Barbados, Mustique and California but she frequently returned alone. When the sun tan faded she would be off again in an eternal search for happiness and sunshine. The latter could be found easily at a price, but the former was more elusive.

'Mind you,' said Pandora, spotting a road sign anouncing 'The South' and feeling greatly cheered, 'the great thing about the Bolter is that she's never boring. It's funny, but the older I get, the better I get on with both my parents. With you it seems to be the other way round. It's sad really because they've obviously sacrificed so much for you and your brother and now you can hardly bring yourself to see them.'

'I don't think that's really fair,' said John defensively. 'I ring my mother every week. I just don't wear my heart on my sleeve, that's all.'

'Thank God,' laughed Pandora. 'There's only room for one bleeding heart in this car!'

'You can say that again,' said John. 'I don't think I've ever met anyone who cries so much.'

'Crying is very good for you.'

'In that case you'll probably live for ever,' said John, resting his hand on her knee and accelerating off the slip road and on to the M1.

Chapter Six

Pandora and John decided on a short engagement, much to her family's horror. She'd managed to track Georgie down at the Acapulco Hilton where she was recovering from her most recent marital breakdown.

'Haven't you learnt anything from my mistakes?' asked Georgie, playing with one of the lilies that were placed in her private swimming pool every morning. 'You're so young, why not wait a few more years at least?'

'There's no point, Mummy, I know John is the perfect man for me. We've been living together for six months now and we've never had a single argument.'

Georgie didn't sound at all convinced. Arguments were the best bit. 'Well, get a pre-nuptial agreement drawn up, darling.'

Really, thought Pandora crossly, John would be terribly hurt if she asked him to sign something like that. And even if something did go wrong, he wasn't the type to sue her for everything like her mother's last husband, the

Argentinian polo player. No, John was one of nature's gentlemen.

But her father was equally pessimistic, trying unsuccessfully to talk her out of it. 'You should go travelling and see the world. Why tie yourself down?' He had met John for a drink one evening during one of his rare forays to London and hadn't been impressed.

'But Dad, you're happy to be single and just work all the time. I'm not like that. I love John and he loves me. We have so much fun together.'

'Well, nothing I can say will make you change your mind. You're wilful like your mother. Still, if your heart is set on this idea, you'll need help planning the wedding. How long have you got?' Really, he made it sound as if she was suffering from a terminal illness.

'Well, we thought three months would give us enough time,' said Pandora. Thank goodness he had offered to help out. Everything would run with clockwork precision now he was in charge. Georgie was too far away to be of any help and it would be too depressing to hear about her latest divorce all the time when she was about to get married.

'Three months! We'd better get a move on. Come down at the end of the week. That will give you time to organize the church and decide where to have the reception. And make a guest list. Do what you can your end and I'll sort out the rest.'

Pandora had shot to Harrods that very afternoon to make her wedding list. Working as a lift operator had given her a geographical expertise that she was longing to make use of. The hours whizzed past in a heavenly blur as she wrote down the code numbers of exquisitely painted china, elegant vases and silver that would hopefully soon be winging their way to their front door.

John was working in Wales for several nights, helping to value a battery chicken farm that was being sold by a client of his merchant bank. Pandora was violently anti battery farms and had been surprised at John's casual attitude. 'But couldn't you refuse to take them on as a client?' she had asked him.

'No!' John had laughed. 'The only thing I care about is getting as good a price as possible. Not everyone can afford your principles, I'm afraid, Pandora.'

They had nearly had an argument about it but the telephone had rung, interrupting their discussion, and later that night as he slept solidly beside her she had smiled. Maybe one bleeding heart *was* enough in a relationship. And he did have to earn a living. Still, she couldn't help but think about all those chickens squashed together in their tiny cages. She shuddered. How she envied John his ability to sleep so soundly; sleep, like contentment, came so easily to him.

Pandora spent the next few days in a fever of activity. She had no idea churches got so booked up and was tremendously disappointed to find that her first choice, where her parents had married and she had been christened, was booked up for months ahead. 'I can't find a church!' she wailed during an hour-long conversation with John that night. 'The only one that is free is on the top of a hill in the middle of nowhere with no road access!'

'Sounds perfect,' said John who had just finished reading *Living Dangerously* by Ranulph Fiennes. 'We can hire a helicopter.'

'That's an idea,' said Pandora. 'I can land in the graveyard in a white helicopter, and maybe we can hire Ranger Rovers for everyone else. I'll ask Daddy on Friday. So shall I go ahead and book the church then?'

'Why not? We can hang on to the helicopter and it can take us to the reception and then on to our honeymoon afterwards!' She had never heard John so enthusiastic about anything. He was right, it was a tremendous idea. All she had to do was sell it to her father.

That Friday she pulled up at the factory and walked over to her father's office. He had had an exhausting week and was looking particularly fed up. She tapped on the window, calling out cheerfully, 'Hello, you miserable old bugger!' James looked a bit happier, he couldn't hear what she said due to the double glazing, but it was always nice to see her.

Pandora made her way into his office, acknowledging the bowing and scraping of various employees who were terrified of James, and thought, quite wrongly, that she had some kind of influence with him.

James was standing by the window, staring at the view of the massive factory before him. Despite his greying hair and increasing girth, he was a distinguished looking man, but a painful marriage and the stresses of running a huge business had taken their toll. Pandora could tell from the set of his shoulders what was coming.

'When I took this place over thirty years ago, it was a

fraction of the size it is today. D'you know, Pandora, that Simpson Industries is the biggest manufacturer of rubber goods in the whole of Europe?'

Pandora did know, he had told her often enough, and she looked suitably impressed. When things were going badly in his personal life, he would often reassure himself with his professional achievements, which were as impressive as his personal life was disastrous.

'I got a call from America yesterday – someone made me rather an interesting offer for the company . . .' He scratched his chin thoughtfully.

'Really! How much for?' asked Pandora excitedly.

'Never you mind.' James changed the subject. 'Your mother has just rung from Buenos Aires. She wants twenty wedding invitations to give to her friends.'

Pandora frowned, she didn't want the day ruined by lots of ageing polo players flashing their expensively capped teeth at her girlfriends.

James continued, raising his voice, 'I told her I had no intention of forking out thousands of pounds to feed a bunch of dago freeloaders. And not only that, she wants to install a Portaloo outside the church!' He banged his fist on the desk. 'Your mother is a very difficult woman. I cannot think why she wants to inflict her weak bladder on the rest of the congregation. The church is in an area of outstanding natural beauty, it's not much bigger than a loo itself. The whole thing is quite preposterous.'

Pandora sighed. Weddings were meant to bring people together but hers seemed to be re-opening all sorts of family wounds.

'How about John and I just elope and marry in Las Vegas?' she joked, trying to cheer him up.

James perked up. 'That's a wonderful idea!'

'Hang on, Dad, I was only joking. Um, I was thinking that it might be fun for us to arrive at the church in a helicopter. You'd like that, it would be just like being in the army again. We could sort of pretend we were going into a war zone . . .' James was always misty-eyed about his days in the army and this was her trump card.

'Wouldn't be too far wrong,' said James, smiling, thinking of his ex-wife's family. 'That's not such a bad idea. I'll look into it. Now, how are you managing everything else? Just go ahead and order whatever you need, we want to do things properly.' The wedding would be the perfect opportunity to show Georgie's family that he had made a success of his life. They had been horrified when she had suddenly announced that she was engaged to James, then a penniless young man from an obscure Surrey suburb. 'Five grand should be enough to keep you going,' he said, unlocking a drawer and pulling out a great bundle of notes.

When John arrived home, he was welcomed by various unidentifiable smells coming from the kitchen. Pandora was heavily into a macrobiotic eating plan that was unfortunately lasting longer than many of her previous culinary enthusiasms. As he bent to kiss her he peered into the saucepan in whose dark, unfathomable depths he could just make out several black strands floating about.

Pandora had just had her hair highlighted at huge expense so they couldn't be hers.

'That looks, um, interesting. What is it?' he asked unenthusiastically. He had had no lunch and was rather hungry.

'Witches' hair soup,' Pandora replied, stirring energetically. 'Only joking, it's a seaweed broth. But I've made us a delicious moussaka we can have afterwards.' John's spirits rose optimistically then fell dramatically as she continued, 'I made it with some tofu mince I found in Healthy Holefillas. They were having a closing down sale and it was reduced to clear but it's terribly good for you.'

As it was a sunny evening, Pandora had laid a table outside on the small terrace. She had spent a fortune buying colour co-ordinated shrubs and plants, so that now in the height of summer the small area was awash with white and purple flowers. She had gone to a great deal of trouble to avoid the merest glimpse of orange or yellow, regarding municipal parks with their clashing yellow, orange, red and purple flower beds as a kind of floral carnage, to be avoided at all costs. Very occasionally she wondered if she might have inherited her grandmother Irma's slightly snobbish streak, but dismissed the thought. Lady Verney would never marry someone like John.

Fortunately, dinner tasted much better than it looked. Pandora was a good cook and although John would have preferred meat and two veg, he was passive by nature and did not complain; Pandora liked her own way and it wasn't worth kicking up a fuss.

They sat chatting and drinking coffee as the sun went down over Chelsea, then Pandora remembered the exciting contents of her handbag.

'I had a bit of a windfall today,' she explained, pulling out fistfuls of £50 notes from its capacious interior. John's mouth fell open.

'What did you do, rob a bank?'

'Not a bank exactly. My dad thought I might need a few quid to buy a trousseau.'

'A trousseau?' John gaped at her.

'You know, all the diaphanous nighties and knickers and stuff the bride buys to impress her husband on honeymoon. Nobody has them any more, but he doesn't know that.'

'It's incredible that your father's agreed to have a helicopter, he seems such an old stick-in-the-mud,' said John, reaching for one of Pandora's homemade organic chocolate truffles made with eighty per cent cocoa solids. Pandora was presently in superwoman mode and everything was homemade and organic. The cupboards groaned with jam she had made from various obscure tropical fruits that never quite seemed to set, and the airing cupboard was heaving with fermenting yogurt and homemade bread.

'I guess it's the nearest he'll ever get to being in the SAS,' said Pandora, clearing their plates.

'I rang my mother today,' said John, the expression on his face similar to that of a patient having his tooth pulled without an anaesthetic. Talking about his family always made him feel uncomfortable. 'I'm afraid nobody wants to wear morning dress, they say it's too expensive to hire and that they're going to wear what they usually wear to weddings.'

Pandora looked confused. How odd. Didn't men always wear morning suits to weddings? 'But what else were they thinking of pitching up in, Bermuda shorts?' she quipped, wincing at the pained expression on John's face.

He laughed bleakly. 'No, no. Suits, I suppose.'

'That's interesting, as long as they're not brown,' she joked.

John looked very uncomfortable. His father's best suit was a brown one.

'Can't you pay for them to hire proper clothes?' she asked. Really, it wasn't as if he had anything else to do except turn up on the day.

'Yes, I guess that if I offer to do that it might shame them into it.'

'Are there any other complaints winging their way down from the north?' she asked tartly, trying to check herself; she wasn't normally this bitchy.

'Well, my mother was also a bit put out that we weren't having a proper receiving line and she doesn't think it's a good idea to have a fish starter because so many people don't eat fish.'

'But everyone eats smoked salmon and caviar blinis are a wonderful idea,' said Pandora firmly. 'It's a wedding, not a convention of food faddists. If they have any more bright ideas, perhaps they might like to pay half the costs.' That would soon shut them up, she thought cheerfully. Such suggestions were really too ludicrous to take seriously. It was funny, John's family had seemed so reasonable. 'Gosh, we're nearly having an argument,' she continued softly, noticing John's worried expression and wrapping her arms round his neck. 'I thought my lot were the only ones who were going to cause trouble. I sort of hoped your family would go along with everything.'

'They will, my mother is just trying to get involved,' John said doubtfully. 'Anyway, don't take it out on me, you know how I feel about them.'

'I feel sorry for your mother. I hope it's not true that men treat their wives the same way as they treat their mothers. I'd better get into slave mode now!' She cleared away the last of the plates and stacked them in the sink. 'It's funny, they say that you marry someone who reminds you of your mother or father or whatever. Neither of us is, though.'

'What?' John was flicking channels hoping to catch the golfing highlights on BBC 2.

'I mean you're not *remotely* like my father, and I'm not like your mother.'

'Thank God for that,' smiled John, wrapping his arms round her waist and kissing her neck. Pandora shut her eyes and relaxed into his arms. John was so solid, so safe and uncomplicated.

'Has your father ever had affairs?' she asked.

'Dad? You've got to be joking. I don't think he's ever looked at another woman. How about your father?'

'God, yes, all the time.'

John frowned. Pandora's *louche* relatives were a source of constant mystery to him, as was the fact that she had survived until now without someone like him to look after her.

Later on in bed they lay chatting companionably side by side. 'By the way, Daniel phoned me at work today and asked us to a party next weekend.'

Pandora's antennae were immediately alerted. 'Why didn't you tell me before?'

'I'm telling you now, aren't I?'

'But if you'd told me before I could have decided whether I need to buy something new to wear,' said Pandora, thinking that she might spend some of her newly acquired loot on something particularly alluring. 'Daniel's parties are bound to be full of exciting and glamorous people.'

'You sound just like a press release,' laughed John.

'That's an idea, maybe I should learn about PR. I haven't done a course in that yet.'

'Must be about the only thing left that you haven't done a course in,' said John drily. 'What was last week's one about?'

'Aerobics. Thank God that's over, I'm surprised it didn't kill me. The worst bit was seeing what years of leaping around had done to the other students. Talk about teenage cripples. Half of them had shin splints, dodgy knees, bad backs, and weak ankles. The only thing that held them together were their trendy leotards.'

John yawned, he was longing to go to sleep. 'Well, I think you gave up too easily. Teaching aerobics would have been perfect. You'd only have to work part-time if you wanted.'

'So I could still do all the cooking!' She laughed, for she was still at the stage when cooking a meal every night was a novelty not a chore. 'No, if I'd carried on I would have ended up in a wheelchair, and then who'd cook your dinner? Besides, you only get so many breaths in life, why use them all up exercising?'

'God, Pandora, you should go into politics, I've never heard so much bullshit. What you need is a nice little job, something to keep your mind occupied during the day. You're quite bright, you could make a real success of something. All you lack is staying power. Let's face it, if you had no money, you'd have to stick at something. God knows what, though.'

'But I have a job, I'm a trust fund hippy, and soon I'm going to be a housewife. It wouldn't be fair if I took a proper job away from someone who really needed one for the money. Besides, when would I find time to see exhibitions, obscure films and plays, use the library, have facials and make jam? Anyway, I like going on courses. I didn't learn to make individual strawberry pavlovas by accident, you know.'

Pandora was a compulsive course goer. She read *Floodlight* and course prospectuses with the excitement that more lascivious people reserved for cookery books and Jilly Cooper novels, though she loved those too. But nothing had really grabbed her and she was resigned to being a committed dilettante. Could one be committed and a dilettante simultaneously? she wondered.

'What you need to do is find something you really enjoy and stick at it.'

'I've always dreamt of writing a novel,' said Pandora wistfully. 'I was quite good at English at school.'

'Come on,' laughed John, 'at least set your sights on something realistic. What could you write a book about?'

'I could write something based on all my diaries, I've got loads of them.' John didn't seem impressed so she went on, 'Anyway, I couldn't possibly get a nice little job because I'm frantically busy arranging the wedding.' This was total fabrication as her father was doing all the hard work. 'Besides, you work hard enough for both of us.' She hugged him affectionately in what she hoped was a sisterly embrace, she wasn't in the mood for any serious action. All the jumping around in class last week seemed to have reduced her libido and had probably made her barren too. Obviously the embrace wasn't sisterly enough because John began to caress her back in long, sweeping movements. Oh God, wasn't seaweed an aphrodisiac or something? She had just had her period and couldn't use that excuse again so she succumbed with false enthusiasm.

'Did you come?' he asked eagerly afterwards.

'Of course, darling, it was wonderful,' she lied convincingly. Making love in the few months since Hugo's shoot had been rather a disappointment; she found it impossible to reach such dizzy heights in the privacy of their own bedroom, despite the *feng shui* improvements. She only seemed to have orgasms in hotels and other people's bedrooms. Maybe she needed sexual counselling. She smiled wistfully, remembering the passion she had felt in Yonathon's arms. The whole episode now seemed little more than a fantasy; what she had felt for him had been too intense to sustain. She had been reading lots of American self-help books recently with irresistible titles like *Find Your Perfect Mate In Ten Days Or Your Money Back!* which all emphasized the importance of marrying your best friend. Apparently, passion didn't last and was no substitute for companionship.

In the corner of the bedroom she caught sight of the tigers she had recently begun collecting, locked away inside a glass cabinet. Pride of place was given to the small tiger that Yonathon had given her. Illuminated in the streetlight seeping through the curtains, it seemed to sparkle in the darkness. A few days before she had taken it to be valued. The jeweller had given it a cursory once-over. 'It's made of glass, not diamond!' he had laughed, handing it back to her. She had felt so foolish. To Pandora it now seemed to symbolize all the insecurity and confusion of her past life. She shut her eyes and snuggled into John's back. Contentedly drifting off to sleep, she knew that now she had John, all the insecurities and nebulous fears that had dogged her for so long were finally fading away.

John left for work early, dropping a kiss on Pandora's slumbering form beneath the duvet before running downstairs. Today she had decided to indulge herself with breakfast in bed and a copy of *Country Life* which she had just started subscribing to. The exquisite pictures of country houses buried tantalizingly within its glossy pages were quite irresistible. She suddenly caught her breath as her eyes rested on a picture of a ravishing garden full of bluebells. It was idyllic. She was getting fed up with London and was longing to grow proper vegetables (the tomato Gro-bags on her patio didn't really count), breathe fresh air and have friends down for the weekend. Perhaps they could have an Aga! She lay back on her pillow for a moment, imagining the smell of freshly baked bread and the long country walks they would take together, returning to homemade crumpets roasted on a roaring log fire – or perhaps they would prefer marshmallows, they were nice toasted too.

Her delicious daydream was rudely interrupted by Lady Robert-Shaw's burglar alarm going off next door. 'Bogus aristos and their bloody alarms,' she muttered, getting up to shut the window, but the piercing sound still filled the house. If they lived in the country miles from the nearest neighbour, they wouldn't have to put up with this sort of noise pollution. No time like the present, she thought, and reached for the telephone to dial the estate agent concerned. She would discuss it with John this evening and persuade him to go on a recce at the weekend.

On the way to Daniel's party that evening she mentioned the idea, cunningly enticing John with ideas about golf club membership – golf was his growing passion.

'Just imagine, we could buy a house next to a golf course so you could play after work every day.' She carefully avoided mentioning the horrors of commuting; after all, men had to make *some* sacrifices for their families.

Daniel lived in a dazzling New York style loft

conversion in Battersea. It had recently been featured in *Zen!*, an upmarket decorating magazine, which generally featured sparsely furnished apartments belonging to overpaid merchant bankers. The editor had been thrilled with Daniel's loft because it contained virtually no furniture at all except a bed and a wrought iron sofa that Daniel usually kept in a cupboard. Tonight it was teeming with beautiful people, models and MTV presenters wearing Lycra cycling shorts that clung to cellulite-free thighs, jostling with gleamingly tanned yuppies, recently returned from weekends skiing in Verbier and Chamonix. Thank goodness she was with John, thought Pandora as they made their way through the braying throng to greet Daniel. Eventually they found him glued to a massive television screen in his eat-in kitchen, his arm draped casually round the shoulders of a stunning blonde whom Pandora recognized from a recent advertisement for Walnut Whip ice cream which had been banned for being too suggestive. They were watching an ice hockey game on cable TV and vociferously supporting the Pittsburgh Penguins. Pandora felt completely wrong in her knee-length sweater dress; if only she had worn her Pucci micro shorts with her thigh-length boots, but John had vetoed that outfit.

'John, Pan-dor-ra,' drawled Daniel in his sexy mid-Atlantic accent, acquired from a two-week stint at Harvard Business School. 'Great you could make it. Let's go and get you a drink,' but John was riveted by the television screen. Pandora followed Daniel into a huge room off the kitchen, dominated by a vast fridge.

'You look gorgeous,' he said, handing her a chilled glass of champagne. 'I saw your father today.' He looked down at her with smiling steel-grey eyes and Pandora felt herself melt in his gaze. Gosh, he was charming.

'Yes, he's thinking of selling his business. I know he was going to see a few merchant banks about it. What a coincidence that he ran into you though.'

Daniel was still looking at her as if she was the most fascinating person he had ever met; it was flattering, when he could have been groping the Walnut Whip model in the kitchen.

'I really admire your father,' he said. 'He's a brilliant businessman. You must have been thrilled when he got his MBE.'

'Oh yes,' trilled Pandora, hypnotized by his gaze and mesmerized by his charm.

'Daniel, darling, there you are.' The Walnut Whip model sashayed into the kitchen and put a possessive hand on Daniel's arm. 'Everyone was wondering where you'd got to.'

'Yes, I must be getting back to John,' said Pandora. If only she hadn't worn such a frumpy dress. Damn. She wove her way back to John's side, stopping to have a few agonizingly tedious conversations with one or two acquaintances along the way. 'Can we go soon?' she whispered. 'This party is full of Wykehamists.' Annabel's father had once told her that he didn't mind who or what she married as long as he hadn't gone to Winchester, and from that time on Wykehamist became slang for any sort of dreadful person that should be avoided at all costs.

Eventually they extricated themselves from the heaving throng and Pandora breathed a sigh of relief.

'God, all those desperate single people. It was exhausting.' She sat back in the car happily. It was so nice being engaged.

Chapter Seven

Pandora made an appointment to see the house in the bluebell wood the following weekend. John, too, had been seduced by the glossy photograph and was now similarly intrigued. After an hour's drive they arrived at the small village of Middlehurst in Hampshire. Geographically challenged at the best of times, Pandora could navigate them no further.

'Here, let me take a look,' said John, patiently taking the map and negotiating their way out of the muddy cul-de-sac that Pandora had insisted he drive down. Ten minutes later they pulled up outside a curiously shaped bungalow. It was a cold, clear day and they could see for miles over a view that took their breath away.

'Nice view, shame about the house,' said John. 'Shall we push off? I don't think they've seen us arrive.'

Pandora was inclined to agree with him. She had no desire to live in a bungalow, especially one as obviously uncared for as this. Still, they wouldn't find a view as stunning in a hurry. While they were prevaricating, the door opened, releasing a delicious smell of baking.

Oh God, it's the old vanilla essence on a baking tray trick again, thought Pandora as they were ushered inside by the jolly householder, obviously used to people taking one look and disappearing, and determined not to let Pandora and John go. There had recently been an article in the *Daily Mail* dispensing tips about how to encourage buyers, and vanilla essence had featured strongly, alongside advice about throwing away potpourri which was no longer 'in'.

Whatever Pandora's reservations, as soon as she saw the view from the drawing room she knew she wanted the house. Acres of bluebells stretched far into the distance in a purplish haze, framed by woodland in the distance. 'If any beauty which I desired and got 'twas but a dream of thee,' she misquoted under her breath. The house was not actually a bungalow, but built into the side of the hill and much bigger than it outwardly appeared. It needed a total overhaul inside and out, but she could make it beautiful. Imagine waking up every morning to the sight of undulating woodland stretching as far as the eye could see. It was as lush and green as Tuscany.

'We've got to buy it!' she whispered excitedly as they climbed back into the car. 'It's so peaceful here. I could decorate the drawing room in different shades of cream, it would look *fantastic* with the wooden floors – they're probably the only thing we won't need to rip out. Didn't you think the kitchen was simply the most ghastly—'

'For heaven's sake,' John interrupted her sensibly,

'don't get carried away! I don't think anyone has spent a bean on it for twenty years. Besides, it's in the middle of nowhere.'

'Hah! That's where you're wrong,' cried Pandora, brandishing the house details. 'It's only two miles from the nearest golf course, and three miles to the nearest station, journey time to Waterloo only fifty-seven minutes.'

John's spirits rose a little, but not much. Although he was quite happy to move out of London, he wasn't sure about the house. But Pandora's mind seemed made up, and as she was the one buying it he might as well go along with her. Besides, he'd enjoy getting to grips with the five acres of woodland. Imagine living in a six-bedroom house. His colleagues would be green with envy. He smiled at Pandora who squeezed his knee in return. Pretty rich wife, nice house, land – life felt good. He put his foot down on the accelerator as they passed a woman riding alongside the road, causing the horse to shy. She waved her riding whip angrily at him.

'Stupid bitch,' he cursed under his breath.

'John, you should slow down for horses. You've no idea how frightening it is riding on roads,' reprimanded Pandora who had terrifying memories of Pony Club hacks on narrow country lanes. 'I'll get the house surveyed next week,' she went on, 'and then I'll make a miserable offer and see how the land lies.' She had bought her first house when she was twenty, and had fond memories of brutal negotiations with the slightly bemused home-owner who had expected her to be a pushover in such matters. She rubbed her hands gleefully and settled down to read her recently acquired Aga cookbook as John successfully navigated their way out of a maze of lanes and on to the M3.

The survey on Bluebell House was fair and the owners accepted Pandora's offer. Meanwhile she received a good offer on her London house unexpectedly soon, which was a relief but also quite sad; she had wanted to keep a foot in the door of London life for a while, but her trustees insisted she accept it. But at least it would mean they would be properly settled in before their wedding which was now only two months away.

Pandora spent hours drooling over glossy brochures depicting fabulously rustic kitchens and gleaming bathrooms, studying fabric samples and country living magazines which were full of pictures of pink-cheeked housewives clutching baskets full of wild flowers and homegrown vegetables. All sorts of magazines had recently sprung up to cater for disillusioned townies and Pandora snapped them up enthusiastically. Many contained interesting recipes. She was so longing to make chickweed deodorant and nettle croissants from her very own nettles. Attempts at growing them on her balcony had not been successful, and the chickweed and dandelions she had carefully transplanted from the country had similarly refused to take.

John was also getting into the spirit of things, and began talking about chainsaws while putting himself on the waiting list of the nearest golf club. Golf was beginning to take up most of his weekends. It seemed such a middle-aged pastime for a young man. She could understand an interest in cricket or rugby, but golf? Still, at least he seemed to be good at it; last weekend he had brought home a silver trophy for winning something or other. He was rather keen that she take it up but as she tactfully pointed out, she was far too busy; perhaps there would be more time after the wedding.

This Sunday John had left at 7 a.m. to play golf in Sussex. She stretched out languorously, it was still only 10 a.m. and she had the day to herself. She heard a thud as the Sunday papers were pushed through the door downstairs and she leapt out of bed to fetch them. As she struggled back upstairs, precariously balancing a cup of tea, a bowl of grapenuts plus six Sunday newspapers, the telephone rang. It was Daniel.

'Hi, Pandora.' She loved the way he said her name and leant back on her pillows with a smile on her face, letting his voice wash over her. 'I was wondering if you and John wanted to come to Soho and watch the Chinese New Year celebrations. We could go out to lunch afterwards.'

Pandora thought for a moment. She couldn't imagine anything she'd like to do more than spend a whole day with Daniel, he was such good company.

'Well, I'd simply love to but I'm afraid John isn't here, he's playing golf.'

'How extraordinary,' drawled Daniel. 'I hope it's not catching.'

'Oh, I don't think so. I've never been near a golf course in my life.'

Daniel really did have the most lovely voice, she thought, rifling through her wardrobe in the hope of finding something really alluring. She finally settled on a fluffy red jumper and a pair of black ski pants. Her godmother, Davina, had once told her that they should always wear red as they had both been born in the Year of the Tiger. Since then Pandora had always felt that it was her lucky colour; it suited her and good things often happened when she wore it.

Pandora hadn't seen Davina for years. She and Georgie had been flatmates and close friends, rather like Pandora and Annabel, but since Georgie had moved to the Argentine they had rather lost touch. Davina's husband George had got badly in debt and, overcome with shame, had put a shotgun to his head, leaving Davina in full charge of the family estate in Cornwall. She was forced to sell the village which had been in her family for generations to an Australian tycoon but was still hanging on to the rest of the estate, which consisted of a crumbling manor house and a large, unwieldy farm that brought in very little income. It had been a mystery to everyone that someone as stunning and amusing as Davina had ever married George who was a typical dyed-in-the-wool country aristocrat. They both came from ancient Cornish Catholic families, their mothers had been best friends and the two of them had drifted amicably into marriage. The arrangement seemed to have worked quite well. George had been very wealthy and had poured money into the estate that Davina had inherited on the death of her parents. Pandora was hoping that her wedding might rekindle something between Davina and her father. Her mother had told her they'd had a short but passionate affair not long before he'd married Georgina and Davina had married George. James had been looking for consolation while Georgina's family tried to block her marriage to him by taking her to Argentina for six months. Davina had been looking for excitement – or so Pandora had always assumed. She thought they were well suited; it would be good if her wedding brought them together again.

Pandora had to rush to beat the clock; this was definitely a heated rollers occasion. She might be engaged, but she had no intention of giving up. It was funny how men backed off as soon as they saw a ring on one's finger. Before John had moved in, she had had so many male friends. Now she suspected that their friendship was just a hopeful prelude to getting her into bed. So much for platonic friendship, she thought glumly. It was funny but she and John were so close she didn't miss any of them.

The doorbell rang just as she pulled the last heated roller from her hair. Glancing out of the window, she spotted Daniel's Mercedes sports car parked outside.

'I'm so glad you suggested doing this.' She smiled at him winningly as he manoeuvred the car into the traffic along the Kings Road. She wouldn't normally have dreamt of driving into the West End on a Sunday to watch grown men dressed up as dragons, but it was fun being with Daniel.

He had taken the car roof down and as conversation was difficult over the roar of the engine she contented herself with covertly admiring his profile and the way the wind ruffled his dark wavy hair. She carefully felt her own. She had gone to so much trouble and now the wind would totally *uncoiff* her. She was sure Daniel liked women to be *coiffed*.

'I'm so looking forward to your wedding, Pandora,' Daniel murmured when they stopped at the lights. 'I bet there will be loads of pretty girls there. Attractive girls always have attractive friends.'

'I expect there will be some,' said Pandora doubtfully. She, Annabel and Beatrice had all avoided the company of anyone prettier than they were like the plague.

'I've been reading a lot about your father in the papers recently,' Daniel went on. James had been profiled in the *Financial Times* the day before, following his announcement that he was selling his company.

The lights changed and further conversation was curtailed; besides, Pandora needed all her concentration to keep her hair from blowing all over the place. She didn't like driving with the roof down, it made one feel so conspicuous in a 'Hey, guys, look at me, I'm so rich' way. And being a blonde in a soft top was such a cliché. She could explain this to John, but Daniel would probably think she was very odd.

The traffic was at a standstill near Soho, and Daniel decided to park some way off. The crowds were very heavy, but he was tall and easy to follow. It was very noisy and Pandora longed to leave. She was amazed that people who worked all week wanted to waste time being pushed around in a crowd of strangers who quite possibly didn't wash very often. Daniel kept peering down at her and saying, 'Isn't this great!' She barely had time to rearrange her features from disgust to a 'Wow, I'm having an incredible time' expression. God, he was so attractive.

Eventually he suggested they wander off to have tea somewhere. 'Let's go to Claridges. I love it there.'

'Oh, I'd simply adore to,' agreed Pandora. This was far more her sort of thing.

She was riveted for an hour by Daniel talking about his fascinating work.

'Are you a Corporate Raider?' asked Pandora hopefully. This was a recently coined term that sounded very glamorous to her.

Daniel agreed that he probably was and the conversation turned to her father's business, and then grippingly to the state of his love life. 'All the girls I go out with want to get married, and I'm just not ready,' he drawled casually.

'What sort of person are you looking for?' Pandora asked, intrigued.

'Oh, someone very work orientated.'

Pandora's heart sank; that was her out of the running. 'Good-looking, bright—'

'A sort of bimbo with brains,' she interjected helpfully.

He sighed wistfully. 'That would be perfect.'

Later, after he had dropped her home, she put her heated rollers away and hung up most of her wardrobe, which was lying on the floor. She didn't want John to think she had gone to a lot of trouble just because she'd spent the day with Daniel.

Half an hour later John appeared, beaming and waving a small misshapen pewter mug at her.

'Look what I've won,' he said cheerfully.

'Gosh, well done!' Pandora responded. 'It's lovely,' she added doubtfully as John reverently placed it beside one of her tigers on the kitchen dresser. Her collection of tigers had increased and the dresser held the overspill from the glass cabinet upstairs.

'I'm starving, what's in the fridge?' he asked, opening it. Various unidentifiable substances on plates and wrapped in foil lurked within. Pandora had been a chalet girl just after leaving school. This had honed her already well-developed skills in economy and recyling. She didn't think she had ever thrown a piece of food away in her life. But luckily John was like a goat, he'd eat practically anything.

'Why are you wearing all that gunk on your face?' he asked, peering at her more closely.

'Daniel phoned this morning and asked if you and I wanted to go and see the Chinese New Year celebrations in Soho, so I thought it might be fun to go along.'

'But Pandora, you hate that sort of thing. So do I. Thank God I was playing golf.'

'Well, you know how interested I am in Chinese astrology. I'm thinking of doing a course in it.'

She busied herself with trying to resuscitate some of the mangled contents of the fridge while John disappeared with a beer to watch A Question of Sport on the television. Thank goodness John wasn't the jealous type, she thought, whisking up some leftover egg whites in a copper bowl – she had decided to make a cheese soufflé. Daniel probably enjoyed her company but as for romance, forget it. Someone like him was far too glamorous for her; after all, he went out with models and spoke four languages, including Mandarin Chinese! And he was probably Jewish – an added attraction – though no one seemed quite sure about that.

She carefully poured the frothy soufflé mix into a large ramekin dish and put it into the oven. 'Dinner will be ready in half an hour,' she called cheerfully to the back of John's head, wiping her hands on her apron and disappearing outside to pick some mint to go with the fresh peas that she would pod in front of the television with him in a minute.

Passing the kitchen dresser, she picked up a wooden tiger and stroked it thoughtfully. Chinese astrology was obviously a load of rubbish; deep down she wasn't remotely tiger-like. There must have been some sort of mistake.

The wedding plans ground smoothly on. James was on a personal mission to organize the most efficient and perfect day possible. All Pandora had to do was to say what she wanted and, hey presto, it was arranged. She had instructed Coriander Angelica, London's most fashionable florist, to drape the church in white lilies which were being specially flown in from Mexico, and cornflowers and autumn berries. Coriander was going to scatter organically grown fresh herbs along the aisle so that their scent would fill the air as Pandora walked up it.

But not everyone was feeling so calm. The Portaloo situation had still not been resolved satisfactorily. Georgie had flown back from Argentina and was making this her special project. She was slightly piqued that there was nothing for her to do, but she soon found that she was fully employed bribing various officials to allow it to be erected on church land. There was all sorts of red tape involved, but her years living in Argentina had taught her that bribery was often the only solution.

There were vague rumblings from John's relatives in the north who continued to make 'helpful' suggestions. As most of these were left on their answering machine, John was able to blame Pandora's technological incompetence for the fact that everyone chose to ignore them. 'We can use the Cuban missile crisis excuse,' he had explained. Pandora had looked at him questioningly. 'You know, when the Russians threatened to bomb America if Kennedy didn't do what they asked. He didn't know what to do so he said that he "hadn't got the message".'

'Couldn't he work his answering machine either?' asked Pandora who had just sent a crisis fax to Annabel: 'Fifty Cumbrians are coming down bearing gifts towards London Town. Send help immediately.' She and John had found out that a bus was being hired in the north to ferry fifty relatives south. Half of them were bringing sleeping bags and were hoping to cadge floor space in their new house. Pandora found the idea very distressing and had to spend a whole day recuperating in Harrods' Hair and Beauty Salon. Since boarding school she had never been very comfortable sharing a room with lots of people.

It was just as well James was taking care of things as she and John had their hands full moving house. To Pandora's relief, John took several days off work to pack everything up with the calm efficiency that she found so reassuring. Without him to chivvy her on she was quite likely to spend the whole morning reading the old newspapers lining her drawers, or gripped by old diaries and letters. She was excited at the thought of seeing Bluebell House again; things had been so hectic in London that they hadn't been down since exchanging contracts six weeks ago.

On the day of the big move she left London early, leaving John to direct the removal men. Putting her foot down hard on the accelerator, the city soon melted away. Driving through the local market town where women still shopped with wicker baskets (so picturesque!), she eventually pulled up outside their new house. The view was stunning. The bluebells had died but the chestnut trees filled the valley in a golden-green haze that stretched for miles.

But once inside, the house seemed much bleaker than she remembered. It was almost gloomy. Had she been seduced by the vanilla essence on the baking tray after all? She wandered from room to room, her footsteps echoing hollowly on the wooden floors. It seemed bigger without furniture and the atmosphere was . . . different.

She sat down on a windowsill with a sinking heart, remembering all the happy times in the house she had just left behind. A girlfriend had just bought a small and relatively cheap cottage nearby which now seemed so cosy and manageable compared to this great place. Pandora realized she had made an awful mistake. She didn't like the house at all.

Once Pandora and John had moved all their furniture into Bleak House, as she now referred to it, things started to improve. John was in his element chopping down vegetation with his new chainsaw and playing golf. The neighbours held a dinner party for them, which John found interminable while Pandora was charmed by everyone. It was funny that although she and John got on so well together, they didn't really like the same sort of people at all. He found most of her girlfriends, especially Annabel, insufferably Sloaney, while his golfing cronies sent her to sleep. But hopefully now they had moved they would start meeting people that they would both get on with.

The wedding plans which until now had been running so smoothly hit a bit of a rough patch during the wedding rehearsal. John didn't endear himself to James when he turned up an hour late and Georgie's father, Lord Verney, had to fill in as an unlikely bridegroom.

'All the man has to do is bloody well turn up, and he can't even manage that!' James fumed at the altar. He regarded John with much the same suspicion as Lord Verney had felt for him.

'Can't you be a bit friendlier, Dad?' Pandora asked, fighting back tears. Honestly, everyone was getting so nervous you'd think they were getting married, not her.

Georgie was cross because the Portaloo hadn't appeared. The final straw came when the vicar refused Coriander permission to scatter herbs and rose petals on the aisle. Pandora burst into tears. She had dreamt of wafting up the aisle, crushing herbs underfoot, since she had founded the Pagan Party at school. Coriander had been shredding rose petals for days in preparation and was severely piqued.

'Pandora, have you tried pulling yourself together?' Lord Verney suggested helpfully.

'Am I allowed a cigarette yet?' asked Georgie irritably.

'Certainly not,' said James, who was longing to light up himself.

'Where is the lavatory?' inquired Coriander sweetly. There was a slightly awkward pause. She knew there wasn't one but had heard about the Portaloo saga from Pandora and wanted to cause some trouble. She was also peeved that although she was ten years older than Pandora she was still single. She smiled winningly at James; he was a bit of a dish if you went for the older man, she thought. James pulled in his stomach and smiled back.

Georgie noticed the exchange and said stiffly, 'The loo hasn't been delivered yet. I told you we would need one. Not everyone,' she looked at James, 'is blessed with a cast-iron bladder. I'm going outside to have a cigarette.'

'Calm down, darling,' said Lord Verney. 'Have you tried pulling yourself—'

'Oh, shut up, Daddy,' said Georgie, storming out of the

church, extracting a packet of chic Argentinian cigarettes from her Gucci bag.

'I'd better go and see that she's all right,' sighed James, grabbing his chance for a smoke.

John suddenly burst through the church door, his best man panting behind him.

'I'm so sorry we're late. There was an overturned lorry on the M3 and we got stuck in a six-mile tailback.' James stormed past him. 'There was nothing we could do, sir,' John added weakly.

'Damn poor show,' said Lord Verney.

'Don't worry, we won't be keeping you long,' James replied icily, shutting the door behind him. He took a deep breath and tried to calm down.

'James,' called Georgie from a nearby bush. 'Have you got a light?'

He fished around in his pocket. 'Yup.' He lit her cigarette and she inhaled deeply, sighing with relief as she exhaled. 'God, I needed that.' She offered him the packet. 'Here, help yourself. You look like you need one. By the way, you'll be completely uninterested to know but the Portaloo is behind those bushes over there. I came across it by chance just now.'

'Christ, you'd need a map and compass to find it.'

'And don't forget the hiking boots.' They both laughed. 'I knew you'd be pleased,' smiled Georgie. 'By the way, I do appreciate everything, you've done a wonderful job. I wish I could have done more.'

'Don't mention it. I just hope Pandora knows what she's doing. He just seems so, so . . .'

'Ordinary?'

'Well, yes. She could have married anyone. But I'm probably saying exactly what your father said to you before our wedding.'

'I don't remember him using the word ordinary. He was more worried about "your people" and that you didn't have any money. Did you hear that he and Mummy have to sell the house?' Lord and Lady Verney had been caught by Lloyd's.

'Yes, I did,' said James. 'Shame about the Rolls having to go too. Don't think much of the motor they've got now.' James had had to give Lord Verney a lift up the hill in his Bentley; Lord Verney's new Mini Metro not being quite up to the task.

'Lloyd's is hoovering up everything, they don't know how much they'll be liable for. They're thinking of moving to Andorra.'

'Well, if they need a loan they've only got to pick up the phone.' He chuckled to himself and then frowned. 'You know, I don't think I've ever heard John express an opinion about anything.'

'Maybe he doesn't have any,' Georgie laughed. 'By the way, I spoke to Davina yesterday. She's looking forward to tomorrow very much. I don't think she gets out much these days, what with trying to keep the estate afloat and everything.' Georgie looked at him but his face remained expressionless. 'Perhaps you should have married her. You always seemed to get on so well.'

'Oh, I don't know about that.' James shifted uncomfortably. 'I haven't seen her for years.' He wondered if

Georgie knew about his affair with Davina; they had both been so careful but you never knew.

The church door creaked slowly open. 'Are you young people quite finished?' Lord Verney shuffled out. 'I think we'd like to be getting on with things now, if you're quite ready.'

Georgie and James guiltily stubbed out their cigarettes.

'Filthy horrid habit,' muttered Lord Verney to himself. Thank goodness Pandora's young man didn't smoke. Though that was the only memorable thing about him. Still, he seemed a steady sort of chap, not the sort to run off and have affairs all the time like James. He thought of the uneasy conversation he and James had had in his Bentley earlier. Damn fine car. Who would have believed a cad like that would have done so well for himself? Irma had never liked him; she didn't like John much either. 'He looks expensive,' she had muttered darkly from behind the confines of her Estée Lauder eye mask, and from then on had remained tight-lipped on the subject. She had stayed at home today, declaring that she had no need to rehearse, she'd been to enough weddings to know the form.

Georgie and James nipped back into the church reeking of smoke and made their way to the front pew as the vicar cleared his throat pointedly.

'Now we're all here, I think we can get on,' said Lord Verney firmly, shutting the church door behind him with a bang.

AFTER

Chapter Eight

Six months later Pandora stood forlornly by a huge empty
skip in the pouring rain. She was doing her bit for the
local Earthchildren recycling campaign but everyone else
was obviously staying at home and watching television.
Since moving to the country she had thrown herself into
local events with great vigour but she was beginning to
wonder if she hadn't been deluding herself about country
life. She and John hadn't made any proper friends, and
they hardly ever saw each other. John didn't return until
eight most nights and at weekends he played golf and she
took part in Earthchildren activities. Even when they were
at home at the same time he was frantically mowing down
the triffid-like vegetation that was constantly threatening
to engulf the house, while she was busy inside it. It was
proving impossible to find a cleaner because local house
prices were so high that the blue collar classes had been
completely frozen out. The house was huge and unwieldy,
and it took her for ever to clean.

Pandora shivered and gazed up at the thunderclouds

billowing above her. The weather reminded her of their wedding day. It had been such a disappointment after the trouble everyone had gone to. Still, apart from the rain it had been a great success and she and John had loved every moment.

She glanced at her watch and noticed with relief that it was nearly five o'clock. Thank goodness, she could push off now. She checked her make-up carefully in the car mirror. John had arranged to play golf with Daniel today and there was an outside chance that he might have brought him back for tea. She had only seen him once since her wedding but she'd been thinking about him all the time. He represented all the glamour her life presently lacked; last week she had opened *Tatler* to find him listed as one of Britain's top one hundred bachelors. She couldn't help wondering if he would ask her out if she was single. He was always so attentive when they did meet.

As she drove up the drive, her heart leapt into her mouth – Daniel's Mercedes was parked outside! She pinched her cheeks and ran her fingers through her damp hair – if only she had time to blow dry it – before opening the door.

'Pandora! We've been wondering where you were!' Daniel was standing by the door. He had his coat on and was obviously just about to leave. 'I'm so glad I managed to catch you before I left; it's a pain but I've got to be in London by half past six. I'm taking Sophie to the premiere of the new James Bond movie tonight.'

'Gosh, you lucky thing,' said Pandora, casually taking off her dripping mac and smiling up at him through glistening lashes. He was standing so close she could smell the faint scent of his aftershave. If she had moved one step closer, or tripped on the doormat, she would have been in his arms. The thought made her weak with longing. He placed a hand firmly on her shoulder and kissed her on both cheeks. 'You're a lucky man, John,' he said, glancing round the immaculate drawing room appreciatively and opening the front door. 'Think of me in a couple of hours struggling into my dinner jacket while you two are curled up in front of the fire!' He climbed into his car and within minutes was swallowed up in the mist that had descended from the surrounding hills.

'It feels like it's been raining for months,' said Pandora, tearing herself away from the window to face John. He was glued to the television and didn't hear her. 'Like a cup of tea?' she asked, longing to escape into the kitchen and be alone with her thoughts and dreams of Daniel. John didn't reply. Really, he was going quite deaf. 'I asked if you would like a cup of tea,' she said loudly.

'Uh, oh, yes,' responded John.

She made the tea and cut a large slice of homemade fruit cake for him. He took it from her without saying anything.

'You could have offered some cake to Daniel,' she grumbled. It would have been a chance for Daniel to see what a good cook she was. 'Men like him probably never eat anything homemade.' She sat down opposite John and sipped her tea. 'What do you and Daniel talk about?'

'Work, sport, the usual stuff.'

'Is it serious between him and this Sophie, d'you think?'

'I don't know.'

Pandora sighed with exasperation. She loved gossiping about other people but John couldn't care less. It was *so* frustrating.

'Is Peter and Wendy's dinner party still on tonight?' she asked wearily.

'Definitely. I saw him at the club this morning. He's asked us for eight o'clock.'

Pandora's heart sank. John had hooked into the local golfing set and weekends were always taken up with dinner parties where the main topics of conversation were pruning rotas, lawn mowers, the perils of commuting and IV fertilization. Everyone seemed desperate to have children but were having great difficulties in doing so. Pandora lived in dread of having a missed period and consequently was on the pill, wore a diaphragm and had recently begun to insist that John wear a condom as well. She had just bought a microwave because she had heard that they reduced men's sperm counts to nonexistent levels. One couldn't be too careful, it would be appalling to get pregnant now when she was thinking about writing her first novel.

'I'll go and get changed then.' She brightened, remembering that she had received some new clothes by mail order this morning. Maybe wearing something new tonight would buck her up a bit. She ran upstairs and slipped into a black leather skirt, which was a bit of a departure from her usual image. She usually lived in black leggings and baggy jumpers but she was longing to break out and wear something different. The skirt could have been made for her, it fitted like a glove. She ran downstairs.

'What do you think?' She twirled in front of John. 'I could wear it tonight.'

John looked very uncomfortable, he hated having to express an opinion. 'It's all right,' he said doubtfully.

'You don't like it, do you?' said Pandora. 'Does it make me look fat?'

'No, not at all. It's, well, it's . . .'

'Yes?' said Pandora impatiently.

'Well, it's just not really you, is it?'

'Isn't it?' She left the sitting room and caught sight of herself in the hall mirror. Who was she? She was a housewife, married to a merchant banker, and she was bored. Bored and unhappy. And the worst thing was that she only had herself to blame. She packed up the skirt ready to send back in the morning and picked out a navy blue sweater dress instead. Who was she trying to kid? She wasn't going to the premiere of a James Bond movie, she was going out for a quiet dinner in the country. Sitting at her dressing table, she counted her blessings. She lived in a beautiful house. OK, John wasn't scintillating but he was faithful, hard-working, kind and reliable. They had plenty of money. Why then did she feel so dead inside?

'Does Daniel ever talk about being Jewish?' she asked John in the car on the way to dinner.

'No, he's a bit sensitive about it, I think,' replied John,

skidding to avoid a rabbit that had just dashed across the lane.

'I wonder why. I've always thought it was terrifically glamorous to be Jewish. Oh, I forgot to tell you, Annabel spotted the General – remember Joshua's father who you met ages ago? – in Annabel's last week. He told her that Joshua has fallen madly in love with the daughter of the PLO finance minister. How's that for gossip?' She sighed wistfully as they pulled up outside Peter and Wendy's immaculate neo-Georgian house. She hadn't been to Annabel's for aeons.

Peter and Wendy greeted them in high spirits. 'Have a glass of shampoo!' said Peter, flourishing a bottle of Australian fizz at them. 'We've just had some good news, Wendy's pregnant!'

Pandora composed her face carefully into an expression of delight while John patted Peter on the back. 'That's terrific news, well done!'

'Come in and meet the rest of the gang,' said Wendy happily. Pandora followed them into the sitting room with a sinking heart. Just as well she hadn't worn the leather skirt, the other three girls were heavily into the Laura Ashley country sackcloth look. Her sensible woolly sweater dress fitted in perfectly. When everybody had finished congratulating Wendy and Peter about their news, conversation turned to Pandora's day manning the skip. Her Earthchildren activities were a source of great amusement to John's golfing cronies who all privately thought Pandora was sweet but a little weird.

'I don't believe in charities,' said Keith proudly. 'Last

week I was auditing Whale Save's accounts. If you knew how much went on administration . . .'

'And most of that waste paper for recycling just gets towed away to the local rubbish dump. There was an article about it in the *Sunday Express*,' his wife Lynda added.

'Oh, I hope not,' said Pandora. 'The chairman of our local branch has looked into it and our skip goes straight to a paper recycling plant in Deptford every Monday. I expect some charity money is misdirected but one has to try to do something.'

'Of course if one isn't working one has time. At weekends I'm so shattered all I want to do is play golf,' said Peter, sawing a lump of roast pork that Wendy had just heaved out of the oven.

'So will you give up work when you have the baby?' asked Pandora, pushing the pink meat around her plate, – pork was the one thing she couldn't stand.

'Maybe for a few months, but I couldn't bear being at home all day, I'd go mad with boredom. I don't know how you stand it, Pandora.' Wendy was secretly envious that Pandora didn't have to work and were it not for their grinding mortgage would have given up her job like a shot.

'Oh, I love it, there's loads to do. It's taken me six months to get the house sorted out, and there's the vegetable garden, having people down for weekends . . .'

'But now you've finished doing the house up, what on earth will you do with yourself all day?'

'Well, I've just started writing a novel.'

Wendy smiled at her indulgently.

'I should write a novel,' said Peter, 'so many funny things happen to me. Now, would anyone like some treacle tart? It's homemade.'

Everyone made enthusiastic noises and the evening dragged on to its interminable conclusion. After dinner the men and women split into separate groups, the men to talk about golf and sport, the women to discuss Wendy's oncoming happy event. Pandora smiled glassily and said very little. She was suffering from excruciating nervous indigestion and was longing to go home. Eventually at midnight goodbyes were exchanged and everybody got into their company cars. Though no one admitted it, there was some discreet one-upmanship which Pandora and John always won because of Pandora's private income. They had the largest house, the biggest garden with a tennis court and swimming pool, a brand new Mercedes and a sports car. They may think I'm two sandwiches short of a picnic, Pandora thought privately, but at least I've got a bit of dosh. That was some consolation in life, she supposed bleakly as John eased his way expertly out of the narrow drive.

'That was a good evening,' he said cheerfully. 'Peter and Wendy were on fine form. Maybe we should try for a baby. What do you think?'

Pandora looked at him in horror. John had never expressed a paternal urge before.

'Um, well, you can't rush into these things. You never know, I might be infertile,' she finished hopefully.

'Well, we're hardly going to find out with you taking

the pill, wearing a diaphragm and insisting on me wearing a condom every time we make love, are we?'

'No,' agreed Pandora. 'Well, perhaps I'll give up the diaphragm and we'll see what happens. But I don't really want to get pregnant until I finish my novel.'

'If you spent half as much time writing this novel as you do talking about it you might finish it before the next century.'

'I've written a synopsis. I could read it to you when we get home, if you like.' She was rather thrilled with the idea she had and was longing to share it with someone.

John pulled into the drive. 'Maybe you could read it to me tomorrow, I'm dead beat.'

When Pandora woke up the following morning, John had already left to play golf. He was going to the airport straight after the game as he had to be in Brussels first thing on Monday morning for a business meeting. She stretched out, relishing the feel of the sun streaming through the windows on her face. It was so nice to have the bed to herself. It was funny, once she had resented John's golfing habit but now she was grateful for it. They had so little in common that she wondered what they would do if they did spend more time together. Any shared activity seemed to involve a huge amount of compromise on one side.

As she jumped out of bed, the telephone rang. It was Annabel. She sounded dreadful.

'I'm sorry to ring so early, darling, but I've had the most bloody news.' She blew her nose. 'You know Daddy put all my money into Lloyd's? Well, apparently I've lost the lot. We thought that my syndicate hadn't been hit, but it has. I'll have to sell my flat, my car, maybe even Merlin,' she sobbed. 'I certainly won't be able to afford the livery fees.'

'I'm so sorry, Annabel. That's dreadful. Look, why don't you drive down here and stay a few days. John's gone to Brussels so we'll have the place to ourselves.'

'Could I? For one night anyway. I'd love to see you, it's been ages.' Annabel spent most of her time in Cumbria with Hugo, and the girls hadn't seen each other for weeks. 'Can I bring you anything from London?'

'Oooaar, could you bring a newspaper? The ones down here are at least a month old.' They both laughed. 'Seriously, you could bring Friday's *Evening Standard*, I can't buy it locally.' Along with mangos, grapenuts, decent yogurts, fresh fish – really, it was a wonder people in the country didn't starve to death.

It would be nice having Annabel to stay, thought Pandora as she made up a bed in one of the many spare rooms that stood empty most of the time. She had once had grand ideas about wild country house parties, but they had had only two since they had moved in. Neither had been a great success, their friends were so different and no one had really gelled at all. The whole experience had been rather embarrassing and incredibly hard work. All she had done was cook and clean all weekend and the sparkling conversation that she had so been looking forward to had never materialized.

On the way upstairs she glanced into her study. It

was a beautiful room and faced south over the chestnut woods. Today sunshine spilled in and her Biedermeier table glowed a deep burnished gold. Her synopsis lay on top of it, she had been working on it in a desultory way for months, and now she was ready to start the first chapter. She read through it quickly, then stuffed it into a large envelope and into a drawer. Who was she trying to kid? John was right, how could someone like her hope to finish a novel, let alone publish one? She didn't have the discipline or the time.

She shut the door behind her and went outside. Everything in the vegetable garden had suddenly sprouted and needed transplanting, she really ought to crack on now before Annabel arrived. As she carefully began to transfer the small plants into a larger bed she remembered with a pang John's disparaging comments and imagined the look on his face if she ever had her own novel published. She quoted softly under her breath, 'I have spread my dreams under your feet, tread softly for you tread on my dreams.' And now fate had squashed Annabel's dream of winning the dressage at Badminton next year. It was awful that she would probably have to sell Merlin, just when she had trained him up so beautifully.

She wondered what John's dreams were, or if he even had any. She had asked him once and he had joked, 'To get a bigger bonus next year.' It had taken her this long to realize that he hadn't been joking, and that he seemed to care about nothing beyond their immediate material concerns at all. At one time she had found that soothing and reassuring but now it just seemed indicative of the huge chasm that lay between them.

'Have you ever wondered if the golf is just a red herring and that he's got another woman?' asked Annabel several hours later as she and Pandora sat chatting in the exquisite Smallbone kitchen.

'God, I wish. It would be better grounds for divorce than boredom. But what d'you think those are?' Pandora gesticulated to the dresser groaning with gleaming golfing trophies. 'Scotch Mist?'

'He could have nicked them.'

'Nooooo.' They both laughed.

'I've always thought that golf was a sure way of ruining a perfectly good walk,' said Annabel, 'but it looks like he's very good at it, judging by all those cups.'

'He's very competitive and he practises all the time. The funny thing is that people feel really sorry for me being a golf widow but I'm actually quite relieved to have the time to myself. I've even started arranging golf matches for him. But I've been boring you for months with my classic bored housewife scenario, we should be discussing what you're going to do.'

'Get a job, I suppose.' Both girls ruminated silently on this appalling prospect. 'I met someone who had a job once,' said Annabel brightly.

'But you do work, you're an equestrienne,' said Pandora loyally.

''Fraid it doesn't pay. You know, I never appreciated how lucky I was till I lost it all. My sisters are in the same boat, but Camilla's just got married to a Palm Beach millionaire – she always was the brainy one – and Emily's got a hotshot career in New York.'

'What's she doing these days?'

'She's still a literary agent with William Morris. Bear her in mind if you ever get round to writing that opus you're always talking about. You should get on and start it while you've got the time. You never know what's round the corner, take it from me.' Annabel got a cigarette out of her bag and lit it with unsteady fingers. She looked thin and gaunt and her grey eyes had lost their sparkle.

'Since when have you smoked?' asked Pandora concernedly.

'It kind of helps at the moment. Don't worry, I'll stop when I'm a bit more sorted out. You see, losing my money isn't the only thing. I had a smear test a couple of weeks ago. There was something wrong and I had to have a biopsy. I have to go for the results the day after tomorrow.' She started crying. 'I'm so bloody scared, Pandora, I don't know what to do!'

'Hang on, don't panic. Remember Beatrice had that positive smear? All they did was keep her under observation for six months and it disappeared. They didn't have to do anything. It's terribly common.'

'But it just might be serious, it might be cancer!'

'Not at our age. Come on, darling, you're as strong as an ox, you look far too healthy to have anything wrong with you. Would you like me to come with you to the hospital?'

'Oh, would you? My appointment's in the afternoon.

Why don't you stay the night and if I'm in the clear we'll go out and celebrate. If it's bad we can throw ourselves out of the window.'

'Have you told Hugo about all this?'

'I've told him about the Lloyd's thing, and vaguely mentioned the smear test, but he's very squeamish. He practically faints if he hears the word menstruation. I'm afraid he'll go right off me.'

'Of course he won't, you guys have been going out for ever.'

'Three years, on and off. He hasn't even rung to find out how I am. I gave him your phone and fax number so hopefully he'll contact me while I'm here.' She burst into tears again.

Pandora hugged her, trying to absorb some of her friend's misery. She had never seen Annabel so utterly defeated and it was quite frightening. Until now she had always led such a charmed life.

'I was reading that a block of marble is an obstacle to the weak and a stepping stone to the strong. You never know what this ghastliness might lead to. You always talked about going into PR one day, you'd be so good at it. Perhaps this will be the catalyst for a whole new life for you.'

Annabel dried her eyes and smiled. 'Maybe you're right.'

'Now, let's have a cup of tea and something to eat. I fancy a bowl of grapenuts and a cup of tea. How about you?'

'Sounds delicious. And some hot chocolate?'

'Perfect. God, it's such a relief not to have to cook a huge great meal for John. Why can't men live off cereal and yogurts like us?' But as she went to put the kettle on she frowned to herself. They said bad luck always came in threes; she hoped with all her heart that Annabel didn't have any more horrors to face.

The next day she got up early to find Annabel was already up and reading a sheet of paper. Her eyes were red and puffy and she looked as if she'd been crying for hours.

'A fax came through from Hugo last night, I checked your machine this morning. I had a feeling something like this would happen.'

'What does it say?'

'I think we can safely assume from it that the chances of my becoming the next Countess of Wolvaston are practically zero. I think the Lloyd's thing and the smear test result have put him right off.'

'Surely not. You've been together too long for him to run off just because of some bad luck.'

'Oh, I think this was just an excuse. His family always thought I was a bit on the racy side, and I think he may have had suspicions about me and Fergus – and one or two others. Can you imagine, being dumped by fax. It's terribly *nineties*, isn't it?' Annabel blew her nose and gazed out over the undulating countryside. 'It's such a fabulous view, just looking at it makes me feel tons better. I've decided I'm going to ring up everyone I know who's involved in PR and see if I can get a job, even if it's starting right at the bottom. I was never going right to the top in dressage anyway. And as for Hugo, well, to be honest, he was pretty lousy in bed.'

'I never could see you locked away in the country opening fêtes somehow,' said Pandora.

'Talking of which, what are you going to do now you've got this place looking like a feature for *Ideal Home*?'

'Well, I've been working on my novel thing, but it's probably a waste of time. John seems to think so anyway.'

'Bugger what John thinks. I remember all those great stories you used to write at school. Mrs Woods used to say you were a born storyteller.'

'But it's so hard to find enough time. This house is like the Forth Bridge – as soon as I've cleaned it, the first bit is filthy again. And the garden is basically a time-eating machine. I can't find a gardener and as the whole point of moving to the country was to grow our own vegetables, I'm determined to give that a shot.'

'But it's not really *you*, is it?' Annabel persisted. 'It's like you're playing some sort of game, playing at country life.'

'I know, it's all been a bit of a mistake really. It's funny, John was the one who had second thoughts about moving out but he's taken to it like a duck to water, he's got loads of chums to play golf with and he loves hacking around with the chainsaw. He even asked if we could start trying for a baby! Can you imagine!'

'Trying for a baby. What a quaint expression. What on earth did you say?'

'That I was far too busy thinking about my novel. I've made an appointment to see my doctor to get a double strength pill just in case he starts refusing to wear a condom or puts a hole in my diaphragm. You hear of men doing dreadful things once they get broody.' They both shrieked with laughter. 'Oh, Annabel, I do envy you.'

'Envy me! Why?'

'Because you're not married. I feel so trapped by all this.' Pandora gestured at the house and huge garden. 'Sometimes I wish I was single and living in a little flat in London. I don't think that John and I really have anything in common at all.'

'But you've only been married six months, you can't be thinking of packing it in already.'

'Oh, I'm not,' said Pandora hurriedly, who had been thinking about nothing else for weeks. 'I mean, realistically I'm hopeless on my own, and John's so easy to live with. Deep down I'm very fond of him but I think that some time apart might be a good idea. It might make me appreciate him more.'

'Or less,' laughed Annabel. 'I know I've never been John's number one fan, but I think you should give it another six months at least before you do anything radical.'

'Yes, I know you're right. But I might go and look at a few flats tomorrow afternoon before I come with you to the hospital. Maybe spending time in London might revitalize our relationship a bit.'

'It might get you out of the clutches of the golfing set at least.' Annabel looked at her watch. 'I'll just grab some toast, then I'll drive back to London and start my marathon phone around. My appointment is at four o'clock at the Portland tomorrow, can you meet me there?'

'Of course. I'm sure everything will be fine, then we can go out and celebrate afterwards.'

'Or throw ourselves out of the window,' grimaced Annabel with a wry laugh.

Two hours later Annabel drove off in a cloud of dust and Pandora retired to her study to write campaign letters for various charities she belonged to. She sat browsing through a newsletter from the Born Free Foundation, a charity which campaigned tirelessly for the welfare of zoo animals that were often imprisoned in appalling conditions. A picture of an elephant locked in solitary confinement inside a dingy cell in a zoo in Belgium was particularly dreadful and the newsletter recommended writing to the Belgian ambassador and her local MEP. Another picture showed a killer whale, abandoned in a swimming pool in Mexico with terrible sores on his back. Pandora wanted to weep. Here she was complaining about being trapped but at least she could change her situation. What on earth could these poor animals do?

She spent the next few hours typing out letters until she heard John's car pull up in front of the house. She sighed, and turned off her typewriter knowing that he would be hungry and that there was hardly any food in the house.

'Hi!' she said cheerfully. 'Did you have a good trip?' She scooted into the kitchen to avoid having to kiss him.

'Yeah, it went really well. I'm starving, though. What's in the fridge?' he asked, opening it.

'Nothing much, I'm afraid. I'll have to get something out of the freezer and defrost it in the microwave.'

John looked irritated. 'Really, it's not as if you work or anything, Pandora. The least you can do is keep the fridge stocked up.'

'I meant to go into town but Annabel came down unexpectedly and I didn't get a chance.' She peered into the fridge. 'There's loads of eggs. How about I make a soufflé omelette *fines herbes*, and for pudding you can have the rest of that mango and meringue ice cream.'

John looked slightly mollified.

'I wrote twelve letters today complaining about zoo conditions. D'you want to sign them too?'

'It doesn't do any good, I should think they just get chucked in the bin. And in some countries they keep files of people who write critical letters and refuse them visas.'

'I don't believe you,' said Pandora, chopping up a handful of parsley, tarragon, chives and chervil that she had picked that morning.

'Besides, what can one person do to change anything?' John helped himself to a can of beer from the fridge.

'Quite a lot. Look at Hitler, he managed to kill six million people.' She began to whisk egg whites aggressively.

'Oh, come on, Pandora, don't get into one of your states.'

'I'm not in a state, I'd just like to see some evidence that you care about something, *anything*!'

'I care about you,' he said rather quietly.

Pandora realized that she probably cared more about the plight of zoo animals in Belgium than her own husband. She was turning into a monster and it was all his fault, she had been a much nicer person when she was single. She melted a large lump of butter in the frying pan and poured in the whisked eggs, waiting until the base was cooked before sliding the pan beneath the hot grill. When the frothy white mixture had risen and turned a rich golden brown she carefully slid it on to a warmed plate and sprinkled some more herbs on top. She paused for a moment, admiring the contrast of green and gold against the creamy plate. 'Here you are,' she said, putting the plate beside him as he sat reading the newspaper. 'Eat it quickly before it collapses.'

'Aren't you having any?' he asked, taking a large mouthful with his eyes still on the paper.

Really, she could feed him dog food and he'd never notice the difference. If only he would just say this is delicious, or this is under-seasoned, over-seasoned – anything! She went to such trouble to cook lovely meals, but his apathy and indifference to her efforts was driving her mad.

'No, I'll have a bowl of cereal in a minute. Is that nice?'

Engrossed in his paper he didn't hear her.

'John, I asked is that nice?'

'Hmmm, yes.' He glanced at his watch. 'D'you mind

if I eat this next door? There's something I really want to watch,' and clutching the paper he removed himself and his plate from the kitchen. Pandora went to the sink and numbly began to wash up. Waves of misery swept over her and she began to cry, her tears mingling with the running water. Her marriage was an empty sham, the strain of living with a man she no longer loved was suffocating her inside. She took a deep breath. Annabel was right, she must stick it a bit longer. After all, going it alone might be even worse, and who else would put up with her? Tomorrow she would ring up her mother's shrink and make an appointment. Maybe talking to a professional would help make up her mind.

Chapter Nine

Pandora left John a piece of fillet steak with instructions on how to grill it for his supper and checked that his wardrobe was full of freshly ironed shirts. He hadn't been very enthusiastic about her spending the night in London with Annabel, he hated coming back to an empty house. But Pandora had explained how depressed Annabel was and he had reluctantly agreed.

Just before leaving the house, she glanced around the drawing room, taking in the shining parquet floor, the creamy silk curtains framing sparkling windows beyond which one could see for miles. Everything was a pleasing blur of rose-gold and cream so that even on overcast days there was always an impression of sunshine within. Lemon and orange trees, jasmine and bougainvillea added splashes of colour and an exotic scent to the silent rooms. It was just how she had imagined it would be. And yet it didn't feel homely; however high they turned up the heating it always seemed cold. It was with a sense of relief that she double-locked the door behind her and set off for London.

'During the examination I was doing this deal with God. I promised that if there was nothing wrong He could take all my money and I wouldn't complain,' Annabel explained during forkfuls of Caesar salad at PJ's later. 'But the awful thing is now I know I'm fine I've started to worry about Lloyd's again, and I promised God I wouldn't. I feel terribly guilty about that.'

'Really, you and your Catholic guilt,' laughed Pandora as she poured them more champagne. 'I told you there'd be nothing wrong.'

'Oh, I didn't tell you,' said Annabel excitedly, 'my sister Camilla rang this morning. She's asked me to stay with her in Palm Beach. All expenses paid!' She took a sip of champagne and eyed the men lining the bar. 'There's a pensioner over there staring at you. I think you'll find you know him.'

Pandora turned round. 'It's the General! I haven't seen him for ages.' She waved enthusiastically and he came over.

'My favourite girl. The Paddington Palace has never been the same since you left. No one makes felafels like you. I heard you got married.'

'Yes, to John Black. You met him.'

The General slapped his forehead dramatically. 'You didn't marry the draft dodger! I don't believe it!' He looked at Annabel. 'Can you believe it? She married him!' The General kissed her hand extravagantly.

'How's Joshua?'

'He is now living in Israel. Yonathon got him a job at the Knesset as a translator. That Yonathon, he is a nightmare, always in scandals with other people's wives.' Yonathon now held an influential position in the Israeli government, and had recently become an international celebrity since appearing on CNN wearing a gas mask during a national crisis.

Pandora smiled. At one time just the mention of his name would have made her heart ache for days. Now she felt nothing.

'It is a shame you are married,' the General went on. 'I have a friend I would like to introduce you to. Do you know Jack Dudley?'

'No, I don't,' said Pandora.

'I do,' said Annabel. 'He used to work with Hugo.'

'Ah well.' The General sighed. 'Since you are married, Jack will just have to take his chances elsewhere. Now, I must leave for a meeting, my friends are waiting.' He indicated a group of swarthy Israelis standing by the door talking excitedly into mobile phones.

'What's the meeting about?' asked Pandora.

'Import export,' the General replied. 'If you give me your card I shall invite you both to my next party.' He took Pandora's card and went to join his cronies by the door.

'You see what I mean?' said Pandora. 'I'd give anything not to be married and to go out on dates with Jack Dudley or whoever. Wearing this,' she flourished her wedding ring, 'makes me feel quite invisible.' She sipped her champagne thoughtfully. 'I looked at a couple of flats today, one of them was really nice. If John likes it I thought I might put in an offer. Then we could spend a few nights a week in town and start doing civilized things again, like going to the cinema.'

'Haven't you got one in Middlehurst?'

'Well, once a week there's a small stir amongst the educated classes when the bingo hall is converted into a kind of makeshift cinema and they show a suitably highbrow film. It's not exactly the Fulham ABC, though.' She was interrupted by her mobile phone. 'Oh, hi, John. Yes, you just heat the grill and put the steak under it till it's brown on both sides . . . No, I don't know how many minutes exactly, it depends on how well done you want it.' She rolled her eyes heavenward. 'There are vegetables at the bottom of the fridge . . . I can't talk because I'm in PJ's. Yes, see you tomorrow. Oh, by the way, I saw a fabulous flat today. D'you want to meet me there tomorrow afternoon and we can drive back to the country afterwards? Great.' She gave him the address, said goodbye and switched the telephone off.

'Poor man,' laughed Annabel. 'You weren't very nice to him.'

'I just can't believe that someone who is responsible for millions of pounds worth of other people's money has to ring up his wife to ask what vegetables he should have with his steak. I find it excruciating.'

'C'mon,' said Annabel, gathering up her bag, 'let's go home and check my answerphone messages. Then we can dial 1471 and see if any gorgeous shy men have called and were too inhibited to leave a message.'

John was as enthusiastic about the flat as Pandora. The relentless commute which involved getting up at six and often not returning home until eight or nine in the evening was taking its toll and he was pale, run-down and tired. Pandora's trustees willingly released the money and within a month the flat was hers. Well, officially it was theirs as she had decided to put it in both their names to make John feel more comfortable.

Spending more time in London gave Pandora a new lease of life. She caught up with old friends, cultivated new ones, held lots of dinner parties and saw the latest movies and plays. At first the plan had been to stay in London two nights a week, but it wasn't long before they slipped into a pattern of returning to the country only at weekends. She resuscitated her novel and embarked on a creative writing course, frequently becoming so involved with assignments that she forgot to shop and cook. John, returning home after a long day at work, had to resort to tins and convenience foods. He yearned for the stews and crumbles Pandora used to make, but when he complained she just laughed and said her earth mother phase had finished and she was developing excitingly urban tendencies that precluded pastry-making. Cooking for John was a soul-destroying exercise and she had decided to give it up. Since he had never expressed an opinion, a preference or an enthusiasm for anything she had cooked, she was rather surprised that he had even noticed that she had turned to Harrods' Food Hall and ready-made meals.

In her dissatisfaction her thoughts turned increasingly to Daniel. He provided an escape from the emotional drudgery of her life with John. In her dreams she could convince herself that he was the man she should have married, and that he might even feel the same way about her. Her longing entered a new intensive phase when a friend confided that Daniel had said that he wished he could find someone just like her.

And so, as her marriage flickered and died, she clung tenaciously to the fantasy of a future with Daniel – as she had once clung to the security that John had provided. If only she could have an affair with him it might even save their marriage, for she longed for excitement and burned with boredom. She didn't know anyone who was having an affair, but then most of her friends weren't married. Poring over a copy of *Cosmopolitan*, she read that two out of three married people had committed adultery during the first five years of marriage. She wondered where they had conducted their poll. Certainly around Middlehurst adultery seemed to be the last thing on anyone's mind; they were far more interested in improving their golf handicap.

When John announced he had booked them a holiday in the Outer Hebrides for a week's golfing with his friends, Pandora's face dropped.

'It'll be fun,' John said. 'You haven't seen Peter and Wendy and the others for ages. They've all been asking after you.'

'Only because they can't find anyone else to bore about golf and pruning rotas and Laura Ashley wallpaper,' snapped Pandora irritably. What on earth was happening to her? She never used to be this vitriolic. But a golfing week in the Outer Hebrides? No way. 'I'm in the middle of my writing course, it goes on for weeks,' she went on more calmly.

'Surely it won't matter if you take some time off.'

'No, I can't, it's important to me,' she replied bitterly. If only he could show *some* interest in her writing. John just thought it was another one of her spurious enthusiasms, more annoying than most because this one had resulted in a deterioration in the smooth running of the household. He had even had to iron a shirt for himself last week.

'Everyone else's wife will be going and it will look very peculiar if I pitch up by myself.'

Pandora sighed with exasperation. What did it matter what other people thought? 'I'm not interested in golf,' she said, trying to keep her voice level, 'and I don't want to go to the Outer Hebrides. I'd be bored stiff. You'll have much more fun without me hanging around being miserable.' She gazed unseeingly out of the window before continuing more calmly.

'Since we've moved back to London and I've started writing, a whole new world has opened up for me. I'm reading more, meeting different people, getting fresh ideas . . .' Pandora's cheeks were flushed and her eyes sparkled. John thought he had never seen her looking prettier. He turned away quickly, she got irritated when he looked at her 'for no reason'. But he looked at her because he loved her, he didn't need a reason.

Pandora spent the next fortnight in a fever of excitement looking forward to John's departure. She hadn't had a whole week to herself since they married and she was longing to practise being single again. She was planning a complex series of social engagements beginning with a party being given by a new friend called Rachel on the Saturday night. Most of her wakeful hours were spent plotting how she might spend some time with Daniel. Annabel suggested that she ring him in the middle of the night in a state, sounding breathless and vulnerable because she was convinced there was a man trying to get into her flat. 'If he's remotely keen he'll rush straight over.'

This was the best idea they could come up with. But Pandora was crushed when she found out that Daniel would be spending the whole week in Frankfurt.

On the Saturday John was due to depart, Pandora woke first and leapt out of bed, rushing downstairs to put the kettle on. He would want to make love before he left and the thought had galvanized her into this uncharacteristic burst of energy. John woke up a moment later and reached out tentatively for her but it was too late. She reappeared with a cup of tea, the paper and a busy expression that would hopefully put the dampener on any nuptial ideas.

'It's not too late to change your mind and come with me,' John said hopefully.

'Oh no, you know how depressed I get in the north.'

She handed him the cup of tea and smiled. The excitement of having a whole week to herself in London had put her in a very good mood. 'Would you like a cooked breakfast before you go?' she asked brightly, longing for him to leave.

'That would be great – if you can be bothered.' It was on the tip of his tongue to say bugger the breakfast, come back to bed, but he didn't. She had scuttled out of the room and was already halfway down the stairs anyway. She knew exactly what was on his mind.

John felt rather hurt that Pandora was so cheerful when they wouldn't be seeing one another for a whole week, but perhaps it might do them good to have a break; maybe absence would make her heart grow fonder. He was disappointed that they hadn't made love for over a month. But then he'd always known that she was undersexed; even when they first started going out she'd never been that keen.

Pandora hummed as the bread sizzled in the hot butter. Out of sight, out of mind, she thought gleefully. John was driving to Edinburgh and then taking a train the rest of the way. She hoped the fry-up wouldn't send him to sleep in the car. Imagine if he had a crash, she'd be a widow . . . She stood for a moment, balancing an egg in her hand, appalled at herself, before breaking it into the pan. Where did such awful thoughts come from? Still, he had a long way to drive, perhaps he'd need another egg. She dropped more butter into the pan and went on to the sunny terrace to cut some parsley.

An hour later she stood at the front door waving as

John's car disappeared in a cloud of dust. She just had to water the vegetables and then she would be free to drive up to London. Wielding the hosepipe she examined the shrivelled green remnants that were the result of months of hard labour. Foraging in the earth she discovered a woody orange stem that looked a bit like a carrot and three potatoes that she had planted five months ago that had refused to sprout. She thought longingly of her local London Waitrose and its tempting array of fruit, vegetables and glamorous bachelors stocking up on bananas and Häagen-Dazs ice cream. How could she ever have thought that the countryside could possibly compare with such urban delights?

Driving into London in the late afternoon she cursed herself for believing the myth of country life so temptingly peddled in the glossy magazines. How could she, a relatively sensible young woman with three A levels and a private income, have succumbed so readily?

Pandora crawled through Putney and down the Kings Road, turning off into the maze of side streets that she knew so well to avoid the traffic. She loved staying in her flat at weekends. The surrounding streets, usually crammed with huge four-wheel drive vehicles driven by harassed mothers, each with a token small, pinched child perched forlornly in the back, were echoing and silent. Everybody was in the countryside relaxing with chainsaws and lawnmowers.

Once inside the flat, she shut the door quietly behind her. Leaning against it, she savoured the silence. A whole week completely alone! She put on her favourite

Kate Bush CD, glad that her immediate neighbours, too, went away at weekends. The music soared and floated sensuously about the flat, and Pandora sank luxuriously into the impractical cream sofa and planned how she would spend her week.

She was looking forward to getting stuck into a particularly absorbing assignment set by Flora, her creative writing teacher, last week. The course was proving to be a great success, despite its odd title, 'Floreat Flora – Creative Writing For Feminists', presumably dreamt up by Flora. It had been the only course with any spare places. There were no men which wasn't surprising given that Flora had written 'men are admitted but not encouraged' on the course leaflet. Flora was a middle-aged poetess and occasional potter who sometimes sold her products after class. She was known as 'the black widow' in potting circles because she had been widowed three times. She was also a Sylvia Plath devotee and when the class were not discussing Sylvia's psychic oppression at the excitingly beastly hands of her husband Ted Hughes, they were set a variety of intriguing assignments. After a particularly long diatribe against Ted Hughes last week, Flora said, 'Hands up if any of you are married.'

Pandora guiltily raised her hand. She knew all the others were single or living with partners of unspecified sex. She had a feeling that Flora had a particularly treacherous assignment in mind.

'Hard cheese, old girl,' Flora commiserated, dropping her habitual dungaree speak and lapsing into the

Cheltenham Ladies tones that outed themselves when she became particularly over-excited.

'How to kill your husband. One thousand words. Pandora will be able to write from first-hand experience,' she chuckled before continuing, 'Enjoy yourselves, this is one of my most popular assignments.'

Pandora had gone a guilty red. 'Why would the High Pottess think that I had ever wanted to kill my husband?' she whispered to Araminta, a glamorous raven-haired actress who had once enjoyed a brief flowering of fame when she had appeared in an episode of *Brookside* as a ravaged lesbian.

'Dahhling, you've got that look about you,' replied Araminta, dramatically rolling her eyes. Pandora thought about John's high cholesterol level and guiltily remembered the steaks, Bearnaise sauces and fry-ups that comprised most of his diet these days. 'RUBBER HEIRESS WIFE SUED FOR MANSLAUGHTER!' What the hell. He wasn't forced to eat it. Besides, it would make a great short story.

Pandora spent the rest of the day getting ready for Rachel's party that night. Rachel lived in Notting Hill in a fashionably run-down and Bohemian street just off the Portobello Road. Pandora didn't like Notting Hill. It had a definite 'wot u lookin' at?' atmosphere that made her feel quite uncomfortable. It was odd how so many of her friends had chosen to live there in recent years when they could have afforded to live somewhere decent like South Kensington.

When she arrived, the party was already in full swing. She squeezed through a crowd of Old Etonian Trustafarians and looked around desperately for Rachel. As she ventured into another room clutching her bottle of Aqua Libra anxiously, someone said in her ear, 'You look like you could use a drink.' She turned round and saw that the voice belonged to a tall, thin man with paint-stained clothes and kind brown eyes.

'Yes, I could, but I can't find a glass,' replied Pandora, relieved that she had someone to talk to.

'Wait here a sec and I'll get you one. My name's Darren, by the way.'

Darren disappeared into a throng of designer baseball caps, reappearing a moment later with a grimy glass full of a surprisingly delicious and innocuous tasting liquid. She soon found herself relaxing and getting into a party mood, soaking up Darren's attention like a rain-starved desert. The relief of talking to a man who had opinions! She soon discovered that he was a 'conceptual artist'. Pandora didn't dare ask him what that was, but he was obviously very creative. By the third glass she was beginning to find him amazingly attractive. The hot room was crammed full of people, Barry White was throbbing away and many people were trying to dance. Pandora thought it rather odd that despite the heat nobody had removed their baseball caps. She and Darren found themselves crushed deliciously into a corner.

'Why don't we go and get something to eat? This place is like an oven,' suggested Darren, and Pandora agreed. She waved at Rachel who was standing at the door and throwing felafels drunkenly into the room. Pandora squeezed past her.

'I've met a man!' she shouted enthusiastically over the din. 'He says he wants to take me away from all this and show me his paintings! Who knows, he might even sleep with me!'

'What? I can't hear you. You can't leave yet!' yelled Rachel, trying to dislodge a piece of felafel from her hair. But Pandora and Darren had slipped past her into the night.

'Phew, what a relief to get out of there,' said Darren, unlocking a rusty bike. Pandora felt disappointed; she thought an artist of his calibre would have a car at least. 'We can have something to eat at my flat. It's only round the corner.'

Pandora's heart sank even further. She had hoped he might take her to a Bohemian bistro. Still, Darren was fascinating company but it was many corners later when he finally parked his bike outside a dilapidated house. She was beginning to sober up and could have sworn she had read NW9 on a road sign. Wasn't that Willesden? She didn't think she had ever been there. What a sheltered life she had led till now. And she hadn't even told Darren she was married. She hoped it wouldn't put him off.

'Darren,' she said, walking up the steep stairs to his flat. 'I don't know if I mentioned that I might be married.'

He turned round and smiled at her. 'I know you are.'

'How do you know?'

'Because you're wearing a gold ring on the third finger of your left hand.'

'Am I?' She glanced down, she must have forgotten to take it off. He'd never want to sleep with her now. Damn.

Darren shared his flat with another conceptual artist called Bruce who was lounging around the kitchen while his girlfriend Jen struggled to remove a huge casserole from an ancient oven.

'You're just in time,' she said cheerfully, once they had been introduced.

'Mmm, it smells wonderful,' said Pandora who was suddenly very hungry.

'Ta very much,' replied Jen. 'It's a new recipe we're trying out in the cafe. We've decided to call it mung bean crush. Good, huh?'

Jen worked round the corner in a local vegan restaurant while Bruce and Darren devoted themselves to their art and trying to break the tight 'bourgeois condom' that was strangling modern British conceptual art, or 'the voice of the kids', as Bruce put it. Bruce looked in his ravaged early forties; surely he didn't still class himself as one of the kids, thought Pandora, tucking in to her supper. Darren barely touched his food, content instead to feed off the vision of Pandora as she ate heartily by his side. Bruce and Jen were keen to share their action-packed experiences of a recent holiday in the Gambia and were oblivious of this display of potential passion. Pandora listened with horror as they described forsaking their luxury hotel to stay with some locals in a succession of mud huts. Their hosts had been eager to visit England, and Pandora wondered if Jen and Bruce would be quite so enthusiastic to wake up one morning to find ten Gambians ringing their front doorbell, clamouring for accommodation. But she nodded and made enthusiastic noises.

When the casserole was finished, they stacked up their plates and Bruce and Jen disappeared to 'hit the clubs'. At last she and Darren would be able to 'talk'. She was longing to see his pictures, he was bound to be incredibly talented. Darren was flattered at her interest and pushed open a door, revealing a gloomy paint-spattered room with hundreds of canvases stacked against the wall. When Pandora peered more closely, she could see that the paint spatters were actually pictures.

'This one's my favourite,' said Darren proudly. 'It's an abstract representation of the agony caused by years of Thatcher government.'

Pandora didn't know what to say. 'It's brilliant,' she said eventually. 'All that red is really effective.'

'It's blue actually.'

'Of course. Blue blood. That's brilliant!'

'I knew you'd understand what I'm trying to get across.' He gazed at her intently. 'You've got incredible eyes, Pandora. I could drown in them, I really could.'

'Could you really?' She was enthralled.

'Come and sit down for a moment.' He pulled her down and kissed her. Her head was swimming with wine and her whole body ached with desire. She pressed herself against him, longing for him to carry her off to bed but he tore himself away from her instead.

'I'm longing to whisk you off to bed, Pandora, but I really like you. I don't want to take advantage of you when you're in such a vulnerable position.' Her heart sank. Distant memories of Joshua – 'I respect you too much to make love to you' – flooded back. She had no idea Darren was a New Man. 'Tell me about your marriage,' he said. 'Obviously you're really unhappy otherwise you wouldn't be here.'

Pandora told him briefly about John, how he didn't understand her, and his addiction to golf.

'Has he tried Golfers Anonymous?' asked Darren.

She laughed delightedly.

'Oh, Pandora, if I was married to you I wouldn't waste my time playing golf.'

'But you see, it's partly my fault. I encourage his addiction just to get him out of the house. I've even started to phone up his friends to arrange matches on his behalf.' She glanced at her watch, it was past midnight and if she wasn't going to get any action she might as well push off.

'Could I ring for a taxi? It's getting terribly late.'

'In a minute.' He got up and pulled her by the hand into his bedroom, shutting the door behind him. She stood rather awkwardly for a moment until he sat her down beside him on the bed and began kissing her hands, face and mouth passionately. Pandora felt wicked and abandoned; the realization that she was about to commit adultery was a potent turn-on. He peeled off her flimsy dress so that she was left spreadeagled on the bed just wearing stockings and suspenders.

Darren was a fantastic lover. Sex with him was a revelation and went on for hours. Pent-up frustration came spilling out of her; the demure, domesticated Pandora was spirited away, replaced by an insatiable tiger.

Finally the frenzy came to an end. They lay, hot, satiated and sweaty in one another's arms. Pandora felt purged, deliciously defiled in this stranger's bed. They lay awake for hours, exploring one another with fascinated fingers and talking. The more they talked, the more there seemed to say. Pandora felt as though they could have talked for ever but as the morning light began to seep through the grimy curtains, exhaustion suddenly overcame them, and finally they slept.

The next day Darren took her to the Tate. She had confessed to him in the night that she knew nothing about art, which wasn't quite true. Her grandfather had been a considerable collector at one time, and she had completed a fine art course at Sotheby's. But Darren was happy to educate her. He wanted her to see a 'conceptual exhibition' which consisted of several piles of old clothes that the public were encouraged to rummage through.

'You mean it's a sort of jumble sale, but you're not allowed to take anything home?' Pandora had asked.

Maybe she was too bourgeois to see the hidden concept, but it seemed like a total waste of time from where she was standing. Darren explained patiently that this exhibition was a 'milestone in modern British conceptual art', as it was helping to re-educate the public about what was really art. 'Art isn't just something you stick on your wall,' he finished triumphantly. 'It's everywhere!'

Pandora was so consumed with lust for him, she would have agreed to anything. 'I see what you're getting at,' she murmured, picking up an outsize drip dry crimpline dress that looked suspiciously like the one John's mother had worn at their wedding.

'Art is organic, not static,' he continued. She looked at him with glazed, loving eyes. He was so *passionate* about things.

On the way out they had to pass through several galleries of fine art. Pandora stood for a moment beneath a glorious sweeping landscape by Poussin. It was one of her favourite pictures and never failed to take her breath away. Darren was unimpressed.

'Look at all this stuff. Art shouldn't be hidden away behind closed doors. The average working-class bloke is far too intimidated to come in here. The whole thing's a middle-class conspiracy and it stinks!'

Pandora felt mildly irritated. 'If they're intimidated, surely that's their problem. It's not as if it costs anything to come here. Besides, wouldn't the sort of people you're talking about rather go to a football match or something? I mean, I'd be too intimidated to go to a football match or a pub but I don't particularly want to go to either, so I suppose it's even stevens really.'

Darren suddenly took her in his arms and kissed her. Pandora melted and all their differences dissolved immediately. This was living, this was life! Being with Darren made her feel so free and unfettered. They wandered down to the coffee shop and stood in the queue. Pandora hoped Darren wouldn't insist on paying. She didn't think he had any money at all and even the small sum required would probably eat into his funds horribly.

Should she offer to pay? She hadn't been on a date for so long she had forgotten what the protocol was.

When they reached the head of the queue, he insisted on getting out his wallet. Pandora could hardly bear to look at it, it seemed so moth-eaten.

'It's hard to sell my paintings. I wouldn't want just anyone to own one,' Darren said as they settled at a table.

'So how do you earn a living?'

'I collect the dole every week. It's not much but Jen brings us food from the cafe and I don't need much myself.'

Pandora wished she had insisted on buying the coffee.

'How do you manage?' he asked. 'You don't work, do you?'

'No fear! No one would employ me.'

'So I guess your husband gives you what you need. That must be difficult for you.'

'Um, not really.' She shifted uncomfortably. 'I have a sort of tiny allowance from my family. Enough for me to be independent, thank goodness.' She changed the subject. 'I'd like to buy one of your pictures. I think they're brilliant. Would you let me buy one?'

'Baby, you're so sweet and understanding.' He grasped her hand. 'I think I'm falling in love with you. Stay with me tonight.'

They gazed into each other's eyes adoringly. 'I'd love to,' she replied. 'I'll take the bus back to my flat and pick up some things, then I'll come straight round to you.'

They bid a passionate goodbye on the steps of the Tate,

and when she was sure he was out of sight she hailed a taxi home.

Once she had shut the door behind her, she kicked off her shoes and ran a long, hot bath. She loved her bathroom. It was big and clean, the white tiles and chrome fittings gleamed in the sunshine streaming through the window. She hadn't enjoyed using Darren's bathroom, it hadn't been terribly clean and she'd noticed mildew growing in the corners.

She was luxuriating in the aromatic foam, daydreaming about possible *noms de plume*, when the telephone went. Damn, she'd forgotten to put the answerphone on. She climbed out and padded towards the phone. It was Darren.

'Baby, where are you? I thought you were just going to pick up some things and come straight round?' His voice had a querulous tone she hadn't heard before.

'I'm just having a quick bath, but now I'm out I'll come right over.'

His tone lightened. 'I wish I was in the bath with you.'

Pandora laughed noncommittally. Bathing was her private dream-time which she guarded jealously. She had no intention of sharing it with anyone.

Instead of getting dressed immediately, she made herself a cup of tea, grabbed a glossy magazine and got back into the bath. Reclining back into the luxuriant foam, she looked forward to the feel of Darren's hands all over her body. She'd forgotten how good sex could be. She could hardly bear the thought of John touching her and had become adept at making excuses to keep him away. On rare occasions she gritted her teeth, lay back and thought of Switzerland. Afterwards he always asked eagerly, 'Did you have an orgasm?' to which she always replied, 'Of course.' She pitied and despised him for accepting her lies so readily and loathed herself for her perfidy. If only he didn't always have to ask her; she always half expected the orgasm police to burst through the bedroom door and arrest her for being inorgasmic. After all, not coming was practically an imprisonable offence these days, requiring counselling and intensive forms of therapy at the very least. But for her brief fling with Yonathon, she might have imagined that she was undersexed, but the truth was that she just didn't fancy John. She had always *liked* him, maybe she had once loved him, but she didn't think she had ever fancied him. Everyone always stressed the importance of marrying your best friend because sexual chemistry never lasted beyond the first flush of a relationship. And she had taken their advice, but she'd been duped! Sex is a lot more than it's cracked up to be, she said to herself, climbing out of the bath. If she was American she'd sue, but sue who? 'Next time I'm going to marry for sex and money like everyone else,' she grumbled. 'Bugger all this friendship nonsense.'

Quickly doing her face, she flung on some clothes that were lying nearest to hand – it didn't matter what she wore, they'd soon come off – and drove to Willesden. Bruce and Jen had thankfully gone out, so she and Darren had the small, grimy flat to themselves. They heated up the remnants of the mung bean crush and went straight to bed. They couldn't get enough of one another and spent another frenzied, sleepless night locked in each other's arms. During an intermission, Darren gazed at her seriously and said, 'I've never said this to anyone before, but I really want to marry you, Pandora.'

She thought quickly. It was bad enough having one husband, the thought of another made her feel quite ill. 'I'd love to marry you too, it's a real bummer that I'm already married.'

'But you could get divorced. We could buy a small cottage in the country. I would paint, you could write your little stories, we'd grow vegetables and make love and have lots of children. I bet you're great with kids.'

Pandora shuddered. 'Yes . . . it's an intoxicating idea, but I don't want to get married again. You've no idea how ghastly it is, knowing the face beside you on the pillow won't change until one of you dies. You'd hate it. Besides, you told me you were a free spirit. Last night you said that marriage was a bourgeois conspiracy to oppress women. You're right, it is.'

'Well, we could live together. Who needs a bit of paper?'

'Ugh, that would be even worse. Commitment without the tax breaks. Yuck.' Pandora hadn't lived with a banker all this time without getting to know the jargon.

'Yeah, but . . .'

She positioned herself on top of him and plonked a breast in his mouth. That should shut him up for a while, she thought, abandoning herself to the delights of his expert lovemaking.

They spent the next two days in bed. Darren would have been happy to stay there for ever but Pandora was beginning to feel a little claustrophobic. Darren kept gazing at her and asking what she was thinking. Besides, she was worried that she might be getting cystitis. After months of using it as an excuse not to make love to John, it would serve her right if she really did get it now.

After eventually extricating herself from Darren she climbed into her car – miraculously it hadn't been broken into – and drove back to the country. She wondered if John would sense anything different about her. Her adulterous interlude had been interesting, but the longer she spent with Darren the more relieved she was to be married to John. Darren was sexy, but such a flake.

She spent the next couple of days drinking litres of Evian water to stave off her cystitis and in between trips to the loo guiltily shopped and prepared a lovely meal for John's homecoming, whisking up a chocolate mousse and filling the house with wilting foliage from the garden. But despite her efforts, her heart sank when she heard his car pull to a halt in the drive.

John was thrilled to be home. 'You look really rested,' he said, taking in her sparkling blue eyes and glowing complexion which was probably a result of all the water she had been drinking. 'Did you take a lover while I was away?' he joked, knowing this was supremely unlikely because Pandora had never been very interested in sex. Pandora laughed cheerfully, raising her eyebrows in a 'the very idea!' sort of way and continued stirring lumps of butter into the Bearnaise sauce she was making.

Unfortunately a week in the bracing Scottish air had done wonders for John's libido and he was very disappointed that Pandora had cystitis *again*. 'Shouldn't you go to the doctor about it? This is the third time in three months,' he said that night.

'Oh, I'll be all right in a few days, I'm sure,' said Pandora.

'And then you'll probably get your period,' mumbled John grumpily. But Pandora had put in her earplugs and was already fast asleep.

Over the next few days Pandora found her mood with John much improved while things with Darren took a nosedive. She spent two afternoons the following week with him but he had started to become possessive, demanding that she tell John about their affair.

'Our relationship won't grow unless I have access to you.' He made her feel like a credit card. It was also boring that they never went out because he had no money and didn't like her paying for him. 'But Baby, we don't need to go out, we can stay in and have a good time,' he'd said one day when she suggested they go out for dinner.

Pandora was beginning to think that this was a one-night stand that had gone on too long. Annabel was staying with her sister in Palm Beach, so she discussed the situation with Rachel during a long nuisance call. Rachel claimed that she had never met Darren before in her life and had no idea how he had come to be invited to her party.

'What does he look like?' she asked curiously.

'Well, he's got these really nice soulful eyes, and he's sort of tall and wiry with mousy hair that's just starting to go a bit grey . . .'

'Enough, enough!' cried Rachel.

'And he's great in bed.'

'What d'you do, put a bag over his head? Dump him. He's a loser.'

'You know, I thought having an affair would make me more decisive but it's made me feel even more confused,' Pandora confided.

'I'm confused myself,' Rachel said. 'Can we recap? You're in love with one man – who you barely know, by the way, – bonking another and married to someone else. Perhaps you ought to see a shrink.'

'But I am seeing a shrink!'

Flora's assignment had caused quite a stir amongst the class and this week there was full attendance. Pandora's article had everyone in stitches; even Flora was quite encouraging, praising her 'vivid imagination'. Pandora had described a perfect wife who created immensely rich and creamy three-course meals for her irritating cholesterol-laden husband every night. He had then died suddenly on a golf course of a massive heart attack. The coroner said that he'd never seen arteries so clogged up with Bearnaise sauce and chocolate mousse, and his beautiful young widow was accused of manslaughter but acquitted. She had gone on to appear frequently on the cover of *Hello!* magazine with a succession of increasingly gorgeous older men. 'Old boys are my toy boys' became her catch phrase.

Araminta sniggered. 'Vivid imagination my foot. Wishful thinking, more like.'

Pandora was offended. 'The story is *totally* fictitious, Araminta. It's not my fault that John won't touch skimmed milk.'

The laughter and enthusiasm of the class still rang in her ears as she sped home, so euphoric she felt she could punch the clouds from the sky. Flora had said she should try and get her story published. Just imagine, something she'd written appearing in a magazine. Nobody would believe it.

John was vaguely pleased for her and thankfully didn't ask to read the piece. It was just as well, but she was rather hurt by his lack of encouragement and curiosity.

Daniel had returned from Frankfurt and invited them to another party, the thought of which kept Pandora in a state of delicious anticipation for days. He was now involved with an MTV presenter called Lisa Grind, to whom he seemed to pay very little attention at the party, to Pandora's great relief. She had wandered into his bedroom at the party 'by mistake' and been tremendously impressed to find *À la recherche du temps perdu* on his bedside table. On wandering into the kitchen she had been waylaid by him and they'd had a memorable conversation about *Madame Bovary*, which she was struggling through and finding very dull but which he had read in French.

'My favourite line is the one where he writes, "If there

is one thing worse than not living with the one you love, it's living with someone you don't love".'

This line had slipped Pandora's attention; she didn't know how because it could have been written for her. She melted inside; Daniel was so perceptive, so intellectual. He was completely wasted on Lisa Grind who had probably never read anything but an autocue in her life.

'I bumped into your father yesterday,' he continued smoothly.

'Oh yes?'

'Yes, he was on his way to have lunch with my boss, Lord Dougall. Apparently he's fallen out with the merchant bank handling his sale and he's looking for someone else to advise him.' He refilled her glass with pink champagne.

'Wouldn't it be great if he used Dougall and Douglas International?' She smiled mistily up at him. She must put in a good word for him with her father. Not that he'd take any notice.

John suddenly appeared and put a proprietorial hand on her shoulder. 'Shall we stay in London tonight or drive down to the country, darling?' He never called her darling, why did he have to in front of Daniel? Really, it was too maddening!

Daniel smiled indulgently at this display of marital harmony. 'I'd better go and fill some more glasses. I'll leave you two to your domestic decisions,' and he was soon swallowed up in a sea of Armani suits and Prada handbags. Pandora's eyes followed him longingly and then she gathered up her bag and accompanied John home.

She ran and re-ran her conversation with Daniel over and over again, looking for clues that might indicate his feelings for her. Had his *Madame Bovary* 'insights' been a sign that he knew how unhappily married she was?

Meanwhile Darren was pestering her with telephone calls demanding 'access' to her. Luckily he only rang during the day, but she lived in fear that he would ring one evening and speak to John. She cursed herself for getting into such a ridiculous situation. It was bad enough being married to a husband who irritated her without walking straight into an affair with someone equally maddening. To give John some credit, he did work very hard, and at least he earned a living, which was more than she could say for Darren. She had actually bought one of his pictures because he was behind on his rent that month and was in danger of losing his flat, but she couldn't find a wall obscure enough to hang it on. Eventually she settled for the swimming pool shed where no one ever went apart from a few spiders.

John was starting to do much more travelling and frequently asked her to accompany him. She usually said no because the trips were a heaven-sent opportunity to dabble with Darren. But she couldn't say no for ever, and when the opportunity came up to visit Lisbon and stay in a luxurious hotel for a week, she decided to go. They hadn't been away together for so long; who knew, maybe it would revitalize their relationship.

It didn't. Things had got so bad between them that she couldn't bear him near her. She would lie in bed after he had gone to work, overcome with lassitude and longing for Daniel. For some reason Portugal was showing full coverage of Royal Ascot and she would watch television for hours as Daniel owned a racehorse and was bound to be attending.

Her spirits soared when she at last caught a glimpse of him in the paddock. They dropped equally quickly when the camera focused on his companion, a gorgeous leggy blonde weather girl called Tracy Sunshine. The camera lingered on her for five seconds then moved away. Pandora felt sick.

That night she and John had dinner in a local fish restaurant. After they had sat down, Pandora noticed a gloomy fish tank crammed full of lobsters in the corner. She begged the waiter to release them back into the ocean, or at least build a much bigger tank, but he didn't have a clue what she was talking about and chivalrously offered her a red rose instead. 'But John, you speak some Spanish, tell him how cruel it is,' Pandora had begged, but John had only laughed and said that he didn't want to make a fool of himself. It was maddening! Didn't he feel strongly about *anything*? No wonder the General had called him the Draft Dodger. She could understand him not sharing her feelings about lobsters if there was some evidence he cared about *something*. A lump came to the back of her throat and she pushed her sardines around on her plate listlessly. 'I saw Daniel on the television today. He was in the paddock at Ascot.'

'God, that man is so flash,' smiled John, relieved the lobster debacle was over. 'He's almost too smooth to be true. I don't know why he's so friendly with us, we're not really his type, are we? I mean, everyone at that party was either a weather girl, a TV producer or a fashion designer. Mind you,' he mused, 'he's always liked you. If I was off the scene he'd be round like a shot.'

'What makes you think that?' Pandora could barely keep the excitement out of her voice.

'Well, even though I might wish you looked more like Michelle Pfeiffer, you're quite pretty, plus your father's business would be a fairly attractive proposition. I shouldn't think Daniel takes a shit without there being an ulterior motive.'

She was prepared to ignore the Michelle Pfeiffer jibe in order to elicit more information. Besides, the guilt and strain of being an adulteress had made her much more tolerant.

'But what possible use would I be?' she asked, intrigued.

'I suppose he thinks that knowing you might help him and his bank get the contract to sell your father's business. That would be a fairly hefty commission. And don't forget, his father's in the same sort of business. There's always the possiblity that the two of them might make a bid for it themselves. Daniel has the City contacts to raise enough capital. If he bought it, he could split the business up and sell it piece by piece. That's his job. We discussed it a while ago when we were playing golf. He wondered if I was planning to do anything along those lines myself.'

'And are you?' Pandora asked innocently. She knew the chances of her father doing any business with John were remote to say the least.

'Well, Peter and a few of us were discussing various possibilities last week.'

Pandora tried not to laugh. The thought of all those run-of-the-mill accountants and solicitors trying to run such a massive business was ludicrous. 'But none of you has any experience in running a business like that.'

'It's quite straightforward, it basically runs itself. It could do with some streamlining though, maybe lose about twenty per cent of the work force.'

'But you couldn't possibly sack that many people, there would be a rebellion. Most of them have worked there all their lives, and their parents before them. Where would Mr Sprout, the forklift truck driver who can only see out of one eye and has a withered leg, get a job at his age?'

'Well, if he's blind and legless he can't be much use as a forklift truck driver,' laughed John.

'Actually, I think he spends most of the day in the canteen. But that's not the point. If you treat people well they reward you with hard work which leads to high productivity.'

John smiled indulgently. 'Pandora, you don't understand. You can't run a business like that any more. You've never had a job so you don't know what it's like. The world is a very competitive place these days. It's quite simple, I'd put someone in to run it from day to day, and I'd drop in maybe three days a week and play golf the rest of the time.'

The whole idea was absurd but she decided to humour him. As far as she was concerned, it was just another nail in the coffin. She always knew John had been attracted by her money, but the knowledge that he harboured ideas about getting his hands on her family company was horrible.

'I thought you liked being a merchant banker.'

'I do, but I don't want to do it for ever.'

After dinner they walked up to the castle in silence, each wrapped up in their own thoughts. The conversation had revealed a side of John that she had rarely glimpsed before. The thought that he would happily sack hundreds of people without a second thought was appalling. He was a good husband and she didn't doubt that he loved her, but realistically she knew that it was probably more than her looks and character that had attracted him. That didn't bother her; what did bother her was his apparent lack of humanity. She seriously doubted that anything lay behind his genial façade at all. Maybe she was naive, but she had always thought that even 'superficial' people secretly had some depth somewhere. People were surely like Russian dolls, consisting of many layers, each one more complex than the last. Some people were so complex they were more like onions, with layers and layers of thoughts, experiences and personalities. But John was a Russian doll with nothing inside except a few opinions that belonged to other people.

Once they had reached the castle, they stood for a moment by the battlements and looked out to sea. Lisbon shimmered and sparkled beneath them, the castle was lit up with a thousand lights and a band was playing. The night air was soft and balmy and a faint ocean breeze caressed Pandora's bare arms. It was an idyllic setting;

with the right person it would have been a perfect evening, but the beauty and romance of their surroundings only emphasized the emptiness echoing between them.

The next day in the blazing sunshine they drove to Cascais, a small town on the outskirts of Lisbon. They lunched outside at a clifftop restaurant on fresh sardines and watched the Atlantic Ocean glinting in the distance. They were surrounded by laughing families, basking in the sun and eating their melting ice creams, but Pandora had never felt so alone. As she sipped her cappuccino, tears rolled silently down her cheeks and into her cup, denting the froth. She was relieved yet irritated that John did not notice her tears and fumbled in her bag blindly for her sunglasses, longing to hide behind them. But suddenly he looked at her and asked, 'Pandora, what on earth is the matter?'

'Oh, nothing, I've just got a terrible headache. It must be the heat.'

They moved into the shade and lapsed into silence again. Pandora imagined her grandfather saying, 'Darling, have you tried pulling yourself together?' It had worked in the past and it worked now. She blew her nose firmly and dried her eyes. It was on the tip of her tongue to ask for a divorce but it didn't seem the right time or place, so she bit her lip and looked out to sea. Maybe things would seem different once they got home.

Chapter Ten

There was some extraordinarily good news awaiting her. *Divorce! Magazine* had accepted her short story!

'Well done,' mumbled John through a mouthful of fried bread. 'How much are they paying you?'

'Paying me? Do you think they'll actually *pay* me?'

'Of course they'll pay you. Have you seen my golf shoes anywhere?'

And that was it. He didn't even want to read what she'd written. The greatest triumph of her life and she couldn't share it with him.

It was only a week now before their first wedding anniversary. Coincidentally, friends of theirs were getting married on the same day so it seemed they couldn't forget it even if they wanted to. She was amazed that John put up with things the way they were. He seemed to think that if he just buried his head in the sand, all their problems would go away. Separation began to seem inevitable. It was just a question of when she would tell him. But instead of feeling relief that she had finally made a decision, she was instead consumed by even more questions. Would their friends take sides? Where would John live? The flat and house belonged to her, although she had put them both in their joint names. John had an excellent salary and he would survive, but she knew he'd baulk at losing the house and flat, the sports car and all the other luxuries her money provided. But surely he would be relieved to escape from a relationship that was making them both so unhappy?

The day of their friends' wedding was sunny and unseasonably warm but Pandora felt bleak and miserable inside. During the service she couldn't stop crying; despite the weather, everything reminded her so much of their own wedding. Angelica Coriander had done the flowers and the beams of the small country church were draped with autumnal fruit and berries; a spectacularly rustic and avant-garde arrangement of unwashed potatoes and runner beans around the altar brought gasps of shock and admiration from the congregation, and the bride wore a headdress of woodland flowers just as Pandora had done.

Daniel was an usher. When it was their turn to be shown to a pew, he winked at her conspiratorially, placing them in one of the best pews near the front.

'I've just had a story accepted by *Divorce! Magazine*,' she whispered excitedly.

He kissed her on both cheeks. 'Well done! I'll grab a bottle of champagne at the reception and we'll toast your success. She's wasted on you, mate,' he joked, slapping John on the back before continuing to deal with the flow of guests into the church. Normally Pandora would have been levitating with happiness at such an exchange but it only made her feel worse. What could someone as glamorous, intelligent and charming as Daniel possibly see in her, a failed suburban careerless housewife?

But he was as good as his word and at the reception he extricated himself from a small posse of admiring girls to come and talk to her.

'It's a real achievement,' he said, expertly pouring the champagne into two flute glasses. 'It's horribly difficult to get anything published. I went out with a girl who wrote for *Harpers & Queen* once. She's in the Priory at the moment, having treatment for writer's block.'

'Oh, how awful,' said Pandora politely. The Priory was a fashionable psychiatric establishment. Pandora went there once a fortnight to consult her psychiatrist about her marital problems. She thought she might stop going now; he didn't seem to be helping much and she got so bored bumping into old school friends in the car park.

'I bet your father is thrilled for you,' Daniel was saying. 'I keep reading about him in the papers.' Before he could say more, dinner was announced. To Pandora's disappointment John had been placed on her left, and someone's deaf, blind and dumb great-aunt – she never managed to find out whose – on her right. Talk about a placement from hell, she thought grumpily.

On the way home in the car her spirits were low. 'Tell him now you want a divorce,' an insistent voice kept saying in her ear. She tried to get the words out but failed. I'll wait until we get home, she thought. I don't want to put him off his driving.

Once inside, she laid her hat and bag on the kitchen table and went upstairs. It was too late to tell him now, she'd tell him tomorrow. But as they were getting ready for bed, she took a deep breath and blurted out impulsively, 'John, I really think we need to talk. I'd like us to separate for a while. We're not making each other happy and I think some time apart would do us good.'

John put down his golfing magazine and looked at her. 'Pandora, you're just being impulsive,' he said reasonably. 'One moment you want to buy a house in the country, then you suddenly realize you don't like the country so you buy a flat in London, then you suddenly decide you don't like any of your old friends so you drop them and find new ones. Then you wake up one morning and decide you're bored of being married. Well, you have to work at being married—'

'I've been having an affair,' she interrupted.

'What did you say?'

'I said I've been having an affair.' She hadn't been going to tell him but it was the only way to make him see how desperately wrong things were between them.

'I don't believe you.'

'It's true.'

John was outraged. 'You're lying. Tell me you're lying.'

'It's the truth.'

'I don't believe you,' he repeated numbly. 'What's his name?'

She expected him to rant and rave but he just sat on the bed and put his head in his hands.

'I asked you a question. What is his fucking name?'

'Darren.'

'You can't love someone called Darren, for Christ's sake!'

'Your brother is called Darren,' she reminded him helpfully.

'You think you're so bloody clever, don't you? Do you love him?'

'No.'

'Well, finish it then. I'll forget everything you said. You can't break up our marriage for someone you don't even love.'

'But if it hadn't been him it would only have been someone else, don't you see? I knew you wouldn't take things seriously unless I did something like this. I've been trying to tell you for weeks, months . . .' She trailed off miserably.

'You're nothing better than a tart. I knew you were a bitch, but Christ, *this!*'

Pandora cowered, she had never seen him so angry. He picked up a vase full of flowers and threw it violently against the wall.

'You fucking bitch!'

Pandora tried to reason with him, but he continued shouting. What would she do if he hit her? The nearest neighbour was miles away; if she screamed no one would ever hear. Anything she tried to say only made him angrier so she lapsed into silence. After ranting for half an hour he suddenly collapsed with exhaustion and started weeping.

She sighed and sat down by her dressing table, preparing herself for a sleepless night. How could they possibly go to bed now? She cursed herself for not waiting until morning.

'So what are we going to do?' she asked. She knew what she was going to do, but it might make him feel more in control to be the one to say it.

'Well, we've got two houses,' he said calmly. 'I'll drive up to London tomorrow and spend the week up there.'

'But I need to be in London next week too.'

'Well, you shouldn't have put the flat in both our names then. Legally it's half mine. So is all this,' he gestured expansively round the room.

'But I bought everything with my own money!'

'Tough.'

They spent the rest of the night wrangling over ridiculous details. As the morning broke, Pandora took a spare duvet into one of the empty bedrooms while John struggled to sleep in their marital bed. He'd known Pandora was restless, but this was a bombshell. He came from a straightforward world of straightforward people; no one in his family was divorced. He had always been in awe of Pandora's family, of their money and *savoir faire*. His boss had recently taken him to lunch at the Turf Club and had pointed out Lord Vesci, a distant cousin of Pandora, and head of a vast sausage-packing business, in the distance. John had said casually, 'Oh, you mean Hugh. He's my wife's cousin.' His boss had been impressed, he could tell. But beyond all that, he loved Pandora. He loved her so much that the thought of losing her made him cry out with pain.

He spent the morning packing up some things. Pandora went for a long walk in the woods to avoid him. In the distance she could hear the maudlin strains of Phil Collins spilling out of the open windows. The same CD was still playing when she opened the front door but he must have just left, the dust in the drive hadn't yet settled. Pandora could sense his pain but felt none of it herself. It was as if a weight had been lifted from her shoulders. She was free at last and it felt wonderful.

She thought about Darren. She hadn't spoken to him since they'd got back from Portugal. She'd left some clothes in his flat and ought to pick them up. Hopefully he wouldn't it take it badly when she told him it was over.

He answered the phone immediately. 'Baby! It's wonderful to hear your beautiful voice. God, I've missed you so much I haven't even been able to paint.'

At least she had provided some service to the world. 'John and I just got back from Portugal. I've left him, or rather, he's left me. It was awful,' she said, sounding thrilled.

'But that's wonderful! We can be together. Why don't I come this afternoon? You can't be alone at a time like this.'

'It's all right, I'd rather be alone. I need time to think.'

'Yes. I understand. I'll come tomorrow then. I'll cook us a lovely supper.'

It didn't bear thinking about. Thank God he didn't have

her address. 'No, really, Darren. I'll come and see you in London.'

'When?'

'Um, soon . . . the end of the week.'

'Pandora, I must have access to you. Don't you understand? We have an extraordinary relationship, but we need to build on it by spending lots of time together.'

'Please, don't use that word.'

'What word?' He sounded deeply wounded.

'Access. I am not a credit card. Though my husband seems to think so.'

'Baby, I'm sorry if I've been putting you under too much pressure. It's just that I love you so much. I think about you all the time.'

Pandora felt exhausted when she replaced the receiver. She'd had no idea that getting rid of a lover would be almost as difficult as getting rid of a husband. They had eventually arranged to meet on Friday and she was dreading seeing him. But if she finished things over the telephone he might rip up her Jasper Conran jacket and Jimmy Choo stilettos which she had left in his flat. It was an appalling thought.

She spent the next two days on the telephone. She put the house and flat on the market and then rang her mother in Argentina.

'Mummy, I've left John. What shall I do?'

'Well done, darling. I don't know what took you so long. How much does he want?'

'He wants me back.' Pandora couldn't hear very well as the line was crackling so much.

'I'm sure he does, darling, but as he can't have you, I expect he'll want a tiny *pourboire* instead, won't he? He looks the type.'

'He says he might want the flat.'

'Well, tell him he can't have it and go and see my lawyer. He's awfully good. And don't marry any more poor people, they cost too much to get rid of. Try to learn something from my mistakes, darling.'

The strangest thing was that she felt so calm. Sometimes she even felt quite euphoric. The only unpleasantness came from so-called friends, some of whom were apparently outraged by what she had done. She had a glimpse of this at a party she dropped into before going on to see Darren. It was her first social engagement as a single woman and she was in a very good mood. It was only a few days since John had left but everyone seemed to know the full ins and outs of the saga already. Just as she was leaving, a mutual friend who had been chief usher at their wedding came up to her with a serious look on his face.

'Pandora. We think you are behaving irresponsibly.'

She was dumbstruck. Irresponsible? Didn't he know she had been a prefect at the convent for two years running?

'Oh dear,' she responded. 'Has my tax disc run out?'

He looked at her with a sad expression. 'It's just that your behaviour tonight was,' he shifted awkwardly, 'well, quite frankly, it was inappropriate.'

'But I don't understand what you mean.' She was very confused.

'You just seem to be so happy all of a sudden. Some of John's friends think it's very tactless of you. Quite frankly.'

In Pandora's family, divorce was usually a cause for celebration not regret, especially where her mother's husbands were concerned, and she couldn't understand this attitude at all.

'Well, I'll try and make myself a bit more miserable next time we run into one another, but I can't promise anything. Now, I simply must fly, I've got a hot date. Ciao for now!'

And with that she sped off to see Darren. Her high spirits soon evaporated in the car. She was dreading breaking things off with him.

He was thrilled to see her. 'Baby, you look wonderful! Come inside. What kept you? I was expecting you hours ago.'

'I had to show my face at some God-awful party that was full of John's golfing cronies. I got told off for being too happy.'

'You should have taken me, I would have told them where to get off.'

The thought of introducing Darren to any of her friends was too horrible to contemplate.

'Oh, by the way, I've got a present for you,' Darren announced. Her heart sank. She hated to think of him spending his dole money on her. He withdrew a large packet from behind the fridge with 'British Gas' emblazoned on it, and handed it to her.

'Oh Darren, you shouldn't have!' She opened it and

drew out a large unwieldy calendar with a picture of a toothless nomad on the front. Inside there were more nomads, each with a bewildering range of dental problems. Wild animals were artfully arranged as a backdrop in the distance. She didn't like it at all.

Flicking through it hopelessly, she said, 'It's absolutely beautiful. Fantastic photographs.'

He was looking at her with rapt adoration, obviously waiting for her to continue.

'I wonder where they found all those nomads?' She put the calendar down. 'The only problem is that I haven't got anywhere to hang it. You see, I'm selling my house. It's such a shame because the calendar is quite beautiful, but it would be wasted on me because I've literally got nowhere to hang it.'

'But it's got pictures of animals in it, you like animals,' he said petulantly. 'Anyway, you can't buy it in the shops.'

'Can't you give it to someone else? Bruce would really appreciate it,' she added helpfully. Really, she couldn't believe this tedious conversation had gone on so long. She had only come round to pick up her clothes and say goodbye.

'But I want to give it to you. If you don't want it you can throw it away!'

She knew she should just accept the calendar and donate it to Oxfam but she was too irritated. He had touched one of her raw nerves. She hadn't been a leading light on the Middlehurst Earthchildren's Recycling Committee for nothing.

'Now that would be the most ridiculous waste. You know how I feel about throwing things away . . .' Pandora worried incessantly about rubbish mountains. Darren got up huffily. 'For God's sake, why do you have to be so wet about everything!' She stomped out of the room and slammed the door behind her. All of a sudden the flat seemed oppressively dark and humid. It was a bit like a tropical rainforest, but at least there one might discover a rare orchid. 'The only thing growing out of the walls in this flat is mildew, to say nothing of the organisms festering in your horrible fridge!' she shouted cruelly, struggling to open the small kitchen window which was always kept locked. 'Good thing you keep all the doors and windows triple-locked. I bet burglars are just panting to get in. I mean, just look at all the silver, the jewellery, the hi-fi equipment.' She cast her eyes around the grimy flat, which contained nothing of any value at all. Darren would have to pay to get rid of his horrible pictures.

She ran out of vindictive steam and took a deep breath. Why was she being such a bitch? Poor Darren had only tried to give her a present, it was just a shame he couldn't get himself a life. She felt sick with shame and this made her feel even more guilty. She must make her peace somehow and go. Gingerly she opened his bedroom door.

Darren responded with a stream of invective. 'How dare you think that you can come round and treat me like this! I want you to get out of here right now!' He started gathering up her things and roughly shoving them into her bag.

Pandora stood, unable to move. She couldn't bear to leave before she had tried to sort things out.

'Darren, I'm so sorry. I know I've behaved unforgivably but I can't stand the thought of leaving before we've had a chance to make our peace. Please, Darren!' She was pleading with him now, but he didn't seem to hear her, the words didn't begin to pierce his rage and hurt. All of a sudden she began to cry, guilt and misery flooding out of her.

Darren leapt off the bed and lunged towards her, making her jump back with terror. She was convinced he was going to hit her, but he flung out his arms instead.

'Don't be frightened, Baby, you know I'd never hurt you in a million years.'

She sagged with relief as he sought out her mouth, kissing her so hard she could barely breathe. She murmured, 'I'm so sorry, I'm so sorry,' but he just carried on kissing her, pushing her on to the bed, deftly unzipping her skirt and slipping his hand between her legs.

'God, you're wet.'

'I know,' she mumbled, fumbling to undo his belt and trousers, the relief of his capitulation making her feel guilt-makingly randy.

A moment later he was pushing himself inside her and for a short time their differences dissolved as she came again and again. He held back, plunging deeper and deeper, but although she called out his name it was Daniel she really called for – the face above hers was just a meaningless blur.

When it was over, he remained inside her, unwilling to

let her go. He kissed her eyes, mouth and skin so tenderly and with such real love that she felt deeply ashamed. If only he would roll off her so she could go home.

She pushed him away gently. 'Darren, I ought to go home now.' But he looked so hurt that she felt horribly guilty which in turn increased her desire to flee.

'But you've left your husband, you don't have to go anywhere, you're free.'

Not in this flat, she thought, getting up and putting on her clothes which were strewn about the room. She normally loved the easy intimacy between them after making love, when they would lie for hours chatting, and in rejecting it, she was rejecting him. He lay there mournfully, watching her dress.

'Will you ring me?' he asked plaintively.

'Of course. We'll speak tomorrow.' God, any moment now he would accuse her of using him for sex. She couldn't bear all this role reversal, it seemed so unnatural. She had just come to the confusing, faintly sluttish realization that it was possible to enjoy sex with someone you didn't like, or even fancy that much. She bent down and kissed him goodbye. 'I'm sorry I behaved so badly.'

'I'll forgive you this time,' he joked feebly.

But as she let herself out she thought, there won't be a next time, we'll never make love again, I'll never return to this flat. And in her mind's eye she was already back in her flat, her excursion into squalor finally over.

She had come to a temporary arrangement with John whereby he spent weekends in the country playing golf, and crossed over with her on Tuesday. It was an uncomfortable agreement, but until the house and flat were sold, it was the best one. Pandora was making huge efforts to maintain friendly relations; if John became vindictive he could make things very unpleasant indeed. He was convinced she only needed time before coming to her senses, that she was only having one of her 'turns'.

She felt a stupendous sense of relief as she stepped into the cool night air, it was so refreshing after the oppressive heat of Darren's flat. She found she was grasping her car keys so tightly that her fingers were numb. They were a talisman, the keys to her freedom. She could get in her car and drive anywhere she wanted. And the one place she wanted to be more than anywhere was her beautiful, quiet, cool flat on whose blank creamy walls she could draw anything.

The argument and frantic sex had exhausted her, yet she felt strangely exultant at the same time. As soon as she got home, she had a blazingly hot bath and went to bed. She tossed and turned, thoughts and dreams filling her head, and before she finally fell asleep she said quietly out loud, 'Tomorrow I shall ask John for a divorce and then I shall ring Daniel and tell him how I feel.'

The next day she was woken by a shaft of sunlight shining through the window. In her exhaustion last night she had forgotten to draw the curtains. She remembered very clearly the resolution she had made the night before. She felt more in control now that she had decided what to do and it was a relief to have a concrete decision to act on. Divorce would surely be better for John in the long run, she thought hopefully. Then at least he would have to come to terms with the fact that things were really over. At the moment he was clinging to the wreckage of their relationship like a drowning man and going nowhere. He rang her every day on vague pretexts – 'How do you work the washing machine? Where do you keep the tin opener?' It made her realize just how much she had done in their relationship. And she was worried that he would sue her. She had discussed the matter with an American girlfriend who had said succinctly, 'Honey, he should be payin' you!'

She glanced at her watch. It was late enough to telephone Daniel. He had probably gone away for the weekend but she couldn't relax until she'd sussed out how he felt about her. Besides, she knew him well enough to ring and arrange to meet for a drink.

She dialled his number, almost hoping to hear the click of his answering machine, but he answered quickly, sounding gratifyingly pleased to hear her.

'Is there any chance of meeting up later for a drink or something? I've got a bit of a problem that I'd like to have your opinion about, as a man of the world,' she joked lightly.

'This sounds intriguing. Why don't you come round to my flat at seven this evening? I can't promise to be a man of the world, but I'm a good listener.'

Pandora felt over the moon as she put the phone down. But what was she going to say to him? Talk about jumping into the abyss. But it had to be done.

Later she walked to Hyde Park, planning what she would say. Crunching through the piles of dry leaves that covered the pavement, the wind blew her hair back from her face with such ferocity her eyes watered. Exchanging the pavement for the grassy park, the leaves seemed to take on a spirit of their own, swirling like dervishes around her feet. She gazed at the penthouses lining the sky at the edge of the park; some of them had roof terraces offering tantalizing glimpses of green. She had always dreamt of living in a huge apartment at the top of such a building and writing a novel. Now perhaps she could. Virginia Woolf suggested a woman needed a room of her own and a private income to be a writer. Well, she had both those things. For the first time she was hit by the full impact of her freedom. If she had known she would feel this confident in her future, she would have left months ago. And now perhaps, she might even have a chance with Daniel.

But on returning home her euphoria collapsed and as she filled the kettle she was so blinded by tears she could barely see. The thought of facing the future alone suddenly terrified her. If John was having trouble working the washing machine (he probably didn't even know where it was), she had huge difficulty changing plugs, driving to parties at night (she had no sense of direction), and mending things. She had bought a hair dryer yesterday without a plug; who would teach her how to put one on? What would happen if she couldn't sell the house or flat, or if John suddenly turned nasty and claimed half her money? Or if Daniel laughed in her face when she admitted her admiration? Was she doing the right thing? She leaned against the kitchen wall and wept.

After a few minutes she took a deep breath, blew her nose and splashed her face with cold water. Going into the bathroom she redid her make-up, sprayed three different gels into her hair, blow drying it to give a false impression of fullness that would last about ten minutes, and then drove over to Daniel's loft at breakneck speed.

She stood at the door and rang the bell. After what seemed like ages but was probably only fifty seconds he opened the door with a deliciously quizzical smile, ushered her inside and poured her a stiff vodka and orange.

'You look like you need this. Now come and sit down and talk to me. What's the problem? Do you need money?'

Pandora laughed politely and took a large mouthful of her drink while Daniel sat down expectantly on the sofa opposite her. She twisted her glass round and round in her hands anxiously.

'I suppose you know that I've left John.'

'No.' He looked shocked. 'I had no idea.'

'But that's not really what I wanted to talk to you about exactly.' She picked an imaginary piece of fluff off her black leggings. 'I'm actually rather nervous. This is the hardest thing I've had to do for . . .' she smiled, 'for hours. You see, I've had a bit of a crush on you for a while, and, well, I know it sounds ridiculous . . .' She lapsed into silence, waiting for him to say something, but he just sat there, barely moving a muscle.

'Well,' she squeezed out a wry laugh from somewhere, 'say something.'

'I'm flabbergasted.'

The phone rang, making her jump. He leaned over to answer it. 'Look, I can't talk now. I'll call you later. Yes, don't make an issue about it, all right?'

Pandora knew he was talking to a girlfriend and felt sorry for her. Daniel sounded so cold all of a sudden. She hoped he would never talk to her like that.

'Sorry,' he said as he put the phone down, rumpling his wavy hair in a charming gesture. 'I had no idea you felt like that about me.'

She had vaguely hoped that he might embrace her at this point and confess that he loved her too, but he didn't. She felt horribly embarrassed and began to gather up her car keys.

'Well, I just wanted to get all that off my chest. I'd better go home now.'

'No, don't go home. Please. I think you've been very brave. I find you very attractive, and I get on better with you than I do with most girls but . . .'

'But what?'

'If circumstances were different . . .'

'You mean if I wasn't married to John?'

'In a word, yes.'

'I didn't realize you were that close.'

'We're not really close, but we play the odd round of golf together, and he's a decent man. I would hate to think someone might do something like that behind my back.

I can imagine how he's feeling. He thought the world of you. Christ, he must be devastated.'

That was that then, she thought. No deal. She glanced at her watch, feeling crushed. She had hoped so much that her feelings for him might be reciprocated. 'I really ought to go now. Thanks for not being embarrassed.'

He helped her on with her coat. 'If you're in London next week, why don't we go out for supper one night?'

Her heart leapt, but she replied calmly, 'That would be really nice.'

'How about Thursday?'

She thought quickly. John was due to fly to Milan on Monday, returning Thursday. He'd want the flat that night. 'That might be a bit difficult. Could we make it Wednesday, do you think?'

'Fine, I'll ring you on Tuesday.'

She felt so relieved that everything was now in the open that instead of accepting the usual goodbye peck on both cheeks, she said jokingly, 'Hug, please,' and he enveloped her, kissing her soundly on both cheeks.

Sliding into her car, she beamed with happiness. Maybe there was a chance for them after all. The weight of yearning at last slid off her shoulders, replaced by a new, exciting glimmer of optimism. She had done everything she could, the next move was up to him.

Pandora spent Monday and Tuesday in a fever of anticipation. She tried to finish that week's creative writing assignment but nothing seemed to emerge. Flora had asked them to write down a person's name, a place and an object on scraps of paper. She had mixed them all up and Pandora had picked Henry the Eighth, Epping Forest and Tom Jones. 'But Tom Jones isn't an object, he's a person!' she had complained.

'No he's not,' said Araminta. 'He's a sex object.'

'I quite agree,' said Flora. 'Women have been sex objects for long enough, let men have a go at it.'

Normally this sort of assignment would have been just up Pandora's street, but instead she wrote a thousand words on the perils of being single, saving Tom Jones, Henry the Eighth and Epping Forest until later. It just didn't seem to grab her somehow.

Having a mobile phone was a mixed blessing. As she kept hers on all the time she couldn't kid herself by thinking that Daniel might have rung when she nipped out. She often 'nipped out', but never without her phone.

She was in a state of great mental agony when Wednesday morning came and Daniel still had not rung to confirm their dinner date. By late afternoon she was lying flat out on the sofa, trying to concentrate on the latest copy of *Divorce! Magazine* and idly wondering whether she should have a bowl of grapenuts or a packet of brownies for supper, or both, when her telephone rang. She scrabbled around anxiously in her shopping bag; she only had five rings before it stopped and transferred to her message service – she hadn't been able to work out how to change that yet. She found it in the nick of time and answered it breathlessly.

'Is that Mrs Black?' asked Daniel cautiously.

'Of course it is, Daniel. There is a one hundred per cent

certainty that all calls on this number will be answered by me,' she laughed, feeling immediately revitalized. Just hearing his sexy mid-Atlantic tones was enough to revive her completely; he was better than a course of royal jelly.

They arranged to meet in an hour's time and Pandora raced to get ready. An hour later she was sitting in his local pizza restaurant toying with a stringy piece of melted cheese. She hoped that the pizza stage of their relationship would soon mature into something a little more upmarket. She wasn't a pizza sort of girl, really. Still, it might be worse, they could be eating hamburgers. Besides, Daniel's company made up for everything. She watched admiringly as he smoothed back his hair. It was thinning a bit but that just made him look even more distinguished.

'Did you know that Desmond Morris says that smoothing back one's hair is a sign of being sexually available?' wittered Pandora brightly. Wine had that effect on her.

'Must be tough on those with no hair,' replied Daniel, loosening his tie wearily.

'Have you had a long day?' asked Pandora sympathetically.

Daniel nodded and frowned slightly. 'Work's really taking it out of me at the moment, and the travelling is a killer.'

'Yes, being an over-achiever must be very stressful.' She smiled sympathetically.

'Not something you'd know about then,' laughed Daniel.

'No,' said Pandora in a small voice. She had just been sent a cheque for her article in *Divorce! Magazine*. It might pay for two pizzas.

'Your father isn't losing his hair though, and I would have thought that running a company that size must be extremely stressful. He must be looking forward to retiring.'

The nice thing about Daniel, thought Pandora, was that he was so interested in her family. 'Actually, I think he's rather dreading it,' she replied as he filled her glass with wine. 'Aren't you having any?'

'I'd love to, but it gives me terrible headaches.'

How strange, he looks so robust, thought Pandora with a twinge of disappointment. 'I mean, goodness knows what my father will do with himself all day,' she continued. 'I wish he'd get married or something, then at least he'd have someone to go on cruises with. But I think it's time I took matters into my own hands. I've actually targeted my future stepmother and I'm plotting to get them together!'

'Oh, who is she? Anyone I know?'

'I shouldn't think so. Her name is Davina Rashleigh – she's actually a countess because her late husband was an earl. She's my godmother and she used to be Mummy's best friend. She had a bit of a fling with my father years ago before they both got married but I think she needed to marry someone with some money to keep her family house going. It's in Cornwall and absolutely huge. My father had no money but he married Mummy who had loads of her own and then he made lots himself so financially everything worked quite well for everybody. But I have this secret suspicion that Davina and my father are made for each other. I think I should play Cupid and arrange a sort of blind date thing.' She paused dramatically and helped herself to a small piece of pizza.

'*Ouch!*' She screamed in agony. A tornado appeared to have gone off in her mouth and she realized to her horror that she had swallowed a chilli. She made a swift grab for Daniel's mineral water but it didn't quench the burning heat and she staggered to the bar where three waiters rushed to her aid with buckets of iced water. Eventually she returned sheepishly to the table, aware that she had turned a savage shade of beetroot. God, Daniel would think she was *so* unsophisticated compared to the models and weather girls he usually dated.

Another waiter materialized and offered her half a hairy coconut containing an unidentifiable substance of indeterminate colour. She stared at it, wondering if Coriander Angelica, who was branching out from floristry into interior design, would describe it as ecru, bone or ostrich spittle coloured. She'd never known there had been so many shades of beige until Coriander had come into her life.

'Gosh, this looks exotic. Are you having one?' she asked hopefully.

''Fraid not. It's got cream in it and I'm allergic to dairy products but I thought you needed something to cool you down.'

Pandora was horrified. Imagine life without yogurt!

It didn't bear thinking about. 'What on earth do you eat then?'

'I'm too busy working to eat very much at all at the moment,' said Daniel impressively.

'But what about the cheese on the pizza?'

'It was goat's cheese. I'm allowed that, you see. I come here so often that they make it up specially for me.'

Pandora smiled at him sympathetically. Poor Daniel. She resolved to buy a special dairy-free cookbook and create lots of delicious meals for him. She managed a few spoonfuls of the ostrich spittle but her appetite had completely gone. Eating in front of Daniel made her feel so nervous. No wonder all her single girlfriends were so thin; one would have to be spectacularly well co-ordinated to manage eating, looking alluring *and* making stimulating conversation all at the same time.

'Shall we have coffee at my place?' asked Daniel, beckoning for the bill.

Pandora agreed readily, gazing at him adoringly. She imagined everyone looking at her and thinking how lucky she was to be with such an attractive man.

It felt awkward visiting his flat as a potential lover instead of in the asexual capacity of someone else's wife. In the past she had always felt comfortable with him but the new goal posts erected an uneasy barrier. She leant awkwardly against the fridge while he put the kettle on. She thought he might have some high-tech coffee-making equipment but instead he reached into his cupboard and pulled out two dusty sachets of instant coffee.

'Here you are.' He offered Pandora a mug full of grey, feebly foaming liquid. 'Let's go and sit down.'

She followed him into the spartan sitting room, and eased herself carefully onto the exquisitely avant-garde iron sofa.

'I won't stay long. I know you've got a long hard day tomorrow.'

Without replying he carefully took away her cup and kissed her. Closing her eyes, she forgot everything and allowed herself to dissolve like warm marshmallow in his arms. When she opened her eyes he was watching her with a detached expression and she found it impossible to read anything from his eyes at all. If only he would throw her over his shoulder and carry her off to bed; she was so drugged with lust that if she tried to walk there herself her knees would probably buckle beneath her.

'What are you up to in the next few days?' he asked casually.

Her heart leapt, he did want to see her again! 'I'll probably drive down to Jane's on Saturday. Have you been invited?' She knew that he had.

'Yes, I have. Has John?'

'No.' She ruffled his hair affectionately. 'Jane is one of my friends, you see. It's funny how people really do take sides. One of John's friends came up to me just after I'd left John and accused me of being too happy! He was terribly disapproving – a Stepford wife had broken ranks.'

Daniel smiled. 'But it's not just your life that you're

shaking up; people get nervous when something seemingly stable collapses. They wonder if they'll be next. How are your parents taking it?'

'Well, the Bolter said she was surprised it had lasted this long and could I hold on a sec while she found her fags – she finds it difficult to talk on the phone unless she's smoking, you see.'

Daniel's face registered a moment of unease; he disapproved of smoking. 'And how about your father?'

'Oh, he just keeps on asking if I'll give him a refund for the wedding. He says I gave him a two-year guarantee that it would work or he could have his money back.' She frowned with concentration. 'I'm sure I didn't. John and I may have been married for only a year but it feels like much longer.'

'Your parents sound very liberal,' smiled Daniel.

'Well, it's sort of taken for granted in my family that divorce is something that just *happens*. I mean I can't think of anyone who has been married who hasn't got divorced quite soon after. My Swedish granny Irma had been divorced twice by the time she was twenty-six. Her first husband turned out to be a homosexual and the second, a Belgian ballooning champion, just disappeared one day. But she and my grandfather are very happy now. I sort of think that marriage is like a house, if you don't like living in it you should just move. Mad Uncle Rupert who's living in tax exile in Bermuda, lucky thing, is campaigning to have the divorce laws completely abolished. He thinks that you should be allowed to just say "I divorce you" three times in a public place, and that would be it. He's been married five times.'

Daniel was laughing. 'God, your family are completely barking! No wonder you're so mad yourself.'

'I'm not mad,' said Pandora a touch defensively, wishing she hadn't been quite so frank with him. She was hoping her revelations might encourage him to talk about his family and what it felt like to be Jewish. Her tactful probing on the subject in the past had always met with an impenetrable wall. He was no more forthcoming now and Pandora looked at her watch. She made to get up. It was getting late and she mustn't overstay her welcome.

'Where are you going?' asked Daniel, gently fingering her cheek.

Pandora was so overcome she couldn't speak and just gazed at him transfixed.

'Has anyone ever told you that you have wonderful eyes?'

Several people had but Pandora remained modestly silent.

'Why don't you stay here tonight?' He reached over and pulled her to her feet. 'Come on, let's go to bed.'

She followed him with a sense of spine-tingling expectation down the corridor and into his white bedroom which was completely bereft of furniture except a rather uncomfortable wrought-iron bed.

'I got that florist friend of yours Coriander Angelica to re-do the colour scheme,' said Daniel proudly.

It must have taken her fifty seconds, thought Pandora, taking in the white walls, white ceiling, white curtains and white bedspread. 'It's beautiful,' she murmured as he deftly removed her suede skirt and silk blouse before quickly struggling out of his shirt and trousers.

Pandora lay back awkwardly on the pillows. The stark room made her feel inhibited and she was beginning to wish she had waited a bit longer before leaping into bed with him. Daniel was hanging up his clothes neatly and placing his cufflinks carefully in a small box he kept inside a hidden wardrobe. The longer he took, the more nervous she found herself becoming, but finally he slipped into bed. He gathered her into his arms rather woodenly and propelled her on top of him. Pandora wished he hadn't; she loved the feeling of being squashed between man and mattress but felt far too awkward to say so. But then, just as suddenly, he switched her round and burrowed beneath the bedclothes and began licking her clitoris with a rather dry tongue. Pandora moaned enthusiastically and simulated great excitement but she was unable to enjoy the experience at all. Chillies were very pervasive, could the one she had swallowed at dinner possibly have worked its way down yet? If so, it would taste dreadful, and Daniel was so sensitive to certain foods. She stifled a yawn. Really, this was becoming very boring. God, had she turned the gas off at home? She couldn't remember.

She wondered if Annabel had met any nice men in Palm Beach. Probably, knowing Annabel. She hoped John was all right and that he wouldn't become unreasonable and make demands . . . Her mental ramblings came to an abrupt halt as Daniel emerged from the bedclothes.

'That was fabulous,' she breathed.

He entered her very suddenly and began rhythmically and silently to pound into her. If only they were comfortable enough to say something, anything, to lighten the awkwardness she felt. Then, just as suddenly, he withdrew, kissed her and asked, 'Did you come?'

'Of course!' she lied expertly. 'I've wanted you for so long – it was unbelievable!' But she hadn't come and neither had he. So it looked as if the orgasm police would have to arrest both of them. All the writhing and moaning had quite worn her out and before she could worry any more she fell into a deep and dreamless sleep.

The next morning Daniel woke her up by sitting down beside her on the bed and handing her a cup of his grey instant coffee. He smiled fondly, ruffling her messy blonde hair. Her heart melted, he looked impossibly handsome in his beautifully cut black suit and crisp white cotton shirt. She'd bet all the secretaries were wildly in love with him.

'I've got to shoot now,' he said. 'Just pull the door shut when you leave. I'll pick you up on Saturday about six o'clock, and then we can drive to Jane's party together. There's one thing I didn't mention last night.' He looked a little sheepish. 'I'm, um, playing golf with John on Saturday. It would look odd if I suddenly cancelled it. You don't mind do you?'

'Oh.' Pandora was taken aback. Surely Daniel didn't expect to continue his friendship with John while he was having an affair with her? But she just smiled brightly. 'Um, no, not really.'

'Good girl,' replied Daniel, shrugging on a black cashmere coat and blowing her a kiss before slamming the door behind him.

Pandora hugged herself with delight. She could hardly wait for Saturday. It seemed unbelievable that she and Daniel were actually going out together, that her fantasy was becoming a reality! It was a little disappointing that the sex hadn't been very good, but people always said that the first time should be banned. It was bound to improve once they felt more comfortable together. It was a little disconcerting to think of Daniel and John playing golf together but perhaps it wasn't such a bad idea. It might stop John getting wind of her romance with Daniel; the last thing she wanted was to antagonize him any further. Besides, an illicit romance would be terribly exciting.

Chapter Eleven

John had always anticipated that he and Pandora would be together for life. Knowing that they could both live comfortably off her capital, he had sensibly tied up a large proportion of his income in a school fees plan and a policy that would mature when he was fifty-five. But out of the blue the rug had been pulled from under his feet. He had loved her, he still loved her, even now he'd take her back like a shot. But the love was slowly turning to bitterness. Reports filtered back to him that she was a different person, that she was glowing with happiness. He resented her happiness, and wanted her to feel the misery that she had inflicted on him. The affluent future that he had taken for granted was fading rapidly. The country house, the Chelsea flat, the two sports cars – he would have to work for years for the lifestyle that Pandora had had the good fortune to be born into. It was so incredibly unfair. But at least his friends had stuck by him. Even Daniel had phoned to arrange a game of golf that weekend. He'd been really kind. Funny, he'd never thought of Daniel as a particularly sympathetic person, but it just went to show that adversity brought out the best in people.

John hated living alone, commuting between the flat in London and the house, in the opposite direction to Pandora. It was bizarre, really. A stranger walking into either place would think they still lived together. Both their clothes hung in the wardrobes, Pandora's magazines and his golfing journals cohabited on the coffee tables. There was no way he could invite a woman home, even if he wanted to. So far he hadn't been tempted but things couldn't go on like this. Last night, when he'd got back from Milan and walked into the dark and empty flat, he'd felt close to despair. A good night's sleep and the knowledge that he'd be on his way to the country this evening and could look forward to a weekend of golf had helped put things in perspective. It was time to talk to Pandora.

He picked up the phone on his desk and dialled her number.

'I suppose I've woken you up,' he said sarcastically when she answered.

'Actually I've been up for three hours,' said Pandora who had woken at 6 a.m. to finish an article she was writing for *Divorce! Magazine* on the delights of being single.

'I think we may as well hurry up and get divorced quickly. There's no point in prolonging this separation business any longer than necessary.' It salvaged his pride to be the one pushing for divorce. Hopefully she'd be taken aback and ask for some more time.

'I think you're right,' said Pandora promptly. This was music to her ears. 'Have you talked to a lawyer yet?'

John paled and gripped the phone tightly. 'Yes. My boss recommended Raymond Rench and he's offered to pay all my legal fees.' This was an exaggeration but it had the desired effect. He heard Pandora's sharp intake of breath. 'He says I should sue you for half of everything.'

'B-but you can't,' stuttered Pandora. 'I paid for the house and flat with my money!' Why should John be entitled to anything when he had been living with her rent free since they had started going out? They had only been married a year, and he had a good job.

'Tough.' For the first time since she had left him, John felt a sense of power. It was a heady feeling. Threatening her seemed the only way to get through and make her suffer what he was suffering. 'Rench seemed to think that I was the injured party and that I could sue you for adultery and mental cruelty.'

'Mental cruelty? That's a joke. You've lived off me since we met, paid no rent, I cooked you a three-course meal every—'

'And I'd like the Biedermeier furniture,' John interrupted her coolly. 'You can keep all the other stuff.'

'That's not fair! I chose each piece individually.'

'You may have chosen it but I paid for half of it.'

That was true, admitted Pandora grudgingly. 'But you don't even like it very much. Until you met me you thought Biedermeier was a brand of Swedish beer.'

'God, you're such a snob, Pandora.'

'If I was a snob I would never have married you,' she replied bitterly, and immediately regretted it when John slammed the phone down.

Daniel called for Pandora on the dot of six o'clock on Saturday. She was surprised. She had expected him to be fashionably late.

Thankfully it was a freezing evening and the car roof remained firmly *in situ*; at least she would be able to remain *coiffed* all evening.

'It's a shame it's too cold to put the top down. I know how much you enjoy the feel of the wind in your hair,' said Daniel flicking a CD effortlessly into the player. A tuneless ballad spewed forth and she glanced at the box – top ten hits from the fifties. It sounded like something you heard in lifts. Oh well, perhaps it had been a present from a friend. He smiled across at her. 'What sort of music d'you like?'

'Oh, everything. Kate Bush, Jo Cocker, Van Morrison. Have you heard his latest album? It's absolutely wonderful.'

Daniel wrinkled his nose. 'I'm not that keen on Van Morrison or Jo Cocker. I'm very mainstream, I'm afraid.'

Pandora winced. She couldn't believe that Daniel didn't like Van the Man. Was he more of a Cliff Richard sort of person? she wondered tremulously. As if in answer, one of Cliff's earlier and more forgettable tracks began to fill the car.

'Aren't you going to ask me how my golf game with John went?'

'Oh yes,' replied Pandora unenthusiastically. She didn't like talking to Daniel about John. 'How was he?'

'He looked pretty dreadful and he seems to have lost a lot of weight.' Not surprising, thought Pandora. He hadn't had to feed himself for over a year, he'd probably forgotten how to ignite a cooker. The price of food must have come as quite a shock too, he hadn't visited a supermarket in aeons.

'You were right not to tell him about us though. He was pretty bitter and a bit chippy about you.'

'Oh dear,' said Pandora nervously. Everything was going so well, John and his financial demands were the only cloud on the horizon. 'He says he's going to squeeze every penny he can out of me and that Raymond Rench will act for him. He can afford to hire him because his boss has offered to pay all his legal fees. I might be left with nothing.' The thought that she might have to get a job made her feel very weak indeed.

'Not Raymond "The Rottweiler" Rench? My poor darling!' said Daniel indignantly on her behalf. 'If he had any pride he'd walk away from it like a man.' He glanced in his mirror. 'Now why is that fucker flashing me?' Pandora cringed, they were driving at 65mph in the fast lane. In desperation the car behind overtook them on the inside. She shrank into her seat. 'Unbelievable! Look at that!'

'So dangerous,' murmured Pandora supportively.

'Still,' continued Daniel, 'I'm sure your father will help you out.'

'No, I shouldn't think so,' said Pandora sadly. James

had told her very firmly that she would have to pay for anything like that herself or ask her mother.

'But things are going so well in the rubber industry. AIDS must have doubled his turnover.' Condom manufacture was a profitable part of Simpson's Rubber Industries.

'Yes, he's very lucky like that,' said Pandora.

'By the way, how are your machinations going with him and your godmother? Have you set up their hot date yet?'

'Yes!' said Pandora excitedly. 'I've been very cunning about it and they both think they're meeting me by myself. I told Davina that I was devastated about the break-up of my marriage and needed to see her for godmotherly advice, and I spun Daddy the same story. We're all meeting in the American Bar at the Savoy next week. I'll do the link-up then I'll quietly disappear and leave them to have dinner downstairs in the Savoy Grill.'

'Sounds fascinating, I'd love to be a fly on the wall,' hinted Daniel.

'It would be nice if you could come along but it might complicate matters. How about I arrange something for the following week?'

'That would be super. Maybe we could fix up a game of golf sometime with him and my boss, Lord Dougall.'

'That'd be a great idea.'

Daniel smiled happily as he parked in front of Jane's house.

* * *

The party passed in a haze for Pandora. She was introduced to someone called Keith who talked for a long time about satellite systems, but she only had eyes for Daniel. It was very exciting having a clandestine affair, and he was definitely the most attractive man in the room.

Daniel drove them home with his hand on her knee and Pandora didn't know when she had ever felt so happy.

'It was a wonderful evening, Pandora,' he said, pulling her towards him once they were inside his flat. 'C'mon, let's go to bed.' She followed him into his bright white bedroom, feeling mellow with wine and love, and lay down invitingly on the bed. She had carefully avoided eating spicy foods all night and had splashed out on some adventurous lacy black underwear in the hope that tonight's encounter might be better than the last.

'I don't know about you, but I'm dead beat,' said Daniel, taking off his black Armani suit and hanging it up carefully. 'D'you want to borrow a nightshirt or something? It gets pretty cold in here.'

'No, I'll be fine,' said Pandora, shrugging off her dress herself as it didn't look as if he was going to remove it for her. She padded into the bathroom but when she returned from performing minimal ablutions and climbed into bed, her heart sank. Daniel was fast asleep.

The next morning she was woken up by a not altogether pleasant sensation between her legs; it felt as if an icicle had attached itself to her clitoris. Daniel's fingers were freezing and the room was so cold that she could see her breath. She shivered and writhed with simulated excitement and pulled him on top of her. She sighed with real pleasure as he entered her, stroking her breasts and kissing her as he did so. She was on the verge of coming when he suddenly stopped and rolled off her. Why had he stopped just when things were going so well? An unbridgeable awkwardness hovered between them.

'I think I'll have a shower,' said Pandora, slipping out of bed.

'OK, I'll make coffee.' Daniel shrugged on a silk dressing gown.

'Why don't we go out for breakfast? We could try that great cafe round the corner, they do wonderful coffee.' Pandora was longing to get out of the flat. It was funny but they seemed much more relaxed outside the bedroom than in it.

'But we can have breakfast here. I've got a deep freeze full of frozen croissants. I'll defrost us a couple in the microwave,' he said, padding cheerfully into his spartan kitchen. He was looking forward to catching a repeat of *The Two Ronnies* on Sky Gold.

Pandora dressed quickly and joined him in the sitting room. An anaemic plate of lukewarm croissants was placed next to two mugs of foul coffee and Daniel was engrossed in *The Two Ronnies*. Pandora *hated* both Ronnies, but when Daniel had told her they were his favourite comedians she had agreed with him. Now she would have to sit through it and pretend to find it hilarious. She realized that she'd told Daniel all sorts of things about herself that weren't true at all just to instil empathy between them. One day he would find out that she didn't like *The Two Ronnies*, Cliff Richard, instant coffee, driving with the roof down, and all the other things she had lied about, and then where would they be?

Daniel offered her a croissant. When she bit into it she found it was still frozen in the middle. She sat beside him, carefully simulating laughter for the next twenty minutes. By the time it had finished, she was so exhausted she wanted to go back to bed, but Daniel had other ideas and began delving into a cupboard.

'I thought we could try out these.' He waved two pairs of his and hers roller blades at her. 'We could roller-blade to the Conran Shop. I love looking around there on Sunday mornings.'

Pandora's face fell. This was the final straw. She'd had *no* idea! All this time and she'd been in love with a *roller-blader*! It was too horrible for words. She glanced at her watch. 'Gosh, is that the time? I've got to pick up Annabel from the airport, she's flying back from Palm Beach today. I ought to leave.' Annabel wasn't arriving until that evening but she just had to escape. Was it her imagination, but did a flicker of relief cross Daniel's face? She gathered up her things and he walked her to the door.

'Send my regards to your father, won't you? Why don't you come round here after you've had drinks with him? I'll take you somewhere for a slap-up dinner.'

'That would be lovely,' said Pandora cheerfully, standing on tiptoe to kiss him goodbye. But later, driving back to her flat, she knew that her feelings for him had radically changed. She still liked him but the raging passion she had once felt had completely disappeared. It was all very confusing. Thank goodness Annabel was coming home today.

Pandora arrived at Heathrow two hours early. She loved airports and was looking forward to a good browse around the bookshop. She had lent all her astrology books to a friend and was longing to look up the Ox, which Daniel had told her was his Chinese sign. She discovered an exciting New Age section in the shop and emerged triumphantly with several new books on Chinese and Western astrology. She quickly looked up 1956, the year he was born. To her *horror* she discovered that he wasn't an ox at all but a sheep! And if that wasn't bad enough, he was a wooden sheep! Maybe that would account for his strange behaviour in bed. Her nightmare discovery was interrupted by an announcement. 'Would Pandora Black please make her way to the information desk to meet Annabel Smythe-Johnson.' Gosh, Annabel's flight had got in early. She gathered up her things and rushed to the arrivals hall.

'Annabel! Over here,' Pandora called excitedly, spotting her friend in the distance. 'Gosh, you look wonderful!' Annabel was golden brown and her blonde hair was bleached practically white from the Florida sun.

'It's amazing what a bit of American positive thinking can do,' grinned Annabel. 'Guess what? I've talked myself into a job working for a PR company based in Palm Beach. They need someone in London to liaise between their celeb clients and the British media. I gave them loads of bullshit, how I knew Nigel and everyone at the *Mail*, *Vogue*, *Tatler* and *Harpers & Queen*. Luckily I had my book of press cuttings with me. I think the picture of me chatting up Prince Edward at a party clinched it. You know how obsessed Americans are with the royal family. So that's my scoop. What's new with you? Are you still madly, truly, deeply in love with the divine Daniel?'

'Um, no. No, I'm not.' They'd reached the car park and Pandora picked up Annabel's case and put it in the boot of her car. 'If you've got the strength, perhaps we could drive to Prêt à Manger for a nuisance cappuccino? I've simply loads to tell you.'

Forty-five minutes later the girls were installed in their favourite corner sharing an egg and cress sandwich, sipping their third round of cappuccinos and screeching with laughter.

'You're nothing but a sheep shagger,' Annabel was saying. 'I cannot believe that you of all people, with your intensive knowledge of Chinese astrology, could have allowed this to happen. You know what tigers do to sheep, they *savage* them! Poor old Daniel, he's probably in hospital recovering.'

'He's a wooden sheep, they're quite resilient, you know,' said Pandora.

'A wooden sheep! What was he like in bed?'

'Um, well, a bit *wooden* actually.' They shrieked with laughter. 'He was very keen on the oral stuff, he used to hang around down there for hours.'

'You should have had him fixed with an anti-suction

device like they give to calves,' laughed Annabel who was familiar with farming matters.

The cafe had suddenly gone silent and the girls looked around nervously. 'You don't think people have been listening to us, do you?' whispered Pandora.

'Well, we do talk quite loudly sometimes, don't we?' replied Annabel. 'Shall I get the next round in?' She left the table, returning a few moments later with two more cappuccinos.

'Death by caffeine. Anyway, it looks like we're jinxed when it comes to men so perhaps we'd better concentrate on our careers. I'm very excited that *Divorce!* has accepted a second article from you. I was thinking on the plane that you and I could really help each other. I've got access to loads of publicity-hungry celebs through my new job. I could easily line up some interviews for you. Why don't you ring up the magazine and see if they'd be interested? It would be great for me to have a journalist I can rely on to write nice things about my clients. That way I'll be able to encourage the shyer ones to be interviewed.'

'That's a wonderful idea, count me in,' said Pandora enthusiastically.

'I'm lunching with Nigel tomorrow and he'll yield some contacts too. Shall I get him to write a story about us?'

'Definitely,' laughed Pandora, 'it'll be fun. If you're serious about making it in PR you're going to need *lots* of exposure.'

* * *

Divorce! Magazine were very interested indeed in Pandora's proposed interviewees; not only that but they offered her the possibility of a regular column entitled 'Diary of an Adulteress' which they wanted to put on the back page.

Pandora put the phone down and leapt for joy, jumping up and down so heavily that her neighbour banged on the ceiling to complain. She sat down immediately at her new word processor and in a burst of inspiration wrote her first column. She spent the next couple of days feverishly writing, only taking time out for regular early morning swims at the Ritzy Marina club, a luxurious new health complex that had recently opened.

Not long after her conversation with Annabel she opened the *Daily Mail*, flicking straight to the Mail Diary. 'Oh my God,' she murmured. Annabel had been as good as her word.

'SAD RUBBER BAND HEIRESS'S MARRIAGE SNAPS!! Saucepot Pandora Black, whose father, James Simpson, is floating his hundred-million-pound rubber goods company, and whose mother, Georgina Verney, is a scion of the wealthy sausage-packing family, admitted that her ill-fated marriage to John Black, son of a Cumbrian post office employee, is finally over. "I know we were only married for a year but it seemed like a lot longer," said the provocative Pandora speaking from her exquisite Chelsea penthouse where she writes articles for *Divorce! Magazine*. "I am still in a state of shock and devastation, and am working hard to make enough money to pay my legal fees. I am hoping that my husband will behave like a gentleman." Pouting Pandora would not go into details but it is believed that her husband is hoping to claim half her fortune. Poor Pandora!'

This sad little story was belied by a picture of Pandora and Annabel clutching glasses of champagne and looking deliriously happy.

Pandora giggled to herself, it was so funny! She, Annabel and a journalist had cobbled the story together over the telephone. Nobody was bound to notice it thank goodness, but she thought she might show a copy to John to shame him into being reasonable. But when she arrived home there were ten messages on her answerphone, mainly from disgruntled elderly relatives complaining about 'dragging the family through the mud'. She erased them brutally, switched the telephone off and got down to work.

'You're famous,' said James drily, as she rushed into the American Bar that evening.

'But Dad, you don't even read the *Daily Mail*!'

'I don't, but the receptionist does,' he smiled. 'Glass of champagne?'

'Yes please.'

'And how is the great love of your life, what's his name . . .'

'Daniel Snodstein. You met him at my wedding, remember?'

James thought for a moment. 'Yes, you told me. I'm just trying to picture him. Not the smarmy bloke with the receding hairline who kept trying to buttonhole me?'

'Yes, that's the one,' said Pandora who had barely

given Daniel a moment's thought since Sunday. 'He works for Dougall and Douglas. He's very keen for you to play golf with him and Lord Dougall sometime. He'd be in seventh heaven if you used his bank to float the business.'

'You've got to be joking. I'd rather do business with Pol Pot. I've got no time for Dougall. When I was buying the business thirty years ago he treated me like scum. Now I'm worth a few bob it's a different story.' He sipped his gin and tonic. 'I had lunch with him recently and he was all over me like a cheap suit, hah! So you're seeing this Daniel chap now, are you?'

'Um, well, I've rather gone off him, actually.'

'I knew it! You're fickle, just like your mother.'

'No I'm not! Yes, perhaps I am,' agreed Pandora. 'But I've given up on relationships, or rather they've given up on me so I'm going to devote myself to my career. My first column appeared in *Divorce! Magazine* yesterday.' She flourished a copy at him. He took it from her enthusiastically.

'Well done! And they paid you for it?'

'Of course,' said Pandora proudly. 'I'm thinking of writing a novel too.'

'A novel? What could you possibly write a novel about? You haven't done anything.'

'Yes I have.' But James wasn't listening, he was transfixed by the sight of Davina, poised at the entrance and looking around for Pandora.

'I don't believe it. What on earth is Davina doing here?' He looked at his daughter. 'You didn't?'

'I did.'

Davina had caught sight of them and was making her way through the bar. 'James, what a lovely surprise! Pandora, you didn't say your father was in town.' Now in her late forties she had retained the glossy dark looks and sex appeal that had made her such a femme fatale in her twenties, and several male heads turned in her wake.

They greeted each other happily. Davina took out a cigarette which James lit with his silver Dunhill lighter.

Pandora wondered when she could conveniently leave. She was beginning to feel like a gooseberry already. Davina turned to her. 'You're looking very well, Pandora.'

'Yes, isn't she?' said James, smiling. 'My daughter appears to have made a remarkably quick recovery. Yesterday you said you were on the verge of a nervous breakdown, the world was collapsing around you and that you simply *had* to see me.'

'You told me your hair was dropping out through stress, that John was threatening you with physical violence and that you were taking Prozac to combat severe depression,' added Davina, crossing her elegant legs and smiling at her.

'Well, yesterday I was having a bad hair day,' said Pandora. 'Besides, I wanted to see you both. But I'm afraid I'm going to have to leave now because I've got a hot date – well, not exactly hot, more lukewarm really.'

'Oh, with that glamorous merchant banker you're so keen on?' asked Davina with interest. 'I'd love to meet him.'

'I'm afraid you're too late, Davina, she's already gone off him, thank goodness. He wasn't up to much.'

'But won't you stay for dinner, Pandora? I haven't seen you for so long.'

'No, I must go, I'm afraid. Daniel is taking me out to a ritzy restaurant.' She put on her coat and kissed them both goodbye. As she left the bar she turned round to wave but they had forgotten her already and were sitting, heads close together, laughing about something or other.

She took a taxi straight round to Daniel's. She was relieved to be going out; it had been thrilling playing Cupid but she felt slightly sad. If only there was someone out there for her, but it seemed that the only relationships she was capable of having were flawed ones. Still, it would be nice to see Daniel. Even if they weren't romantically involved, they could still be good friends. She paid off the taxi and rang his doorbell. After an interminable wait he eventually opened the door. His large feet were bare and he was clutching a piece of pizza. 'Hi. I hope you don't mind but I ordered us some pizza. I know how much you like it. I couldn't face going out to dinner.'

She followed him in wordlessly. Not only were his feet bare but he was wearing a revolting pair of baggy grey tracksuit bottoms.

'Here, help yourself, I ordered us a choice.' He opened a box and sighed crossly. 'Shit, they sent me the wrong one! This one's got bacon on it. I told them not to send anything with pork on it!'

'Can't you eat it for, um, *religious* reasons?' inquired

Pandora gently, feeling her irritation vanish. Perhaps now they could have an interesting conversation about his inner Jewish conflict; she knew she was the right person to help him come to terms with it.

'Of course not,' replied Daniel crossly. 'I'm allergic to milk and I can't eat pork because pigs are fed on dairy products.'

'Actually, I'm not terribly hungry,' said Pandora coldly. 'I had a snack at the Savoy.'

'Oh, how was your father?' asked Daniel eagerly.

'Very well.' She yawned. 'It's been a long day, if you don't mind I might make a move.' She was suddenly longing to return to her flat.

'Have a coffee before you go.' He smiled appealingly at her and headed towards the kitchen.

'Um, no.' Pandora backed out of the room. The thought of his instant grey coffee made her feel sick. 'Bye, Daniel.'

She quickly let herself out of the house and ran towards the main road and a taxi home. But instead of offering the relief she craved, the spacious, uncluttered flat oppressed her. She checked her messages. There was an unpleasant one from John saying his lawyer thought he should make a claim for half her shares in her father's business, as well as everything else, a desperate one from Darren pleading with her to ring him, and one from Daniel, left that afternoon saying how flattering the picture was of her in the *Daily Mail*, and would she please pass on his regards to her father. She smiled grimly. John wanted everything, Darren wanted her body and Daniel wanted her father. Why couldn't they all just leave her alone! And yet it was partly her fault, she had invited them all into her life and now she was taking the consequences. And how. She dialled Annabel's number, fearing that if she didn't talk to someone she might burst into tears. But Annabel was out. She dialled Rachel and six other friends. Nobody was in. She even called her mother in Buenos Aires but all she got was a message saying that she had flown to Monte Carlo and would be back on Monday. Allowing her legs to buckle beneath her, she sank on to the floor with her head in her hands and wept with the sudden aching realization that she was well and truly alone.

She sat huddled miserably on the floor, weeping, her mind drifting over the past. A conversation she had overheard on her wedding day between two of John's friends flickered through her mind: 'John can cash in his Premium Bonds now!' they had laughed. *Was* that why he had married her? For her money? She cried for herself, she cried for John, she cried for her parents. As the sobs wracked her, she felt as if her body was swelling with grief for the whole damn world, its disappointments, its pain, but most of all she cried for love. She had a photograph of her parents taken thirty years ago that revealed a young, good-looking couple, madly in love, blissfully confident that the world would remain their oyster for ever. But that same world had soon crashed, leaving everyone involved scarred by the fall-out. Where had the love that lit up that picture disappeared to? Where did love go? Everything turned into something; what did love turn into? A lawyer's bill? She knew what her grandfather would say at this point: 'Have you tried pulling yourself together?' She smiled bleakly and hauled herself to her feet, splashed her eyes with cold water and blew her nose.

She picked up a pen and her notebook and sat down to write. All the questions, all the pain, all the melancholy and confusion came pouring out of her heart and into her pen, which raced feverishly across each page. Eventually, she put her notebook down and went to stand by the window, watching the bare branches of the trees silhouetted in the moonlight in the gardens below. She opened the window and breathed in the cool night air. Turning round she stooped to pick up a piece of paper that had blown to the floor. It was her cheque from *Divorce! Magazine*.

Shutting her eyes, she clasped it tightly to her mouth. This was it, the ticket to her freedom. Let John take her money, her house, her flat – let him take the whole damn lot. There was one thing even the toughest, cleverest lawyer couldn't get his hands on, and that was her heart, her hand, and her pen. She was going to write her novel. No one seemed to think she had what it took, but she'd show them.

Early the next morning the telephone rang shrilly.

'You bitch!' It was John. 'How dare you tell all the newspapers about our private business. Everyone at the office is laughing at me, thanks to you and your big mouth!'

'But the piece in the *Daily Mail* was very innocuous, and all true, by the way,' said Pandora crossly.

'I'm not talking about that, I'm talking about the double-page feature in the *Daily Telegraph* about husbands that sue their wives for money.'

'I don't know anything about it. I haven't talked to anyone from the *Daily Telegraph*.'

'Well, there's a whole spread about us and your crazy family. It says I've hired the Rottweiler and that I'm suing you for millions.'

'Well, you are, aren't you?'

'I was only joking, for heaven's sake. I haven't even seen a lawyer yet.'

'But you said your boss was fixing it all up.'

John was silent. 'Look, maybe I was angry, maybe I was exaggerating. But now, thanks to you, everyone thinks I married for money and that I'm suing my poor vulnerable young wife for everything! It's a nightmare. A complete fucking nightmare.'

'Look, I don't know what to say. How about we settle out of court and call it quits?' she asked hopefully.

'Well, I don't see that I've got much choice. My boss is livid with me.'

Good for the boss, thought Pandora. 'What did he say to you?'

'Oh, some rubbish about a gentleman never taking money off a woman, and how this sort of publicity would make people think that everyone in the company is a crook. He said he was a great admirer of your father. Jesus! The whole thing is so bloody unfair. I'm only trying to teach you a lesson for the appalling way you've behaved! Now everyone thinks I was living off you and that I never paid for anything.'

'Well, tell them. Take out an ad in *The Times*. What did you pay for, out of interest?' asked Pandora sweetly.

'God, you're such a bitch!' repeated John.

He was probably right, thought Pandora. 'Well, how much do you want?'

He mentioned a figure, she halved it and he agreed readily. Damn, thought Pandora, I should have gone for less.

'Right, now we're agreed, let's get everything sewn up so we can both move on.'

'If you're quite sure that's what you want, Pandora. I'd forget everything you've said and done if you want to try a second time,' said John hopefully.

'I don't think so.' Pandora felt a wave of pity for him. 'You'll find a better woman than me and be much happier. You were always telling me how difficult I was. If I were you, I'd look on this as a blessing.'

John didn't sound terribly convinced, she thought, once their conversation had drawn to its bleak conclusion, but at least he wasn't ranting and raving at her any more.

As soon as she replaced the receiver it rang again. It was Anouska, the features editor of *Divorce! Magazine*.

'Darling, just *loved* your pix in the *Mail* and the *Telegraph*. You're *frightfully* photogenic. How about a teensy photo shoot modelling some of the latest frocks from the Bruce Oldfield collection? I'm planning a feature about what the fashionable *divorcée* is wearing in court this winter. Oh, I had lunch with Annabel yesterday. I had no idea you and she were friends. I was at Benenden with her elder sister Camilla.'

'The Queen Bee of Palm Beach, by all accounts,' said Pandora cheerfully.

'Yes, good old Camel. Anyway, Annabel says that Camilla has arranged for you to interview a host of celebrity *divorcées* from Palm Beach, the only provisos being that they get to plug whatever rubbish they're into, freak religions, colonic irrigation, you know the sort of thing. We'll fly you to Palm Beach and put you up at the Breakers, it's a fab hotel and that's where you'll do all your interviews. How does all that sound?'

Pandora could hardly take it all in. 'It sounds wonderful. I'm sure I can fit it in with my other commitments . . .'

'Well, perhaps we could meet for lunch on Monday. How does one p.m. at Daphne's sound?'

'Perfect,' agreed Pandora.

'Good. If we like what you fax us from Palm Beach we'll offer you a contract to work exclusively for *Divorce!*. You came along just at the right time, we've been looking for a socialite *divorcée* for a while, and if the articles you've sent us so far are anything to go by, it appears you can write like a dream. The Adulteress's Diary had us all in fits! There's just one thing that I hope won't be a problem.'

'What?' asked Pandora nervously.

'Well, we need someone who has absolutely no strings, who will be free to up sticks at a moment's notice and go anywhere. You don't have a serious boyfriend or a secret baby or anything, do you?' She laughed shrilly.

'Absolutely not. Just give me five minutes' notice and I can be anywhere.'

'That's the spirit! See you at Daf's next Monday then. *Ciao* for now!'

Ciao for now, thought Pandora weakly. Darling Annabel had obviously done the most brilliant PR job on her. But could she live up to it? Of course she could. From now on she was going to Think Positive! She was no longer a frumpy housewife from the suburbs who couldn't grow vegetables, she was a writer, for heaven's sake. Palm Beach! She could hardly believe it. Life really did turn on a sixpence. Last night she had felt so hopeless, but this morning luck seemed to be raining down from the skies. This was the opportunity of a lifetime and she *had* to make it work.

Chapter Twelve

Pandora threw herself into her writing, working late into the night polishing her articles and in spare moments working assiduously on her novel. Her trip to Palm Beach had been a great success, the interviews had been well received and had led to other assignments so that now her byline was becoming a regular fixture in the magazine. To her great relief she had now sold Bluebell House and was living full-time in the London flat which, though small, suited her very well. John was staying with friends while he looked for a place of his own.

'I can't open a glossy magazine without seeing either a picture of you "sharing a joke" with some poor sod at a party, or something you've written,' said Rachel who was in London briefly before returning to Israel where she was spending most of her time. 'It's great, I can catch up on what you're up to when I'm in Tel Aviv. I loved your piece – what was it called? The one about gambling.'

'"Unlucky in love but lucky in cards – looking on the bright side",' said Pandora, scooping the froth off her cappuccino and licking her teaspoon. 'I enjoyed writing that. It's true, you know, you just have to look at my family. The Bolter's a whizz at *vingt et un* and my dad ran his business like a game of poker.'

'Someone said he got a hundred million for it. Is that true?' asked Rachel, widening her dark eyes incredulously.

'Thereabouts,' said Pandora vaguely. 'But you know the scoop on him and Davina? It's going great guns. I spoke to her last week and I think they've practically moved in together. It's rather sweet, he said that the Rashleigh estate has been mismanaged for generations and that he's going to sort it all out for her. He needs something to get his teeth into now he's sold the business. You know, their story really does make me think that dreams can come true.'

'So he's not only lucky at cards but lucky in love too. Rather goes to disprove your theory.'

'Actually he said he lost ten grand at the Truro races, so I'm afraid the theory still holds. Perhaps I should take up gambling,' said Pandora thoughtfully.

'Oh, come on, you get asked out all the time.'

'Yes, but by such odd people. A really sexy man took me out for all these lovely dinners but he didn't make a pass or anything. Then he takes me to Paris to stay in the George V for the weekend—'

'See, you have all the luck!'

'No, wait, so I packed all this slinky underwear and had my hair done and everything, then when we were in bed the first night he said he couldn't make love to me because sex was terribly important to him and he didn't want to make a commitment until he knew me better.'

'So what did you do?'

'I said, "Who said anything about commitment, we're only here for two nights," and turned over and fell asleep. He still rings me up. I suppose he likes me for my mind,' she finished sadly.

'Perhaps he's got crabs and he's waiting for them to clear up,' said Rachel helpfully. 'They take ages to die. You've got to poison the first lot and then—'

'Spare me the details,' begged Pandora.

'Maybe he's HIV positive, or impotent—'

'—or a woman!' They both shrieked with laughter.

'So tell me, Rachel, how is your latest romantic interest? It all sounded *deliciously* painful when you rang from Tel Aviv.'

'The irresistible Benjamin is driving me wild with misery!' said Rachel happily. 'He didn't call for weeks, then out of the blue he rang and asked me to stay with him in Ein Hod, this blissful artists' colony just outside Tel Aviv, where he has a studio. He wants to sculpt me in the nude. I simply can't wait.' She sighed dreamily, then patted her solid thighs crossly. 'I must shift some of this weight. I've only been to the Ritzy Marina club once since I joined and that was to have a pedicure.'

Pandora smiled. 'I hope you'll be here for the ball that Annabel and I are organizing for the Dolphin Free charity next month. She's managed to talk the Hyde Park Hotel into letting us use their ballroom, and Möet and Chandon are providing free champagne. I'm so pleased for her, if she hadn't lost all her money in Lloyd's she would probably never have known how talented she is. She's getting loads of new clients and making some quite serious money, I think.'

'You and she both,' said Rachel. 'If you hadn't left John you'd still be growing wonky vegetables and trying to make chickweed deodorant.'

'Please, don't remind me,' shuddered Pandora. 'I'd better make a move, I'm flying to Zurich tonight to interview Ted Shred, the world's number one ski jumper who's just got divorced. I can't wait!'

'Yoga was fabulous today, he's such a good teacher,' said Annabel. She and Pandora were lying on one of the squishy sofas at the Ritzy Marina club. They had just finished a yoga class and were analysing their cappuccinos with some intensity.

'Not as good as Prêt à Manger, I'm afraid.'

'The cup is too small and there isn't enough froth,' Pandora agreed. She had been commissioned to write an article about the best cappuccinos in London. 'Can I have a bit of your muffin?'

'Go ahead,' said Annabel, flicking idly through a magazine. 'Oh look, here's a picture of me and Dai Llewellyn at the Dolphin Ball.' She passed it over to Pandora and continued, 'You don't think we're becoming a bit New Age with all this yoga and dolphin saving, do you?'

'Course not,' said Pandora, munching Annabel's sugar-free rhubarb muffin. 'The ball raised fifty thousand pounds. That's enough to rehabilitate all the dolphins at Ocean World so they can be released back into the ocean.'

'Rehabilitate! You make them sound like alcoholics.'

They sipped their cappuccinos thoughtfully.

'By the way,' continued Annabel, 'how are your father and Davina getting on?'

'Brilliantly! They've just left on a first class, round the world trip. I think they're in Antigua at the moment. I'm half expecting them to slip off and get quietly married somewhere. They've asked me if I want to join them for two weeks in Hawaii. I just can't wait. I've been running round in circles since I left John, it'll be great to take some time out and really think about the future.' She sipped her coffee thoughtfully. 'You know, when we were doing our head stands just now, I was thinking of all the Earthchildren meetings I used to go to in Middlehurst, all the tins I shook outside supermarkets and all the letters I wrote that were probably just thrown away. I know people complain about publicity, but if I hadn't had all this exposure recently we wouldn't have got nearly as many people interested in the ball.'

'And it's nice getting our pictures into the papers, isn't it, sweetie?' said Annabel, admiring her picture closely. 'By the way, I saw John driving down the Kings Road in a brand new Porsche *with a woman*!'

'Huh, didn't take him long,' said Pandora. 'Someone told me he's put a downpayment on one of those fantastic flats overlooking the Thames.'

'I know, he's telling everyone he's just had a humungus bonus from the bank.'

'Humungus bonus indeed! Well, it would have been much worse if you hadn't leaked that story to the *Telegraph*. I probably deserve it anyway. I was an *adulteress*. In Saudi Arabia they might have beheaded me. Or, worse, chopped my hands off so I couldn't write!' She sighed bleakly.

'Now, how is our latest idea coming along?' asked Annabel. In a bid to meet some decent men they had dreamt up the idea of doing a guide to the world's most eligible divorced bachelors. Anouska had lapped it up.

'God, don't remind me. *Divorce!* gave me a shortlist of a hundred men – heaven knows what a long list would be – and told me to research them and come up with the ten most interesting for an *in depth* feature.'

'Just how *in depth* are we talking?'

'Well, I have to take them out for dinner and ask them personal questions,' grinned Pandora. 'I said I'd need an assistant to help me with my research, and that's where you come in. Now, Annabel, can I rely on your utter *commitment* to this project?'

Annabel snorted with laughter. 'Does the Pope pray?'

'I knew I could count on you. I've brought the list with me.' Pandora dug it out of her bag and passed it over. 'Take your pick.'

Annabel swiftly scanned the typed pages. 'Anouska's range is pretty wide, isn't it?' she commented. 'Still, we should be able to whittle this down to about twenty gorgeous men without too much trouble. I mean, I don't think

I could road-test more than about ten in the next couple of weeks. How's your stamina in the field, Pandora?'

'Limited,' said Pandora. 'And anyway, it's got to be done before I go to Hawaii.'

Annabel turned back to the first page. 'I see Anouska has included that chap Jack Dudley.'

Pandora looked blank.

'You know, he's brought out all those educational computer games that have been selling everywhere. He was the man the General wanted you to meet that time we were in PJ's celebrating my clean bill of health after my biopsy.' Annabel winced at the memory.

'Oh, him. Now I know who you mean. I doubt he'd talk to anybody even remotely connected with *Divorce!*. His ex-wife got six pages in the magazine recently, slagging him off. I'm surprised we weren't sued.'

'Pity,' said Annabel. 'He'd be perfect. I read something about a charitable foundation he's setting up in Africa. Maybe you could try that avenue. And I'm sure Hugo would give you a few tips. They used to work together years ago at Dougall and Douglas. I met him a couple of times and now I come to think of it, the General was right, he's definitely your type, Pandora.'

'Please, I need someone like him like I need a hole in the head,' lied Pandora convincingly. 'In future I think I'm going to put my faith in something a little more reliable than love, like corn circles.'

One month later Pandora sat glued in front of her word processor. She had returned from a glorious two weeks in Hawaii with James and Davina only the day before and was feeling surprisingly un-jet lagged. As she had anticipated, they had indeed got married in Antigua. Pandora smiled to herself. She had never seen her father look so happy – he was a changed man.

The grinding years of running the business and the past few months of selling it had taken their toll on him and this was the first proper holiday he had had in years. Davina, too, had begun the trip pale and exhausted from the continual strain of trying to keep the family estate together, and Pandora, who had been priding herself on coping with divorce and moving out of Bluebell House, as well as working all hours on her articles and her novel, had collapsed on to a sunlounger on her first day and been unable to move for a week. But Hawaii had worked its subtle magic on them all and after a few days Pandora found that the stresses and strains with which she'd arrived had been replaced by a new vigour and sense of optimism. She had done very little but lie on the beach every day and plan her novel from behind a large pair of sunglasses, while Davina and James had gone for long walks and spent the rest of the time recovering from them in the bar.

Pandora had made pages of inspired notes in Hawaii, and now, after several hours of frantic typing, she got up and stretched, suddenly feeling very sleepy. She glanced at her watch. It was time for *EastEnders*. There was nothing she felt more like doing than crashing in front of the television with a TV yogurt or two.

Grasping a six-pack of 'lite' Marks and Spencer yogurts

from the fridge, she switched on the television and settled down with a blissful sigh. It was so heavenly living alone, she couldn't understand why it was most people's dream to shack up with someone. The thought of having to fight for the remote control after a tough afternoon slaving away at her computer was just too awful to contemplate. Now, should she start with the rhubarb, the starfruit, or the gorgeously named Exotic Heaven yogurt?

The phone rang, brutally interrupting her indecision. Damn! She'd forgotten to put the answerphone on. She couldn't be bothered to answer it, best to let it ring. One minute later it was still ringing, and it was impossible to concentrate on the television.

'Hello,' she answered in her 'I've got six calls waiting and I've got to finish a novel by nine p.m. so hurry up' voice.

'You sound busy,' said a deep voice with a South African accent that was so compelling, Pandora completely forgot about yogurts and *EastEnders*. His voice had the amused tone of someone who knew her very well. She didn't recognize it, perhaps he'd got the wrong number. But it was essential that she kept him on the line as long as possible.

'Oh no, no, I'm not busy at all. I'm, um, Pandora. Can I help you?' she asked hopefully.

'Yes, Pandora. I think you can. My name is Jack Dudley. I believe you've been trying to reach me.'

Jack Dudley! She'd given up hope of ever tracking him down. Of course, he would be the sort of man who'd have a voice like sun-warmed honey.

'Y-yes, I, um, I've been trying to get hold of you,' she stuttered pathetically. 'I've been working on an article about the world's most eligible bachelors and you were suggested.' Damn. It was far too late to include him now, the piece was coming out in next month's issue. Still, he didn't know that. Maybe she could still 'interview' him anyway.

'I guess it's too late to include me now. That's a pity.' He sounded relieved. 'Actually, I wasn't really calling you about that. I wanted to discuss the possibility of you doing some work for me.'

Anything, anything, Pandora drooled silently.

'I recently bought an environmental magazine called *Environment Today* which sells about ten copies a month. I'm convinced something could be made of it. The new editor was reading some of your articles and suggested that you'd be the perfect person to give us a few ideas about how to glam it up a bit. We'd pay you a consultancy fee, of course.'

'Gosh, it sounds like a fascinating project,' said Pandora enthusiastically. 'I'm sure I could help you de-grunge it a bit.'

He laughed. 'Well, how about we meet for dinner next week to discuss it?'

Pandora pinched herself to check that she wasn't dreaming.

'I'm flying to Hawaii tonight,' he continued, 'but I'll be back a week on Tuesday. Would the Wednesday be any good for you?'

Pandora pretended to think. 'Um, yes, Wednesday

would be good for me, too. I envy you going to Hawaii. I've just got back from there myself; it's one of my favourite places in the whole world.'

'Mine too,' agreed Jack. 'Trouble is, it takes so long to get to. I've got a beach house on Oahu that I haven't had time to stay in for years so I've rented it out. It's ridiculous, I'll end up staying in a hotel.'

'Hey, that's a coincidence. I was staying on Oahu too! I probably walked past your house every day. Will you get the chance to relax or will you be working?'

'Bit of both, I hope. I'm thinking about involving the magazine in a few things that are going on out there. We can discuss it when we meet. Can I get someone to send you a copy? It's quite difficult to get hold of.'

'Oh, don't worry; when I worked on the Earthchildren Action Committee in Middlehurst it was required reading.'

Jack laughed. 'I knew you were the perfect girl for the job. I'd been wondering who was buying those ten copies.'

'I know Harrods stock it,' Pandora added helpfully.

'Sadly, they're about the only place that do.'

'Well, we'll change that. Maybe you could run a series of articles about what celebrities are doing for the environment – interview Sting and people like that.'

EastEnders was finishing and the theme music droned drearily down the receiver. She tried to reach the television to turn it down but knocked over a bowl of jaded potpourri by mistake. Damn, Jack must think she was frivolous enough already with her dippy celebrity profiles without him knowing that her idea of a perfect evening was sitting down with six yogurts and *EastEnders*.

'Is it *EastEnders* tonight?' asked Jack. 'What's happening?'

'Do you watch it?' asked Pandora with surprise.

'Of course. I love it.'

'I don't believe you. Who's your favourite character?'

'Umm . . .'

'See, I knew you didn't watch it!'

'My wife used to watch it all the time so I couldn't avoid getting sucked in really.' He thought for a moment. 'I liked the guy who was always thumping people he didn't like.'

'You mean Grant "if nothing else works threaten physical violence" Mitchell. Yes, I agree, he's deliciously Neanderthal. It must be wonderful to have such an uncomplicated attitude to life.' They both laughed.

'Well, Pandora, it's been lovely talking to you. I'd better leave for the airport if I'm going to make my flight. I'll ring you a week on Wednesday, you can fill me in on plot developments then.'

Pandora felt her insides sizzle up in excitement. A whole evening with the elusive Jack Dudley! What would she wear? Did her roots need retouching? Had she time to go to a health farm before next Wednesday? Get a grip, she thought, rifling through her wardrobe, he was only a *man*, for heaven's sake; even if he did have a house in Hawaii, it wasn't worth losing her head. He was bound to be a disappointment like all the others. Damn, there was nothing remotely suitable for her to wear, she'd have to splash out on something new. She remembered a wickedly expensive slither of cashmere she'd tried on in Harrods and rejected. How could she justify spending so much money on a dress? But it would be *perfect*.

Pandora spent the following days in a fever of antici-pation. As she had feared, she was unable to resist the slither of cashmere and it now clung irresistibly to a wooden hanger in her wardrobe.

She looked up Jack's press cuttings and discovered an old *National Geographic* magazine which had carried an interview with him after he had left the South African army and before he had gone into business. He had been trying to break the world record for climbing Mount Huascarán in Peru, and the story was illustrated by a grizzled picture of him with a beard, looking into the camera, impatient to get on. There was determi-nation in the eyes and a sense of energy and pur-pose in his stance. The picture made rather a stun-ning impression on Pandora and she cut it out and stuck it on her fridge. He was often mentioned in the business pages of the newspapers, but he kept a low social profile. His marriage to Atlanta on an obscure Caribbean island had attracted some media attention, but that was all.

On Wednesday he rang as promised and arranged to

pick her up at eight. He could have said three in the morning and she would have agreed, Pandora thought feebly, pouring seaweed extract into the bath. It smelt disgusting but promised a thrilling all-over inch reduction which would be necessary if she was to wriggle her way into her new cashmere dress.

She fingered it reverently before she put it on. It was the colour of sun-warmed lemons and felt deliciously soft beneath her fingers, managing somehow to be discreet and sexy at the same time. Then she selected her most impractical dolly handbag, which was too small to carry money but just big enough to squeeze half a lipstick into, and practised *slithering* around the kitchen until the buzzer went. 'Don't panic,' she panicked, forgetting how to slither, grabbing the nearest bag and her keys in a frantic rush before dashing downstairs. She wondered if she would be able to recognize Jack from her memory of his picture.

He was leaning against the wall and straightened up as Pandora burst out in a flurry of bags and keys.

'Hi, you must be Pandora,' he said, looking at her for what seemed like an interminable time before stooping down to retrieve her keys which had slipped through her fingers.

Pandora had the feeling he was examining her and hoped she had passed the test. She wouldn't have recognized him. The beard had gone and the tawny hair was darker than in the *National Geographic* picture. But the determination in the eyes and the power in the stance hadn't changed. The one thing she hadn't been prepared for was the sheer physical size of him. He was at least six foot four and heavy with it. And he had *wonderful* forearms.

'I thought we'd go to Daphne's, if that's all right with you,' he said, opening the passenger door of an enormous four-wheel drive. The seat was very high off the ground and Pandora's new dress made agility impossible. She wondered if she could jump into it somehow, but thought it unlikely.

'Um, Jack, have you got a stepladder or something? I don't think my dress will be able to take the strain.'

He laughed, put two large hands round her waist and lifted her into the seat. Maybe the seaweed extract had worked, she felt like a feather in his hands. The inside of the car was as impressive as the outside. The dashboard was filled with as many gadgets and winking lights as a small aeroplane.

'Jack, I simply love your car. What is it?'

'It's a special edition Range Rover. It's a bit big for London but I own a shoot in Scotland and it really comes into its own out in the wilds. I'm a bit of a car freak, I'm afraid.'

'Oh, so am I. I'm saving up for a Porsche at the moment. Well, for the insurance at least.' She was keeping all the money she earned in a separate account; that way she would really appreciate a decent car. She just hoped she'd be young enough to drive it by the time she'd saved enough. She glanced covertly at his suntanned wrists resting on the steering wheel.

'How was Hawaii?' she asked.

'Magical. Absolutely magical. It's the one place where I can really relax.'

'Yes, I know exactly what you mean,' agreed Pandora, gazing wistfully out of the window.

Sitting beside him so high above street level and other motorists made Pandora feel very superior. It was like driving a tank or something.

'You know, you remind me of someone,' Jack said, pulling brutally out into the Fulham Road, causing a line of cars to brake suddenly in his wake. 'I know, Lady Penelope! You look just like her.'

'Gosh, do I really?' She was very flattered. Lady Penelope had been her heroine and role model since childhood.

'You're not a bit like Parker,' she added.

As Jack manoeuvred the tank into an impossibly small space near the restaurant, Pandora tried to work out how she could slide out of the vehicle elegantly without her dress riding up to her crotch. She wasn't wearing knickers, her dress was so close-fitting she couldn't afford a VPL beneath it. In the event, her exit was far from elegant.

Daphne's was packed with beautiful people, as usual, but Jack had enough clout for them to be seated immediately. This was very impressive, customers had been known to age years in the long wait for a table. Pandora followed him to a secluded corner, aware of mutterings from wilting customers, unhappy at this obvious display of queue-hopping.

Jack ordered champagne and a waiter smoothly filled

their glasses. 'Here's to a long and productive association,' he said, raising his glass and toasting her. In the flattering light it glowed a deep, burnished gold. Pandora, transfixed by the tiny bubbles spinning around the glass, felt a tiny stab of disappointment. She had almost forgotten that this was a business dinner.

'I chose this champagne because it matches your dress,' he said lightly.

'Did you really?' Pandora took a sip. 'Mmmm, it's delicious.' She made an effort to be business-like. 'I bought a copy of *Environment Today*. I'm afraid it sent me to sleep.'

Jack was looking at her very intensely. To her surprise he seemed to be taking her quite seriously. Encouraged, she went on, 'Basically, I think the whole magazine needs to be more people-orientated.'

'Less of the heavy-going stuff and more froth?'

Pandora looked at him carefully. She was a bit sensitive about her superficial celebrity profiles. Was he making fun of her lightweight style? 'Yes. Up to a point. We don't have to take the magazine downmarket, just make it more appealing to the modern reader. People haven't got time to wade through long, technical articles about sewage.'

Jack tried not to smile, she looked so irresistibly earnest. 'When you feel strongly about something, do you always wrinkle up your nose?' he asked.

Pandora went pink with embarrassment. No one ever took her snub nose seriously. Intellectuals had long, elegant, aquiline noses, not tiny blobs in the middle of their faces. Damn.

'It's a wonderful nose,' said Jack seriously. 'I know women who've paid thousands of pounds to get one just like it.'

'How do you know I haven't bought mine?' asked Pandora.

'Because you're not the type,' said Jack firmly.

Pandora felt a little cheered. Maybe he was taking her seriously after all.

'You've got a nice nose too,' she said. 'It's sort of . . .' She paused to find the right word.

'Crooked?' Jack finished, smiling at her.

'Robust. I did a course in how faces determine a person's character. Large noses mean a person is good at making money.'

Jack looked sceptical.

'It's true, you know,' she persisted. 'Look at Getty and Onassis. They had whoppers.' Apparently noses also had something to do with penis size, but she didn't want to discuss *that* with Jack. 'How come you've got a crooked nose?' she asked curiously.

'I had a bit of a fight with someone once.'

'What about?'

'Oh, I can't remember. It was years ago.'

'I'm sure you tried every peaceful means of persuasion first,' she said.

'Something like that,' smiled Jack, 'but as Grant in *EastEnders* is always saying, "if nothing else works, threaten—'

'—physical violence",' she finished with a laugh.

'I'm only joking,' added Jack unconvincingly.

'Did you have to do national service in South Africa?' asked Pandora.

'Yes, when I was eighteen. Two years in the Angolan bush. It wasn't something I'd want to repeat.'

'Two years! What did you live on?'

'Anything we could get our hands on. We had army rations, but we'd hunt stuff.'

'Monkeys?' asked Pandora, digging into her delicious pumpkin risotto.

'No, but we ate snakes when we could get our hands on them.' He sounded as if he was describing a delicacy from Fortnum & Mason.

Pandora gazed at him in admiration. 'Do you know how to catch snakes then?'

'It's not difficult. You just get a double-pronged stick and trap it.' He demonstrated with two fingers on Pandora's arm. A course of electricity surged down it.

Lucky snake, she thought. 'What does it taste like?'

'It's very good, a bit like tender chicken. It's a lot better than tarantula.'

'You're kidding me!'

'I swear I'm not. I once spent six months in the rainforest taking photos of a tribe of Indians for the *National Geographic*. These tarantulas are the size of dinner plates and they have inch-long fangs. The Indians roast them.'

Pandora shuddered. She wasn't the only one. The elderly occupants of the next table had gone quite silent and were hanging on to Jack's every word.

'Can you eat the legs?' she inquired, quite sure they would want to know.

'Absolutely. The legs aren't too bad if they're cooked properly. They taste a bit like crab. The abdomen is sort of gooey, a bit like poached egg. The eggs from the pregnant female are considered a real delicacy, they make omelettes out of them. They're very nutritious but they taste like shit.'

Pandora silently digested this information. Her life seemed so tame and parochial in comparison. She scooped up a small mouthful of pumpkin risotto, trying not to think of tarantula omelettes. Jack ate his steak and kidney pie with enthusiasm.

'Haven't had this for years, it's delicious,' he commented.

After Daniel's obscure dietary restrictions, dining with Jack was a treat.

The waiter cleared away their plates. 'Would you like some pudding?' he asked.

'Just a cappuccino please.'

'And I'll have a double espresso.'

Pandora took a deep breath of relief. She thought of Daniel and his horrible instant coffee, and shuddered.

Jack noticed and asked what was wrong.

Before she could reply a stunning blonde materialized from nowhere and put a predatory hand on Jack's shoulder. 'Darling Jack! I had no idea you were in town! Bunny said you were still in New York!' She spoke in a series of breathless exclamation marks and had a charming lisp.

Jack stood up. 'Pandora, this is Saffron. Saffron, Pandora.'

Pandora's heart sank. Saffron was a knockout, she *had* to be a model with a name like that.

Saffron looked at Pandora. 'Oh Jack, she's *sweet*.'

Oh no I'm not, thought Pandora, crossly wondering about the possibility of having a nose augmentation to make her look more substantial.

Saffron quickly turned her attention back to Jack. 'I'm in London for two days doing the shows, and then I'm back in Paris. Promise me you'll look me up when you're next over, darling. I can get you a front row seat at Dolce and Gabana next month if you like.'

Jack looked faintly appalled and stooped to kiss her goodbye. 'It's not quite my thing, Saffron, but thanks anyway.'

Saffron wafted off to the bar looking crushed.

'Sorry about that, Pandora. Who on earth are Dolce and Gabana, by the way? Are they a band or a Panama hat company or something?'

Pandora smiled. 'They're a fashion house, and they do ready-to-wear as well. Their clothes are really popular with girls under three stone.'

'Just as well I turned down the invitation then.' He glanced towards the bar. Pandora followed his gaze. Saffron's etiolated form had been absorbed by a crowd of braying Eurotrash types.

She was laughing and flicking back her hair girlishly.

'She's very lovely,' said Pandora pleasantly.

'Yes, she is. I took her out a few times when I was in Paris.'

Pandora wondered crossly if he had slept with her. He

was obviously the sort of man who could get under a girl's skin very easily. Well, he wouldn't get under hers, that was for sure. Theirs was a business arrangement and nothing else.

Jack had finished paying the bill. 'Shall we go and have a drink somewhere?' he asked. 'I could take you to Monte's. Monte's was a five-storey house in Knightsbridge that had recently been converted into a chic new club.

'I think I've had enough,' said Pandora. 'I ought to get home.'

The champagne had enhanced her agility considerably and she was able to hop into the Range Rover with no assistance. She giggled to herself as she bounced into the seat. Really, she was having a wonderful time. Jack was such good company. He made everyone else who had ever taken her out seem quite wishy-washy. Except perhaps Yonathon. But even he hadn't eaten tarantulas. Jack was probably a complete bastard to women as well, she told herself sensibly, admiring his deft driving and the way every other vehicle on the road made way for his.

He squeezed into a space several doors down from her house and turned off the ignition. Pandora felt a bit nervous, she longed for the evening to continue but knew it had to end here. Jack obviously expected to come up, otherwise he would have just dropped her off outside and left the engine running.

They walked towards her house, pausing as she fished for her keys.

'I really enjoyed myself tonight, Pandora. I know you'll

give us some brilliant ideas for the magazine.' He gently tilted her chin and kissed her good night. Pandora had prepared herself for a chaste kiss and a hasty exit into her flat. She had no wish to join the hordes of women discarded by Jack. If someone as ravishing as Saffron so obviously bored him, what chance had she? But she couldn't draw herself away from him in time and the kiss passed the point of friendship and moved towards the place of no return. Pressed between her neighbour's shiny new Golf GTI and Jack, she melted into his arms. They were so engrossed that when the Golf suddenly edged forward Pandora was thrown completely off balance. Jack pulled her away.

'Did the earth move for you too?' he smiled.

'God, how embarrassing,' said Pandora. 'I didn't notice anyone getting in. Do you think they didn't notice us?'

'They were probably just being English about it,' said Jack. They looked at one another for a second and Pandora felt her stomach turn. She couldn't move, she felt like a rabbit caught in the glare of a car's headlights.

'I must go up, it's so late,' she gabbled, letting herself into the flat as if her life depended on it. Jack stood for a moment, watching the door slam shut, before turning back to his car.

Once inside, Pandora leant against her door. She felt dizzy as if someone had banged her over the head with a sledgehammer. She went over to the window and looked out. It was a full moon and the white stucco buildings opposite gleamed in the white light. And then she saw Jack's car, still parked outside. She stood gazing at it blankly for five minutes until he eventually pulled away. She wondered if he felt that his life had just been turned upside down, like hers, but somehow doubted it.

Chapter Thirteen

Pandora was behind on a deadline but so far all she had managed to do was switch on her computer. Every time she tried to think about anything but Jack, her brain went completely dead. It was ridiculous! It was time to snap out of it and *pull herself together*. Not for the first time, she wondered if she should abandon writing her celebrity profiles. She used to enjoy it so much, but she was becoming tired of the suspicion in the eyes of her interviewees who didn't see her as a person but as a snake, waiting to catch them out. Journalists in her field had such a dreadful reputation. It was still a thrill to see her words in print and know that they were read by millions, but people could be so scathing. 'Careful what you say to Pandora, she writes for *Divorce! Magazine*,' friends would joke. 'But I'm not like that!' she would protest like a feeble Miss World contestant. 'I just want to help people and be kind to animals!' But it was true. She longed to do something useful, to write something that would really make a difference.

Jack had made a difference. He had worked his way through a system he disapproved of and now, due to sheer hard graft, was in an influential enough position to really change things. She had read about his radical profit-sharing schemes and knew all about the high esteem he was held in by his employees at Dudley Enterprises, who reacted with increased productivity. The City was suspicious of his methods but his charismatic hands-on approach made him popular with the business editors of left-wing newspapers.

She reached into a desk drawer and pulled out the file of newspaper clippings she had collected. She had been amazed at how much money he had poured into his animal sanctuary in Africa, and now he was about to build another one. He hadn't talked about any of this at dinner, and she hadn't raised the subject. She didn't want him to know she had been looking into his background. So that was Jack, he was doing something useful with his time and money, he had dreams. What were her dreams? She had no desire to remarry or even to have children. She had no financial constraints so she had the freedom to do whatever she wanted.

I'll pack it in, she thought suddenly. Yes, I'll pack it in! I don't have to do this any more.

She reached into another desk drawer and pulled out her novel. She had still only written three chapters of it, journalism took up practically all of her time. Why couldn't she replace the celebrity journalism with some work for *Environment Today* and devote the rest of her time to the novel? The doubting voice crept into her head.

But what's the point? Everyone knows how difficult it is to get a novel published.

'But it's not impossible!' she shouted excitedly, banging her fist on the desk and making her computer judder. She didn't need to look too far for inspiration, her father had proved that with plenty of grit and lots of luck the sky was the limit. She was lucky too and she had a fair amount of grit.

Gazing out of the window she imagined the book launch party, admiring friends and relatives clamouring around her, 'Pandora, please sign your book for me.' She wondered what the cover would be like. Could she be on it, elegantly coiffed and reclining seductively on a chaise longue?

The phone rang, breaking into a dream that might well have lasted all day. She lunged for it.

'Hello,' she panted.

'Wouldn't it be nice if need and desperation were attractive?' It was Annabel. 'You sound very *eager*, sorry it's only me. Who were you expecting?'

'Oh, no one special. Someone is meant to be ringing me about some work, that's all. Where are you nuisance calling from?'

'I'm at the Carlysle in New York.' Annabel sounded peeved.

'Oh, poor you. I stayed there once. The rooms are *awfully* small, aren't they?'

'You're telling me.' They both sighed petulantly.

'Are we just a *bit* spoilt?' Pandora asked, laughing.

'Not at all. Girls like us deserve the best. I don't know

why Robert didn't book us in at the Royalton. He's *so* hopeless, I'm thinking of letting him go. By the way, I've just been speaking to Emma Theobald.'

'Who?'

'She was dining at Daphne's last night and told me that a certain stunning mystery blonde was dining with the elusive, charismatic, eligible Jack Dudley last night. It was you, wasn't it?'

'Yes. He tracked me down out of the blue and asked if I'd do some ecology pieces for a magazine he's just bought.'

Annabel snorted with laughter. 'The closest you've got to a green issue this year was deciding not to go to the Rainforest Ball because it clashed with a fashion show at Horrids.'

'That's not quite true actually. I buy most of my make-up at MAC and they have a very strong recycling policy. And from now on all my loo paper is going to be recycled.'

'I really haven't phoned you long distance to have this sort of tacky conversation. All I really want to know is are you shagging him or not?'

In my dreams, thought Pandora weakly. 'No, I am certainly not!'

'I told you he was your type, didn't I?' Annabel crowed.

'It's purely a business arrangement. He wants to use me as a consultant.'

'Hah! You a consultant? Does he need anyone to do his PR for him?'

'I shouldn't think so. He hates publicity.'

'Well, maybe he needs someone to keep him out of the limelight and stop the press getting wind of his mystery assignations.'

'I'll run it by him if you like.'

'I wonder what went wrong between him and his wife,' mused Annabel.

'He didn't talk about her at all.'

'I'll do some digging and find out how the land lies for you. And by the way,' Annabel went on quickly before Pandora could protest, 'I've got a great person for you to interview.'

Pandora's heart sank. Annabel's last client had been a micro celeb of such miniscule proportions that even Anouska had never heard of him.

'I'd love to help you but I've decided to give up nuisance journalism and write my novel.'

'I think I've heard that line before,' sighed Annabel. 'Do you know what it's about yet?' She paused for a moment. 'What about me?'

'What about you?'

'You can write about me of course. It would be fascinating.'

'Well, that's an intoxicating thought, but I've worked out the plot already. It's going to be a deep and meaning-ful Alpine bonkbuster. This chalet girl falls in love with a Mossad officer in a beautiful mountain setting.'

'Ooh, it sounds wonderful. Jilly Cooper, eat your heart out!' Pandora smiled, she loved the way Annabel was so enthusiastic about everything. 'So do I say no to my client then?'

''Fraid so.'

'That's a real pisser. You always manage to find nice things to say about them, you must be one of the best barrel-scrapers in the business. I mean that in a loving and caring way, darling. Never mind. I respect your need to go on to higher things. Does Jack "I'm worth a billion but I still care about the environment" Dudley have anything to do with this pre-midlife career change?'

'No, he jolly well doesn't. I've been thinking about packing in journalism for ages,' lied Pandora.

'You know, if you're serious about your novel, you should send the synopsis to Emily, my sister. Remember I told you she's a literary agent. She's just been head-hunted by Smith and Godson and is back in London. I know she's always on the look-out for new writers. I'll give her a ring and tell her to expect to hear from you.'

Pandora gripped the receiver tightly. Smith and Godson were the oldest and most prestigious literary agency in the country. This sounded like a dream contact. 'Oh, would you, Annabel? I'd be so grateful.'

'Of course I will. You've helped me out of enough jams. I'm meeting up with her next Wednesday, why don't you come along? I'm going to drag her out to the opening of that new club in Covent Garden I'm doing the PR for, A Paper Bag. It'll do her good to get away from all those manuscripts. I keep telling her that it's not enough to read about romance, she ought to try having one of her own.'

'Thanks, I'd love to come along. If you like, fax me through some stuff on your client and I'll show it to

Anouska, see if she'd be interested in a half-page spread on him. A quid pro quo and all that.'

The conversation was terminated abruptly by the arrival of room service. Pandora could hear the discreet rattle of a trolley and the clink of silver. Lucky old Annabel.

'My delicious clam chowder has arrived. Must go before it gets cold. Chowder for now.'

Pandora went back to her computer with a weary sigh. The phone rang again. This time it was bound to be Jack!

It wasn't.

'Is that Pandora Black?' asked an unknown voice.

'Speaking.'

'Hello. My name is Sven Arvidsson, I'm the editor of *Environment Today*. Jack Dudley suggested that I take you out to lunch to discuss some ideas for the magazine.'

Pandora was disappointed. She'd thought Jack would ring himself. Sven arranged to meet her at the Savoy the following Monday, by which time Pandora was to have come up with some ideas.

She put the phone down feeling suddenly galvanized. Maybe she really would be able to do something useful for a change. Thus empowered, she opened a new file on her computer and began to sketch out some proposals.

Pandora was busy squeezing herself into a Pucci micro dress, getting ready to meet Annabel and Emily at the opening of A Paper Bag when the telephone went. The dress was over her head and both her arms were trapped, so she let the answerphone take the call.

'Hi, Pandora. Sorry to miss you. Can you ring me when you get in later? Any time before two a.m. I really enjoyed seeing you last week.' She stood, hypnotized by the sound of Jack's voice. Damn this dress. But if he'd liked her as much as she'd liked him, why had it taken him over a week to call her? Thank goodness he had phoned! She hugged herself with pleasure. Perhaps she'd call him back tonight after the party. There was no point in appearing over-eager.

Things were buzzing at A Paper Bag when she arrived but Annabel took time out from her duties to introduce her to Emily. She was weighed down with the most enormous briefcase Pandora had ever seen. She wondered if her synopsis lurked in its capacious depths. She had spent every waking moment over the past week torn between longing for Jack to ring her and agony about what Emily would say about her writing. Oh God, she thought now, clenching her mouth into a smile, she probably hates it, it's too frothy, too lightweight. I knew I should stick to nuisance journalism.

'Thanks for sending me the synopsis, I absolutely loved it,' said Emily promptly. 'I'm longing to have a chat with you.' Pandora sagged with relief.

'I told you Emily would love it.' Annabel turned to her sister. 'I can just see Pandora on the front of the *Sunday Times* book section. "Rubber heiress writes bonkbuster to die for!"' Press releases weren't Annabel's strongest point.

Pandora tried to look embarrassed. 'She owes me a few favours,' she whispered to Emily. 'That's why she's being so nice to me.'

Annabel's eyes were darting around the bar anxiously. Her face suddenly brightened. 'Oh good, Nigel's here! Cross fingers we'll get a mention in the *Mail Diary* tomorrow!'

'By the way,' Pandora went on, 'Anouska said I *can* do a couple of columns on that client of yours, Zorro the hairdresser. I just have to emphasize how his celebrity clients are sticking by him despite his being HIV positive.'

'Well, the article might have to take on another slant because none of his clients have stuck by him, but he needs lots of publicity to help him sell his book which is coming out next month.'

'What's it about?' asked Emily.

'A hairdresser who contracts HIV and loses all his clients. Oh look, Dai's here too, I'd better go and say hello.' Annabel dashed off and her elegant figure was soon lost in the crowd.

'Let's go and sit down,' said Emily, 'before *How're Ya Doin'?* or some other magazine photographs us. Every time I come to one of Annabel's dos she makes them snap me, then three months later I spot some horrific photo of myself when I'm at the hairdressers. I'm not very photogenic, you see.'

Pandora found that hard to believe; if anything Emily was even more stunning than her sister. She had the same rangy figure and feline grey eyes framed by glossy blonde hair. But that was where the resemblance ended. Whereas Annabel was nervous and excitable, Emily seemed grounded and almost serene.

'There's a room through here where we can sit down,' said Emily, grabbing three glasses of champagne as she led the way. 'I want to hear more about your book.'

Pandora grabbed another three glasses for Dutch courage. At this sort of event the good stuff tended to run out early so it was sensible to grab while the going was good.

Once they had sat down and finished carefully arranging their stockpile of Moët and Chandon in front of them, Emily drew out Pandora's lengthy synopsis from her huge briefcase.

'You can see why I've got one arm longer than the other,' she laughed.

Pandora peered curiously at all the scripts bulging out and almost felt guilty for adding to them. 'Have you got to read *all* that lot?'

Emily nodded. 'It's not as bad as it looks, I'm a fast reader. But it's a bit of a struggle at the moment, I'm still finding my feet at Smith and Godson. This should liven things up,' she flourished Pandora's synopsis at her. 'Of course, I need to see a bit more before I can make a proper judgement, but on the strength of this and the articles you write for *Divorce! Magazine*, I'm sure you'll get a publisher.'

Pandora beamed with delight. 'You mean I might actually get this book published?'

'Of course,' said Emily. 'You've got a zippy plot,

interesting characters and you write like a dream. And it's very funny too. And, as Annabel says, you're a publicist's dream. A glamorous, well-connected author is a real plus in this business. You're not publicity shy, are you?'

'Oh no, not at all,' said Pandora reassuringly.

'Rather you than me. There's just one thing that I don't think works very well. You're planning to write it in two parts which is a bit muddling for the reader. I think you should merge them. And try and avoid flashbacks, they're difficult to do and can be terribly confusing.'

'I know what you mean,' agreed Pandora. 'I wasn't quite sure about them myself.'

'So now all you've got to do is go and write it,' said Emily. 'I'm sure you want to shop around a bit, but I'd love to represent you if you're interested.'

'Would you really?' Pandora was amazed. 'Could I ring you tomorrow once I've had a chance to absorb all of this?'

'Of course. I'd better be making tracks now if I'm going to read some of these manuscripts.' She groaned. 'Unfortunately not everyone has your light touch, Pandora.'

'You'd better slip out without Annabel seeing you, she'll never let you leave this early. It's interesting that even though you both look so similar you have such different characters.'

'I know, we used to fight like cat and dog. She's probably told you.'

Pandora nodded. Annabel had once shown her a scar on her arm from a milk bottle Emily had thrown at her.

She couldn't believe that someone as nice as Emily could ever do such a thing.

'I was horrible when we were younger. Really angry and jealous,' she shuddered, 'and then I got married and we didn't speak for two years because she couldn't bear my husband. She turned out to be quite right, I ended up divorcing him after nineteen months.'

'Snap. I lasted twelve months.' They clinked glasses. 'To divorce.'

'It was almost worth getting married just for the bliss of getting divorced afterwards,' said Pandora.

Emily nodded sagely. 'A bit like the agony of losing something followed by the bliss of finding it again.'

'Or banging your head against a brick wall and then having the wall taken away.'

'Or your head!' They shrieked with laughter. The champagne was really very good.

'But was it actually that easy for you?' asked Pandora.

'Well, not really. But by that time I was working in New York and had become a Buddhist and that got me through it. I wouldn't have coped otherwise because he was out to make my life a misery. But somehow it all turned round and amazingly enough we're reasonably good friends now.'

'Gosh, a Buddhist.' Pandora was impressed.

'Yes, I have been for five years.'

'That must be why you seem so serene. It was the first thing I noticed about you.'

'Serene? You should try telling that to my secretary. At my first job my nickname was Panic because I was so neurotic. Still,' she smiled at Pandora, 'it just goes to show how much I've changed, which is a relief.'

'And do you go to that temple in Battersea Park?' Pandora was riveted. Like many Pisceans she took a keen interest in religion and had narrowly escaped being seduced into Catholicism. She still harboured fantasies of wearing a mysterious black veil and being introduced to the Pope.

'No, I've never even been there. We tend to get together and chant in each other's homes.'

'Could I come along one day?' asked Pandora. 'It sounds very interesting.'

'Of course. I'll teach you how to chant if you like. Are you Church of England?'

''Fraid so, though I long to be something more original. My father is a Catholic, but he got so guilty about all his sinning that he gave it up. My glamorous step-mother is very staunch though, she's even got her own chapel attached to the house. She's very keen on smells and bells, and everything has to be in Latin. It's rather romantic really.' Pandora was just starting on her third glass of champagne and feeling very misty-eyed and spiritually inclined.

'Goodness, are you two still talking?' asked Annabel crossly. She was under a great deal of stress. Nigel Dempster had only stayed five minutes, and nonentities kept climbing through the lavatory window in a vain attempt to meet George Michael who had never even been there. And if that wasn't bad enough, Michael Winner was criticizing the canapés. He was right, they were disgusting, but it wasn't very polite. Things couldn't get *any* worse.

'I want you both out there,' she gestured to the heaving throng beyond the door. 'There are far too many men here, *please* take some of them on for me,' she wheedled.

Pandora smiled at her rather blankly. She was having some trouble focusing and the thought of having to get up and talk to A Man suddenly seemed terribly complicated.

'Look at you two, the place is literally *heaving* with eligible men and all you want to do is talk about books.' She sighed and sat down next to them, withdrawing a packet of cigarettes from her bag and offering one to Emily.

'Could I have one please?' asked Pandora.

'But darling, you don't smoke,' said Annabel.

'I know, but I'm trying to give up.' Pandora lit a cigarette with difficulty. 'I'm trying to give up being a non-smoker but it's terribly difficult. If I could smoke like Lauren Bacall I'd take it up tomorrow. I just love all those smoky *films noirs*.' She started to cough horribly.

'You mustn't start,' said Annabel, inhaling complacently and tapping ash on to the floor with a perfectly manicured finger.

'You're probably right,' wheezed Pandora, mopping her watering eyes.

'Well,' said Annabel, 'if I can't tempt you to return to the throng, I'll leave you to it. Come and say goodbye before you go. The *Mail* photographer wants a picture of us all together.'

Emily groaned and Pandora tried to look appalled but failed.

'I think I'll make a move now,' said Emily. 'I'll just slip away quickly before Annabel notices.'

'I'll ring you tomorrow. Thanks so much for your encouragement, you've made my week – no, make that my year,' said Pandora, getting to her feet slowly and retrieving her shoes from where she had kicked them beneath the table. 'I'd better say goodbye to Annabel and tell her my good news,' she added, touching up her lipstick and hoping the photographers hadn't gone home yet. After all, she had a book to publicize!

Chapter Fourteen

Pandora had given much thought to her new role as potential consultant to *Environment Today*, partly because she hoped it would lead to her doing something useful and partly because it was a link between her and Jack. She'd been trying to return his call for five days, but every time she started to dial his number her fingers froze. It was ridiculous, she was behaving like a neurotic schoolgirl. Still, if he was that keen, wouldn't he have rung back by now? She rifled through her wardrobe trying to find something suitable for lunch. She had been surprised when Sven had suggested meeting her at the Savoy, she'd thought it might have been more of a Windymill Wholefoods sort of occasion.

'I don't come here every day,' explained Sven once they had introduced themselves and were sipping drinks in the American Bar, 'but Jack insisted I take you somewhere decent. He's extremely keen to lure you away from *Divorce! Magazine* so you can write lots of features for us. I hear you're brimming with ideas.'

Pandora dug into her exquisite Gucci briefcase which she had just bought to consolidate her new image and pulled out a slim folder. 'Yes, I've outlined some of the points I discussed with Jack. I have some quite strong views about the magazine, I don't know if you'll agree with any of them.' She hoped she wasn't being too forceful.

'I'd certainly like to take a look. Jack and I had a meeting last week and we both agree the magazine needs a complete updating. The present format isn't working and it's losing far too much money. I'm still finding my feet myself, but I've known Jack for years and when he asked me to become editor it was too good an offer to turn down.'

'What were you doing before?' asked Pandora.

'I was the campaign manager for Greenseas, and I used to write most of the press releases. I write a column in the *Times* every Saturday too, though I'm going to wind that down now because I just haven't got the time.'

'And how did he get rid of the last editor?'

'That was very easy. John Silkes had been wanting to retire and grow lentils in the country for years. When Jack offered him a pile of cash to leave he couldn't believe his luck. I'm basically rejuvenating the team and getting some fresh blood in. It's make or break really. Jack is happy to pour in lots of money to get us started, but after that we're on our own.'

'I'm very excited at being involved with this,' said Pandora. 'I've been longing to do something a bit more useful for ages. I think there's a real gap in the market for a glossy, easy-read environmental magazine. How do you know Jack?' Despite her enthusiasm for matters environmental, she wanted to get the conversation back to what really mattered.

'Well, like all pacifists, we met in the army,' joked Sven. 'We did our national service together in South Africa and we've stayed great mates. When I moved to England and started working for Greenseas, Jack used to get involved in the campaigns too. We spent our life being arrested.'

'I think it's wonderful that you had a cause you'd go to prison for,' said Pandora earnestly.

'I don't know about that,' laughed Sven, 'I think we just liked causing trouble. Coming to England after two years' fighting in the Angolan bush seemed pretty tame and we needed to let off steam. Plus we believed in what we were doing. But we're too old for all that stuff now so I guess you could say we're taking a more law-abiding approach to achieve the same ends. At the end of the day, a really well-presented magazine will probably reach more of the people who matter than blowing up whaling ships, though there's a place for that too,' he said wistfully, easing a finger behind his collar.

'The pen is mightier than the sword,' Pandora smiled. She imagined that he would probably feel much more at home dressed in oilskins and carrying explosives than wearing a suit and tie in the Savoy.

'Exactly. Which is where you come in, Pandora. We need bright young writers with exciting ideas. You come very highly recommended, by the way.'

285

'Do I?' She flushed with pleasure. 'Who by?'

'I've got some contacts at *Divorce! Magazine*. I'd really like you to start coming to our editorial meetings and to throw your ideas into the melting pot. The next one is a week tomorrow. Can you make it?'

'Definitely.'

'And as editor I'll give you carte blanche to write any features you like. Just run the ideas by me first. I'm hoping you'll exploit your celebrity contacts for some stuff that will really jazz things up a bit.'

'What I could do is speak to ten well-known people and write, say, a hundred words on what each of them is doing to help the environment. They'll probably make it up but it could produce a nice double-page spread. I know of one supermodel who waters her window boxes with urine, for example.'

Sven choked on his wine. 'That's an interesting idea – talking to supermodels, I mean. But you write regularly for *Divorce! Magazine*. Will you have time to take on more work?'

'I've actually made up my mind to stop doing those celebrity interviews, my heart's just not in it any more. What you're suggesting sounds perfect for me. I've got loads of ideas for articles.'

'Great.' Sven leaned back expansively in his chair and beamed at her. 'Welcome aboard. Maybe I'm an optimist, but I've got a good feeling about this magazine. And no venture of Jack's has ever failed.' He thought for a moment. 'Apart from his marriage, of course. I wouldn't wish what he's gone through on anyone, poor bugger.'

Pandora's ears perked up. 'But I thought he left her?'

'Yes, he did eventually, but only because she became quite impossible.'

'In what way?'

'Well, despite being a knockout to look at, she's very insecure. Jack's a bit of a workaholic, to put it mildly, and Atlanta is a real party girl. She just couldn't hack not being the centre of attention.'

'I've seen pictures of her, she's very lovely,' said Pandora sweetly.

'Christ, yes. Jack used to say that whenever they walked into a room together every man wanted her. I guess it gave him a buzz. God knows what they found to talk about though.' The waiter refilled his glass with claret. 'Are you sure you don't want some?'

Pandora shook her head. 'So then what happened?' she asked casually.

'Well, he was very much in love with her and he tried desperately hard to make it work but she wasn't having any of it. Then when he left she decided she wanted him back, but by then it was too late. And now she's stinging him for a huge settlement. He was cut up about it all for a long time.' He signalled for the bill. 'God, I'm rambling on, I shouldn't drink at lunch. No wonder you're such a good journalist, people probably tell you their darkest secrets at the drop of a hat.'

'I'm just very nosy, I'm afraid.'

'I really ought to be getting back to the office. Well,

Pandora,' he pushed his chair back, 'I'll look forward to seeing you at the editorial meeting next week.'

On her way home in a taxi, Pandora began to make a list of ideas for articles on the back of an envelope. She had recently heard about a swan that had been horrifically clubbed to death by a vandal in front of its mate. Apparently the remaining swan had not eaten for two weeks and was slowly dying. Pandora had found this unbearably sad. Could it be true that swans, and all animals for that matter, really did fall in love, just like people? She wondered if Sven would allow her to investigate and write a piece about it. She would ring him and ask as soon as she got home.

She gazed idly out of the window. The traffic had seized up completely and her taxi was at a standstill. Though it was only half past three the light had already faded and the pavement was crowded with harassed shoppers scurrying towards the Tube, trying to avoid the drizzling rain and the belching car fumes. She shivered and pulled her coat round her tightly. Then she smiled, remembering a winter she had spent as a chalet girl in Switzerland. In Klosters they would be expecting the first flurry of snow just now. She imagined the cosy village cloaked with soft white powder; shutting her eyes she could envisage the view from the Weissfluhjoch, the jagged mountain peaks stretching into the distance beneath the clear blue sky. It would be such a perfect setting for her novel. *Casablanca* in the Alps . . .

She pulled herself together. For heaven's sake, she had

just been offered a fantastic new opportunity to write about things that really mattered. And she had met Jack. She couldn't just push off. But part of her longed to pack a suitcase, escape to the mountains and just write. If she set the novel in the Palace Hotel in Gstaad, could she perhaps stay there and offset her bills against tax? But no one had actually agreed to publish it yet, so there was no point in jumping ahead too much. She had rung Emily after the opening of A Paper Bag and asked if she would represent her. Emily had readily agreed and said she would send the synopsis and three sample chapters to several suitable publishers and that she should just sit tight and be patient, but to keep on writing. She wanted to see each chapter as it came out of the printer.

On Friday Jack called. Pandora was arranging flowers and totally gripped by an American chat show on Channel Four.

'Sorry to drag you away from your computer.'

'Oh, I needed a break,' lied Pandora, quickly turning down the television.

'Sven tells me you've got a wonderful idea for the magazine. Something about swans?'

'Well, there was an appallingly sad story about a male swan that was clubbed to death three weeks ago, and his swan mate is literally pining away.' A lump was forming in the back of her throat and she had a dreadful feeling that she was about to cry. She pinched herself hard. 'I thought it might be interesting to investigate whether animals fall in love like humans do.' She hoped he wouldn't laugh at her; she had always found it difficult to sell articles over the telephone.

'I think it would be fascinating,' said Jack quietly.

Reassured, Pandora went on, 'It would be nice to introduce some romantic interest into the magazine. I'm afraid that's the only thing I'm any good at writing about.' This was amazing given her romantic track record. 'Where are you?' she asked, curious about the strange background noise.

'I'm in the car, I just flew in from Zurich.'

'Oh,' said Pandora, her eye momentarily caught by a trailer for a new James Bond film. 'Was it a successful mission, I mean trip?'

Jack laughed. 'Mission sounds much more exciting. Yes, it was reasonably successful. There's nothing much to do in Zurich but try and make money.'

'Yes, I've heard it's very boring there,' empathized Pandora, who had visited Zurich twice and absolutely loved it.

'I quite like it,' said Jack, his voice fading out slightly on his car phone. 'I'm just about to go into a tunnel. I was wondering if you'd like to go to the theatre tomorrow. A friend of mine is producing a play that's just opened. Would you like to come along?'

'Yes, I'd love to,' said Pandora, her stomach turning over with delight.

'Great. I'll ring you tomor . . .' His voice faded out.

'Oh, divine man!' Pandora put the phone down and whooped and danced around the kitchen with delight.

*   *   *

As the lights dimmed and the curtain went up, Pandora found it very difficult to concentrate on anything but Jack shifting uncomfortably in his small seat like a caged animal beside her. From what she could gather, the play seemed to revolve round an impoverished Swedish family at the beginning of the century. Maybe she had been anaesthetized by her compulsive reading of glossy magazines, but she found it impossible to take in anything that was being said. She glanced at Jack's legs, massive as tree trunks, stretched out in front of him and only inches from her own. His big hands rested on the arm rests and in the dim lighting appeared practically black against his white cuffs. He had come straight from a meeting to pick her up, and he hadn't rung first to say what time she should expect him. Good thing he hadn't caught her in the bath or anything. Then again, if he had, maybe they would have missed this interminable play . . .

At last the curtain drifted down to ecstatic applause and Jack turned to her, his eyes racked with boredom.

'Pandora, did you understand any of that?'

'I think it was about a poor Swedish farming family trying to grow turnips,' said Pandora vaguely.

'I just about picked up that much. Jesus, I haven't been to the theatre for years and now I know why.' He eased himself out of his seat and stretched. 'These seats must be designed for midgets. They should stick a few first-class plane seats in here, then at least you could fall asleep in comfort.' He glanced at his watch. 'If we're quick, we could just make the James Bond movie, it's on round the corner. Have you seen it?'

'No, but I'd love to,' said Pandora, excited and relieved she didn't have to sit through any more suicidal Swedish monologues.

'A girl after my own heart,' said Jack, grabbing her hand and pulling her up the aisle.

The seats were much more comfortable in the cinema and for the next hour and a half they were totally absorbed. The combination of the thrills and spills of the movie and the feel of Jack's hand on her leg made the time whizz by, and when it ended and he removed his hand, she felt quite bereft. As they stood up to go, she said wistfully, 'Oh, Jack, I wish life could be like that all the time.'

He pressed her nose affectionately, helping her on with her coat. 'You mean you want to be a James Bond girl?'

'Well, it would beat writing celebrity profiles. Still, at least writing for *Environment Today* is sort of almost saving the world. I'd rather be a spy though.'

'You're not duplicitous enough.' He looked at her closely. 'Hmm, perhaps I'll take a raincheck on that. Now, where do you feel like eating? How about the Ivy?'

'Sounds perfect.'

The Ivy was busy but a waiter led them to a table, thankfully without Jack being waylaid by anyone he knew.

'You're looking very pretty tonight,' he said thoughtfully. 'Red really suits you.'

'Thanks. I was born in the Year of the Tiger and red is meant to be my lucky colour. D'you know what your Chinese sign is?'

'A Hong Kong friend once told me I was an Aries Dragon which sounds a bit ferocious.'

'But that's a great combination. You see, Dragons are very lucky and Arians are very dynamic – but they do like their own way,' she wrinkled up her nose in concentration. 'I should think that once you've made up your mind about something you'll try all available means of persuasion . . .'

'Before threatening physical violence?' finished Jack, smiling at her. 'I don't think that sounds like me at all.' She met his glance and their eyes locked with an intensity that belied the lightness of their conversation. Pandora had the sensation that she was being sucked into two dark whirlpools. It was the most extraordinary feeling. 'By the way,' Jack went on casually, 'Sven thinks the editorial meeting next week should be quite interesting. The sparks are definitely going to fly between the old guard and the new, that's for sure.' He chuckled. 'Shame I can't be there, I'd give anything to be a fly on the wall. I know, you can be my mole and report back to me.'

They were interrupted by the arrival of a steak tartare for Jack and a salad niçoise for Pandora. She picked at an olive and thought how nothing would please her more than being Jack's personal mole. It would be as good as being a James Bond girl. Better in fact.

'I just wish I had more time to devote to the magazine but life is crazy at the moment. I'm raising finance to buy another company.' He sighed and scooped up a large mouthful of steak. 'If I have to deal with any more idiot merchant bankers I think I'll go crazy.'

'When have you got to raise the money by?' asked Pandora.

'Well, the deadline for bids is in less than a fortnight and I've got to have all the finance in place by then. This week is going to be very tough, I'll be spending most of it trying to convince the banks to invest in me.' He was silent for a moment before continuing almost to himself, 'I tell you something, if I bought those companies I could revolutionize the software industry in this country, create hundreds of new jobs.' He reached over and smoothed back a strand of her hair. 'Not very glamorous, I'm afraid.'

'Where there's muck there's brass,' said Pandora lightly, hoping to lift his mood. 'I think what you're doing is tremendous. Think of all those new jobs, not to say all the editorial jobs you've probably saved by buying the magazine and saving it from extinction. You're out there hustling and risking your money and putting yourself on the line to create something new and exciting.'

'Anyone could do what I'm doing, really,' said Jack modestly, refilling her glass. 'I'm not cleverer than anyone else, just a bit more determined – and luck plays a part too. I probably shouldn't have bought the magazine but I just couldn't resist it. Besides, I got it for peanuts. You know, I really think Sven will be able to make something of it.' He sat back thoughtfully and sipped his champagne.

'So do I,' agreed Pandora. 'It's the right idea at the right time. How's the African animal sanctuary going? That must take up a lot of time too.'

'It does, but I kind of believe that if you've been as lucky as I have, you should put something back. Still, perhaps my motives weren't purely altruistic. It's great to have an excuse to go back home and fool around. It keeps me sane. You must come out and see it.'

'What d'you think would have happened to the magazine if you hadn't bought it?' asked Pandora lightly. She was thrilled at the invitation but didn't know whether it was meant seriously enough to acknowledge.

'It would probably have gone into receivership and been scrapped.'

'I would have thought that those bankers should be bending over backwards to help you. After all, everything you've done has been a real success.'

'They're cautious, it's a complicated industry and they don't want to be over-exposed in something they don't really understand.' He covered his face with his hands for a moment and yawned. 'It's just such a bore having to deal with them at all. Bunch of wankers. And they don't even get my jokes.'

Pandora smiled. 'But why are you putting yourself through all this? You could probably retire tomorrow and be quite comfortable.'

'Sometimes I wonder myself. But I like being in the cut and thrust, doing deals, making money.' He glanced unseeingly out of the window into the dark street beyond. 'The money's nice, but there's more to it than that. I guess I'd like to make a mark on the world, build more animal sanctuaries, not just in Africa but in Europe too. I'd like to invest in breeding programmes and make old-fashioned zoos and marine parks completely redundant. Christ, I hate those places.' He reached for her hand. 'Oh, Pandora, it's so good to talk to you.' It was true, just looking at her lovely face, earnest in the candlelight, relaxed him.

'Tell me, how is your article going, the one about the lovesick swan?'

'I've rung up the park keeper and made an appointment to see him next week. She's barely eating and the keeper says she's literally pining away.' Pandora's eyes were shiny with tears and too much champagne. Ever since she'd met Jack she'd had even less control over her emotions than usual.

Jack thought for a moment. 'I've got a great friend who runs a sort of bird sanctuary from his stately home – actually it's really a castle. He keeps swans. I could ask him if he'd take this one. Maybe she'll find another partner.'

'Oh, Jack, would you?' Pandora beamed with pleasure. 'It would make a great story, too. We could keep tabs on her and in six months' time I could write an update on how she's doing. I'll call it "The Swan's Progress". Actually, talking of writing, I had a bit of success last week. I sent the synopsis of my novel to a literary agent and she liked it! She's agreed to represent me.'

'That's wonderful news! So what happens next?'

'I sit tight and chew my nails while she tries to interest a publisher with some sample chapters. She seemed quite confident.'

'Are you sure you weren't born in the Year of the Dragon too?'

'Yes,' laughed Pandora. 'I'm definitely a tiger. But they're lucky too. Well, they're lucky in their work apparently, but unlucky in love. Whereas dragons are meant to be lucky in everything.'

'Oh, I don't know about that,' reflected Jack. 'I've been lucky with money but other things have been a bit rocky.'

'I guess that getting divorced is never a piece of cake,' said Pandora tentatively.

'You're telling me. I mean, one's used to things going wrong in business and sorting them out, but the disintegration of a marriage has got to be about the most awful thing that can happen to anyone. When things have got rocky at work I've always been able to find a solution, but when my marriage collapsed,' he shrugged, 'well, I tried everything but nothing worked.'

'Why did things go wrong? People must have thought you were a golden couple.'

'I think we were for a while. But I was building up the business and was away a lot, and when I was home I was too knackered half the time to go out. Atlanta wasn't working so she wanted to go out. Then she got in with a crowd of losers and started doing drugs. By that time she had become totally irrational. I stopped travelling and put her through rehab. That didn't work so I took her to a whole string of shrinks. That didn't work either. I was so desperate I even started seeing one myself, but he was hopeless, just sat in total silence and occasionally shook his head.'

'Nice job if you can get it.'

'I hate all that psycho-babble crap anyway.'

Quite right too, thought Pandora.

'What happened then?'

'Well, by this time things were getting really hectic at work and I had to do a lot of travelling again. Atlanta became convinced I was having an affair. She wouldn't let me near her and we hadn't made love for over six months so I can't say I hadn't thought about it. Then one day I came back from work to find she'd chucked all my stuff outside the house. I thought to hell with it and went and checked in at Blake's Hotel. I ended up staying there for eight months.'

'Oh, how heavenly. It's one of my fantasies to live in a wonderful hotel. Still, I expect you were pretty upset.'

'I felt bloody awful. But I just threw myself into work.' He smiled thoughtfully. 'I made a hell of a lot of money.'

'Did you carry on trying to make things work?'

'Yes. We'd had a couple of wonderful years together. I wasn't going to give up on it without a fight. But gradually I started to quite like being independent. I took a few girls out and decided to file for divorce. Then she decided she wanted me back, so I agreed to give it another go. We struggled on for a few months. It was so awful that I moved back to Blake's.'

'And does she still want you back now?'

'She did for a while.' He lit a cigarette and inhaled deeply. 'She's shacked up with some other bloke now.'

'In your house?'

Jack smiled. 'Yup. And I'm being sued for half of

everything I've got. If she wants a fight, I'll fight. But I'm moving heaven and earth to keep things out of court because it's just not worth the aggro.'

'How much are you offering her?'

'I thought five million was fair. We didn't have any kids, after all, and she can keep the house and all the stuff if she likes.'

Pandora swallowed. Five million! 'God, Jack, that's really generous. I obviously divorced the wrong man.'

'How much did your husband give you then?' asked Jack curiously.

'I should have been so lucky, it was the other way round. He even wanted me to pay him back for the honeymoon.'

Jack was horrified. 'You mean you had to pay *him*?'

'Well, he made some nasty threats.'

'God, you poor thing. I thought only men had to put up with that sort of crap. Still, it's behind us both now.' He lifted his glass.

'Here's to your novel, Pandora. If you were selling shares in it I'd buy the lot. Can you tell me what it's about?'

'It's going to be a sort of *Casablanca* in the Alps.'

'My favourite movie. Will you read it to me?'

'I'd love to. I wouldn't want to bore you, though.'

'No chance of that.'

'It would be nice to read it on a long car journey or something,' said Pandora. A long car journey to a romantic country house hotel with a nice swimming pool, she thought dreamily, sipping her champagne.

'How about coming with me to Zurich next weekend? You can read it to me on the plane.'

Pandora's eyes shone with delight but she replied casually, 'I've got a few things on next weekend, but I should be able to rearrange them.'

Jack was a little crestfallen at her lukewarm response but he continued, 'We could fly out on Friday and stay the weekend. I could do with a break.' He signalled for the bill. 'I'll ring you tomorrow and we'll fix it up.'

After he dropped her off at her flat, Pandora danced around with glee. Jack and Switzerland! Talk about her cup running over. She didn't quite know why she hadn't asked him up. Fear that once they had made love he would tire of her? Wanting to prolong the suspense? She wasn't sure. But she was certain of one thing. She had waited years to be kissed the way Jack kissed her, to be talked to the way he talked to her, to be listened to the way he listened to her. The chemistry that crackled between them had thrown her off balance, she was being sucked into the vortex of his charm and it terrified her. But it wasn't just his charisma that made him so compelling, he was a curious mixture of brutality and integrity. He had the 'vision thing'. While most people just sat back and thought about changing things, he had dreams that he had already partly fulfilled. She remembered John and his refusal to stick his neck out and be counted, whereas Jack had actually been arrested trying to board a whaling ship. That must have taken real courage. She smiled, imagining the shock the Norwegian whalers must have got seeing Jack's massive angry frame materialize on deck. The vision was a potent turn-on. She hardly dared look forward to the weekend. The thought of being squeezed next to Jack on an aeroplane followed by two nights in a sumptuous hotel in Zurich was just too much for one lifetime.

Chapter Fifteen

Jack didn't ring the next day or the day after. Two more days passed. Why can't he ring when he says he'll ring? thought Pandora, mournfully feeding paper into her printer. She wanted to send Emily two more chapters today. But her printer had other ideas and flashed PAPER JAM! rebelliously at her. She kept a tight rein on her temper. She tried to avoid swearing at her computer and printer, whatever they did to her. Bitter experience had taught her that they had minds of their own and as she depended on them completely she had no wish to antagonize them. Normally she could sort out a paper jam without too much bother, but today her computer decided to join in too and flashed an incomprehensible message on to her screen.

'Oh God!' wept Pandora. 'Don't do this to me!' If someone had asked her what was the worst thing that could possibly happen, she would have replied, 'My computer going down.' In fact she could barely bring herself to say, 'I'm *going down* to the shops' without shuddering, the phrase had such appalling connotations. Her computer was an old friend, she'd had it since the very beginning of her writing career. Of course this wasn't the first time it had behaved irrationally, but combined with the uncertainty she felt about Jack, it was all too much.

Feeling hysteria rise in the back of her throat, she took deep breaths, cleared her mind and made herself a cup of tea. She thought of her grandfather, Lord Verney's timeless response to emotional outbursts: 'Have you tried pulling yourself together?' and managed a smile. Really, she must try and be rational about this. After all, she had saved everything on a floppy disk so in theory she could just get anyone to print it out for her. But she was loath to ask Emily, who had already been so helpful. And she had discovered that her software didn't seem to be compatible with that of any of her friends. Either that or they were as technophobic as she was.

She sat, thoughtfully sipping her tea. What was the point of having a crush on the boss of a computer company, valued at one hundred and twenty million pounds, according to yesterday's *Financial Times*, if she couldn't ask him to get someone to print out a floppy disk for her? But that would mean ringing him. No, she would rather die than risk such an indignity. She decided to go to the Ritzy Marina club for a swim instead.

Slicing through the clear blue water half an hour later, her mind drifted back to her novel. If it was set mainly in a glitzy ski resort, what was she doing in London? She could write it anywhere. But then again, London was exciting, she had created the life she had always dreamt of having. She had friends, her work for *Environment Today*. And Jack. Well, sort of.

Soothed by the feel of the water against her skin, she let her mind drift aimlessly. She remembered Yonathon and the feelings of grinding, desperate misery his rejection had triggered. It was terrifying to care for someone so much that you depended on them for your happiness, to be controlled by a force that was outside yourself. And now Jack had reawakened in her that same passionate longing. She had the strangest premonition of exquisite pain whenever she thought of him, which was most of the time. What would happen if he disappeared, like Yonathon or her father had done? She felt as if a Berlin Wall round her heart was melting without her permission and leaving her totally vulnerable.

Lying in the sauna a little later she dreamt of snowy mountains and clean trains. A calm environment to calm her unquiet mind. Escape. She smiled, thinking of her mother, the Bolter, and her eternal quest for love and the sun that took her round the world. Maybe it was time to think about bolting herself.

She had barely arrived home and unlocked the front door when the phone started to ring. It was Jack calling from his car.

'Hi, Pandora, still OK for the weekend?'

'Um, well, a few things have come up,' she lied, 'but I can put them off if you like.'

'Don't sound so enthusiastic.'

If you're so keen, why didn't you ring when you said

you would? she wanted to say. Instead she relented. 'Sorry, I'd love to come. It's just that I've been having problems with my printer and I can't find anyone with compatible software.'

'Why didn't you ring me? It'd be the easiest thing in the world for me to get sorted out. I'll come round tonight and pick up the disk. One of the guys here can do it first thing tomorrow.'

'Oh, Jack, could you?'

'Of course. They love doing that . . .' His voice faded out for a moment and then faded back in. '. . . got a meeting in the City after work but I'll come round about nine.'

'Who are you meeting?'

'The partners of Douche Bank. If they give me the money it'll be the final piece in the jigsaw and we'll be ready to go. But I'll be glad when it's over, it's still a bit touch and go.'

'Sorry, I didn't catch that, which bank are you meeting?'

'Douche – I mean Dougall and Douglas.' Pandora smiled.

'Didn't you used to work for them?' she asked.

'Years ago. I'm afraid that doesn't help though. They didn't like me much then and I don't think they like me any better now.' He laughed wearily.

'I used to know someone called Daniel Snodstein who works there.'

'He's the guy I'm meeting. He's a real sh . . .' His voice faded out again. '. . . Wish me luck!'

'Jack, I know you'll do it. Remember, you're brilliant. You could sell snow to the Eskimos.'

'Keep talking, keep talking, I need to hear this.'

'I'd lend you the money if I had it,' she reassured him.

'That's nice to know.' She could feel him smiling. 'D'you think I should be nice or nasty to them?'

'Be nice. Remember, even they love their children.'

Jack grunted. 'Maybe you're right. But if that doesn't work, I'll just have to . . .'

'Threaten physical violence!' They spoke in unison.

Pandora smiled to herself, she did so love talking to Jack.

She worked most of the evening, only stopping to watch *EastEnders* and to prepare several nuisance snacks. She found she wrote better when she had something in her mouth.

Nine o'clock came and went. Maybe he was held up in his meeting, she thought kindly. By 11 p.m. she was completely pissed off. In a fit of pique she left a message on his answer machine saying that something had come up and she couldn't travel to Zurich that weekend after all. Serve him right. Then she sank into a fit of feverish regret, longing to cancel her message. Half an hour later the phone rang. Pandora leapt on it and then forced herself to let it ring four times before picking it up.

'What's this about you not coming to Zurich?' asked Jack crossly.

'I've got to stay and get my computer sorted out,' said Pandora.

'Oh Christ, I said I'd come round and pick up your disk, didn't I?'

'Look, it doesn't matter.'

'Don't be silly, I'll come round right now and pick it up.'

'No, please don't bother, I'm just going to bed.'

'Oh. Well, I could come round tomorrow on my way to work.'

'Please, Jack, it's not a problem. I can get it sorted out myself, I know you're busy at the moment. I'm sorry to be a bore about it.' Why the hell was *she* apologizing to *him*?

'So shall I cancel the trip to Zurich?'

'Um, actually, I'd still quite like to go really,' Pandora backtracked feebly. She couldn't pass up the opportunity to combine Jack *and* her favourite city. She might never be able to coordinate the two of them again.

'Great. I'm really looking forward to it. We'll catch the four o'clock flight and I'll pick you up at about two.'

'OK. By the way, how did your meeting go?'

'Pretty well. I took your advice – being nice worked, they gave me the money.'

'That's terrific!'

'Perhaps you're lucky for me, Pandora. Sleep tight now. I've got to do a bit more work and then I'm going to crash.'

Pandora hugged herself with pleasure as she climbed into bed.

When Pandora awoke the next morning, the first thing

she remembered was that in forty-eight hours she would
be waking up next to Jack in a hopefully sumptuous hotel,
the second was that she was due at the *Environment
Today* editorial meeting in one hour! She rushed to the
bathroom to perform speedy ablutions and flung on her
nearest available powerless suit.

Thankfully the offices were only a short drive away in
Notting Hill, an area she was particularly familiar with
since her brief foray into squalor when romancing Darren.
She shuddered, remembering his mildew-ridden flat. The
past was indeed another country. All she knew about
Jack's house was that it was in Mayfair and had eight
bedrooms. His housekeeper was Swiss, so it was probably
terribly tidy. She wondered if he had a swimming pool
in his basement. Probably not. If he fell wildly in love
with her, perhaps he would build one. Her fantasy came
to a potentially disastrous end as she braked suddenly to
avoid a dazed looking roller-blader with dreadlocks who
was completely out of control.

The offices of *Environment Today* were run-down,
but there was a very buzzy atmosphere with lots of
girls wearing Doc Martens charging about enthusiastically.

'Hi,' said Pandora to one of them. 'Could you tell me
where the editorial meeting is, please?'

'Yes,' smiled the girl pleasantly. 'Go up two flights of
stairs, walk down the corridor, turn first right, first left,
go down another corridor and it's the third room after the
meditation room. You can't miss it.'

Pandora suspected that she probably could and prepared for a long search. Luckily she was intercepted by Sven halfway up the stairs.

'Pandora, it's great you could make it. You should know a few people. I've invited a couple of chaps from *How're Ya Doin'?* that you might know, Max Chister and John Blackiston. They should liven things up a bit.'

Pandora's heart sank. Max Chister was known as Max Shyster and would stop at nothing to get a good story. He had trained as a gymnast, and was famous for his ability to contort his body into elongated shapes in order to slither through the lavatory windows of the rich and famous. He specialized in minor royal stories. She couldn't imagine what he could possibly contribute to an environmental magazine. Maybe, like her, he just wanted to do something positive for a change.

Pandora recognized several faces round the table as she walked in, but as luck would have it, the only seat free was right next to Max.

'Pandora, darling, how are you? I'm so pleased we're sitting next to each other. Now tell me, what are you doing here?'

Pandora explained that she was a friend of Jack's, and then immediately regretted it.

'Darling, and I thought you were just a good writer! Where did you meet him? I hear he's terribly elusive.'

'Oh, I wouldn't say that I've actually *met* him,' she lied. 'I sort of bumped into him at a party. He said he had just bought this magazine and I begged him to let me write for him. So he got Sven to ask me along today. More to the point, what are you doing here? I thought you were working full time on *How're Ya Doin'?* these days.'

'Well, I am, more or less. But should a window of opportunity present itself, well, let's just say I have a flexible attitude.' He chuckled to himself.

Pandora wouldn't trust him as far as she could throw him. 'Were you lured by the promise of a juicy expense account and free travel?'

'Christ, I shouldn't think this outfit could stretch to a free Tube ticket. How could you even *think* such a thing!' He raised his voice. 'I'm here because *I want to make the world a better place for our children.*'

The room fell silent and everyone turned to look at him.

'Glad to hear it, mate,' said Sven genially. 'Now that you've all shut up, we'll start. I'm Sven, the editor of *Environment Today* which, as you all know, has recently been taken over by Jack Dudley, whom most of you have probably never met.'

'Sorry to contradict, but he and Pandora are great mates,' Max interjected.

'Oh, shut up!' hissed Pandora, going bright red. Twenty faces looked at her with renewed interest.

'Thanks for sharing that with us, Max. Now, moving swiftly on, Jack's happy to bail out the magazine for two reasons. One, because he genuinely believes there is a gap in the market for an environmental magazine that can put across a message in an entertaining and profitable way. And two, because he really cares about the environment. Jack's main business is computers and that's the cash cow that provides the finance for his other, um, more *interesting* ventures.' Sven smiled before continuing, 'Dudley Enterprises invests some of its profit into an in-house venture capital company which funds, amongst other things, medical research into rainforest medicine. He also started a charitable foundation five years ago that rehabilitates zoo animals into sanctuaries in Africa. Now Jack and I go back a long way. He's not a saint, but he strongly believes that altruism and profit can go hand in hand. We both agree that it's time to chuck out the lentil image and replace it with something far more glamorous that will appeal to the sort of person who reads *Tatler*, for example.'

There was angry murmuring round the table.

'You mean sell out and become just like all the other rubbish,' said a pale young man wearing a parka and sandals, and clutching a bicycle helmet. 'Why don't you go the whole way and have society pages as well?' He sniffed in disgust.

'That's a good idea,' said Max. 'I wasn't lured on board to write about *ecology*, for heaven's sake.'

The room erupted. It was obvious that there was a clear division between the greens and the glossies. Pandora felt somewhere in the middle but feared that her chic red Kookai suit marked her out in the latter camp.

'Having a social diary, fashion pages and celebrity articles won't stop us from writing about mung beans,' shouted the trendy Doc Marten-clad girl who had directed Pandora when she arrived.

'Oh, shut the crap up, Tabitha!' replied a thin young man angrily.

'I think you've confused me with someone who gives a flying fuck about your opinion!' replied Tabitha.

'Christ,' whispered Max, 'these vegans are so *aggressive*!'

'Now that you've had a chance to express your opinions, perhaps we can move on,' said Sven firmly. 'I did anticipate some disagreements and I fully sympathize with you all. I know that some of you have been with the magazine for many years and may be resistant to change. But we've got to face facts. The magazine isn't selling which means it isn't making money. All of you have had to take a pay cut this year already. If things don't pick up we'll all be out of a job in three months.'

'I'd rather be out on the streets living in a box than sell out to the enemy,' said the bicycle helmet fiercely.

'Oh, for heaven's sake, get a grip, Lionel,' said Tabitha, tapping a brutally shod foot irritably against the floor.

Sven banged his fist on the table. 'This won't get us anywhere. I'm going to outline what I've got in mind for the magazine, and I don't want any interruptions, do you all understand?'

'Yes, boss,' mumbled several disgruntled members of the green troupe.

'Right. We're going to start covering society events that have relevance to the magazine, for example the rainforest conference next week. I've lined up some great celebrity interviews, Kate Twig—'

313

'Kate Twig! What the hell does she know about the environment? She probably can't even spell it!'

Sven ignored the interruption. 'She's agreed to appear on the front cover for nothing to launch the new issue. Max here has kindly agreed to travel to Kenya with Joanna Yummy to report on Jack's animal sanctuary there. We'll get some great photos out of that one.'

'It's a tough job but someone's got to do it,' said Max smugly.

'I don't *believe* this,' protested the thin young man. 'Some of us have been working here for over ten years, and suddenly, without a by your leave, you change the entire editorial policy overnight.'

'And give the best jobs to some lowdown scumbag,' said Lionel, glaring at Max jealously. Lionel had a huge crush on Joanna Yummy.

'Who the hell is this Jack Dudley anyway? *I've* never heard of him,' shouted one of the greens.

As if on cue, the door swung open. 'I think that's one small matter I can clear up.' It was Jack. His presence filled the room which immediately fell silent. Pandora wondered if he had been standing outside and waiting for the right moment to burst in. Sven pulled up a chair and Jack sat down, removing his jacket and rolling up his sleeves.

'I should think that some of you are feeling a bit fed up. Some South African big shot walks in, buys the magazine and destroys the editorial policy overnight. I'd be pretty pissed off myself.' His hands rested on the table and Pandora could glimpse the Rolex on his large wrist. Her mouth went dry. She had a thing about his wrists. Those who had been so vociferous a moment ago had softened immediately under the force of his considerable charm.

'I didn't buy this magazine to make a fast buck.' He laughed drily. 'If things stay as they are, I'll lose five grand an issue. But things aren't going to stay as they are, they're going to get better. You know how things are going to get better?' He looked round the room. You could have heard a pin drop. 'Simple. We're going to produce a magazine that people buy, that manufacturers want to advertise in. To do that we'll change the title, the layout and the content. This isn't a sellout but, believe me, we'll do more good in the long run by working within the system than outside it. Maybe our ten loyal readers from the Middlehurst Earthchildren Action Committee will cancel their subscription but that's a risk we'll have to take.' His eyes met Pandora's for a brief moment; she couldn't be sure but he appeared to wink. Her heart flipped.

He continued, 'This magazine is going to make the environment a real political issue again. People are busy, they haven't got time to wade through long articles on sewage,' he glanced at Pandora, 'they've been getting lazy and they've stopped caring. But we can change that. Each one of us has a vital role to play. That's why you're here. Some of you are great writers, or great administrators, but the bottom line is that you all really care about what you're doing. I've been in business long enough to know that your sort of commitment is worth its weight in gold. Bearing that in mind, I'd like to propose a profit-share scheme. The more issues we sell, the more money each of you will make.'

Glancing round the room Pandora noticed that everyone was sitting up straight and looking attentively at Jack.

'Unfortunately, I'm not going to be around as much as I'd like because I'm busy selling my soul to make the money to keep this show on the road. But I believe in this magazine. It's really going to change things. Trust me. Now,' he looked round the room, 'can I count on all of your support? I need each and every one of you, but if you can't work with Sven and me, let me know now, or after the meeting.'

There was silence. Pandora didn't know about the others, but she would have followed Jack to the ends of the earth, profit-share scheme or not.

Lionel broke the silence. 'I must say, speaking for a few of us, we did have one or two small doubts. But, well, I don't know about you lot,' he looked at his colleagues, 'but I feel rather excited about the future of *Environment Today*, or whatever it's going to be called. Maybe it *is* time to be more forward looking.'

Everybody nodded in agreement.

'After all, there's no point in slogging our guts out producing a magazine that nobody ever reads,' said Tabitha, looking misty-eyed at Jack.

'Good,' Jack nodded. 'I hope I've managed to put your minds at rest.' He got up and put on his jacket. 'Thanks for your support. You're a great team and you've got a great editor.' He scooped up his briefcase, whispered something to Sven who grinned, and left as suddenly as he had arrived. Everybody started talking at once.

'The Emperor has spoken,' whispered Max. 'I'd marry him if I were you, Pandora.'

Pandora looked at him. 'What?'

'Come on, I saw the way he winked at you.'

'OK, everybody,' said Sven, 'now the pep talk's over we can get down to business. Next issue. I've got a few ideas for feature articles . . .'

Pandora arrived home feeling exhilarated. They had all gone to the pub after the meeting, which had melted any remaining barriers between them all. Jack's talk had miraculously pulled the whole team together and everyone was full of ideas and optimism. She had never really worked with other people, writing was a solitary business, but she adored the easy camaraderie and jokes that came with being part of a team of disparate people united by a similar goal. She had attended editorial meetings for *Divorce! Magazine* but they had been rather terrifying occasions, with everyone jealously guarding their features ideas and toadying like mad to the editor. Everyone had loved her idea of the pining swan and was crossing their fingers that it could be matched with one of those belonging to Jack's friend in the country. She must remember to remind him about that, he was so busy he had probably forgotten. She decided to put in a nuisance call to Annabel to describe Jack's impressive performance that morning.

She dialled the number but got Annabel's answering

machine. Her recorded voice warbled into action: 'For reasons that I can't go into right now I am unable to take your call but please leave your name and number and I'll call you as soon as it is humanly possible to do so.'

'I know you're there,' shouted Pandora into the phone. 'Wake up, I have urgent news that concerns YOU!'

Annabel picked up the phone immediately. She sounded very sleepy.

'I haven't woken you up, have I?' asked Pandora.

'Goodness no!' lied Annabel who was recovering from a hideous hangover and had decided to spend the afternoon in bed to prepare herself for the evening's excitements. 'I was defrosting my deep freeze, if you must know.'

Pandora let this blatant untruth pass and continued excitedly, 'He's taking me away with him tomorrow afternoon!'

'I know he is. You've been talking about it all week.' She settled down for a comfortable chat. 'I can't remember where you're going. Is it somewhere impossibly romantic?'

'Yes, Zurich.'

'Zurich? That grey place where people with lung infections stop to change trains on their way to sanatoriums?'

'Yes,' breathed Pandora.

'It's great to hear you so enthusiastic about a decent chap. I hope it all works out for you and Jack.'

'We get on pretty well, but I wouldn't read too much into it. It's fun having someone to go out with, but it's not as if I'm interested in living with anyone again, I've become far too selfish.'

'I'd love to live with someone,' sighed Annabel. 'I'd really like a man to cook for and to curl up with at night.'

'I don't believe you. You'd miss the parties and being taken to glamorous restaurants by lots of different gorgeous men.'

'But I've been doing that for ages. I promise you that if I met the right man I'd give it all up tomorrow and live in the country, have babies and grow vegetables.'

Pandora shuddered. 'I suppose I did all that when I was too young. The thought of that sort of life now fills me with terror. I'd like to be wined and dined and taken to glitzy places for the rest of my life. But I won't be, so I'm making the most of it while it lasts. Besides, if you lived in the country you'd have to commute to Tramp every night. It'd be *exhausting*.'

'Yes, you're probably right. Actually, a rather gorgeous Italian is taking me out tonight, we're going to Blake's for dinner.'

'See, there you are. No more hot dates if you lived in the middle of the country. You'd die a slow natural death on top of your Aga.'

'So you mean to say that if Jack Dudley said he was madly in love with you and wanted to spend the rest of his life with you, you'd say no?'

'I'd say can we discuss it over dinner at the Cipriani next weekend,' said Pandora flippantly.

'I bet Jack is really confused.'

'I'm very nice to him really. But that's not difficult. You should have seen the way he handled everyone at the editorial meeting today. He was brilliant. That man has more magnetism than God. But you know what I really like about him?'

'No. Surprise me.'

'Well, he has this sort of *brutal* look. You don't know whether he wants to bonk you or just kill you. You know what I mean?'

'Ugh, Pandora, you make him sound horrible! Like a gun runner or something. You be careful with him in Zurich, he might do anything.'

'I should be so lucky.'

Later that evening, Pandora put down her yogurt spoon and just listened, breathing in the blissful silence. Sometimes she thought she might now be totally incapable of really sharing her life with anyone. There was a wonderful phrase that summed up how she felt: the eroticism of solitude. How did people manage with the day-to-day detritus of sharing their lives with other people, the noise, the messes, the eternal compromises? Even Jack would be difficult to live with. He had told her that he only needed six hours' sleep and never went to bed before 1 a.m. Her idea of heaven was to go to bed at ten and sleep for nine hours. But then she supposed that if you really loved someone, none of that would really matter very much, would it? This time in seventeen hours she would be sitting next to Jack on their way to the airport. She was so looking forward to seeing him. Seventeen hours seemed like an eternity!

Chapter Sixteen

Seventeen hours and five minutes later Pandora was twitching around her flat like a cat on hot bricks, waiting for Jack to appear. Her suitcase was packed, she had checked her make-up several times, she had taken her vitamins. She rushed to the kitchen to check the digital clock. Eight minutes past two! Where on earth was he? She wasted several minutes trying on hats and wondering which of them, if any, she should take.

The phone rang.

'Pandora, I'm a bit held up this end. Would you mind if we caught the eight o'clock flight instead?' It was less a question than a command.

'Oh no, not at all,' said Pandora casually. 'It'll give me a bit more time to pack.'

'Great.' Jack sounded distracted. 'I'll pick you up at six and we'll catch the eight o'clock flight, all right?'

Pandora thought quickly. That would mean they'd hit the rush hour and if they missed that flight, they'd have to wait until tomorrow morning. It didn't bear thinking about.

'Um, Jack, the traffic reports on the M4 are *dreadful*. There are roadworks and the traffic is apparently backed up for miles. Perhaps we should leave a bit earlier.'

'OK, I'll pick you up around five thirtyish then. Look, I've got to go now . . .' His voice faded out.

Pandora didn't like the sound of five thirty*ish*. Still, if he was aiming for five thirty, maybe that would mean he'd pick her up at six. Really, Jack was so difficult to manipulate.

The door bell rang just after six. Jack was sitting in his car, talking on the phone as she panted out of the house, lugging an embarrassingly large suitcase (it was important to be prepared for every eventuality, after all). Jack climbed out, ruffled her hair and stowed her case in the back, still talking on the phone.

She glanced towards him as he pulled out and headed towards the motorway. He looked tired and distracted. She hoped there hadn't been a crisis. It was obviously going to be a long call so she settled down comfortably with the latest issue of *Divorce! Magazine*. It felt very cosy to be sitting alongside Jack like this, and she didn't mind in the least taking a back seat to his phone call. Besides, the conversation was audible on the voice box, so she could hear everything. Jack was discussing the details of the takeover with his partner; it all sounded incomprehensible and very high-powered. He reached over and caressed her neck. The gesture was so unexpected it made her melt.

Eventually the call finished. 'Sorry about that. I must

get this sorted before I leave. I've just got a couple more calls to make.'

'Don't worry about me, I've got bags to read,' said Pandora cheerfully, picking up a tabloid and flicking through it. Her gaze froze. Oh my God, there was a piece about her and Jack! He would hate it! 'Blonde trust fund hackette, Pandora Black, who supplements the meagre five million pounds she received upon the sale of her father's multi-million-pound rubber goods company by writing celebrity interviews, has found a new beau, I can exclusively reveal. Obviously inspired by Ms Black's august literary talents, Jack Dudley, chief executive of Dudley Enterprises, the worldwide computer conglomerate, has offered her carte blanche to write for his latest acquisition, the dreary *Environment Today*, the world's least read magazine. Jack Dudley was married to the gorgeous Atlanta Du Ville who is presently drying out at the world-famous Betty Davies clinic . . .'

The article droned on. Should she show it to Jack? His press cuttings service would be bound to pick it up if she didn't. Illustrating the story was a rather flattering photo of herself, alongside a picture of Jack and Atlanta on a beach. Jack looked as if he was about to thump someone and Atlanta looked fragile and totally gorgeous. What a pisser. She decided not to show it to Jack and turned the page irritably.

Jack had just finished his call and picked up her irritation. 'I'm sorry, are you fed up because I've been ignoring you?' he asked solicitously.

Nothing could have been further from the truth. Pandora was like a pot plant and thrived on neglect.

'Of course not,' she laughed. 'It's bliss to catch up on some reading.'

He glanced over at the paper on her lap. 'Anything good in the *Snoop*?'

She gave him a sidelong glance, he met her gaze and raised his eyebrows. She had that strange feeling again that he could see straight into her mind and read her thoughts.

'Um, I wasn't going to tell you because I just know you'll be cross.' She immediately regretted opening her mouth and feebly tried to change the subject. 'Gosh, we're making really good time. They must have finished the roadworks ahead of schedule. That's a relief.'

'What makes you think I'll be cross?'

Oh well, she'd tried. 'Actually, there's a tiny piece about you in the gossip column.' Pandora looked at him but his expression was inscrutable. She wittered on, 'I mean, I would have missed it completely, it only caught my eye because there's a picture of me next to it. And it mentions the magazine, which is good, isn't it?'

'Show me,' said Jack. 'Christ, I wonder where they dug that old photo out? It was taken on our honeymoon.' He sounded rather wistful. 'Good picture of you though. Did they mention your novel?'

'Unfortunately not,' said Pandora sadly. 'It's not a very nice piece really. Still, Emily says that no publicity is bad publicity when you're selling a book.'

Jack was gazing moodily ahead at the darkening road.

He didn't appear to have heard anything she had said. She wondered what he was thinking and was just about to ask him but stopped herself in the nick of time. It was her personal relationship policy never to ask men soppy questions like that. It was a dead giveaway. 'You don't mind the article, do you?' she asked casually.

'*No*,' he growled. Pandora's spine tingled. 'I'm used to all that crap by now. There's nothing one can do about it so there's no point in getting worked up.' He lit a cigarette. 'But I get a bit pissed off when they write about Atlanta because she's so fragile. You're much more robust than she is.'

Robust! What a horrible word. Perhaps she should develop an eating disorder.

'I don't mean that you're physically robust,' he said, 'but that you're quite strong emotionally, which is a great relief. I'm fed up to the back teeth of going out with limpets who expect me to run their lives for them.'

Perhaps Jack was just changing his karma, thought Pandora rather sadly; she quite fancied the idea of being his limpet for a while.

They made it to the airport in good time. Jack glanced at his watch and laughed. 'God, I don't think I've ever had so much time to spare before a flight, you're a good influence! Tell me, were there really roadworks on the M4 or did you make that up?'

Pandora bit her lip and looked confused. 'Well, there normally are roadworks somewhere. We must have been lucky. Besides, you'll have time to make some more phone calls which is always useful.'

'That's true.' Jack heaved out her suitcase. 'What on earth have you got in here? Ten travel kettles filled with rocks?'

'Only one actually,' replied Pandora seriously. She only ever travelled light when she knew she'd have to carry her own luggage.

Jack swung his impossibly small case on one hand and hers in the other and strode off towards the Swissair ticket collection desk. She wondered if they would be flying business class or economy; hopefully the former but she couldn't be quite sure. 'Hang on, I'm right behind you,' she panted, catching up with him.

'Can I have a look at that paper a sec?' asked Jack when he had collected the tickets. Business class, yippee! thought Pandora, looking forward to making lots of free nuisance calls in the lounge. He pushed their trolley through customs, glancing at the paper at the same time. Pandora studied his face for signs of irritation, she was dreading their weekend getting off to a bad start. To her relief he burst out laughing and handed the paper back to her. 'We'll talk about it on the plane, I just want to make a few calls.'

Pandora snooped around the lounge, helping herself to free drinks, aware of being eyed up by several jaded businessmen pretending to read *FT*s. Armed with several drinks, she made her way to one of the telephone booths and got out her address book, only to put it away again when she realized one could only make free 0181 calls. But I don't know anyone with an 0181 number, she thought crossly. Jack was using one of the phones round the corner and she could hear him quite distinctly. 'I don't bloody care, Max. You shouldn't have written it. Pandora is a friend of mine and I don't want her upset.' He was silent for a few minutes. 'Well, that's too bad, Max. I hired you on good faith that you wouldn't write this kind of crap about me. OK, maybe you didn't write it, but you tipped them off . . . *No!*' Pandora's spine tingled. 'It's none of your bloody business if I am seeing her. She's an excellent writer and a wonderful girl. She deserves more than this sort of rubbish innuendo. Anyway, the last thing I'm looking for right now is a relationship.' Pandora's heart instantly dropped.

'Max,' Jack went on, 'we go back a long way and frankly I don't trust you an inch, but I'd still rather have you pissing with me inside the same tent than pissing on me from outside it. Look, I'm about to catch a plane, but if you still want to go to Kenya with Joanna Yummy, bloody well leave off.'

Pandora was touched that he seemed so genuinely outraged on her behalf and was disappointed when the call came to an end. She gathered up her things quickly and went to sit in the bar area; she didn't want to look as if she was eavesdropping. Jack was making another call now, she could hear him laughing about something into the telephone. It was very pleasant listening to him, she loved the way his laughter carried round the lounge. God, she must be pretty far gone if the sound of Jack's voice was more compelling than the lure of the duty free lotion counter.

Half an hour later as they settled into their seats Jack

caught Pandora's eye and smiled. A frisson of anticipation and unadulterated lust passed between them. She just couldn't *wait* to go to bed with him. He reached into his breast pocket and withdrew an envelope.

'I forgot to give you this.' He handed it to her.

She opened it curiously. Inside lay a share certificate for one thousand shares in the gloriously named Pandora's Mines. 'What are Pandora's Mines?' she asked, laughing delightedly.

'They're a little South African diamond mine. I'm afraid they haven't discovered any diamonds there for years and the shares aren't worth the paper they're written on, but with a name like that I thought they were worth a punt.'

'Oh Jack! It's the nicest present I've ever had! I'll treasure them.' She kissed him lightly on the cheek and then went bright red. 'Will this work in Switzerland?' she asked, picking up his mobile telephone, to cover her confusion.

''Fraid so,' said Jack. 'I shouldn't be going away at all this weekend; my partner wants to shoot me, but it was either that or shooting myself.' He stroked her cheek with his finger.

She sat, entranced by his touch. The mood was broken by the arrival of their heavily cellophaned inflight meal. 'Gosh, the Swiss really hate germs, don't they?' said Pandora, studying the impregnable packaging. 'It's amazing how they make such good yogurt, considering how many bugs that's got in it.'

'Ugh, I hate that stuff,' said Jack firmly.

'Just wait till you try a coffee-flavoured one, you'll never want to eat anything else.'

Jack looked unconvinced.

'I've heard that when the Swiss go abroad they get iller than anyone else because they have no resistance,' wittered Pandora brightly, gazing with disappointment at the high-tech television monitor that revealed they were already halfway through their flight. She peered out of the window. The sky was inky black, but somewhere beneath them Europe was flashing past. 'I wonder where we are now,' she mused.

Jack glanced at the monitor above them. 'Looks like we're somewhere above Belgium. We'll be arriving in,' he glanced at his watch then back at the screen, 'twenty-five minutes.'

'How did you work that out?' asked Pandora, not particularly wanting to know but impressed anyway.

Jack launched into an incredibly complex explanation which Pandora found impossible to follow because she was too distracted by Jack's wrists. She was fantasizing about undoing his cufflinks and rolling up his shirtsleeves to see if the rest of his arms were as compelling when he said, 'It's fascinating, isn't it?'

'It certainly is,' said Pandora, wishing she could think of something more intelligent to say. 'D'you like my watch?' she asked, flashing a garish Swatch watch at him.

He grasped her wrist firmly and examined its fluorescent colours closely. 'It's lovely,' he said doubtfully. 'You know, for someone who likes Switzerland so much you should at least have a decent watch. I'll buy you one tomorrow.'

'Oh Jack, I couldn't possibly . . .'

'Just see it as part of your consultation fee.'

'Oh, all right then,' said Pandora happily.

'Besides, I feel responsible for that nasty tabloid piece. I should have realized Max Chister would stay true to form.'

'If he's such a loose cannon, why do you want him working for you?' asked Pandora.

'Because he's got the best contacts in Fleet Street, and he'll really help put the magazine on the map. He can reel in celebrities like no one else. And he's great chums with the editor of the *Daily Mail*. He's been twisting their arm to do a fundraiser for the foundation.'

'That would be fantastic! They ran a campaign to raise money for the release of that poor killer whale in Mexico last year and they got thousands of pounds.'

'I know. Max was behind that as well.'

'Never!' Pandora was very surprised. 'So he's not nearly as bad as he pretends to be.'

'Actually, he's far worse. But he has his uses.'

The plane had landed and Jack got up to collect their hand baggage. 'I've booked us a car so we'll just go and pick it up and drive into town.'

Pandora wafted through the airport on a cloud of duty-free perfume behind Jack, dangling a Kelly bag delicately from one hand and her passport in the other. Jack seemed to have commandeered the services of the only porter in the airport, and they were soon being handed the keys to a sleek indigo-blue Porsche which was waiting for them outside.

'Jack! What a smashing motor!' said Pandora, lapsing into estuary motor speak in her enthusiasm.

'I wanted to try it out before I ordered one myself. It's not available in England yet.'

Pandora fingerered the gear lever reverently. 'It's got six gears. Amazing.'

Jack roared out of the airport with such ferocity that Pandora gripped her seat. This was the life!

'I've booked us into the Dolder. D'you know it?'

The Dolder was the ritziest hotel in Zurich. Jack really was pushing the boat out.

'I've been in there for coffee but I've never stayed the night.' Pandora didn't add that it was far beyond her means – whatever Max Chister might say.

Shooting through the silent Zurich suburbs they soon glimpsed the old town rising mysteriously from the lake in the distance. 'The Venice of the north!' breathed Pandora, who had never actually been to Venice.

'I thought that was St Petersburg.'

'Oh no, I'm sure it's Zurich,' replied Pandora confidently. 'I love all those narrow little streets full of shops under the arches. There's the lake . . .' She gazed out of the window as Jack took a detour over the bridge, transfixed by the still water, lit up with the reflection from thousands of illuminated banks on the lake edge. 'All this and the loos work too! And you can swim in the lake in summer. They have a women's section, a men's section and a section for homosexuals, too. I bet the only things that swim in the Rialto are dead rats.' Really, she could see very little point in going to Venice at all.

'But Venice has a certain something, the Cipriani is one of the best hotels in the world.'

Pandora thought she had read somewhere that he and Atlanta had gone there for part of their honeymoon. Huh! Another good reason not to go to Venice.

'Shall we stop here a moment and walk by the lake for a bit? I could do with stretching my legs.'

'Oh, I'd love to.'

They climbed out of the car and their figures soon melted into the darkness. An icy wind suddenly blew off from the lake, winding her chiffon scarf round her face and neck. She shivered.

'Are you cold?' Jack asked, putting a warm hand on her neck.

'Not really, someone just walked on my grave, that's all.'

'C'mon,' he said, steering her back to the car, 'let's get to the hotel and check in.'

Their suite was huge. When the bellboy had shown them how the television, telephone, curtains and shower worked and finally shut the door, Jack unlocked the mini bar and drew out two half-bottles of Krug. 'Like a drink?'

'Yes please,' said Pandora, not quite knowing where to sit herself. She wandered into the bedroom and perched awkwardly on the edge of the enormous double bed, glancing at the televison which the bellboy had left on. The 1936 version of *Dorian Gray* whispered sinisterly.

Definitely the sort of spooky film to watch in Zurich, she thought idly, smiling her thanks as Jack walked over and handed her a flute of champagne.

'Here's to you.'

As Pandora held his gaze, she again had the sensation of drowning into some place beyond; it was almost as if she could see right into him and he into her. The spinning intensity left her quite unable to speak. Jack put down his glass and kissed her. 'God, you're so pretty,' he said. 'I love you in this.' He slipped his hands beneath her red silk shirt and with practised ease undid her bra. 'I've been longing to do this since the night I first met you.'

That makes two of us, thought Pandora, but she said nothing, just shut her eyes and succumbed to the whisper of his mouth on her smooth skin; this moment was an island lost in time, nothing existed beyond it, the past was forgotten and the future blurred. The only thing that mattered was his body, pressed against hers, shutting out everything. She longed to shout out, 'My darling, darling, darling Jack,' but remained silent, not sure enough of his feelings for her to let him know how she felt. Jack caressed the back of her neck, dextrously undoing the zip of her skirt. He wrenched off his tie and undid the buttons of his shirt with one hand, kissing her at the same time, relishing the feel of her soft breasts pressed against him. The room was dark, only illuminated by the flickering black and white film in the corner of the room. Pandora had the sense that they were in a film themselves, seamlessly spinning through time and lost in a vacuum that she hoped would never come to an end.

'Please, please,' she murmured, drawing him to her, coiling her arms about his neck, as Jack lightly touched her breasts before exploring between her legs, caressing her with small, subtle movements until he found the most sensitive part of her and concentrated on that, driving her wild. Still he stroked her, the weight and strength of him pushing her into the bed so that she thought she might die with the desperate need to feel him inside her. At last he entered her, still caressing her, and she came immediately, wrapping her legs round his back and crying out into the night.

She opened her eyes and saw Jack looking at her, and through her; his eyes were black pools of nothingness and she couldn't reach him. He was locked in his own private world of desire and longing. Again she coiled her arms about him, loving the feel of his hard, strong back against her hands, and kissed his mouth, face, eyes and ears, whispering to him, until he saw her again. He rested on his elbows and pounded into her with such intensity she was almost frightened. Out of the corner of her eye she caught sight of the withered portrait of Dorian Gray and heard a crash of music as the film came to its excruciating end, and she came again, clenching her eyes shut against the tidal wave of intensity that surged out of her as Jack climaxed, his back slippery with sweat. 'I love you, love you, love you,' she repeated silently to herself, 'and I always will.' Then fear gripped her, fear of love, fear of loss, a fear of something so deep she couldn't put a name to it. Jack had collapsed into a heap of pleasure and exhaustion in her arms. He propped himself with effort on to one elbow, stroked her nose and moved a wisp of hair from her face and kissed her.

'Ouch,' said Pandora, wriggling against his bulk which suddenly seemed quite oppressive.

'Sorry, darling, are you uncomfortable?'

'Um, just a bit. I must get up a sec.' She disentangled herself from him and the pile of damp clothes she was lying on and went to the bathroom. She had a sudden urge to escape and be alone. Turning on the shower she stepped beneath it, taking pleasure in the strong jet of water against her skin. She felt her sanity return and stepped out and dried herself with a big fluffy bath towel, before enveloping herself in the soft, warm bathrobe hanging on the heated towel rail beside her. She padded silently back to the bedroom and wandered over to the window.

'No moon tonight,' she said conversationally to Jack who was sitting up in bed and smoking a cigarette. 'The shower's great,' she said cheerfully, getting back into bed. Really, she might have been having a chat with the hotel receptionist rather than the man who had just given her the two most memorable orgasms of her life, but she just couldn't snap out of her flippant mode. Jack had touched a place in her that was so tender, and hidden so deeply, that she didn't dare expose it to herself, let alone him.

'You're so lovely, Pandora, I could become addicted to you,' Jack smiled, burying himself in her hair. She snuggled up into his arms and then turned on to her side away from him, burying her back into his chest and resting her head on his arm. Thus entwined and with her emotions firmly under control once more, she fell into a deep, easy sleep.

Despite his exhaustion, Jack found rest impossible. He envied Pandora her deep sleep and her lack of responsibilities. Her seemingly casual approach to their relationship was at once tantalizing and disconcerting; he couldn't make her out. She was different. It was so odd the way she had just got up after they had made love, almost as if she regretted their intimacy.

She shifted away from him in her sleep, releasing his arm as she did so. Jack crept quietly out of bed, and went into the sitting room. He felt restless and uneasy. Jack was intuitive; that and the courage to follow his hunches had made him very rich indeed. In principle the finance was now in place but Dougall and Douglas still had two days left to change their minds. Something about the last meeting he had had with them made him think they might be stringing him along a bit. Bastards. He stubbed out his cigarette viciously. He had hoped this weekend away would take his mind off things at home. He helped himself to a whisky from the mini bar and thought of Pandora, fast asleep in the next room. Her presence soothed him. Eventually he drained his whisky and got back into bed. He longed to wake her up and make love to her again, it was the only thing that could empty his mind, but instead he contented himself with the sight of her, admiring the silky spread of her hair over the pillow. There would be plenty of time to make love in the morning, after all. At last he fell into a deep, uneasy sleep.

Chapter Seventeen

Pandora woke early. It was one of her more anti-social habits that she immediately felt wide awake the moment she opened her eyes. Jack was snoring faintly and still fast asleep. It would be a pity to wake him, he was obviously exhausted. She had a sudden desire to walk by the lake. Maybe she could get a coffee somewhere. She had woken up with some interesting ideas for a possible plot development and she was longing to write them down while they still made sense. Jack had said he was hopeless in the mornings; it was just before eight, he'd probably be asleep for another couple of hours at least.

She padded into the sitting room where their suitcases lay, still unpacked. The room was horribly smoky and she went to fling open the window, noticing an ashtray overflowing with cigarette butts and an empty glass beside it. Jack must have got up in the middle of the night. She wondered what could have disturbed him to keep him awake, and what he had been thinking about as he kept his vigil. But all thoughts of Jack and his problems were driven from her mind as she flung open the French windows. The medieval city was covered in a soft lacing of snow, in the distance church spires soared into the clear blue sky. It was magical! Pandora rummaged through her suitcase – thank goodness she had brought so much stuff – selecting a bright red jersey and a pair of soft cashmere leggings which went well with her red cashmere coat with its black fake fur collar. She was longing to wear a fur hat that had belonged to her mother. She strongly disapproved of fur, but it suited her so well. Besides, it would be freezing outside. And she'd better put some make-up on, she didn't want to shock Jack.

She stole one more look at him. He had thrown off most of the bedclothes and she could see his broad brown back and a muscular arm, flung untidily over the crumpled sheets. Her heart turned over, he looked curiously vulnerable. 'If any beauty I desired and got, 'twas but a dream of thee,' she quoted silently, drawing the door quietly shut behind her.

She slipped out of the hotel and took the funicular railway and then a tram down to the lake. The city was deserted, the stolid Zurich citizens sensibly preferring to stay warm inside. Her breath was visible in the frosty air and she rubbed her gloved hands together as she walked briskly towards the old town. Zurich was definitely the capital of Narnia, she thought dreamily, remembering the C.S. Lewis books from her childhood. Any moment now she almost expected to see the White Queen whizzing past in her wicked carriage, on the way to indulge in some evil urban pleasure. Pandora gazed up to the mountains, shrouded in cloud, their peaks scraping the sky in the misty distance. The city was surrounded by acres of pine forests. Definitely Narnia country.

Jack woke up soon after Pandora left. Eyes still closed, he turned towards her side of the bed, looking forward to the feel of her silky skin against his hand, but as he opened his eyes, instead of the sight of her glorious body he was confronted by a dent in the pillow and a pool of clothes hurriedly ripped off the night before. She was probably in the bathroom. Either that or she'd done a runner. He chuckled at the unlikelihood of that. Women never ran away from Jack. He shut his eyes and promptly fell asleep again.

He woke an hour later with an erection and a raging appetite. Still no Pandora. Damn. He glanced at his watch. It was 10 a.m. Oh well, she'd probably gone for a walk. He ordered breakfast from room service and mused about what they were going to do that day. He had a sudden urge to visit his old school, Ecole Lemania. It was miles away but it would be great to put the Porsche through its paces. He knew of a fabulous place where they could stop for lunch on the way. Ecole Lemania was not far from Gstaad. They could spend the night at the Palace before flying back from Geneva the next morning.

Just as he was cracking into a plate of ham and eggs Pandora returned, her face flushed with the cold air and her hat flecked with snowflakes. Jack gazed at her, hypnotized for a split second; she looked absolutely gorgeous. Her eyes sparkled as she sat down, dripping snow and enthusiasm all over the bed.

'You look like Julie Christie in *Dr Zhivago*,' he said, returning to his ham and eggs.

'I've just had the most wonderful walk. Did you know it's snowing?'

'Yup,' said Jack, his eyes straying to his share price in *The Times*. 'D'you want to order something to eat?'

Pandora scanned the menu card and rang room service, ordering birchermuesli, a large bowl of prunes, a pot of Earl Grey tea, emphasizing carefully that the bag must be put in in the kitchen. She couldn't bear the way continentals provided a teapot of lukewarm water and a tea bag separately.

She caught his eye, he was laughing. 'And I would like the bag put in the pot *in the kitchen, please*,' he mimicked. He sounded so funny imitating her high-pitched voice that she burst out laughing. 'And they say I'm a control freak!' he grinned.

Pandora was embarrassed at having exposed her spinsterish ways. 'If you were English you'd understand.'

'You're right.' He put on an exaggerated Afrikaans accent. 'In S'thifrica we don't have tea just bits of dung that we pour water on, end if you want it hot you've got to crawl on bended knees for sixteen miles, find a horse and use its urine while it's still warm.' Pandora shook with helpless laughter so hard that she began to have hiccups. She lay down on the bed and gurgled with laughter. Jack carefully removed her hat and kissed her, his warm hands caressing her beneath her coat. Pandora's hiccups subsided and she responded passionately.

There was a knock on the door. 'Room service.'

'Oh shit, your bloody tea,' said Jack. 'Let's hope for their sake they've made it properly.'

Thankfully they had, and Pandora, who was starving after getting up so early, tucked into her prunes with relish. 'They're absolutely delicious. I think they must have soaked them in Armagnac and cinnamon. Can I tempt you, Jack?' His head was buried in *The Times* and he didn't hear her. She helped herself to an English-language Swiss newspaper and was soon engrossed reading about various Swiss foibles. 'Goodness,' she exclaimed. 'Switzerland has grown one and a half kilometres since the war. Is that a lot?'

'Enough to build two more banks on I guess,' said Jack, heaving himself out of bed. 'I thought we could head over towards Geneva and check out my old school on the way.'

'I didn't know you went to school here,' said Pandora.

'Only for a couple of years. My father was working for a while in France and he and my mother thought Switzerland might teach me a few airs and graces.'

'And did it?' smiled Pandora.

'No! The only useful thing I learnt here was how to ski down moguls backwards,' said Jack, heading for the shower.

Pandora shivered. God, he was so cool. She spat out a prune stone, relieved that she could now do so without Jack seeing. It was important to preserve *some* mystery in the early stages of a relationship, after all.

After breakfast they quickly packed up their things and hit the road. It was very quiet and it didn't take long to leave the city behind. Soon the Porsche was speeding out on to the autobahn, overtaking everything in its way. Jack seemed in a rather bad mood; he had barely said a word since they had got in the car. Pandora wondered if he was getting bored with her and stared out of the window truculently. Huh, she thought, see if I care. She got out her newspaper and soon became engrossed in more Swiss foibles.

Jack was worrying about work. He couldn't rid himself of the feeling that something was wrong. At lunch he'd better ring and check everything was OK. He'd forgotten to recharge his telephone last night, most unlike him, but then there had been distractions. He glanced at Pandora's earnest face, buried in her newspaper. God, it was such a relief being with a woman who didn't talk all the time!

'Anything interesting in the paper?' asked Jack, longing to be sidetracked from thinking about work.

'Well, yes. Actually there is. There's *going to be a referendum*,' Pandora said dramatically.

'That's hardly news. The Swiss have referendums every five minutes.'

'Yes, but this issue could affect the whole of Europe!' She paused, holding her breath as Jack overtook a juggernaut lorry. The moment of terror past, she continued, 'The government wants to abandon carrier pigeons but the Swiss carrier pigeon club is up in arms, so they're going to take the issue to the country.' Her voice was full of admiration.

'You're a bit of a Swissie, aren't you?' said Jack, smiling at her.

'Well, if I could move the Ritzy Marina club to downtown Zurich it would probably be my idea of a perfect country. I mean, you've got everything, money, mountains, beautiful scenery . . .' Jack glanced doubtfully out of the window. They were driving past a particularly uninspiring grey landscape full of industrial units. 'And it's terribly reassuring seeing banks everywhere.'

'Only if you've got something in one of them,' said Jack, his mind returning to the nagging worry about his deal. 'I was sent to work in Zurich for six months, years ago.'

'Lucky you,' said Pandora.

'I rented a flat with a couple of guys from the New York office. We went skiing every weekend. Those were the days, no responsibilities, no worries . . .' The sun had come out and he rummaged around for his sunglasses. They made him look faintly sinister. God, he was gorgeous.

'Would you read me some of your novel? You did bring it, didn't you?'

Pandora was flattered that he was showing an interest. 'I brought a few chapters along with me just in case we got snowed in and you got bored of reading the *FT*. I'm not sure it's your sort of thing though.'

'It will be if you wrote it,' smiled Jack, resting his hand on her knee.

'I'll start with the synopsis, just so you get the gist of the plot.'

As she began reading, Jack felt the tension easing out of his back and shoulders. The feel of her warm thigh beneath his hand was as erotic as it was soothing, while the synopsis, read by Pandora in a breathy Nancy Mitford-style voice, had him laughing out loud.

'It's great,' he said, when she'd finished. 'Can you read me some more?'

'You don't have to be polite.'

'No, seriously, I loved it. It's clever the way you've interwoven the business with the romance.'

'Actually, I'm getting a bit stuck on some of the business bits. The romance is easy, but I've never even worked in an office, unless you count the time I worked the switchboard at my father's but he sacked me after five days. I need to find out about how people buy and sell companies, but it's so confusing.' She hoped Jack would take the bait and offer to advise her.

He did. 'I'm sure I can help you. After all, that's what I'm doing at the moment.'

'Oh, would you?' Pandora's eyes sparkled. He was the fifth man who had offered to help her with the confusing business bits of her novel that month, but the thought of collaborating with him was very alluring.

They had left the autobahn and were now driving along a narrow winding road. Jack had been forced to reduce his speed as they were stuck behind an Aston Martin. He sighed impatiently and tapped his fingers irritably on the wheel. 'Flash bastard!' he muttered, and Pandora shielded her eyes and cringed into her seat; she knew what was about to happen. Jack put his foot down and nipped in front of the Aston just before a juggernaut came rumbling round the approaching corner. 'Hah!' said Jack, adrenaline coursing through his veins. He loved taking risks. Pandora didn't.

'Did you really have to do that?' she asked, fear making her tetchy.

'Yes,' said Jack firmly.

'But why? It was completely unnecessary and we might have all died,' said Pandora crossly.

Driving dangerously and making love were the only things that took Jack's mind off things but he said nothing. Instead his mouth tightened into a thin line. 'If you don't like the way I drive, you could always catch a train. You might miss rather a good lunch, but I hear that the railway buffets are excellent.'

She reeled from the sarcasm in his voice and her eyes filled with tears. If he really liked her, he wouldn't dream of talking to her like that. Then hurt changed to anger. Sod him, she thought. How dare he talk to me like that! But she said nothing more and engrossed herself in her paper.

Jack had already forgotten his sharp tone and in the silence his mind returned to his nagging business fears. 'Will you read me some more of your novel?' he asked, eager for distraction.

'I wouldn't want to put you to sleep,' she said lightly, flicking through the paper. 'I mean, you don't read novels, do you?'

'Too busy earning a living I guess,' he mumbled, but Pandora was gripped by an article that asserted that single women lived longer than married ones and were generally much happier. She must show it to Annabel, it might stop her feeling so broody. She ripped it out carefully and put it in her bag.

'Sorry,' she said, 'did you say something?'

'Nope,' said Jack, fiddling with the radio. 'Did you bring any tapes with you? There's nothing on the radio.'

'Yes, I did.' Pandora delved into her bottomless bag and fished out her favourite cassette. 'I've got the latest Van Morrison tape. He's great, don't you think?'

Jack didn't respond. He had another car in his sights and was about to overtake and he was wondering if he could remember exactly where the restaurant was. It was one of his favourites and he was looking forward to showing it to Pandora.

Pandora put the tape back in her bag and returned to her reading.

Jack glanced at her, earnestly engrossed in her strange little Swiss newspaper, admiring the way her glossy blonde hair fell to her shoulders, and smiled to himself. If only he could put work out of his mind for a while, everything would be just perfect.

The restaurant was deeply embedded in a pine forest in the middle of nowhere.

'Gosh, Jack, how did you find this place?' said Pandora admiringly. He might have a closed mind when it came to music but he had a brilliant sense of direction.

'I've been here a few times. I know the *patron*, he's very keen on truffles. If we're lucky he might give us some.'

'Gosh, how wonderful,' said Pandora doubtfully. The

only truffles she had ever tried were the Belgian chocolate ones, and she had a feeling that the knobbly ones that were ferreted out of the ground at enormous expense by pigs were probably vastly overrated.

The *patron* was very much in situ, and having had a successful morning truffle hunting was in an excellent mood. He was delighted to see Jack, firstly because he liked him and secondly because he always brought pretty women with him.

'Meester Dudley, you are looking reeely well. And Mademoiselle,' he kissed Pandora's hand, 'you are looking charming also.' Pandora blushed girlishly as he pulled out her seat.

'Now, Bernard. What's the truffle situation today?' asked Jack firmly.

'Eees difficult,' said Bernard, sighing dramatically. 'Theese year they are, 'ow you say, theen on the ground, but for you 'an your charmeeng companion I theenk there will be no trubble.'

'I guess that means he'll charge the earth for them,' said Jack as Bernard slipped away on tiny feet.

Distracted and a little edgy, Jack gazed into the distance, wondering if he could phone his partner Tom from the restaurant or whether he should wait until they got to the hotel. But he longed to have his mind set at rest. 'I really ought to phone Tom and check things are OK at home. Do you mind?'

'Of course I don't mind,' said Pandora. Growing up with a workaholic father she thought it was perfectly natural for a man to eat, drink and sleep work. It was how a proper man should be, she thought firmly. It was pleasant to be alone for a few minutes to savour the delicious champagne which had automatically been brought as an apéritif and gaze at the distant mountains through the window. No one had ever spoilt her quite so deliciously as Jack. Even doing everyday things seemed to be out of the ordinary. Perhaps everyone felt like this in the early stages of a relationship, though she never had until now.

Jack was making his way back to the table, frowning slightly.

'Did you get hold of him?' she asked.

'No, I left a message telling him where we'll be tonight. He'll only ring if there's a problem, but it'll put my mind at rest to talk to him.' He smiled but the smile didn't reach his eyes. At that moment Bernard reappeared, flourishing a small plate.

'Now, Meester Dudley, I would like you to try theez.' He offered the small plate of what looked like three tiny potato peelings to Jack and beamed at Pandora proudly. Jack tried one of the withered slithers and rolled his eyes in pleasure. 'Try one, Pandora, they're delicious.'

Pandora pasted an excited look upon her face and helped herself enthusiastically. 'What a treat!' she said, savouring the tiny shrivelled morsel carefully. It tasted a bit like some raw celeriac she had once discovered in the back of her fridge. 'Fabulous,' she added convincingly, not meeting Jack's eye and busying herself with her napkin. Compared to eating tarantulas in the rainforest, truffles probably did taste like manna from heaven.

The waiter scurried over and reverently placed two very small plates of scrambled egg adorned with more truffle shavings in front of them. The helpings were so tiny Pandora wondered bleakly if they had been made with quails' eggs. She was terribly hungry after Jack's death-defying driving and longed for a baked potato but rather doubted if this august establishment could provide such a thing. Jack began a long, well-informed discussion about the truffle season with Bernard who then disappeared to find an obscure bottle of white wine that would apparently set off the rest of their truffle meal to perfection. At least Jack was starting to look less worried and Pandora challenged herself to cheer him up.

'Are you still worried about the deal? I thought the finance was all in place now.'

'Well, it is,' said Jack, relieved to discuss what was on his mind. 'Douche Bank—'

'You mean Dougall and Douglas?' interrupted Pandora.

Jack nodded and continued. 'They've agreed to lend us the money but they can't, or won't, sign the agreement until Monday because Lord Douche, I mean Dougall, is playing golf in Gleneagles for two weeks and is apparently incommunicado.' Jack rolled his eyes. 'Can you believe it? Like they don't have faxes in Scotland, for Christ's sake.'

'So you're worried they might pull out and then you won't have the money to bid for the company.'

'Precisely.' Jack took a gulp of wine and lit a cigarette, ignoring the aromatic plate of pasta that had been put in front of him. Despite the ubiquitous truffle shavings scattered over the top, it was delicious.

'It's nice to take out a girl with such a good appetite,' said Jack admiringly, stubbing out his cigarette and getting stuck into his pasta. 'All the girls I've been out with seem to be on ridiculous diets or something. I think the last girl I took out had anorexia.'

'Must have saved you a fortune in restaurants,' said Pandora. Jack's girlfriends was not a subject she wanted to pursue – at least, not while eating truffles. 'You don't think that Lord Douche will pull out of the deal, do you?'

'I don't know but the whole thing makes me feel very edgy.'

'If he does, you'll just have to try all reasonable methods of persuasion and if that doesn't work . . .'

Jack smiled. 'I'm getting too old for threatening violence.'

'Never!'

'Anyway, I mustn't bore you about business, I want this to be a nice weekend for you.'

'But I find it interesting. I might learn something I can put in my novel. Besides, I've got a strong intuition that everything will pan out fine. Remember, you're a dragon, and people like helping you because you're so charming. You had the left-wing greenies positively eating out of your hand at the editorial meeting. Your entrance was great – perfect timing. How long had you been eavesdropping outside the door?'

Jack grinned. 'About ten minutes.'

Bernard reappeared bearing pudding menus. 'I 'ave jus' the theeng to round off your meal perfectleee.'

Jack looked at Pandora inquiringly. 'D'you want a pudding?'

'No thanks, I'm completely truffled out, I'm afraid. It was all delicious.'

'Meester Dudley, can I tempt you wiz our luverrly truffle cake?'

'Um, no thanks, Bernard. Just a double espresso and a cappuccino.'

And hold the truffle shavings, please, thought Pandora. She liked her cappuccinos unadorned.

Once back in the car, they lapsed into silence. Jack seemed impenetrable behind his dark glasses and Pandora, sleepy with wine and truffles, soon dozed off. When she woke up they were driving at some speed up a narrow mountain road. She yawned and stretched her arms.

Jack glanced over and ruffled her hair. 'At least one of us is never going to die from sleep deprivation. You've been out for over an hour.' Pandora sat up and tried to look animated; she hoped she hadn't been snoring or dribbling or anything. 'I can't remember exactly where the school is,' Jack was saying. 'I think it's somewhere up here . . .' He trailed off vaguely. 'Hang on, this bit looks familiar.'

He parked the car by the side of the road and they got out. It had started snowing again and though Pandora didn't feel in the least bit cold she decided to put on her hat for aesthetic reasons. Anything that made her look like Julie Christie was probably a good idea.

The place was completely deserted. 'It must be half-term. Either that or they're off on an expedition somewhere. Shame we can't go in, but at least we can snoop around outside.'

They wandered past some very basic buildings and stood in silence gazing at Lake Leman stretching into the melancholy grey beyond. Both were hypnotized by the stillness and the swirling mass of snowflakes drifting slowly to the ground. Pandora tried to focus on one but couldn't: in the clear light they formed a spinning, shining mass and she had the gloriously surreal sensation that she and Jack were dancing with a million tiny diamonds. They might have been the only people left in the world, and she couldn't imagine anyone else she would rather be left alone in the world with. She imagined the place full of children. Perhaps she and Jack would send theirs here. She checked herself suddenly. The idea had arisen from nowhere. Heavens, she didn't even *like* children! But the thought of Jack's children . . . It was completely ridiculous, the beauty and stillness were playing tricks on her frazzled London nerves.

As if with one mind, they both turned to go, Jack's hand still resting proprietorially on her neck.

'It's a magical place,' he said as they got into the car, 'wasted on kids – at least it was wasted on us lot. I even tried to blow it up with some stuff we nicked from the chemistry lab but we got caught.'

'What happened?'

'They decided I was a subversive influence and expelled me. I was pretty upset about the whole thing.'

'Yes, it must have been very disruptive for your education,' said Pandora sensibly.

'Oh, I didn't mind about that, I was upset because I never found out why the explosive didn't go off.'

Pandora laughed. 'I'd give anything to stay here for four months and finish my novel, it would be so inspiring.'

She shut her eyes, imagining the possibility. A bit later she glanced out of the window. It was getting dark.

'God, I must have dropped off again. What's the time? Are we nearly there?' She realized that Jack still hadn't told her where they were spending the night.

'Yup, we're about a quarter of an hour away,' said Jack, yawning. 'You might recognize the hotel when you see it. I'll give you a clue, there was an aerial view of it in *The Great Escape*.'

'That's one of my favourite films, but I don't remember a hotel in it.'

They drove in silence for a bit longer, entering a charming village which would have been rustic if it hadn't been for all the exclusive designer shops that lined the quiet main street.

'Look up. That's where we're staying tonight,' said Jack.

Pandora raised her eyes. At the top of a mountain stood a large Gothic building lit up with a thousand lights. It looked like something out of a fairy-tale.

'I'll give you three guesses where we are,' said Jack.

'It's the Palace Hotel and we're in Gstaad,' said Pandora, who had stuck a photo of the hotel on her fridge a year ago because it was so pretty. She sometimes looked at it wistfully and thought what a wonderful destination it would make for a romantic weekend.

'I knew you weren't just a pretty face,' he said as they climbed up the steep hill that led to the hotel.

'So which bit of *The Great Escape* was the Palace in?' asked Pandora.

'There's a long aerial shot when two of them are just about to fly over the Swiss border into safety and you see the Palace Hotel in the distance. It owes a lot to poetic licence, as we're nowhere near the German border.'

'I remember that bit – they're shot down just before they reach Switzerland. It's agony. My favourite part is the motorbike chase when Steve McQueen is trying to get here. I know just how he must have felt.'

'You might not have felt quite so enthusiastic about the country if you'd been one of the Jews they turned away at the border during the war,' said Jack.

'Did they? How appalling. I had no idea.'

'Probably because your grandparents were never turned away.'

Pandora looked over at him. 'You mean *your* grandparents were turned away?'

'Yup. They had to go back to Germany and then they were taken to Dachau. My father was at boarding school in England so he was all right.'

'But you never said . . . I mean, I didn't even know you were Jewish.'

'You never asked,' smiled Jack. 'Besides, I'm only half Jewish, and probably not even that because it's carried

through the female line and my mother's not Jewish. I
don't really know much about what happened. As soon
as he was twenty-one my father changed his name and
emigrated to South Africa. Then he married my mother
and sort of took up her Catholicism. He hardly ever talks
about it but apparently my grandparents stashed a load of
cash in a Swiss bank account which no one has ever been
able to get at. Some story about needing identification
papers. One of these days when I'm not so tied up I might
look into it myself. Like you said, it's a great country,
but you don't have to dig too deep to find some pretty
murky stuff.'

They pulled up outside the hotel and a doorman sprang
into action. As they entered the lobby, Pandora glanced
around, hoping to clock a minor member of a deposed
royal family: she was familiar with most of them from
her regular perusal of *HOLA!! Magazine*. To her disappointment, the lobby and bar yielded little glamour. She
wondered how she and Jack looked to outsiders. She'd
noticed that people always stared at them and wondered
if they were 'a glamorous couple'. Jack wasn't classi-
cally handsome, but he had real presence, she thought
admiringly as he stood at the reception desk.

'I'd like a suite please,' he was saying.

'You've got an urgent message, sir.' The receptionist
handed over an envelope.

Jack ripped it open and Pandora scanned his face for
clues about its contents but it revealed nothing. 'What's
in it?' she asked nervously, touching his arm.

'Just a message from Tom,' he said, screwing up the

paper and dropping it on to the reception desk. 'He wants me to ring him. I'll call him from the room.'

Oh God, thought Pandora, it's about the deal, something's gone wrong, I just know it. It was too unfair that a crisis should blow up now, when things were going so well between them. Staying at the Palace with Jack – well, it was too good to be true. Things like this just didn't *happen* to demoted Hampshire housewives. Well, perhaps they happened, they just didn't last very long.

Jack's face was grim and he didn't say a word as they made their way to their suite on the top floor. Pandora knew that anything she said would sound unbearably contrived and kept silent.

As soon as he had tipped the bellboy, Jack picked up the phone while Pandora went into the bedroom, not wanting to stand over Jack. She could eavesdrop from there anyway. Sinking into the luxurious kingsize bed, she could hear him quite clearly and her stomach churned with nerves. It didn't sound good at all. He was firing questions rapidly down the phone.

'What d'you mean they've pulled out? I don't believe it!' His voice was tight with anger. 'When did you find out? Shit, and I've been pissing about while all this was happening. Look, I'm going to catch the next flight out of here.' He glanced at his watch. '*Shit*, we've missed the last plane, it left at eight thirty. The Swiss are so bloody ridiculous about flying at night . . . Yes, I'm with someone. No, she won't mind . . . It's not important.' Pandora's ears strained. What wasn't important? The cheek of it!

The conversation continued and Jack became less heated. When he had put the telephone down, she went into the sitting room. He was gazing out of the window.

'Bad news?' she asked quietly.

'Lord Douche has pulled out. Unless I can raise the money by Wednesday, the whole deal's off.' He spoke matter-of-factly but she could see that he was seething with anger. 'British two-faced bastards.' He continued to gaze out of the window. 'I've been putting this deal together for two years, it's a brilliant idea. It's so short-term of them not to be able to see what we're doing. Tom suggested I sell my land in Kenya where I'm building the sanctuary but I can't do that. Christ, I'd rather starve.'

'So when are we going home?'

'We can catch the seven thirty flight tomorrow morning.'

'You wouldn't be able to do anything tonight anyway,' said Pandora soothingly, relieved that they would have at least one night in this gorgeous suite. She gazed round, taking in the fine furniture and exquisite pictures. The view was the best picture of all though; jagged mountain peaks glistened eerily in the moonlight against the inky black sky.

'At least they've given us a decent room. Last time I was put in a shoe box.' Jack sat down moodily on the sofa and began channel hopping. He obviously didn't want to talk so Pandora went into one of the bathrooms to examine the freebies. It seemed unlikely that Jack was in the mood for dinner, which suited her; she felt weary after the long drive despite sleeping much of the way. Jack must be completely shattered. She poked her head round the door. 'Can I run you a bath, Jack?' She smiled to herself. Jack seemed to be bringing out the geisha in her.

'I'll have one later,' he replied. He was watching the CNN business news and barely glanced at her. She ran herself one, adding copious amounts of gloriously scented bath oil. She wasn't particularly fazed by Jack's moodiness, it made him seem more interesting in a strange sort of way. It was new for her to have to anticipate a lover's moods, it was usually the other way round. Emily had told her about the Buddhist law of cause and effect – what you gave out always came back to you, there was no escape from your karma. God, was Jack going to be her bad karma concentrated in one person?

After an interesting hour ruminating over all the bad causes she had made in her love life, she got out of the bath and slipped into a long white bathrobe. Jack was now watching what looked horribly like a Sylvester Stallone movie, and must have called for room service while she was in the bath. A trolley was laden with the remains of a hamburger and chips and various other bits of junk food.

'D'you want to order up something?' he asked, flicking back to CNN as she sat down on the sofa.

'No, I'm not very hungry, I had such a big lunch. I might just go to bed, I'm completely knackered.'

'All right then.' Jack smiled at her and his eyes returned to the screen. A group of soldiers were being interviewed about food shortages and appalling living conditions. They were all smoking heavily.

'Have you ever noticed that they run out of food, water and medical supplies but they never run out of fags. Lucky bastards.' He was itching for a cigarrette but had thrown his last packet out the car window in a vain attempt to cut down. He flicked channels. 'I'll just catch the end of this movie then I'll join you.'

Pandora closed the door as a volley of gunfire emanated from the television. She vaguely wondered if his change of mood was solely due to business worry or whether he had just gone off her, but she was too tired to care and thankfully fell asleep as soon as her head touched the pillow. Half an hour later Jack got into bed beside her. He reached for her hand but in her sleep it felt like a butterfly trapped in his big airless palm and she withdrew it, turning away from him as she did so. She slept fitfully after that, dreaming of trapped birds in dusty rooms, flying round and round in a frantic bid to escape.

Later, as the Alpine dawn seeped in through the curtains, she woke in fright, disorientated and confused. Sweat was running down her back and her hands were clammy with fear. Jack wandered in from the bathroom, a towel tied round his waist. In the dim light Pandora thought he was the sexiest man she had ever seen and her heart contracted. She felt suddenly awkward with him and didn't know what to say. They could have been strangers.

'Five a.m., time to get up, I'm afraid,' he said, sitting on the bed and roughly towel-drying his hair. 'Will you be ready to leave in about quarter of an hour?' The tone of his voice suggested that he would be leaving then whether she was ready or not and she sprang out of bed.

'I will if I motor,' she said briskly, deciding that casual and friendly indifference was probably the best approach to adopt from now on.

They drove to Geneva in silence punctuated only by trivial news reports from Swiss Radio International. Geneva was golden in the early morning sunshine and the *jet d'eau* gushed from the lake with such velocity that it appeared to graze the sky. You could just glimpse Mont Blanc rising majestically above the clouds in the distance.

Pandora forgot about being brisk and indifferent and craned her neck excitedly out of the window. She'd forgotten how stunning Geneva was.

'It's so *beautiful* here,' she said, remembering long walks up steep, cobbled streets lined with immaculate fountains decked with flowers.

'Looks good but it's about as interesting as a kicked-over bucket of sick,' said Jack grimly as they raced through the empty streets towards the airport.

God, he's such a killjoy, thought Pandora grumpily. It's not my fault his deal's in crisis, for heaven's sake.

When they pulled into the airport she left Jack to sort out the car and raced down to the supermarket on the basement level to stock up on Swiss yogurts to keep her going in the long, bleak London months ahead. Who knew when she would next return?

Laden down with plastic bags, she staggered into the Swissair lounge to meet Jack.

He was pacing around the empty lounge and saw her

before she saw him. He smiled, she looked so pretty and disorganized with her jumble of plastic bags. 'Pandora! What the hell have you been buying?'

'Oh, nothing very interesting, just a few boring bits and pieces.'

Jack was impatient to leave and strode off towards the check-in counter with their luggage. Pandora trailed after him.

'You look like an illegal immigrant with all her worldly goods stashed in both hands,' he laughed. 'They *do* have supermarkets in England, you know.' He glanced inside the bags. 'Christ, Pandora, what will customs say? You'll be arrested with this lot. I'd better declare it . . .' He strode off in the direction of customs.

'No! Jack! Come back with my yog,' she lowered her voice, 'yogurts. You're allowed to take them abroad . . . I do it all the time.' She couldn't stop laughing; Jack was marching through the airport pretending to look for an official.

'If there is a listeria outbreak in England I'll know who to blame. Pandora, you're quite daft, d'you know?' he said as they made their way on to the plane. Thankfully they were the only people in business class and there was plenty of room for her yogurts.

'Jack?'

'Mmm?'

'D'you like my watch?' She proffered her wrist and showed him the garish specimen. Jack grasped her slim wrist for a closer look, then slapped himself on the forehead.

'God, I'm sorry! I promised to buy you one, didn't I? I know, let's do a deal. You can choose any one you like from the duty free if you read me some more of your novel.'

'I'm afraid it's in my suitcase,' said Pandora sadly.

'Never mind, choose one anyway. It'll make up for cutting short our weekend.' He handed her the duty free magazine.

'I shouldn't think Swissair sell anything naff enough for me,' said Pandora, flicking through the glossy catalogue doubtfully and then putting it aside. She quite fancied one with a picture of a Swiss flag or a train on it, but they only had exotic Gucci and Cartier ones for millions of francs. She couldn't ask him for one of those.

Jack sat beside her gazing out of the window, his head full of strategies for the coming two days. The whole thing was a complete nightmare. He'd been waiting for the chance to buy a company with such perfect synergy to his own for years. The bids had to be in by next week; if he didn't have the money in place by then, the opportunity would be lost for ever. The plane suddenly jolted and he shuddered involuntarily. He hated flying. Pandora glanced over at him, noticing him grip the seat for a moment, his knuckles white. This rare glimpse of vulnerability made her heart turn over.

'Help!' she laughed. 'I've been reincarnated as a dead person!' She was relieved to see Jack's anxious expression replaced by a smile. 'That's one of Emily's. You know, my agent,' she said proudly. 'She's a Buddhist. I'll get her to chant for your deal if you like.'

'God, I'm so desperate I think I ought to try it myself,' said Jack grimly.

'OK, I'll find out what she chants and we'll have a session. Jack?'

'Hmm?'

'It'll be fine. The deal, I mean. You'll pull it off. Call it female intuition but I just know you will. You are brilliant, you know. But I guess you get bored of people telling you that all the time.'

'You're the only person who does.' He took her hand and kissed it.

An hour later, he dropped her home, helping her in with her luggage. He stood in the hall, eager to leave and get back to work.

'Good luck with the bankers,' smiled Pandora. 'I'm sure you'll persuade them.'

He was already halfway through the door. 'I'll survive. It's only money!' And he laughed.

The door closed and Pandora stood blankly in the hall. A phrase from a novel breezed through her mind: 'And long after you have stopped laughing I can hear your laugh running up and down my veins.' As she turned to go upstairs, she realized rather sadly that he hadn't even kissed her goodbye.

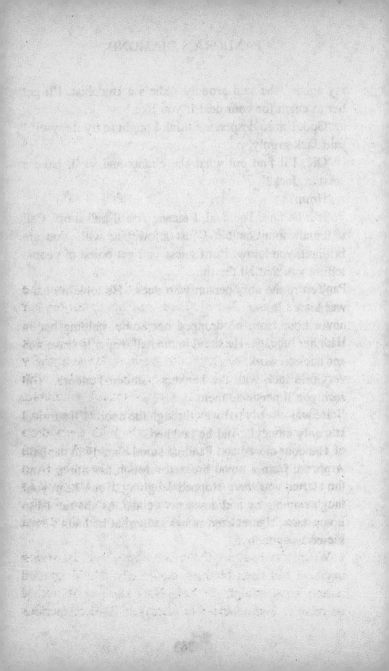

Chapter Eighteen

Pandora woke up at 7 a.m. feeling wiped out from the weekend's drama. She stretched out languorously in her new kingsize bed which she'd bought for a fortune in the Harrods' sale, pulling the soft downy duvet up to her neck and snuggling into her goosedown pillow. It was actually very pleasant waking up alone. This time yesterday, with Jack, she had woken up in a sweat feeling miserable. Being in love, or infatuated, was terribly tiring, she didn't know whether she liked it very much. With every drop of exquisite pleasure – the sight of Jack with his towel wrapped loosely round his brown waist, glistening from the shower, the feel of his hand resting on her neck as they stood by the lake – came an equal measure of pain. It was a package deal. She didn't even know if she'd ever see him again.

When she had got home last night, her answering machine had been blinking mournfully. She'd ignored it and gone straight to bed. Now she put it out of its misery. There were five messages. Two mysterious hang-ups (so maddening), a dull man to whom she had given her telephone number a while ago because she had felt sorry for him, and a hysterical message from her downstairs neighbour complaining about a leak. She sighed bleakly. Then Emily suddenly came on the line.

'Pandora, I've got some rather interesting news. Red Duck really liked your synopsis and sample chapters and they want to meet you. Can you ring me as soon as you get in?'

Pandora shrieked with delight. Red Duck were a well-respected publishing house whose novels were sold everywhere. It was a miracle! Quickly she dialled Emily's number.

'Emily, I'm thrilled about your message. Where do we go from here?'

'Well, the editor I sent your material to is about to go to America for two weeks and would like to see you before she goes if possible. How does lunch tomorrow sound?'

'It sounds perfect.'

'It really is extraordinary to get this sort of interest so quickly. Editors normally take ages to get back to me. I've sent the manuscript to three other publishers, but if Red Duck make us a worthwhile offer I really think it's worth running with them. They've got a good reputation and they're very commercial.'

'I quite agree. I'm not aiming for the Booker Prize, after all.'

'I'm delighted for you, Pandora. You must have been born under a lucky star.'

Pandora replaced the receiver and wondered who to

telephone with her wonderful news. It was all very well being single and relishing her independence, but there were times when it would have meant the world to share something like this with someone really special. Someone like Jack.

She went into the kitchen and opened the fridge for a freshly imported pot of Swiss yogurt. The shelves were crammed with the stuff. Maybe she shouldn't phone anybody, she thought, selecting three yogurts. She probably spent more time on the telephone than doing anything else. If she was going to be offered a contract for her novel, things would have to change. A contract would mean a deadline for finishing the book, and it was too easy to be distracted, especially by the telephone. Since most of her friends were on diets or trying to give up smoking, they tended to reach for the phone instead of a fag or a biscuit. Perhaps she should just disappear from London leaving no forwarding address and rent a cottage by the sea or something. And she wouldn't tell Jack where she was going, then he'd be sorry! Or then again, perhaps he wouldn't even notice she'd gone.

Virtuously she got down to work. The weekend seemed to have been quite inspiring; Pandora pounded away at her computer for several hours before the phone rang. It was her father, calling from the depths of Cornwall.

'Oh, hi, Dad,' said Pandora. 'I was going to ring you and ask for your advice about something.'

James groaned. 'Oh God. What's his name?'

'It's not about a man actually,' lied Pandora. 'Emily thinks she's found a publisher for my novel.'

'That was quick. Congratulations! But that means you'll have to finish it.'

'Exactly. And I think I'll have to get away from London to do it. There are too many *distractions* here.'

'Good idea. Why don't you borrow one of the cottages on the estate for a couple of months? There's bugger all to do down here.'

'That's true,' she agreed, 'but I'm not quite ready for a slow and natural death just yet. I was thinking of going to Switzerland. You see, it's *imperative* that I leave the country as soon as possible.'

'Like I said, what's his name?'

'Jack Dudley.'

'Hm, that rings a bell. What does he do?'

'He owns Dudley Enterprises.' She waited for him to open his *Financial Times*.

'Really?' James sounded unusually impressed. There was a rustle as he scanned the share price index. 'Hmm. Dudley Enterprises. Seven pounds a share, the company is capitalized at two hundred million pounds. Why are you running away? He's obviously worth a few bob, unlike the rest of them.'

'But Dad, you don't know him, he's very *difficult*. He always has to have his own way and—'

'Talk about the pot calling the kettle black.'

'Difficult? Me? Seriously, though, I quite like him and I need to leave England before it's too late.' She tried to inject some necessary pathos into her voice but James just laughed at her.

'You say this every time, Pandora. In a few weeks'

time, when he's all over you, you'll be fed up with him. Got no staying power, that's your trouble. I think I ought to ring him and let him know what he's getting into. But enough of that. What are you doing about Christmas?'

'I haven't a clue.'

'Well, if you don't have a better offer, Davina wants to return to Hawaii. We thought you might enjoy a few weeks at the Kahala Hilton.'

'Might enjoy! I'd give my arms and legs to go back there! The thought of it might even cure my potentially broken heart.'

'Well, it's still weeks away, you'll probably be in love with someone else by then. You're fickle—'

'—like my mother,' finished Pandora. 'How's Davina?'

'Praying, I think,' said James drily.

'I should think she's run out of things to pray for at the moment. Everything is going so well for both of you.'

'Yes and no.' James had never been so happy but superstitiously didn't dare admit it. 'The church spire appeal has been so oversubscribed that everyone's fighting about what we're going to do with the spare cash. If the church is renovated any more it'll collapse. My suggestion that we build another pub didn't go down too well with the Women's Institute. And—'

'But Rashleigh has more pubs than any other village in England,' interrupted Pandora.

'And the pub landlady has run off with one of the film crew who came to make a documentary about the village.'

'Dad, you're a victim of your own success.'

'And the Queen wants to make me a knight.'

Pandora sat down. 'You mean you'll get a K at last? That's fantastic news. It was only a matter of time.'

'It's for services to the British rubber industry, whatever that means,' he said gruffly but Pandora knew that he was thrilled to bits.

'So you'll have a title. Sir James Simpson. It sounds *wonderful*. And Davina will become—'

'Your stepmother is already a countess,' said James. 'It'll surprise your mother's family,' he chuckled to himself.

'First the Beatles, now you.'

'Your grandfather always said the country was going to the dogs. This will just confirm it for him.'

'Oh, I think he'll be delighted for you,' said Pandora doubtfully.

'And how is life in Andorra these days?' Lord and Lady Verney had recently moved to Andorra.

'Cheap.'

'Well, it's a sad old world,' said her father drily.

It certainly was odd the way things worked out, thought Pandora when she put down the telephone, but rather wonderful too. Her father had started off with nothing and now had the world at his feet, whereas her grandfather had begun life with everything and had lost it all. Nothing could be taken for granted. Money was so transitory, one moment you had it and the next it could just disappear into thin air.

Still, in many ways her grandparents' life was enviable. They adored one another, and Irma, who had never quite come to terms with leaving Sweden, was much happier in Andorra than in England. At least the place had snow in winter. Lord Verney was quite content provided he had a *Daily Telegraph*, a supply of Fortnum's Darjeeling tea, and twenty-four-hour access to the BBC World Service.

At the end of the day it all boiled down to love, mused Pandora idly. As long as one had that, one could probably cope with most things. Her father was a changed man since he had got together with Davina. His habitual world-weariness and cynicism had evaporated, and the sale of the business, which everyone had feared would destroy him, had been replaced by a multitude of new interests. Still, there were plenty of people who were happy who didn't have partners. Emily for example. And plenty of people who were as miserable as sin who did have them. Life was a mystery that way.

At eleven o'clock the following morning Pandora was flicking through the recesses of her wardrobe, eyebrows knitted together in concentration. What did one wear to lunch with a publisher? A power suit perhaps? She didn't have one. She pulled out her red Kookai suit. The skirt button had popped off and she hadn't had time to replace it yet. She'd just have to make do with a safety pin.

Her taxi drew up outside the small Italian restaurant in Shepherd's Market in Mayfair an unfashionable twenty minutes early but Pandora decided to go in and order a quick cappuccino before Emily arrived with the publisher, and practise looking cool and unflustered.

'Signorina! Allow me!' oozed a waiter, whose accent

owed more to Stepney Green than Naples, as he took her coat.

Half an hour later Emily appeared, followed by a tall woman in her early forties.

'We're so sorry we're late,' said Emily, kissing Pandora warmly. 'This is Mary, from Red Duck.'

'Hi there.' Mary extended a friendly hand. 'Hope we haven't kept you waiting too long, the traffic was backed up all the way down Shaftesbury Avenue.' The voice was unmistakably American.

'No, not at all,' replied Pandora. 'I always have plenty to read with me.' She brandished her well-thumbed copy of *Divorce! Magazine*.

'Pandora writes regularly for *Divorce!*,' said Emily.

'I know,' said Mary. 'I really like your work.'

'Do you?' Pandora tried not to sound too amazed. 'Actually, I've told them that I'm giving up nuisance journalism for a while to concentrate on more serious things, like writing a novel, but that was an excuse. I've been longing to give it up for ages.'

'I'm sure you're doing the right thing,' said Emily reassuringly. 'You've proved that you can make it in journalism now, and rightly or wrongly people are much more respectful of authors than journalists.'

'I know. When I tell people I'm writing a novel they melt but when I say I'm a journalist their eyes harden with suspicion. And yet they all buy newspapers.'

'Double standards, I'm afraid,' drawled Mary, lighting a cigarette and inhaling deeply. 'You don't mind if I smoke, do you?'

Pandora shook her head.

'The British are so tolerant, it's one of the reasons I love living here.'

'Mary used to work with Doubleday in New York,' explained Emily.

'Until the country became completely obsessed with this non-smoking thing,' interjected Mary. 'I wasn't even allowed to smoke in my own office.'

Pandora wondered when they could start talking about her novel, but Mary continued with her theme.

'If Britain goes the same way, I'll probably end up living in Cuba or somewhere. Shit food but at least the cigars are cheap.'

Their Caesar salads arrived and Mary became more serious. 'Emily may have mentioned that Red Duck would love to make an offer for your novel on the strength of the synopsis and the three chapters you've sent to us. I'd be your editor which means that I'll be kind of holding your hand through the whole process and suggesting any changes that need to be made.'

'Do you think I need to change very much?' asked Pandora, hoping she would reply, no, absolutely nothing.

Mary smiled and said, 'Well, the overall structure needs a bit of reorganization – we can discuss that at my office – but basically it's a great read. It's just the sort of thing I'm looking for at the moment.'

Pandora beamed with pleasure. 'Is it really?'

'Oh, definitely. It's light and funny, what I call a frothbuster.'

'A what-buster?' asked Pandora.

'A frothbuster means a romance with, um . . .' Emily hesitated.

'Hidden depths?' asked Pandora hopefully.

Mary looked a bit uneasy.

'Sort of,' smiled Emily.

'Well, the main thing is that it has lots of gold letters on the cover and is sold at airports,' said Pandora sensibly.

Mary visibly relaxed. 'That's right,' she beamed.

They talked about Pandora's ideas for the rest of her story and how the book might best be promoted. Remembering how for so long her friends and relations had all dismissed her dream of writing a novel, Pandora could hardly believe she was having a serious business lunch dedicated to discussing nothing else.

Emily had an appointment in Knightsbridge after lunch and shared a taxi home with Pandora.

'I really think we should go with Red Duck,' she said. 'Mary is the best editor I know, she's got a real instinct for what people will read. Are you happy with her?'

'Definitely,' said Pandora enthusiastically.

'I'll get her to draw up the contract. I'll go over it with you and we can go in and sign it next week. If you like you can get a lawyer to look it over as well. It'll be a pretty standard one, I should guess.'

It was all too good to be true, thought Pandora happily.

Late on Thursday night, just when she was convinced she would never hear from him again, Jack rang and left a message on her answering machine. Pandora carefully saved it and then decided not to return his call. Love was for wimps. She was crossing her fingers for his deal and that he had been able to raise the money in time, but having a relationship with him was too potentially difficult and would distract her from her work. This wasn't quite true – since meeting him she had been feeling unusually inspired, but she probably would have felt inspired anyway. She rewound his message and listened to him again. He really did have a lovely voice, she thought wistfully, saving it once again. 'Now you are trapped in my answering machine *for ever*!' God, she was going mad. It was all Jack's fault. She was becoming addicted to him, the same way a smoker was addicted to cigarettes and an alcoholic craved drink.

'I'm a Jackoholic!' She raced up the stairs a little unsteadily for she had spent the evening with Annabel and Rachel. Rachel was on a diet that forbade solids and was living on liquids for a week to give her digestive system 'a rest'. It was apparently perfectly all right to ingest large quantities of alcohol on this diet, and they had worked their way through the cocktail list, carefully avoiding solid things like the cherry garnishes. 'I feel marvellous, as if I've spent the week at a health farm!' Rachel had screeched, narrowly missing being run over in the Strand by a taxi. 'You stupid . . .' The taxi slowed down, its driver about to unleash a stream of invective at them. Pandora, whose celebrity radar was always finely tuned no matter how much she had drunk, recognized Pierce Brosnan in the back. Annabel and Rachel chanted, 'Pierce, Pierce, we love you,' and they started singing the James Bond theme tune very loudly, but by then the taxi driver had pulled away, fearing damage to his cab. By this time half the Strand had sensed that a celebrity was in its midst and was screaming and running towards the commotion. The three girls quickly hailed a cab and jumped into it before they were mobbed themselves.

'I don't know what you're getting so excited about,' Pandora said grumpily. 'He's far too thin.'

'Not every man can be beefy and bald, Pandora!' Rachel reminded her.

'Jack isn't bald. At least I don't think he is.' After three Bonk Me I'm Yours cocktails Pandora was finding it difficult to remember very much at all.

'If he's not bald now he soon will be by the time you've finished with him!' And Rachel and Annabel rolled around the cab, shrieking with laughter.

Pandora continued to look puzzled.

Rachel stared at her. 'You *have* bonked him, haven't you?'

'Emily says it's easier to get a book published these days than get laid,' said Annabel gloomily.

'That's true,' agreed Pandora. 'Did you ever hear from that glamorous Italian after he disappeared?'

Annabel had recently been wined and dined by an eligible Italian scion of a motoring dynasty who showed little inclination to move the relationship on to a more physical footing. Eventually managing to lure him home, he had passed out mid-snog on her expensively re-upholstered sofa and then disappeared out of the window in the middle of the night while she slept.

'No!'

'Men aren't what they used to be,' Rachel intoned, between hiccups. 'Mummy says it's the oestrogen in the tap water.'

Yes, it had been a good evening, thought Pandora, climbing into bed wearily. Thank God for girlfriends, without them to confuse reality even further she would go completely mad.

She was busy cleaning out a kitchen cupboard the following morning when the telephone rang. Damn. She removed her rubber gloves. What was the point of having a cordless phone if it was never there when you wanted it? She turned into the sitting room, located the phone under a pile of magazines and answered it.

'Not interrupting anything, am I?' drawled the familiar voice.

'No. I'm desperately looking for crumbs of inspiration in the back of my kitchen cupboards and having no luck at all,' said Pandora, sitting down on the floor. Jack was one of the few people she actually sat and talked to without doing anything else at the same time.

'Late night?' he inquired casually.

'Horribly late, I'm afraid. We were dancing and drinking till two in the morning.' She didn't elaborate on who 'we' might have been. Let him imagine the worst, it would do him good to think she was constantly in demand. 'But never mind about that, how's the fundraising going?'

'Well, we've scraped the money back together and put in our bid. I've got to give a presentation in a minute. Yet again,' he chuckled.

377

'You're a natural hustler, Jack.'

'A hustler! Yeah, I guess I am. I don't want to be, though. I just think I can turn that business round. It could be very exciting.'

'I've been reading this great book on positive thinking. You have to *know* that you're going to succeed right from the beginning and keep a picture in your mind of how you want everything to turn out. But I know you'll knock 'em dead, you're very persuasive, you know.'

'It's so good talking to you, Pandora, you always manage to say the right things.'

'Well, it's worked for me. Since I last saw you I've been offered a publishing contract for my novel.'

'Pandora! That's absolutely terrific! Listen, I've got to go, the meeting's about to start. Are you around at the weekend?'

'There are a few parties going on, but nothing particularly exciting.'

'I'll give you a ring tomorrow then.'

Pandora replaced the receiver in a deliriously happy mood. The sound of Jack's voice had blasted her hangover clean away. She pirouetted around the sitting room humming her favourite song of the moment. There was an unpleasant smell coming from somewhere and she pirouetted quickly into the kitchen. Her rubber gloves had melted all over the electric hob. But who could blame them? It wasn't just the gloves that were in a state of meltdown.

As she settled down to work, she realized that she

hadn't discussed the first edition of *Action!* as *Environment Today* had been rechristened, with Jack. It was due out in several weeks. She had gone to the magazine's offices on Wednesday and Sven had shown her how the layout was getting on. She'd been very impressed. Kate Twig had modelled for the cover and persuaded some of her supermodel friends to pose for a spread on fake fur bikinis and to reveal their most ecological beauty tips. Max Chister had been as good as his word and had persuaded the editor of the *Daily Mail* to run a fundraising campaign in tandem with *Action!* to raise money for the release of Maddie, a whale that had been performing tricks in a Florida aquarium for twenty years. There had been a real buzz and a sense of purpose in the scruffy offices. Pandora had a feeling that the magazine was going to be a tremendous success. It was so well put together and the articles so entertaining that even if people weren't remotely interested in the environment they would still want to read it. Then, having read it, there was always the chance that they might be inspired to do something. Jack was the catalyst who had made it all happen. It just went to show that it wasn't only tree huggers who cared; petrol-guzzling Porsche-driving entrepreneurs who refused to take public transport could create value too.

Jack didn't ring the next day. Pandora was getting used to the unreliable nature of their relationship. But she was determined to play him at his own game, reasoning that like most people he probably found the lure of the unattainable irresistible. Rich men in particular only valued the things they couldn't have. The trouble was, he had got under her skin. She thought about him all day and long into the night. Whereas she had always sneaked looks at men in the Ritzy Marina club gym, now she only glanced at them to compare them unfavourably with Jack. 'Huh, bet *they* wouldn't last long in the jungle,' she would mutter dismissively.

Pandora decided to give him until midday Saturday; if he hadn't rung by then it would be *too late!* After all, she might have hordes of men queuing up to take her out on a Saturday night. She might. There *were* men, but no one like Jack.

Twelve o'clock came and went, but by then she had glanced at the paper and seen that *The Great Escape* was on television and that after a tiring week she didn't want to go out after all. Nothing seemed more appealing than a delicious cheese soufflé followed by her last Swiss yogurt in front of the television and a long bath reading the latest issue of *Tatler*.

She was just whisking up some egg whites with a pinch of salt in a copper bowl while watching *Blind Date* (it was so important to use all of one's senses at the same time), when the phone went. It was Jack.

'D'you feel like having dinner with me at Blake's?'

'Oh, I'd love to, but I've been asked to a party. What a shame.'

'What time d'you think you'll be able to leave?'

'Ooh, probably around midnight.' This could get a bit confusing.

'Well, why don't you come round for a late drink

afterwards.' It was a statement not a question. 'I'm living here for a while while my flat's being redecorated.'

'God, you lucky thing.'

'Well, it's an open invitation. I'll see you later.'

'Perhaps, it sort of depends what time I leave the party,' lied Pandora cagily. Really. Who did he think she was? His beck and call girl?

Still, she thought, settling down to eat her perfectly risen soufflé in front of *The Great Escape*, it was nice to know that he had rung. But according to her bible of dating behaviour, *Hook Him!* he would have to learn that if he really wanted to see her she would need at least three days' notice. And if he wanted to see her on a Saturday, he would have to ring by Wednesday. Girls like her were in demand and spontaneity could only be taken so far.

Half an hour later the telephone went again. Sighing, she went to pick it up, dreading that it might be Jack, checking to see that she had really gone out. But it was Annabel, in a terrible state.

'You know I was going out with Russ tonight?'

Pandora didn't, but she said, 'Um, yes, I think so.'

'Well, he rang half an hour ago to say that he'd been unavoidably detained in Manchester at a rugby match and he couldn't make dinner. I've been cooking all day!' she wailed angrily.

'God, I'd be relieved if I were you. *The Great Escape*'s on the telly tonight. I mean Russ is very nice,' Pandora hesitated, 'but given the choice between having to cook dinner for him or drool over Steve McQueen biking over to Switzerland, well, let's just say I know which lap I'd rather plonk my bum in. Quick, turn on the telly, he's on now!!'

Both girls sat whooping to each other on the telephone, getting quite carried away. 'Oh, look, it's the Palace. Jack told me you could see it!' cried Pandora.

'I suppose this is what executives call a conference call,' said Annabel.

'It might be,' agreed Pandora. 'Well, I'm glad you sound a bit more cheerful. I think you should sit down and eat your delicious dinner and have a restful night.'

'But I hate eating alone. It seems . . . so sort of sad really.'

'That's probably why you're so lovely and slim,' said Pandora, looking at the remains of her delicious soufflé and wondering whether she had room for any more. 'I love staying in by myself, especially on Saturday nights. I'll be able to get up early tomorrow morning and be the first person in the swimming pool.'

Annabel groaned. 'But what about Jack? You were in love with him two days ago.'

'Yes, I know. He asked me out for dinner tonight but I said I was busy.'

'You're mad!'

'You're right, I'm crazy about him. It's just that I don't like the way he phones up out of the blue and expects me to be instantly available. Especially on a Saturday night. *Hook Him!* says one should never be available for a Saturday night date after Wednesday. I mean, what does he think I am, a social failure?'

'Bugger that,' said Annabel, who favoured the instantly

available school of dating. 'If everyone did what that book says the human race would be extinct.' She laughed. 'Poor man. He probably doesn't know if he's coming or going.'

At that moment Jack was driving past Pandora's flat on his way to the office. His new Porsche had been delivered and he had been looking forward to showing it to her. She would love it. He was very put out when she'd said she was busy. Hadn't she said she was free this weekend? Driving past her flat (well, it was sort of on the way) he noticed that her light was on and that her car was outside. He couldn't make her out. Was she playing hard to get, or was she just not that interested? And at the end of the day, was it really worth the trouble?

The collapse of his marriage had hardened something in Jack. He had loved Atlanta, and her erratic behaviour and the ensuing breakdown of their relationship had devastated him. Even now, when they had been separated for over a year, he still found it impossible to get really close to a woman. But Pandora was different from the other girls he had gone out with. Despite her openness and vivacity there was an intriguing coolness about her and he wondered if she had ever really loved anyone. He remembered how after they had made love she had cut off, retreating into herself. If they had been in London she would probably have put her clothes on and shoved off home! He smiled to himself wrily. Only men were meant to do that. He'd certainly done it enough times in the last year. He wasn't proud of himself, but it was as if by hurting someone else he could offload some of his own hurt. It hadn't worked; he had just felt even worse. He'd sworn not to get involved with another woman for as long as possible. He felt so dried up inside that there was very little to give to a relationship anyway. And work was so absorbing. But then Pandora had come along when he had least wanted to meet anyone. In many ways she was perfect for him, she had her own life, was independent and had lots of other friends. She didn't pester him or demand his time. Sometimes he wished she would – she was so damn elusive! Trying to have a relationship with her was like playing a game of chess.

Women! Christ, who needed any of it? He turned his car round and decided to let off steam on the M4. He was longing to put the car through its paces and driving fast always helped him think. The last few days had been stressful but productive. Everything was back on track and he felt quietly confident that his offer would be accepted and the company become his.

Stopping for petrol, he bought a sandwich and a cup of coffee. Traffic was crawling out of town because of roadworks so drinking it wouldn't be a problem. He was just wrestling with the sandwich wrapper when Tom rang on his car phone.

'If you're not doing anything tomorrow, why don't you come down and see us? You haven't been down for ages.'

Tom lived with his wife and two children in an exquisite manor house in Kent. He had the sort of life that Jack had once dreamt of sharing with Atlanta. They had even gone so far as to look at country houses, but it was just as well it had never materialized. He couldn't see Atlanta in the country somehow; the idea had appealed to her but she would have been bored out of her mind in a week.

'I'd love to, there are a few things we need to discuss before next week. Besides, I need to get out of London. Been getting a bit bogged down in stuff recently.'

'God, Jack, not another woman?' Tom followed Jack's complicated love life with a mixture of exasperation and humour.

'I should be so lucky!' laughed Jack. The traffic had thinned out and he put his foot down, taking a slug of coffee at the same time.

'Well, if you'd like to bring anyone down, they'd be more than welcome.'

Jack glanced into his mirror and noticed a police car flashing at him. 'Shit. Tom, I've got to go. I'm being flagged down by the bloody fuzz.'

He pulled over. A very young policeman got out of his car, eyeing up Jack's brand new Porsche with a mixture of envy and dislike. He'd enjoy throwing the book at this one.

'Did you know that it is illegal to speak into a mobile telephone while driving a motor vehicle, sir?' he asked, peering into the Porsche and taking in the black leather upholstery and the state-of-the-art music system. The alloy wheels didn't help his mood either. 'Looks like you forgot the blonde. Thought one of those always came with the motor.'

Jack said nothing; if he did he might thump the little shit.

'I'm afraid I am going to have to book you for jumping a red light, speaking into a mobile telephone and drinking a cup of coffee while driving at a speed of one hundred and ten miles an hour.'

'Christ, is that all? I thought I was going much faster,' said Jack.

'I'd like you to step out of the car and breathe into this. You have the right to remain silent but anything you say . . .' The policeman was enjoying himself immensely.

Jack got out of his car and stood, towering over the policeman. The urge to thump him was very strong.

The policeman began to feel nervous. Jack was a foot taller than he was and he'd bet he didn't get that broken nose judging bake the cake competitions.

Jack remembered asking Pandora, 'Shall I be nice or nasty to the merchant bankers?' 'Be nice,' she had advised. 'Remember even they love their children.' The policeman only looked about fourteen, he probably didn't have any children. Perhaps he loved his mother.

Jack blew into the Breathalyzer. He hadn't been drinking and it was negative.

As soon as the formalities had been dealt with, Jack drove off, breathing a sigh of relief despite the threat of losing his licence hanging over him. He'd nearly given that copper a real hiding.

He rang Tom.

'Tom. It's me. Some bastard copper has gone and booked me for speeding.'

'Christ, man, you didn't hit him, did you?' Tom had

had to bail Jack out once before and didn't relish the thought of doing it again.

'No. It would have been the best thing that had happened to the little Nazi in ten years if I had though.'

'Thank God for that. I don't know if you can bid for a company while you're standing trial for GBH.'

'You can back home.'

'Yeah, well, they're much more civilized about these things in South Africa. So we'll see you for lunch tomorrow. And if you'd like to bring someone, feel free.'

'I might, if it's not a problem.' He'd ask Pandora to come along. Tom and Samantha would love her.

When he returned to Blake's there was a message waiting for him from Pandora, saying she had been detained and couldn't make it that evening. He scrumpled up the piece of paper irritably and went into the bar to have a brandy. No doubt Pandora was having a ball somewhere, surrounded by admirers. Well, who could blame the poor sods? She was gorgeous, and funny and nice. It would be fun driving down to the country with her in the Porsche. He'd ring her first thing.

As Jack was sipping his second brandy and discussing the failings of the English cricket team with the barman, Pandora was unavoidably detained in her bathroom, surrounded by scented foam and avidly reading a gripping article about luxury travel for single people, entitled 'She travels fastest who travels alone'. Maybe when she'd finished her novel she should just take off somewhere, cruise around the Arctic or walk across the Israeli desert . . . And then she thought of Jack and sighed, wishing she was seeing him later after all. Being his beck and call girl suddenly seemed a very enticing prospect. She shut her eyes for a moment, imagining being wrapped up in his big arms. But it was too late now, she couldn't change her mind again. He'd think she was horribly indecisive. Maybe he was right. It was so hard to make up one's mind about such matters.

At 7 a.m. Pandora leapt out of bed, flung on her bathing costume and her favourite leggings and jumped into the car. At this early hour she had London all to herself. She roared down the deserted Fulham Road, relishing the empty streets. She switched on a Kate Bush tape and screeched along to it. One particular song always made her want to weep, it was so wistfully romantic. Her mind turned automatically to Jack. Why was he so inconsistent? Taking her away for lovely weekends, then not ringing her for days. She was pleased that he had rung last night, but her pleasure was tainted by the uneasy feeling that he had left ringing her to the last minute again. Surely if he liked her as much as she liked him he would think ahead more? What on earth did he want? More to the point, what did *she* really want?

Two sybaritic hours later, having swum, had a sauna and a blissful read of the Sunday newspapers, she slipped out of the club, past the crowd of harassed parents and children who were forbidden entry until 10 a.m. After this time the club was uninhabitable to child-free members. The television channels were switched from CNN to the cartoon network and the swimming pool became crowded with excitable infants peeing in the water.

Pandora shuddered at the thought that one day she, too, might become A Parent. She imagined foregoing her early-morning swims and silent perusal of the newspapers and having to play noisy water games instead. It didn't bear thinking about. But wasn't that what happened when you fell in love with someone? After the passionate, cosy dinners you became 'a couple'. You looked at sofas together in the Conran Shop on Sunday mornings, you got married, had a baby, bought a Renault Espace to transport the infant around, did 'big shops' at Sainsbury . . . Could she do that? Was falling in love just a biological ruse for perpetuating the species, selling more Renault Espaces and keeping supermarkets in business?

She made herself a cup of tea and settled down to work, turning towards the window and refreshing her face in the early morning breeze rippling through the bare branches of the trees below. She didn't know what had come over her recently; normally she had to make at least three pots of tea and five nuisance calls before she could settle down. Now she couldn't stay away from her computer. Her novel was rattling away. If she was dating someone she'd never work at weekends. She'd be too busy *shopping* at the Conran Shop.

She wrote feverishly for an hour, and then stretched out her arms, wondering idly what Jack was doing. Gorgeous unattainable man, the perfect romantic hero . . .

The phone rang.

'Are you busy?'

'Well, I'm vaguely writing.' Pandora held the receiver tightly, it was so good to hear his voice. 'How are you?'

'Not bad, considering. I got booked for speeding last night. I'm rather afraid they'll take away my licence.'

'Oh God, you poor thing! You'll need a *chauffeuse*. You can employ me when I've finished my novel. I like travelling.'

'Unfortunately, chauffeurs need to know how to change a wheel and read a map,' Jack said drily.

'Well, I guess that rules me out then. I was reading about South Africa in the paper today. A top government minister has just admitted shooting twenty people and he's outraged that somebody wants to send him to prison—'

'But he was only cleaning his gun, you can't be too tough on the guy.'

Pandora laughed delightedly, she loved it when Jack was in one of his *brutal* moods.

'I was wondering if you wanted to drive down to Kent. Some friends of mine have asked me for lunch.'

'You mean they're a couple?' asked Pandora dubiously.

'Yup, they've been married five years and have two kids.'

'When I was married I lived in the country. It was pretty horrible but I think I've blanked out the worst bits – you know, like when you have a baby you forget the pain. But some things I'll never forget.' She shuddered.

'Like what?'

'Growing vegetables. The local library – they hadn't bought any new books for twenty years. And I'll never forget the night when my husband came back from work with two tickets for the golf club dinner. Since I got divorced and sold the house, I haven't been back to the country on principle. I'd love to come with you but I've actually got to work today. Emily wants my next chunk by tomorrow. By the way, how's the deal going?'

'We're just waiting to see if our bid's been accepted.'

'So things have gone to plan despite Lord Douche.'

'Despite Lord Douche.'

'I once had a big crush on his lordship's right-hand man, Daniel Snog-Option. He used to play golf with John and date MTV presenters. I thought he was the great love of my life.'

'And what happened?'

'Well, we had a few dates and then I went off him.'

'Has anyone ever told you that you're very fickle?' said Jack.

'Yes. All the time. But it was just as well I did go off him. I think he was using me to get close to my father who was selling his company. I read recently that Daniel's father, Merve, lost a lot of money from diversifying into rubber fan belts. He even had to sell his white Rolls. Pretty tragic really,' said Pandora cheerfully.

'I've had a few run-ins with Daniel – what's his real name?'

'Snodstein.'

'Of course. You can't forget a name like that.'

'I know. But Snog-Option suits him much better. He's just got engaged to Lord Douche's daughter, Daphne. Have you met her?'

'God, yes. Old Daffy Douche! Reckon Daniel's got his

work cut out with her. Still, at least he'll get the bank. He's pretty smart.'

'She's not that bad, is she?' asked Pandora.

'No, she's not *that* bad. She's got thick ankles though.'

'How awful,' said Pandora, examining her ankles nervously. 'Jack?'

'Yes?'

'Have you seen my ankles yet?'

'Of course. I checked them out the first time I saw you. Ankles are *very* important, and yours are superb.'

'Are they?' Pandora looked at hers with renewed respect. 'Thank you very much.'

'So were you involved with your father's business before he sold it?'

'Apart from being fired from the switchboard, you mean? Well, only through hearing him talk about it, and he never talked about anything else really. It ruled our lives when I was growing up, and since then I've always found business rather intriguing. That's why I'm so thrilled with what you're doing. You're taking risks and really creating something new from scratch. It's very brave. You could just sit in a bank all day and lend brave people money that doesn't belong to you and then drive around in a Porsche the rest of the time.'

'Sounds just like my first job. But you told me you liked Porsches.'

'I do, specially the new one that's just come out.'

'That's a coincidence. I just bought one.'

'Great!' said Pandora enthusiastically. 'Is it like the one we drove in Switzerland?'

'Identical.'

'But I thought you couldn't buy it in England yet.'

'Well, let's just say I—'

'Tried every means of persuasion before being forced to—'

'*No!*'

'Bet you did.'

'No, I didn't!'

'How did you get your broken nose? Hospital visiting?'

'Someone was hassling Atlanta at JFK airport. I stepped in and thumped the guy and then I asked her for her telephone number.'

'How romantic. But you must have been in agony if you had a broken nose.'

'You should have seen the other guy.'

'Did you kill him?'

'No!'

'It was very chivalrous of you to wade in and help her.'

'Yeah. But I might not have bothered if she hadn't had such great ankles.'

'I expect she was very grateful to you.'

'She was even more grateful when I upgraded her to first class.'

'I wish my husband had done something like that.' She thought hard. 'But he was very good at mending things.' She didn't want Jack to think that she had married a total loser. 'But when he threatened to sue me I realized I'd have been better off staying single and keeping a plumber on permanent retainer.'

'I can't get over you having to tip him. It's terrible.'

'Well, he could have cost me a lot more. Mummy's had a terrible time getting rid of all her husbands. She's hardly got any money left now and things are so bad she's even been considering getting a job.'

'My God. Not *a job*! I didn't realize things were that bad.'

'Well, she might be able to hang on for a bit longer. You see, she's not really qualified to do anything very lucrative.' Pandora remembered her mother's performance in Harrods' cruisewear department. 'She's very good at shopping though.'

Jack laughed. 'I'd better make a move now, I'm still lying in bed. Can I take you out to dinner tomorrow?'

'Um, yes, tomorrow would be fine.'

'OK. I'll ring you tomorrow morning and fix something up.'

Why couldn't he fix it up now? She sighed, replacing the receiver. But it had been *wonderful* to talk to him, she thought happily, wandering into the kitchen and stacking her phone in the dishwasher along with her breakfast things, just wonderful. She couldn't *wait* until tomorrow night!

The following morning Pandora was typing up a poem about Jack that she had written during the night when the telephone went. She hunted round the kitchen anxiously before discovering it in the dishwasher. It was Annabel.

'Hey, I've got some *shagtastic* news!'

Pandora cringed, this could only mean one thing: Annabel was about to insist she attend some Godawful party with her.

'I've got a spare ticket for the Ritzy Marina club's Very Early Christmas Party so you can come along.'

'But it's only the beginning of October.'

'Oh, don't go chronological on me, darling, members get very booked up around Christmas. We're talking about the social *crème de la crème*, after all.'

'I'd really like to come, but my romantic disinterest is *meant* to be taking me out tonight. He said he'd confirm this morning, but he's so hopeless I don't know if he will.'

'Why don't you ring him then?'

'Oh, I couldn't!'

'Why ever not? We are living in the twentieth century, you know.'

'Look, I've got an idea. If I haven't heard from him by five o'clock this evening, I'll come along with you if you haven't got rid of the ticket. OK?'

'It's a done deal,' said Annabel cheerfully.

Five o'clock came and went. Pandora had been so looking forward to seeing Jack that she could hardly bear it. Still, she wasn't going to stay in and be pathetic about it, she may as well go out with Annabel and be pathetic about it in public.

Annabel raced round to Pandora's flat immediately for a consoling glass of champagne before they set off. Three glasses later life suddenly seemed much rosier.

'Being in love is so *deliciously painful*. Annabel?' Pandora paused dramatically. 'I've decided I might want to be the Mother of his Children.'

Annabel groaned.

'I had a mystic realization in Zurich about it. We were

standing looking over the lake, snow was falling and Jack had his hand around my neck in a vice-like grip then—'

The phone rang.

'The phone's ringing!' The girls stood transfixed, dazzled like rabbits in a car's headlights.

'Where is it?'

'Where's what?' asked Annabel.

'The phone!' Pandora began to search desperately behind the sofa. 'It's one of those cordless ones. Last night I put it in the dishwasher by mistake after I spoke to him. Oh dear, I can't remember where I put it. It might be *him*!'

The answerphone clicked into action and the caller hung up.

'Here it is!' cried Annabel from the kitchen.

'Where was it?'

'In the fridge. Quick, call 1471 and find out who it was.'

Pandora punched in the numbers. 'Agony! They don't have the caller's number. Now I'll never know if Jack loved me or not!' she sighed. Pisceans were meant to be absent-minded but this was getting ridiculous.

Stimulated by the drama and fortified by champagne, the girls jumped into a taxi.

'Damn!' said Pandora. 'I've left my swimming things at home.'

'They'll have shut the pool, they always do when they have parties.'

They lapsed into silence for five seconds.

'Annabel? Why don't we drive to Monte Carlo in my car? I can write about it in my novel. What d'you think?'

'But what about your romantic interest? Won't the mind?'

'Disinterest,' Pandora corrected her. 'I shouldn't think he'd care if I lived or died.'

The taxi pulled up outside the club and they joined the stream of sequined members making their way into the building.

Within ten seconds, Pandora had seen five people she had been trying to avoid all year. Annabel was snapped up by her doubles partner and Pandora decided to do a runner. On the way out, she bumped into Daniel.

'Pandora! How are you? How's your father?' Daniel hadn't changed a bit, still as good-looking as ever. But he had zero sex appeal. How could she *ever* have fancied him?

'He's about to get a knighthood. How's yours?'

'Business hasn't been so good recently.'

'I'm sorry to hear that. Maybe he should try Andorra. My grandparents moved there after Lloyd's and they're having a great time. By the way, I hear you're engaged to Daphne Douch – I mean Dougall. Congratulations.'

'Oh, thanks. I'll send you an invite to the engagement party. We're holding it on Lord Dougall's estate in Hampshire, should be quite a do.'

'I'd love to come. By the way,' continued Pandora with studied casualness, 'have you run into someone called, um, Jack Dudley at work? A friend of mine rather likes him but he seems to have quite a bad reputation.'

'Christ, yes. I know Dudley. We were going to give him the finance for some company he wants to buy but we decided to pull out. He's not the sort of person we're used to doing business with.'

'Why not?'

'He's a bit of a rough diamond, to put it mildly. His ways of doing business are a little unconventional. And he's a bit flash, the sort of person who would drive a brand new Porsche,' Daniel shuddered, 'and he makes incomprehensible jokes.' He looked at her closely, he had always been able to read her like a book. 'Friend, my foot. He's your latest victim, isn't he? Now everything is fitting into place. A mate from the office spotted him at Heathrow with a, and I quote, "mystery blonde with legs up to her armpits".' Pandora looked alarmed. Who had Jack been lurking around airports with? Beastly man! 'Hey, don't look worried, it's a compliment,' said Daniel.

'But who is this woman?' asked Pandora bleakly.

'Well, the description sounds just like you. I bet you're his type. Great hair, great legs . . .' He was glancing disconcertingly over her shoulder into the heaving sequinned throng at the bar. 'Pandora, I must just say hello to Jamie Robertson. He runs a computer software company that I'm thinking of investing in. Send my regards to your father.' His stiff, besuited figure was soon lost in the crowd and Pandora smiled to herself. Good old Daniel, he had quite cheered her up. Marrying for money must really agree with him.

When Pandora arrived home the first thing she did was check her answering machine. It wasn't on. She must have accidentally switched it off somehow before she left. Someone had rung at 7.30 p.m. but 1471 refused to divulge their identity.

Right, that was it. Running into Daniel had been a mystic

sign. How could she take her infatuations seriously? She had been so in love with him and now he meant nothing to her. She thought she was madly in love with Jack, but who knew what she would be feeling tomorrow? But it was hard to be logical when she couldn't stop thinking about him, when the sound of his voice made her knees tremble and the memory of his body on hers was so blissfully etched into her mind. It was disturbing to lose control of her emotions in this way. Still, it seemed as though everyone went through it at least once. When she next saw Jack, *if* she ever saw him again, she would casually explain that neither of them had the time for any sort of relationship and that it was best to stop seeing each other for a while. But how could they stop seeing each other when they never saw each other anyway?

Pandora didn't know if Jack was responsible, but since she had met him something seemed to have fundamentally changed within her. The wall around her heart that had existed since childhood, providing a barrier against real emotional involvement with anyone, seemed to be melting away. On the one hand it made her feel quite vulnerable, but on the other it was somehow helping her to tap into a great reservoir of human feeling that at its highest level expressed itself so beautifully in literature and music. There were so many different types of love one felt for friends, family and lovers, but until now she had just been skating the surface and not really *feeling* anything. It was almost as if someone had come along and tuned her in, changing her vision from black and white to colour. Her writing reflected this and had developed depth and intensity. Perhaps she was at last ready to write a book that included every flavour that life had to offer.

Meeting Jack had been an interesting experience. She had dipped her toe into the great reservoir and now she thought she would remove it. A glimpse of what it had to offer was enough for the moment. He had been too badly hurt himself to offer her anything and she knew it was best to get out of the whole thing now before she lost the use of her legs as well as the use of her mind.

That was that sorted, she thought sensibly, and having rationalized the irrational and applied logic where only intuition would do, she fell contentedly to sleep.

Chapter Nineteen

In the weeks that followed Pandora tried to lock her feelings away in an iron grip. But it was no good, they kept gushing out whatever she did. Cheerfully listening to the radio in the car, she would hear a song that reminded her of Jack and tears would suddenly spill from her eyes. Oddly enough, she quite enjoyed these outpourings of emotion, revelling in the drama and the indulgence of giving in to her feelings. The heroine in her novel was going through agonizing romantic trials and Pandora was able to explore her real-life situation through her eyes. Was this virtual reality? Was she using Jack just so she could write about him?

She discussed the situation with Annabel during one of their irregular lunchtime tennis sessions. Very little tennis was ever played, and sometimes Pandora thought it would be more sensible to just meet for lunch instead. But they both agreed that they would miss wearing their decorative tennis dresses too much to give up the game completely.

'D'you like my new tennis knickers?' asked Annabel as they stood chatting energetically at the net. She flicked up her micro skirt revealing a frilly pair of knickers studded with pink rosebuds that matched her rosebud appliqué socks perfectly.

'I love them, they're deliciously *sportif*. Where did you find them?' asked Pandora enviously.

'In the Horrids' sportswear department. And you'll never guess who I spotted in the ski-wear section.'

'Who?'

'Jack Dudley!'

All pretence at playing tennis was abandoned.

'And he was with *a woman*!' Annabel paused for dramatic impact.

'What sort of woman?' asked Pandora, feverishly.

'I think it may have been his wife. I recognized her from *Divorce! Magazine*.'

'What did she look like in the flesh?'

'Sort of waif-like. I was with Peregrine, he couldn't stop drooling at her. I had to drag him away before we were spotted.'

'You don't think he's still in love with her, do you?' asked Pandora, frowning.

'I don't know. He seems pretty keen on you.'

'But what did their body language reveal?'

'I think she was keener on him. He was frowning a lot.'

Pandora thought for a moment. This dramatic news added a whole new slant to things, she was looking forward to mulling it over later in great detail.

'I can't imagine going shopping with my ex-husband. I think it's all very odd.'

'Talking of husbands, I think John's still in love with you, you know.'

'Ugh, how boring. Everyone's in love with the wrong people. It's a miracle anyone ever gets together at all when you think about it. D'you think Jack does like me?' asked Pandora.

'Of course. But you're making it very difficult for him. He probably thinks you don't like him very much. After all, every time he asks you out you say you're busy.'

'I just don't want him to think I'm too keen.'

'Not much chance of that. I think you should ring him and ask him to the theatre or something.'

'But neither of us likes the theatre. The seats are too small for him.'

'Ask him to the cinema then! I think you're just making excuses. Perhaps you don't really want a relationship. You seem to be sabotaging this one before it's begun.'

'I don't want anything too heavy, but I wouldn't mind going out with someone who travels a lot and lets me live my own life. And I wouldn't want to go to the Conran Shop every Sunday morning with him.'

'God! I don't think you know what you want. I feel sorry for Jack. Perhaps he knows you wouldn't come so he had to take his wife shopping instead.' Pandora looked doubtful. 'I love looking around the Conran Shop with boyfriends at the weekend,' Annabel continued, 'then wandering across the road to Joe's Cafe for lunch, holding hands . . .' She looked mistily into the distance.

'Yuck and double yuck,' said Pandora. 'Oh good, our hour's up now, we can go and have a drink. I'm worn out.'

They packed up their state-of-the-art tennis kit and left the court.

'I'm thinking of going to Abu Dhabi for six months,' said Annabel once they were installed at the bar. 'There's a chance I might be able to do some PR for a sheik that Peregrine knows. The money's fantastic and it's really not very far when you think about it. Guess how many hours away it is on the plane?'

'About five?'

'Ten. I mean, it's nothing when you think about it.'

'But ten hours is ages away!'

'Yes. Well, I think I need a change of scene.'

'It would be rather an adventure. I wonder if we're both so restless because we're tigers. D'you think we'll ever settle down?'

'I hope so,' said Annabel, 'but maybe not just yet.' She sipped her cappuccino thoughtfully. 'If all the Chinese horoscopes were rearranged and you and I became, say, chickens or goats or dogs, do you think our personalities would change?'

'You mean would we turn into a couple of old dogs overnight? Probably. But the Chinese wouldn't make a mistake like that. After all, Jack's an Aries dragon, there's no way he could become something like a . . . a . . .'

'Soup dragon?'

'Exactly. It would be quite impossible.'

*　　*　　*

Pandora spent the next few days wallowing blissfully in the agonies of unrequited love, convincing herself that Jack loved his wife and she would never see him again. The situation had all the poignancy of *Brief Encounter*, *The Go-Between* and *Casablanca* rolled into one. 'It's excruciating!' she would say to friends on the telephone, and she frequently found herself bursting into tears at traffic lights. So it came as a bit of a shock when Jack rang her on Friday morning.

After trying to call her at seven thirty on Monday, Jack had finally ended up having dinner with some of his backers which had been very useful. And since then work had been so frantic and Atlanta had been giving him so much aggro that he hadn't been able to get his head round the thought of seeing Pandora as well. But the weekend stretched ahead, and with it the promise of escaping from the office for at least a day. There was nothing he felt more like doing than having a quiet chatty dinner and catching up on all her bizarre news; it would be like a breath of fresh air after the interminable week he'd had.

'Hello,' said Pandora, picking up the telephone. No one answered but she knew it was Jack because of the crackling.

'Jack? Can you hear me?'

The crackling mercifully died down. 'Pandora, how's it going?'

'Oh, I'm bearing up, thank you.'

'That good? Shit, I'm about to go into a tunnel . . .' The phone went dead.

Pandora put down the telephone with a sigh of exasperation. Really, she'd heard of people being elusive, but Jack was one step beyond that. The phone rang again.

'Sorry about that. Will you have dinner with me tonight?'

Pandora thought carefully. She had planned to go late-night shopping and treat herself to an egg and cress sandwich and a perfectly formed cappuccino at Prêt à Manger afterwards. Why couldn't Jack ever give her more notice? Still, she was longing to see him so much her knees were aching.

'I'm not sure, I'd arranged to go late-night shopping,' she said doubtfully.

'Oh, is that all?'

'How do you know that late-night shopping isn't the highlight of my week?' Pandora joked. Late-night shopping followed by an egg sandwich really was the highlight of her week, but Jack didn't need to know that.

He chuckled. 'I'll pick you up later. I want to find out how your novel's going.'

'Oh, all right then,' said Pandora cheerfully. The line started crackling. 'Jack, Jack, are you still there? What time will you—' The line went dead again. Damn. She would have rung him back but she'd lost his car phone number. It seemed that if she wanted to see him it would have to be on his terms or not at all. This was one relationship over which she had no control. It was *maddeningly* addictive.

At 9 p.m. he still hadn't rung. She felt torn between feelings of disappointment, anger and worry. What if there had been an accident? Rain was beating down against the windows and the candles flickered in the draught. She kept meaning to change the lightbulb but she quite liked the long shadows cast by the candles. Sitting down at her computer, she tried to draft a features idea she was working on, but she was too distracted. The phone lay, inert and useless on the floor beside her.

She switched off her computer. It was hopeless, she just couldn't focus on work. Lighting the gas fire, she stood back as the flames leapt high into the air, mesmerized as they danced and flickered in the grate. She knew what she should do. When, if Jack eventually arrived, she would tell him that whatever passed for their relationship was over. She could probably just about walk away now; if she left it any longer she would probably turn into an emotional cripple. It was pathetic.

When the phone rang half an hour later, it was Annabel. Pandora gave a brief recap.

'God, men are so unreasonable,' Annabel commiserated. 'But cheer up, I've got a riveting snippet of gossip for you. Last night I went to a party and met a man who works with a girl who went out with Jack just after he left Atlanta. Apparently, when they split up this girl completely went to pieces and had a nervous breakdown. No one could believe it, she was drop-dead gorgeous *and* held down a brilliant job. She could have had any man she wanted.'

'Annabel, this is a *fascinating* piece of undercover research. Why did he dump her?'

'Apparently she just got too keen. The poor girl would

phone him up twenty times a day and was terribly jealous. She once threw a gin and tonic over him at a drinks party.'

Pandora's call waiting signal beeped in. 'I've got to go, Annabel, it'll probably be the monster himself.'

It was. 'I've just left a meeting in the . . . went on hours longer . . . I'm so sorry.' His voice faded in and out on his mobile phone. He sounded distracted and tired.

'Have you had a nightmare day?' asked Pandora.

'The worst. Shit, and the traffic is backed up for miles.'

Pandora's heart sank. She wondered if she ought to cancel the evening before he did.

'Perhaps we ought to forget tonight if you're tired,' she said.

'No, I'd like to see you. I'm literally round the corner now anyway. I'll take you to Blake's.' She could hear the bleak sound of rain against his car window and the rhythmic wipe of his windscreen washers in the background.

Five minutes later the door bell went. She switched off the fire, grabbed her bag and went downstairs to meet him.

Once they were sitting in the discreetly lit bar, Pandora took a deep breath.

'I've been thinking that perhaps we should stop seeing each other.'

Jack's tired face paled beneath his tan.

'I mean, you've got such a lot on your plate and you haven't got time for any distractions at the moment. You should be at home now, catching up on some sleep, not drinking champagne with me.'

'But why? We get on so well,' replied Jack, looking puzzled.

If Pandora had been honest she would have said, 'Because every time you touch me I melt inside, because I'm starting to do pathetic things like saving all your messages on my answerphone just so I can hear your voice, because I'm falling in love with you and the thought of losing you makes me shrivel up inside.' But she just shrugged and said, 'Well, it just seems that it's bad timing for both of us. I need to be single for my work, you're caught up with the business.'

'Look, I know I haven't been able to see you as much as I'd like.' He paused for a moment and looked away from her. 'It's no consolation, I guess, but I've been so wrapped up with work and the divorce and everything. You're lucky for me, you know.'

'Yes, but you were born lucky anyway,' she replied.

'Lucky to have met you.' He laughed softly, fiddling with his signet ring. 'Or maybe unlucky.' He pulled off the ring and slipped it on to her middle finger. It was too small so he put it on her ring finger. It fitted perfectly. She fingered it absently then handed it back. 'I don't think we should stop seeing one another.'

Pandora agreed with him. In fact, she had caved in immediately when she saw how seriously he was taking her threat, but she was enjoying seeing him sweat.

'Stay here with me tonight.' He caressed her hair.

Under the circumstances, refusal was quite impossible but she thought she'd say no for the hell of it.

'I don't think that's a very good idea, Jack,' she responded primly.

'I think it's the best idea I've had all day.'

'But . . .' It was impossible to speak coherently as Jack was winding her hair irresistibly around his fingers.

'No buts,' said Jack, kissing her. 'Come on, little one, time for bed.' He pulled her to her feet.

'Oh, all right then,' she tried not to sound too eager, 'just to check your mini bar.'

They wandered out of the bar into a scented courtyard. White jasmine gleamed in the moonlight and ivy spilled out of pots, brushing against Pandora's legs. But she barely felt it, her skin was numb to everything but the feel of Jack's hand resting on the back of her neck. His door was hidden behind a mass of foliage. As they entered, a breeze rippled through the airy room, lifting the flimsy white muslin draped over the four-poster bed and making the strings of seashells hanging from the ceiling shiver. The sound reminded her of Hawaii.

'I love this room, it reminds me of my house in Hawaii,' Jack was saying, dropping his key on the mother-of-pearl bedside table and scooping Pandora up in his arms and kissing her. The dreamlike quality of the room had dissolved her inhibitions and she felt herself instinctively melt into him as he littered her body with kisses.

'I love you in this dress,' he murmured, peeling it from her so that it fell like a silken pool at her feet.

Reaching out, she tried to turn off the bedroom lamp.

'Leave it,' he commanded. 'I want to see your face when you come.'

The combination of his weight and scent and the way he touched her in all the places she longed to be touched made her climax immediately. He seemed to know her body so well, it was like an extension of his own; everything she did to him and everything he did for her was just what the other wanted.

Eventually, overcome with exhaustion, they fell asleep, melted together like spoons in the darkness, Jack's arm resting lightly on Pandora's shoulder. But as the night drifted towards dawn, his arm slipped on to her neck causing her to wake with a terrified start. Used to freedom of movement in her big bed at home, she felt trapped. Jack slept soundly beside her. She shut her eyes but sleep proved elusive. Besides, she was dying to go to the loo. She glanced at Jack. His face looked peaceful and untroubled. Asleep, he looked years younger, almost boyish. It was a treat just to look at him, to trace every feature with her eyes, and to engrave every detail of his face on her memory for ever. She was getting cramp. Slowly she got out of bed, slipping on her mac and gathering up her clothes. Turning the door handle stealthily, she took one last glance around the room. The diaphanous white muslin curtains and the strings of seashells shivered in the draught and the wooden floorboards shone in the early morning light. An arrangement of white lilies in the corner gave the room a heavy, sensuous scent. Everything was simple and elegant. In that one glance she was transported to Hawaii; instead of the distant murmur of traffic she could almost hear the wind chimes and the roar of the sea.

Jack opened a bleary eye and watched her as she stood thoughtfully at the door. Her hair was tousled and her make-up was faintly smudged; he couldn't imagine waking up to anything lovelier.

'Where on earth are you going?'

Pandora's hand rested on the door knob, the other clutched her shoes. 'I've got to go. I'm on a schedule.' It was one of her favourite Americanisms. Besides, it was true; she wanted to go swimming.

Before he could respond, she opened the door and slipped into the garden. She stood for a moment, inhaling the heady scent of jasmine and listening to the birdsong. In the cold misty dawn the garden was still and lovely, dew clung to its foliage and Pandora had the feeling that if she remained still for long enough she might see a fairy darting about in the undergrowth. Shivering, she wrapped her mac tightly round her naked body and slipped on her shoes, slinking out of the hotel and into the street. Her shoes echoed on the deserted pavement and a milk float drove slowly past. She smiled, feeling deliciously sluttish. This was sin! This was life! She could have been wrapped up in Jack's arms right now but she had chosen to escape. If I had stayed in bed a moment longer, she told herself sternly, I might have fallen asleep and woken up *shopping* in the Conran Shop.

Although she no longer attended editorial meetings – nothing could ever live up to the first she had attended –

Pandora was still enthusiastically involved with *Action!*. She had agreed to submit an article every month and contribute ideas for features which she no longer had time to write now that she was working full time on her novel.

Her determination for its success was growing steadily; for the first time in her life she had the bit between her teeth and *nothing* was going to stop her. She began to leave her answering machine on during the day so that she could write undisturbed, resenting anything that took her away from her computer for long periods. It was almost as if she was scared that once she stopped she might never be able to start again, and her deadline, which had once seemed so far away, started to loom ominously close.

'If only I could escape to a desert island for three months,' she complained to Emily one day over lunch. 'There seem to be so many distractions here, either the phone's going or something's breaking down. Like today. I spent the whole morning just mopping up water in the kitchen because the washing machine is leaking again. My downstairs neighbour is having a fit because it's dripping on to her bed and this is the second time it's happened. Tomorrow I have to get my car fixed and I've got to get my car residential permit sorted out which will mean six days standing in a queue—'

'Before being told that you've left a relevant document at home, like your water bill or smallpox vaccination certificate or something equally vital,' Emily laughed.

'But some people work twelve-hour days and have children. How do they fit everything in?'

'I don't know. Just stop sleeping I guess,' said Emily. 'Mary was thrilled with the last five chapters I sent her, by the way. I know you're working hard, but do you think you'll be finished by the deadline? You've still a long way to go, remember, and you don't want a mad rush to finish it at the last minute.'

'I know, I have sleepless nights just thinking about it.' She paused for a moment then smiled. 'You know the most irritating thing people ask you when you're writing a novel?'

'I can guess, but tell me.'

'"So what's your novel about then?" And the look in their eyes says, but I only want the sixty-second version. Also when people say, "But haven't you finished it yet?" Or, "How near are you to finishing it?" Christ, I wish someone would tell me!'

'I know. It must be like building a house when you don't know how many floors it's going to have.'

'Precisely.'

'Now, shall we have an egg mayo sandwich and another cappuccino on expenses?' asked Emily.

'Yes, please. This is the life, being wined and dined by my literary agent. If we were men we'd be sloshing it back at the Savoy or somewhere ritzy.'

'I'm afraid it's not like that any more. Maybe for Jeffrey Archer or Jilly Cooper, but for the likes of us it's egg mayo or nothing. By the way, how is Jack "it's only money" Dudley?'

Pandora looked sheepish. 'Well, I suppose you could say he is a vague inspiration.'

Emily sipped her coffee thoughtfully. 'How keen are you on him?'

'I think you could say that I'm pretty keen. But I haven't even spoken to him for over a week. He took me to Blake's for dinner and we had a *wonderful night of passion*. Then I crept out dramatically into the dawn, clutching my shoes and naked beneath my mac . . .' She sighed and looked mistily into the distance. 'It broke my heart to leave him but I had to.'

Emily just smiled.

'He hasn't rung me since. It's *excruciating*!'

'Well, look on the bright side. This multiple confusion is doing wonders for your writing.'

'Maybe that's the point of this whole Jack thing. Perhaps when I've finished writing the novel I'll go off him. I wonder what on earth he'll think when he reads it. I went to a party the other day and a man asked me what he had to do to be in my novel and I replied, "Sleep with me".' They both roared with laughter. 'He thought I was joking,' added Pandora.

'Emily!' A stocky dark man stopped at their table.

'Oh, hi, Jeremy. Have you met Pandora Black? She's one of my frothbuster authorettes.'

'I'm a first-timer so I'm only allowed an egg mayo sandwich on expenses,' explained Pandora. 'When my novel comes out I'll be upgraded to the Chelsea Bun down the road and allowed to have a pudding as well.'

'Can I join you?' Jeremy plonked his tray down at their table. He was quite good-looking with a kind, open face, but he had far too much hair for Pandora, who preferred her men big, brutal and broken-nosed whenever possible. She sighed inwardly; now she and Emily would have to stop talking about men. It was funny how men were often much more interesting to talk about than to.

'So what's your novel about then?' Jeremy asked.

Emily caught her eye.

'It's about living on the edge with a private income in Knightsbridge and Klosters,' replied Pandora.

'Jeremy is another one of our authors,' said Emily. 'He writes extremely successful thrillers based on his high-powered job in the City.'

Pandora was impressed and regretted her flippant evaluation of him.

Emily began packing up her bag. 'I really must get back to the office. I'll leave you both to discuss your creative impulses.'

Pandora turned to Jeremy and smiled. She wondered if he was any good at fixing leaks.

'How on earth do you find the time to work and write?' she asked.

'Well, when I first started I wrote at weekends and at night, but six months ago I handed in my notice, rented out my flat and went to Venice to finish my fourth book. I'd always wanted to learn Italian.'

'Just like that.'

'Just like that. And now I've handed in the manuscript I'm thinking about going to Tuscany to write the next one. It's a treadmill!' he said happily.

'It sounds perfect to me. You weren't born in the Year of the Tiger, were you?'

'Yes, I think I was.'

'I knew it.' Pandora smiled triumphantly. 'I'm a tiger, too. We're compulsive travellers and we find it very difficult to *commit* ourselves to one place.'

'Ugh. I hate that word.'

'So do I,' agreed Pandora. 'I'm fascinated by the idea of you packing in your job and disappearing to Venice for six months. I'd love to do that. London is so distracting and I've been vaguely thinking about shooting off to Switzerland and finishing it in the mountains.'

'What's stopping you?'

Pandora thought for a moment. 'The Ritzy Marina club. I'd miss the pool dreadfully.'

'You wouldn't be leaving some poor besotted man behind?'

'Goodness no!' she laughed shrilly. Jack wouldn't even notice she'd gone.

'Just do it. I'd love to hear more about your novel. Why don't we go out one evening and discuss it over a meal?'

He was a fast worker, thought Pandora, handing him her card willingly. It was interesting to meet someone with whom she had so much in common. She wondered if he wrote about his girlfriends like she wrote about her boyfriends. He wasn't remotely her type but his interest was just what she needed. Her ego had taken quite a battering from Jack's on/off courtship. It was only later when she got home that she realized that she hadn't even found out if he was any good at mending things.

* * *

Jeremy rang her the next afternoon inviting her to 'supper' the following week. Pandora wondered whether he had a Daphne's supper or Chelsea Bun supper in mind, but didn't feel it would be polite to ask. As long as he didn't try and cook something himself she didn't care either way. How she missed Jack. It had been ten days since their last meeting but she couldn't stop thinking about him. During the day it was easy to be flippant about her feelings, but at night alone in the darkness she couldn't run away from the longing she felt. She would replay their conversations in her head and sometimes when the ache became unbearable she would turn her face to the wall and cry her eyes out. Shutting her eyes tightly she would scan the streets that lay between them, wondering what he was doing, who he was with and what he was thinking.

She couldn't go on like this. It was time to get out of the boxing ring and take a break. After Christmas she would go to Switzerland. There were only five million men there compared to twenty-five million in England. Statistically, at least, her life should be made much easier. And if she didn't give her number to Jack he wouldn't be able to not ring her and she could just cut him out of her life completely.

She decided to spend the weeks before she flew to Hawaii with James and Davina attending to the backlog of personal administration that she had been putting off for the last ten years. If she was organized she would be able to return from Hawaii in the New Year, swap suitcases, and fly straight out to Switzerland. Bin bags of old clothes were taken to Oxfam, ageing kitchen produce was tossed away ruthlessly and Jeremy showed her how to use a Psion organizer, enabling her to throw out drawers full of scrap paper, whose arcane information could now be filed away on this miraculous gadget. She had her windows, curtains, sofas and carpets cleaned, and after a few weeks the flat gleamed. It looked so wonderful that she managed to rent it out from the middle of January for six months to a wealthy American couple, who offered her so much money she thought she was dreaming.

She was trying to squeeze a pair of langlaufing boots into the enormous trunk she was having freighted to Gstaad (langlaufing was so much *chic*er than downhill skiing), when Jack rang.

'Oh hi,' she said casually.

'What are you up to?'

'I'm planning my great escape from London. I'm off to Hawaii for Christmas and then I'm going to Switzerland to finish my novel. I may be gone for quite some time.'

'Lucky you,' said Jack. He didn't sound in the least bit upset.

'Was your bid successful?' Pandora asked brightly, trying to hide her disappointment.

'Yes, they accepted the offer a few weeks ago.'

'What a relief! You must be thrilled.'

'Yeah, I guess. Now I can stop "hustling", as you call it, and get down to some real work. I envy you escaping to Hawaii. I don't think I could even get away for a weekend at the moment.'

'Oh Jack!' She suddenly felt so sorry for him. 'You

must take a break. The graveyard is full of indispensable people, remember.'

'It is a break after grovelling around all those merchant bankers. So when do you leave?'

'In a couple of weeks.'

'Perhaps I can take you out to dinner before you go.'

'Oh, all right,' said Pandora, unenthusiastically.

'Well, you don't have to. It would just be nice to see you, that's all.'

'I don't think I can. You're too unreliable. I've been thinking that it was a bit of a mistake that we slept together. Perhaps it would be better if we were just friends.'

'Look, sometimes I can make it and sometimes I can't,' he said curtly. 'That's just the way I am.'

'Oh dear, my call waiting signal is beeping, I've got to go. I'll ring you sometime. 'Bye.' Pandora replaced the receiver, pleased at the way she had handled him. 'I'll ring you sometime' – like hell she would. The cheek of it! Who on earth did he think he was? It had been an interesting experience trying to have a relationship with a dysfunctional tycoon but it was definitely time to call it a day.

Several weeks later, Pandora was lingering over a coffee at the Kahala Hilton's open air restaurant in Hawaii, feasting on the view. The ocean lay in front of her, smooth and azure against the white sandy beach. If she stretched out her hand she could touch the palm tree that shaded her table. Behind her, soft green hills, the nearest of which was called Diamond Head, stretched into the distance. It was their last full day and James had dragged Davina off to look around Pearl Harbour so she had the rest of the afternoon to herself. Giving in to a sudden urge she decided to watch the sun set over Diamond Head one last time.

Wandering along the beach, soothed by the rhythmic ebb and flow of waves over her bare feet, she inhaled the warm balmy air and sighed blissfully. Really, she must be the luckiest girl in the world. How she relished having no ties. She was as free as the ocean lapping around her. She could write her book anywhere, she certainly didn't have to return to London and get sucked into the endless merry-go-round of parties and people with tired, pinched faces. She strolled past the exclusive empty beach houses. Though she never saw anyone, often when she walked past a sofa had been moved to catch the sun, or a bowl of immaculate fruit had appeared from nowhere. The melancholy sound of wind chimes lingered in the air, mingling with the roar of the ocean. If she had a house here she would never want to leave it. Jack's house was near Diamond Head; she wished she knew which one.

Turning left off the beach she strode up the well-worn path towards Diamond Head, relishing the warm sun on her neck and the occasional breeze from the ocean behind her. Lush green vegetation stretched far into the distance like soft grassy clouds and the air was thick with the scent of tropical jasmine. After walking for half an hour she sat down on a mossy rock and took a swig from her bottle of water. It was good to be alone with her thoughts in this magical place. Last year had been wonderful; next year her novel would be in the shops. People might actually buy it! She hugged her knees to her chest with excitement. She could still sometimes hardly believe it was really happening to her. She, Pandora Black, who had slogged her way through school, ending up with a handful of mediocre exam results, would actually have a novel published. It was a miracle! She got up and stretched her arms above her head, climbing on to the rock for a better view. In the distance she could see the back view of Ocean Zoo that was hidden from the public. Four small swimming pools were crammed full of dolphins swimming round and round frantically. It seemed so unfair that she was standing in this beautiful place, dreaming of freedom when directly below her, creatures of perhaps equal intelligence were imprisoned in filthy old swimming pools. This must be where they lived when they weren't performing for tourists. If only she could do something about it. Perhaps she could write something for *Action!* to tie in with their dolphin rescue campaign with the *Daily Mail*. She would ring Sven when she returned to the hotel.

She lingered for a moment, watching the sun sink like a great ball of fire into the ocean, and savouring the silence and the balmy wind blowing her hair back from her face. How Jack would love to be here now, she knew he felt the same as she did about this place. He would be as outraged about the dolphins doomed to swim in endless circles for ever as she was. The difference was that he had the financial clout coupled with the determination to do something about it.

She scrambled down the hillside, making her way back along the beach towards the hotel. Dusk was falling and in the distance she could see welcoming flares lit outside her hotel, their fiery tongues licking the darkening sky. Davina would be dressing for dinner and James would be in the bar watching the American football and chatting to the barman. She smiled to herself looking forward to the evening ahead. Imagining wings on her feet she broke into a run, summoned by the flares and eager to see her parents' welcoming faces as she walked into the bar.

Pandora let herself into her flat and wearily dumped her suitcase on the floor. After the tropical heat and colour of Hawaii, London seemed drab and grey and she couldn't wait to leave for Switzerland. Her tenants weren't arriving for three weeks but she was free to go at any time. She glanced at her heaving trunk in the corner. She really ought to buy another suitcase. She yawned, suddenly overcome with exhaustion after her eighteen-hour flight, and collapsed into bed.

The next day, feeling much more cheerful after a fifteen-hour sleep, she let herself loose in the Harrods luggage department. She brushed her fingers against the fine leather cases and Louis Vuitton trunks, inhaling the smell of expensive luggage and the rich aroma of coffee from the adjoining expresso bar. The tantalizing combination of smells summoned her away from Knightsbridge, beyond Swiss mountains to Kenya, Columbia, Jamaica,

Costa Rica . . . She forgot about sensible suitcases and found herself drifting into the vanity case department. Before she could say Joan Collins she had given into temptation and bought herself one. It was the colour of deep chocolate and contained an irresistible supply of mirrors and make-up brushes. A suitcase would have been far more useful but she didn't want to ruin the trip by getting bogged down in practicalities.

She was unwrapping the case from sheets of delicate tissue paper when the telephone rang. She picked it up enthusiastically. It was probably Annabel who was telepathic when it came to things like shopping.

'You sound in a good mood,' Jack said drily.

'I've just bought the most divine vanity case. I really think it's going to change my life.'

'Are you going on a cruise?'

'No!' she laughed. 'Though that's a luscious idea. I'm off to the Alps. I've just got to finish packing my vanity case then I'll be ready to leave.'

'Can we meet up before you go? What are you up to this weekend?'

She thought quickly. This was a trick question. If she said nothing he'd think she was a social failure, if she said she was busy she might never see him again.

'I'm reasonably flexible,' she hedged.

'So am I. Would you like to go to Cliveden for the weekend?'

Pandora felt her strong resolutions melt away. 'Yes, I'd love to. I could practise using my vanity case.'

He laughed. 'Well, I'll get it booked up. I'll come by at sixish this Friday.'

'You sound in very good form. What does it feel like to own the new company?'

'It's hard work, but a real relief. I've inherited a brilliant secretary, I can't believe how smoothly my life is running now.'

'She's probably madly in love with you.'

'Sonia? You've got to be joking. She's about fifty and married to her job.'

'Secretaries are always in love with their bosses.' Especially bosses like you, she thought.

'Hold on, Pandora.' She could hear someone talking in the background. 'I've got to go, my chairman's on the other line. See you on Friday.' Pandora hugged herself with excitement. It was unbelievable that Jack had called her back after the bitterness of their last conversation, but thank goodness he had.

She spent the rest of the week finalizing her preparations, and by Friday she had packed up her flat and air-freighted her trunk to Gstaad. Jack had miraculously confirmed the weekend and all she had left to do was have a quick medical check-up and she'd be ready to relax and enjoy herself. She was rarely ill and was looking forward to being told how healthy she was.

After scraping, prodding and squeezing various parts of her body, the doctor carefully examined her breasts. This was the worst bit, and Pandora's anxious eyes didn't leave the doctor's for a moment.

'Have you noticed any changes?' asked the doctor, suspiciously casual.

'Um, no.'

'I'd quite like you to get a second opinion about a small lump in your left breast. Can you feel this?'

Pandora anxiously prodded her breast. 'I can't feel anything different, they've always been a bit lumpy . . .'

'I'd still like you to get a second opinion. You can go along to the hospital on Tuesday, they have a breast clinic from ten to twelve in the morning.'

'But that's five days away! I can't wait that long!' Pandora felt hysteria rise in her throat.

'Don't worry. It's probably just a little cyst, nothing to worry about.'

'But I'm meant to be going away for the weekend. And I'm leaving for Switzerland next Tuesday, everything's booked up . . . my schedule . . .' She started to cry uncontrollably. The whole thing was a nightmare. If only she hadn't left the check-up to the last minute.

The doctor took her hand sympathetically. 'Look, you can't go home in this state. Is there anyone you can ring to come and pick you up?'

Pandora was unable to reply, her mind was fogged with fear and her chest heaved. She was having a panic attack. The doctor delved into a cupboard, quickly removing a brown paper bag which she told Pandora to breathe into. After a few minutes Pandora had recovered enough to write down Annabel's telephone number which the doctor quickly dialled, keeping an eye on Pandora's ashen face. '. . . could you come and collect her? No, nothing wrong, just a routine examination . . .' Her voice weaved in and out of Pandora's consciousness as she found herself slipping inexorably towards the floor where she crumpled in a dead faint.

After what felt like hours but was only a few seconds, she came to, her head between her knees and with a nurse sitting beside her.

'Here, drink this.' She handed Pandora a cup of strong sweet tea. Pandora sipped it obediently. Perhaps she was dreaming, she thought hopefully, pinching herself surreptitiously, but to her horror she didn't wake up.

'Now take some deep breaths and stay calm,' said the nurse. 'There's probably nothing to worry about but these days we are very cautious. The chances of having any serious problem at your age are miniscule but it's a good idea to get things checked out before you go off travelling.'

'Yes,' said Pandora weakly. She was starting to feel very tired. 'I'm feeling terribly sleepy.'

'I put a light sedative in your cup of tea so that you can go straight to bed when you get home. I'm going to give you one to take away just in case you feel another panic attack coming on over the weekend.'

The door was suddenly flung open and Annabel raced in.

'Here comes the Light Brigade,' smiled Pandora weakly.

'Pandora, how are you feeling? The doctor said that you'd fainted.'

'Yes, I did. It was rather nice actually.' Pandora's voice

was slightly slurred and her eyes kept closing. She was longing to go to bed. Annabel and the nurse had to clasp her by the arms and practically carry her outside into Annabel's car.

'I'm taking you back to my flat,' said Annabel firmly. 'You can stay in the spare room so I can keep an eye on you.'

'But I'm meant to be going away with Jack this weekend, and Mummy's coming to stay in my flat.'

'Don't worry. I'll ring Jack and tell him you're not well. Has your mother got a key?'

'Yes.'

'That's all right then. I'll ring her tomorrow.' Annabel parked outside her flat and helped Pandora from the car.

'I'm going to tuck you up with a hot water bottle and then I'll telephone Jack,' she said, steering Pandora into the bedroom and helping her into bed. Closing her eyes, Pandora's fears soon melted away in the blissful oblivion of sleep.

Annabel rifled through Pandora's address book and dialled Jack's work number. She was put through to Sonia.

'I'm afraid Mr Dudley isn't available at the moment, can I give him a message?'

'I'm a friend of Pandora Black who is meant to be meeting Mr Dudley later,' explained Annabel. 'I'm afraid she's had some bad news and is under sedation at my flat. Perhaps I could leave my number so that Mr Dudley could ring her over the weekend.'

'Of course. I'll call him immediately on his mobile

telephone and let him know. I'm so sorry about Pandora, I do hope she feels better soon,' Sonia said sympathetically.

'She'll be fine in a day or two, I'm sure.' Annabel replaced the receiver, reassured by Sonia's kind, efficient voice. She'd be sure to get the message to Jack in time.

'Right, Sonia, I'm off now,' said Jack, wandering into her office. 'Have there been any messages?'

'Oh no,' replied Sonia brightly. 'Are you doing anything nice this weekend?'

'Yes, I'm going down to Cliveden for a couple of nights. I'll keep my phone on so you can get hold of me any time.' He shrugged on his jacket. It was such a relief having Sonia, she was so competent. Miranda, his last secretary, had been hopeless but charming. Her charms had almost made up for her inefficiency and she had certainly raised morale in the office but he had been quite relieved when she had got engaged to the son of a Greek shipping tycoon and decided on early retirement at the age of twenty-four. Sonia had appeared at the perfect time. Within two weeks she had totally reorganized the office. She had also fallen head over heels in love with Jack.

'I'm sure I won't need to bother you,' she said. 'You go away and have a complete break, you deserve it.'

'Maybe you're right.' Jack smiled at her. He wasn't used to being fussed over and it amused him, Sonia reminded him of a mother hen. 'You have a good weekend too.'

She heard him humming to himself as he walked down

the corridor. He had been in an unusually good mood all day. Sonia frowned as she tidied her desk. She was sure she had done the right thing, she'd seen pictures of Pandora in the gossip columns. A flibbertigibbet girl like that couldn't possibly make a man like Jack happy. She would only end up upsetting him like that silly wife of his who kept ringing him up in various stages of hysteria. It wasn't often that Jack left before her and she decided to nip into his office and see if anything needed tidying away. Jack had cleared his desk and left everything spick and span. One of his desk drawers was half open and she bent to close it. Inside lay an old copy of *Divorce! Magazine* on top of a pile of *Economist*s. She pulled it out curiously, drawing her lips into a tight line as her eyes rested on a picture of two glamorous blondes, one wearing a catsuit and the other a mini dress and shiny white boots, clutching five glasses of champagne. The picture was captioned, 'PARTY GIRLS – Pandora Black and Annabel Smythe-Johnson sharing a joke and a bottle of Bolly at the opening of A Paper Bag.' Sonia tutted disapprovingly to herself as she replaced the magazine carefully. Party girl indeed! Yes, she had definitely done the right thing. If Jack found out that she hadn't passed on the message she would just plead forgetfulness. Everyone was allowed to make a mistake now and then.

She put on her coat and glanced around the office carefully. She was sure there was something she had been meaning to check. Ah yes, biscuits. They were nearly out of Jack's favourites. She made a careful note on her shopping pad. She could pick some up on her way home.

Jack was in an excellent mood as he drove round to pick up Pandora. He was so looking forward to seeing her that he didn't quite know why he had left it so long. He had neither the time nor the inclination for a serious courtship at the moment but during the last few days he had been suddenly consumed by a longing to see her.

Pulling up outside her flat, he leapt out and went to ring her bell. He waited but there was no reply. He rang it again. He tapped her number into his mobile phone but all he got was the answerphone. It had started to rain and he sheltered beneath the porch for a moment, scratching his head in bewilderment. It would be just like her to change her mind and fly off somewhere, she could be so erratic. He dialled her number again. 'Pandora, where the hell are you? It's six o'clock and I'm standing outside your flat. Get back to me if you feel like it.' He strode back to his car, his good mood quite evaporated, and made another call. 'Hi, Tom. Are you up to anything this weekend? Can I? Great.' He lit a cigarette and pulled out into the road, causing the Mini behind him to break abruptly. The driver hooted, gesticulating in anger. 'Go fuck yourself,' muttered Jack as he put his foot down and roared off towards Kent.

Pandora woke late the following morning feeling bleary-eyed. 'What time is it?' she asked Annabel who had brought her a cup of tea.

'Ten o'clock. You've slept for fourteen hours.' She sat down on the bed. 'If you slept for that long every day you would significantly reduce the risk of premature ageing.'

'But who would ever see me? There wouldn't be time to do anything else but sleep. My youthful bloom would be totally wasted on you.'

'God, you earth signs are so practical,' said Annabel scathingly.

'I'm not an earth sign, I'm a Piscean as you jolly well know. Now be nice to me, I'm living through a nightmare. I might be dying.'

'Rubbish. You must speak to Emily, she's always having false alarms.'

'Is she? I'd love to talk to someone who's gone through this.'

'You are. Remember when I had that smear test?'

'How can I forget? You planned your funeral in great detail just in case. Oh God! Did you remember to ring Jack? He'll think I stood him up!'

'Relax, I left a message with his very nice-sounding secretary.'

'That would be Sonia. Jack says she's a paragon. She's probably a dead ringer for Miss Moneypenny.'

'So, no worries. Why don't you leave a message telling him what's happened?'

'Oh, I couldn't ever tell him about something like this. He'd go right off me.'

'You know, if he was the right man and you really did like him, you'd be able to tell him, I'm sure.' Annabel frowned slightly. Pandora looked absolutely washed out. 'Well, let's at least ring Emily and see what she says about all this.' She dialled her sister's number.

'Hi, Em, it's me. Could you have a word with Pandora? She's having a boob scare. OK, I'll pass you over.'

The sound of Emily's sympathetic voice made Pandora burst into tears again. She blew her nose and quickly explained the situation.

'But the funny thing is that I haven't noticed anything myself, it always feels like that.'

'I'm convinced you've got absolutely nothing to worry about. I've put my boobs on sheets of metal, in fridges, in microwaves, you name it. Three years ago some woman smeared jelly all over them and then wired them up to this huge cinema screen and invited all these medical students in to watch. Talk about horror movie.' They both laughed. 'Really you've got more chance of winning the lottery than having the remotest thing wrong with you,' Emily went on cheerfully. 'Please don't worry. The surgeon will probably just prod you around on Tuesday and send you packing. I'll chant for you to be fine and to stop worrying.'

Pandora put the phone down, immensely reassured, and then remembered that Georgie was staying at her flat that weekend. 'Can I ring my flat? I'd better let Mummy know what's happening.'

'Of course. I'll leave you to it. I'm off to Waitrose to look at men.'

Pandora groaned and dialled her home number.

'Hi, Mummy, it's me. I'm with Annabel. The doctor thinks I have a lump in my breast which needs examining.' Her voice wavered.

'Oh, darling, how awful for you. But I'm sure there's

433

nothing wrong. Remember when I went through all those problems with my fibroids? I was convinced I had cancer. Would you like me to come and pick you up?'

'I think I might stay here tonight. I fainted at the surgery and the doctor gave me a sedative. I could sleep for a week. Besides, you're flying to Deauville tomorrow aren't you?'

'Yes, but I can easily stay a few more days.'

'No, I'll be fine, honestly. It'll make me feel even worse if everyone starts changing their plans for me. It's bad enough having to delay my trip to Switzerland.'

'Well, let me drop round to see you on the way to the airport. Does Annabel still live in that nice flat by the river?'

'Yes, number two, Rumbold Road. Top floor. Oh, Mummy, just one thing. Could you check my answer-phone messages? I want to see if my romantic disinterest has telephoned.'

'Of course, darling.'

'You do know how to work it, don't you?' Georgie was famously technophobic.

'Of course. I've got one myself, you know.'

Pandora replaced the receiver and shut her eyes. How could anyone feel so tired after sleeping for fourteen hours? Maybe she did have cancer after all. How would she cope if her breast was removed? What would she tell Jack? Would she tell him? Probably not. Jack wasn't the sort of person you could tell something like that, he'd probably disappear for ever if she had some sort of physical deformity. A tear spilled down her cheek. She'd been so looking forward to the weekend.

Georgie lit a cigarette and made herself a cup of coffee before wandering into the sitting room to check Pandora's messages. Thankfully it was just like the one she had at home. The first message was a long one from herself – how very dull. She took a sip of coffee and grimaced. 'Ugh!' It tasted of ground up dandelions. Knowing Pandora, it probably was ground up dandelions. 'Really!' she exclaimed, carrying the brew into the kitchen and pouring it down the sink. She had left such a long message that she'd have time to make another cup. Her eyes alighted on a jar of Gold Blend. That's more like it, she thought, quickly spooning coffee into another cup. She returned to the sitting room just in time to hear the bleep signalling the end of Jack's curt message. It was followed by an equally long one from Pandora's neighbour downstairs complaining of leaks. Georgina rolled her eyes. 'And I thought my daughter led such an interesting life.' She went to pack up her things, oblivious of Jack's message. Lost somewhere inside Pandora's machine, it would soon be wiped away for ever.

An interminable three days later Pandora sat in the plush waiting room of the London Clinic waiting to have an ultrasound. She wondered if her editor would extend her deadline if she needed radical surgery. Even if she did manage to finish her book on time, she would look terrible on the dust jacket. She might even have to wear a wig . . .

A voice broke into her grim musings. 'The doctor's ready to see you now, dear.'

Pandora jumped up suddenly, knocking a pile of ancient *Country Life* magazines and a dried-flower arrangement on to the lap of an Arab sheik sitting impassively by the door. He appeared not to notice the onslaught of elderly petals upon his person and continued to gaze blankly ahead. Pandora scrabbled around the floor picking up the magazines and started to cry.

'Now, now, don't worry,' said the receptionist ushering her out of the room. 'Don't worry about Sheik Mahmood. He's on so much Prozac he won't have noticed a thing.'

Prozac! Why hadn't she thought of that? She shrugged on a white hospital gown and followed a nurse into a troglodytic chamber where she could just make out a doctor sitting in front of a television screen. As Emily had predicted, an unguent was smeared all over her breasts – thank goodness the doctor was a woman – and then a metal wand was massaged over them in order to pick up any abnormalities. The doctor concentrated impassively on the screen while Pandora concentrated on her face, desperately looking for clues from her expression. After an interminable amount of time, the doctor put down the metal wand and smiled at her. 'You'll be relieved to know that there is absolutely nothing wrong with you. Your breasts are completely normal.'

Pandora squealed with joy and her eyes sparkled with

relief. 'Thank you *so* much!' She bounded out of the room and went to make a telephone call.

'Annabel! There's nothing wrong with me. I'm free to leave the country at last!'

'Oh, Pandora. I'm so happy for you. When do you want to leave?'

'How about half an hour ago?'

'Hang on,' laughed Annabel. 'I can't leave work till four o'clock. If I pick you up around four thirty, is there a plane you can catch?'

'Certainly is,' said Pandora who had been unable to focus on anything but her medical encyclopedia and the Swissair timetable for the last three days.

Six hours later Pandora wandered excitedly around the first-class lounge, dizzy with relief and surreptitiously slipping tea bags into her vanity case. She couldn't resist them, and tea bags always came in handy. She glanced around the lounge and sighed. There were no decent men to practise eye-meets with, it was very boring. Annabel said it was worth forking out to travel first class because one never knew who one might meet. So far, both of them had nearly bankrupted themselves but had never met anyone worthwhile at all. But in a triumph of hope over experience both girls continued to shell out in the unlikely hope of sitting next to Mr Suchard, Mr Roche or Mr Swissair.

During the past four days she had been so terrified that she hadn't been able to think about Jack at all. She had tried to ring him to confirm that he had got her message but he had been out of the office.

She had been hurt and disappointed when he didn't return her call, but hardly surprised. Being married to Atlanta had probably put him off women with problems for ever.

'Swissair flight to Geneva is now boarding at gate number four.' It was time to go. Pandora took a deep breath and bent down to pick up her vanity case. It weighed a ton but looked divine. She smiled to herself. It was astonishing how much a handful of tea bags could weigh.

Chapter Twenty

Early in the morning four weeks later Pandora woke up and stretched sleepily, allowing her mind to drift languorously over the chapter she had just finished yesterday afternoon and to plan what she was going to write today. She was relishing the opportunity to devote herself to her writing with no distractions. Every day she woke up with the glorious feeling that she had acres of space to fill exactly how she wanted. When she considered how other women lived their lives, bringing up families, with no time to themselves, she felt so grateful. No wonder so few female artists made it; one needed more than a room of one's own, one needed great acres of time too. And most women just weren't selfish enough to demand it.

She jumped out of bed and pulled back the curtain. Her room faced on to a quiet street beyond which soared two mountains that she had named Weetabix and Narnia. 'God, I really am losing it,' she smiled to herself. 'What sort of person names a mountain after a breakfast cereal?'

She flung open the door to her balcony and wandered outside, breathing in the freezing air and stretching towards the sun, which at this early hour was just a glimmer in the distance. 'I wish I could stay here for ever writing nuisance novels and undisturbed by *things*.' She had worried that she might get lonely for her friends and London life but now, if anything, she worried that she didn't miss them. Was it normal to enjoy such isolation? Annabel had said it would make her suicidal.

Now, which would be her first yogurt of the day? She decided on a cappuccino-flavoured one and settled down to work.

Two hours later the phone rang and Pandora leapt to answer it. It would probably be Annabel. She was one of the few people who had her number and Pandora relied on her regular updates to keep her in touch with the outside world.

'Pandora! You're in! What a surprise.' It was a standing joke between them that Pandora never went out and had managed to avoid having a conversation with anyone except the lady at the local yogurt shop since she'd arrived.

'Yes, my one-night stand has just left.'

'Really?'

'No! I've given up men until I've finished my novel. I've got far too much to write about as it is.'

'Have you seen Roger Moore yet?'

'Unfortunately not, but I'm keeping my eyes open. How is Enrico?' Enrico was Annabel's latest squeeze.

'It's over.' Annabel sighed dramatically. 'He was twenty minutes late picking me up last night, and his car was *filthy*.' For reasons Pandora had never been sufficiently interested to go into, Annabel had an absolute horror of men with dirty cars. 'Besides, he was starting to bore me anyway. He was always going on about his boss.'

'Yuck. You mean you were going out with someone's *employee*?'

'Only for three weeks. Chaps are a bit thin on the ground at the moment in town.'

'It doesn't sound like I'm missing much in my hermetically sealed Swiss isolation unit then.'

'No. By the way, Jeremy rang, he says he can't get hold of you.'

'You didn't give him my number?'

'No. I told him that I wasn't sure where you were, but that if anyone needed you urgently they could leave a message with Father Hubert at that church in Cranley Gardens next to your flat.'

Father Hubert was an old friend of Davina's who kept a spare key to Pandora's London flat and had occasionally saved Pandora's bacon when she had locked herself out in the past.

'Well done. Father Hubert will fob him off, he's a real brick.'

'But I thought you and Jeremy were such chums.'

'We are, sort of, but he might want to come out and see me. The great thing about living in a hotel is that you never have to do anything remotely grungy like changing lightbulbs, so if he did come out there wouldn't be very much for him to do.' Pandora and Jeremy's relationship was based almost entirely on the latter's DIY skills. 'And I'm really trying to avoid social distractions at the moment.'

'What about Jack? Bet you wouldn't mind a bit of distraction from him.'

'Huh! If I never see that arrogant, unreliable, pig-headed douche bag ever again it'll be too soon,' lied Pandora energetically.

'Yes, you're probably better off without him. It was mean that he never got in touch. After all, we did leave him two messages. D'you think he'll get back together with his wife, Alaska?'

'You mean Atlanta. I don't know. He might, I suppose,' said Pandora glumly. 'Let's make a pact,' she went on. 'Both of us have to stay single for six months in order to develop "a stand alone spirit". It could be a very interesting experience for both of us.'

'*Could* being the operative word,' said Annabel doubtfully. 'It's all right for you, you're living in a hotel with twenty-four-hour access to a handyman. I *need* gentleman callers for practical reasons. Anyway, I better go now and let you get on with your life's mission. I'm off to the hairdresser. Out of interest, the pact wouldn't preclude one-night stands, would it?'

'One night is fine, but no longer. And no shopping afterwards.'

Pandora returned to her computer and was soon immersed in the exploits of her romantic hero who bore a startling resemblance to Jack. She sucked her yogurt spoon dreamily. Would he have had time to squeeze in membership of the SAS, the Royal Marines, the Mossad, the British Secret Service and have made sixty million pounds, much of which he gave away to good causes, all before the age of thirty-five? Definitely, she thought firmly as she began to type once more.

But did South Africa have an SAS and a Royal Marines? she wondered later that afternoon, wandering down to the very cosmopolitan newsagent to buy her *Daily Mail*. Her eyes alighted on that week's *Hello!* magazine. Oh good, she thought, fumbling in her purse for change. Now she would be able to find out what all her friends were up to without having to go to the bother of telephoning them all.

As January drifted into February, Pandora became more and more consumed with her novel. Annabel and other friends kept her up to date with London life and her mother rang frequently to ask when she intended to return to London. 'You're wasting yourself out there, darling. You're in your prime, don't lock yourself away all day. At least look up Alicia Bearman – you remember, my friend from finishing school. She'll take you about, I'm sure.' But Pandora just couldn't be bothered and preferred to fill her days with long stints at her computer followed by a stroll down to the newsagent and a cappuccino. When the weather was fine she would ski over to the idyllic village of Saanen which had a very tempting yogurt shop. Listening to the rhythmic swish of skis on snow she would feast her eyes on the ragged mountain peaks scraping the clear blue sky like knives. How lucky she was. The sight of them never failed to take her breath away. It was like living in a touched-up photograph all the time.

The Palace Hotel was nearly as omnipresent as the mountains. When walking down the busy main street or emerging from a shop she would suddenly catch sight of it hovering above the village, its turrets disappearing into the clouds. It was an extraordinary looking place, more like a castle than a hotel, and set against the distant snow-laden pine forests in the distance, was the sort of place the White Witch of Narnia would definitely take her holidays. Seeing it would remind her of Jack and cause a *frisson* of exquisite melancholy to surge through her.

The only time she thought about London was to wish that she never had to go back. Her writing was flowing like a dream, the mountains were her muse, shielding her from the outside world and enabling her to focus totally on the words pouring out from her heart and on to the page.

One afternoon after a four-hour session at her computer she went out on to the balcony. It was five o'clock, the sun had nearly disappeared behind Weetabix Mountain and the sky was the light aquamarine that is unique to Switzerland. It was paradise. No wonder Steve McQueen had been so desperate to get here in *The Great Escape*. But maybe she was escaping too. Was she abnormal? Did she need therapy? Surely not. She had never felt so fulfilled and happy.

In two months she would, hopefully, have finished her

novel. She would hand it to her editor, do the rewrites and then she would be really free! Perhaps she would return to London, perhaps she would go to Hawaii and campaign for dolphin release. She was looking forward to working again for *Action!* She had told Sven she was taking a six-month sabbatical to finish her book and then she would love to start submitting regular articles once more. She had been careful not to tell him where she was going and had given him Father Hubert's address but not her Swiss telephone number. He might pass it on to Jack, though he had probably forgotten all about her by now. Besides, it would be depressing if she thought Jack had her number – she'd only be disappointed if he didn't ring.

She hugged herself against the cool mountain breeze. Try as she might she couldn't forget Jack and not a day went by when she didn't wonder how he was or what he was doing. Still, she was better off without him, she had done the right thing. She must have, otherwise she wouldn't feel so happy all the time. Any lingering regret that she might feel was serving to feed her muse and give her writing a poignancy that it would not otherwise have had. Besides, sensible people knew that love was just an illusion, perpetuated by romantic novels and the music industry. She decided to ring Emily and ask her advice.

'Emily, I'm worried that I'm turning into a recluse. Do *you* think my lifestyle is abnormal?'

Emily laughed. 'It's unusual, but I wouldn't say it's abnormal. Lots of writers choose to live in an unconventional way. Look at Daphne Du Maurier – she virtually lived in a shed at the bottom of her garden and insisted that her husband sleep in a separate bedroom.'

'That sounds quite normal to me,' said Pandora, remembering how she had longed for her own bedroom during her marriage and feeling even more worried.

'And I know of writers who rent houses in France and Tuscany by themselves and don't emerge for days. Writers are often very solitary people, artists tend to be much more gregarious. I think that if you're happy with the way you're living, you shouldn't worry. After all, you're not going to live like this for ever. Are you?'

'Um, no, I suppose not. I'd quite like to though. Life inside my Swiss isolation unit is very comfortable and totally stress-free. A bit of writing, a bit of skiing, and if I want a bit of excitement I just go shopping and clock a few celebs – and I'm not joking!'

'I wouldn't worry about it. The most important thing is that Mary loves what you're writing. If it helps to be stuck in the mountains living a quiet life then carry on doing it. Maybe it's only by cutting yourself off from distractions that you'll finish the book in time. After all, it's not so easy for you because you've never had the discipline of a nine to five job.'

'Yes, you're right. I do miss you all though.'

'Liar,' said Emily affectionately.

Pandora laughed. 'What's your news? Are you in love or anything dramatic?'

'Well, I've just been made a director of the agency so I'm thrilled about that.'

'Emily, you're brilliant! You really deserve it, well done!'

'And I've sort of met a man . . .' She trailed off cautiously.

'Yes?' prodded Pandora. 'Who is it? Anyone I know?'

'I don't think so. He runs a film company called Glow Pictures.'

'I've heard of them. Gosh, Emily, he's obviously very eligible.'

'Yes, he is.' Emily sounded unusually dreamy. 'He's taking me to Venice next weekend, and the weekend after we're going to Paris. He says he wants to wake up with me in a different city every Sunday.' She sighed blissfully.

'Emily, you're in love! Love and promotion in one month – you're living proof that a woman can Have It All!'

'Hardly,' laughed Emily. 'I've only known him a month, but yes, I'm pretty happy about life at the moment.'

'You were single for ages though, weren't you?'

'Oh yes, for about three years. But it didn't bother me because I wanted to concentrate on my career for a while. The funny thing was that I met Jonathon just after my divorce, but he didn't really make a particular impression. Then we ran into each other recently and it was *pow*, immediately. These things are all about timing, I guess. By the way, how is Jack Dudley?'

'Locked away inside my computer where I can keep an eye on him. Talk about the wrong man at the wrong time. I think I only met him so that I'd have a model for my frothbusting hero.'

'The funny thing is that before I practised Buddhism I used to worry all the time about meeting the right man and finding the right job, but these days things seem to fall into place. I just *know* that whatever happens, it's for the best. It's very reassuring.'

'Yes,' said Pandora thoughtfully, 'I've been doing some chanting and it does make one feel very centred somehow. I liked that article in the Buddhist magazine you sent me about the rich man who sews a diamond into his poor friend's robe while he's sleeping, so the poor man doesn't know about it and wanders about feeling hungry and depressed. Then he discovers it and realizes he needn't have suffered because he was rich all the time. It said that real happiness was inside and not dependent on whether you had a hot date for Saturday night or whatever. Just as well really, I'd have thrown myself off a ski lift by now if it was. Hot dates are definitely a thing of the past.'

'The diamond within,' mused Emily. 'It's a struggle to remember that sometimes. But it's true, happiness is right under our noses, but most of the time we're looking in the wrong direction—'

'You mean looking outside rather than inside.'

'Exactly.'

'Hmm, wonder if this would interest *Divorce! Magazine*. I could do a sort of spirituality for beginners.'

'Bit of a long shot, unless it had a major celeb angle . . . but don't you get distracted. You've got a frothbuster to finish. And when you've finished that I want another one as soon as possible.'

'Slavedriver!'

Pandora replaced the receiver feeling inspired. The 'diamond within': she liked the sound of that. It reminded her of Diamond Head. She gazed out of the window. It was getting dark now and instead of Weetabix Mountain she saw Hawaiian hills drenched in fragrant coffee bushes stretching into a green haze as far as the eye could see. But it was impossible to think about Hawaii without remembering those dolphins swimming round and round their tiny prison. But Emily was right. She must finish her novel and then she would definitely do something about that.

By the end of March the snow in the village had melted away, along with the *beau monde* who had disappeared to their other residences in the Caribbean, London, The United Arab Emirates and New York. Gstaad was even more delightful devoid of people. It was now possible to get a seat in a cafe and wander down the main street without being jostled.

Today she was sitting in the warm spring sunshine sipping cappuccino at her favourite cafe, The Rialto, and watching the world go by. Occasionally a blue and white train, its windows sparkling in the sunshine, would trundle over a distant bridge on its way to Montreux. It was all very soothing. Some would say boring, but Pandora found the orderliness of Switzerland provided a restful contrast to the turmoil that usually existed in her mind. Even the news that Father Hubert's vicarage had burned down – fortunately he had been away shooting at the time – had hardly dented her equilibrium. She had a sudden vision of bits of paper containing messages for her blowing around the charred remains of the vicarage, and sighed contentedly. Now it would be practically impossible for anyone to get hold of her. It was a wonderfully liberating feeling. She opened her day-old copy of the *Daily Mail* and flicked to the *Mail Diary*. Her blood ran cold. A picture of Jack and Saffron illustrated the main story. 'Jack In The Box!!!' began the accompanying article.

'Workaholic tycoon "Mad" Jack Dudley, chief executive of Dudley Enterprises, valued at two hundred million pounds, emerged from court yesterday a poorer man. His ex-wife, stunning saucepot Atlanta Du Ville, who recently signed a million-dollar television deal, emerged smiling after winning a record-breaking twenty million pound pay-off. "This is a victory for women everywhere," she exclaimed, flanked by her close companion and lawyer, Raymond "The Rottweiler" Rench.

'Mad Jack, who recently lost his driving licence after being charged with speeding through a red light while using his mobile phone, smoking a cigarette and drinking a cup of coffee, declined to comment. He has recently been linked to beautiful "new waif" model Saffron Whisp, who created a stir when she was caught climbing out of devout Buddhist Richard Gleary's hotel window last year. She later claimed that they had been discussing China's oppression of Tibet and had "lost track of the time". Miss Whisp lisped enigmatically, "Jack and I share a deep interest in Buddhist philosophy. We are close friends and he stays on my sofa bed when he comes to Paris." Miss Whisp inhabits a charming studio flat in Montmartre so one presumes overnight visitors must be on very friendly terms indeed. Keep spinning the prayer wheel, Jack!'

Huh! Miss Whisp indeed, thought Pandora flicking through the paper angrily. God, what sort of a man *was* Jack? First of all marrying someone like Atlanta and now bonking that ridiculous Saffron Whisp. I bet her real name is Maureen Smith and that she was born in Woking. They were welcome to each other. She glanced at the picture again. Jack had raised his arm, presumably to prevent the photographer from taking a photo. He looked very cross and very sexy. Wretched man. Destroying her equilibrium just when it was settling down nicely.

She quickly flicked to the horoscopes for some light relief. 'Pisceans are easily confused and love to escape from brutal reality into their own peculiar private worlds. Unfortunately this week's disastrous clash between Mars and Venus is likely to leave you feeling even more confused than ever!' Load of old cobblers, thought Pandora gathering up her things briskly, longing to get back to work. It would be a relief to return to the characters in her novel. If only real people were as easy to manipulate.

Two weeks later Pandora switched off her computer with a feeling of finality. She had re-read and picked over everything to death and could do no more, the rest was up to Emily and Mary. It would be such a relief to share her novel with someone. She hugged her knees to her chest. Now what? It was April, if all went according to plan the book was due out in December. Say the rewrites took a month, she would have six months to play with!

She went out on to the balcony and breathed in the soft, balmy air and sighed wistfully. It would be so difficult to leave this lovely place. The last four months really had been a dream time and she wondered if she would ever have the opportunity to indulge herself like this again. Writing her novel had been cathartic, somehow freeing her from the countless fears and anxieties that had always plagued her. For the first time in her life she could hold her own in the world. When people asked what she did, she could now reply 'I'm a writer' with conviction and real pride. Looking upwards, shielding her eyes against the glare of the sun, she watched a solitary bird winging its graceful way across the sky. At that moment she, too, had wings, and in her mind's eye she was as light as the bird, soaring and swooping in a world where anything was possible. 'They build too low who build beneath the skies,' she murmured to herself. No one had thought she could do it, but a small nugget of determination had grown into a great ball of fire and now she knew that *anything* was possible, provided she wanted it enough.

She went inside and picked up *The Diary of Anais Nin*, and re-read a favourite passage: 'Dreams pass into the reality of action. From the action stems the dream again; and this interdependence produces the highest form of living.' Who knew, maybe the end of this Swiss dream would signal the beginning of an even bigger, better dream.

Chapter Twenty-one

'Would you like me to do any interviews or any kind of publicity yet?' Pandora asked Poppy, the long-suffering publicity director at Red Duck. Pandora had been back in England for a month and she and Mary had now finished editing the novel. There was nothing more for her to do, and while she was thrilled, she was also surprised at the sense of loss she felt. She had been working on it for so long it had become a part of her. Perhaps this was how a mother felt when her only child left home. It was a strange mixture of relief, pride and sadness. It was so difficult to let go.

Poppy sighed inwardly and smiled brightly. First-time authors were the worst, they imagined their book was the only one that Red Duck had to publish. They clucked and fussed away like anxious mother hens. At the last editorial meeting she had suggested that funds be made available to send nuisance novelists away for long cruises. Very long cruises, thought Poppy wistfully.

'I'm afraid it's a bit early for that,' she said in the

soothing tones that female authors found so reassuring, and male authors so alluring. 'We still haven't decided on the cover yet. I think you should go on a nice long holiday and take it easy for a few months. There really won't be much for you to do before November.'

'Oh, all right,' said Pandora, a little disappointed. 'Can I come in and talk about the cover again? I've got some great ideas.' She was hoping that she and Annabel could be photographed clutching glasses of champagne and surrounded by hordes of divine looking men, hand-picked by them at parties.

'Yes, come in next Monday. We'll have something to show you by then. And don't worry, we'll get the publicity ball rolling when it's the right time. If we start too early we'll lose momentum. Besides, it's summer now and lots of people are away on holiday. Trust me.'

'Oh, I do, I do,' said Pandora hurriedly, deciding not to push things any more. The last thing she wanted was to be considered a nuisance. It was only later when she had put the phone down that she realized she had forgotten to ask what the chances were of appearing on *Desert Island Discs*. Or the *Selina Scott Show* perhaps. That was broadcast all round the world. And shouldn't someone be contacting *Divorce!* and *Hello!* magazines? The possiblities were endless.

She was having a lovely time back in London, it was wonderful to use the Ritzy Marina club, to drink cappuccino at Prêt à Manger and indulge in long nuisance calls to friends she hadn't spoken to in months.

Since her disappearance various rumours had been circu-
lating around London as Annabel, forbidden to divulge
Pandora's whereabouts, had given full rein to her imagination. 'Pandora, we thought you had died!' joked several.
'How was Mongolia? Is it true that you've had radical
plastic surgery/had a baby/got married?'

However, after a month of rampant socializing she
found she wanted to go away again.

'There's nothing for me in London,' she protested to
her father and Davina one weekend. 'I've been back a
month and I've already run out of debauchery. I think I
need a change of scene. After all, I'm meant to be getting
inspiration for my next novel.'

'Have you any idea what you might write about?' asked
Davina.

'I thought I could write about a girl who runs away to
Switzerland to escape from the absentee ministrations of
her totally dysfunctional tycoony boyfriend.' She thought
for a moment. 'Not that it would be autobiographical or
anything.'

'Have you heard anything from Jack Dudley since
you've been back?' inquired Davina casually.

'If you two are going to start talking about men for
the next two hours I'm going out for a pint,' complained
James from behind the *FT*.

'Nonsense. You stay here. We may need a man's
opinion.'

James turned to the crossword.

'After all, we could be discussing your future son-in-
law,' said Davina hopefully.

James turned to the share price index.

'Oh please!' exclaimed Pandora. 'That man was rude, unreliable and aggressive. And that was on a good day. Anyway, he's bonking some daft model called Saffron Whisp at the moment.'

'Share price is looking good though,' muttered James from behind the paper. 'Dudley Enterprises, capitalized at two hundred and ten million pounds, nine quid a share. Not bad. Why don't you give him a ring?'

'Oh Daddy, please. Anyone would think you were trying to marry me off!'

'And they'd be right!' exclaimed James. 'I can't afford to pay for any more expensive holidays for you.'

'Oh, that reminds me, are we set for Hawaii this year?'

'Of course,' said Davina. 'Your father booked up Christmas in January, and got me to confirm the reservation last month, just to make sure.'

'Any chance of a little mid-year holiday treat?' inquired Pandora hopefully. 'I think we're all looking a bit peaky.'

'Certainly not. You've only just got back from Switzerland. Next time you come down I'm going to put a sign up: "Do not ask for credit, refusal often offends." Now, Pandora,' he put down his paper, 'I want to know what you're planning to do now you've finished this book we've been waiting to read for the last ten years.'

'Mrs Button, who works in the post office, keeps asking me when you're going to settle down.' Davina adopted a Cornish accent. '"That Miss Pandora, she's such a card. Is she ever going to settle?"'

'I've been making inquiries about German courses in Vienna. There's one starting in a few weeks.'

'How long for?' asked James.

'Just a few months. I've got to be back by November to do some publicity for the book.'

'You're a loose cannon,' remarked James drily, returning to his paper.

A loose cannon. Yes, that just about summed her up at the moment. A loose cannon about to go off and land somewhere in Europe. It was so exciting!

A few days later Beatrice telephoned from Zurich. Although they no longer saw very much of one another she had recently moved into her own office and was able to indulge in nuisance calls and keep up to date with her old flatmates once more.

'I'm just going to give in to my wanderlust, I'm afraid,' said Pandora, explaining her latest travel proposition.

'I think it's a marvellous idea,' said Beatrice warmly. 'I'll come and see you, Vienna is wonderful. We can sit in cafes and eat *sachertorte*. I've got some friends out there, maybe I could get us invited to one of the Viennese balls.'

'Oh Beatrice, would you?'

'No problem.'

'I wish you'd come and stay for a couple of days. Annabel and I want to take you clubbing before you turn into a Zurich gnome.'

'I turned into one ages ago. That's why I don't dare come to London. I've shrunk.'

'Oh, I do envy you living in Zurich in your wonderful

flat overlooking the lake, taking one of those lovely trams to work, getting dressed up and going to the opera in the evening . . .' Pandora sighed dreamily.

'And I envy you in London, going to restaurants, clubs, meeting new people. All people really do in Zurich is work. But the grass is always greener on the other side, I guess.'

'You must keep December free because that's when we're having the book launch. I'm hoping that lots of love affairs will start that evening. Wouldn't that be a wonderful way to be remembered? I can imagine people asking for years afterwards, "Where did you meet your husband?" "At Pandora's book launch, it was so romantic." By the way, how is your gorgeous German doctor?'

'Somewhere in Stuttgart, I think,' replied Beatrice casually. 'To tell the truth I'm quite relieved he's returned to Germany. Work is hectic at the moment and I don't have time for much else. He was becoming a bit of a pain, always nagging and telling me I worked too hard.'

'God, what a bore,' agreed Pandora. 'I can't bear it when men get whiny like that. Still, don't worry, you'll meet someone in December. Then you can have a long-distance romance which is far more exciting. How's the Swiss franc doing?' She liked to show an interest in Beatrice's job.

'It's gone up three points since we started to talk.'

'Gosh, has it?' Pandora racked her brains for something intelligent to say and failed. 'Can we start talking about men again now?'

*   *   *

Later that week she was alerted by Davina early in the morning.

'There's a piece about that gorgeous man of yours in the *Daily Mail*. Go out and buy a copy quickly!'

Pandora was sufficiently intrigued to slip on some clothes and race down to the newsagent. There was something very exciting about staying up to date with one's ex-lovers through the newspapers, she thought, eagerly scanning the pages. Gosh! There was a big picture of Jack and Saffron on the third page. She stopped in her tracks.

'Jack in the box again! Tycoon's secretary sues boss for unfair dismissal and sexual harassment. "Mad" Jack Dudley, chief executive of Dudley Enterprises, the two hundred million pound software company, is being sued by his former secretary, Sonia Smith. Ms Smith alleges that Mr Dudley made improper advances to her over several months, eventually sacking her when she refused to comply with his increasingly bizarre sexual demands.

'Mr Dudley, emerging from court yesterday, would only say, "She should be so lucky," before getting into his waiting car with top model and close companion Saffron Whisp. Witnesses, including Miss Whisp, confirm that Ms Smith had become obsessed with her employer, refusing to pass on messages from women she thought were romantically involved with him and making up rumours about their relationship. The final verdict will be delivered tomorrow. Mr Dudley is no stranger to the courts, he was recently sued for "unreasonable behaviour" by ex-wife Atlanta Du Ville. Over the past few years Jack Dudley has poured millions of pounds into a charitable foundation which rehabilitates unwanted zoo animals preceding their release into the wild. He also owns *Action!* the successful glossy environmental monthly.'

Phew, thought Pandora. Talk about drama! She was alternately gripped and piqued by the story. Maybe Sonia hadn't passed on her message. It was extraordinary, she had sounded so friendly on the telephone. Still, it looked as if Jack was being happily consoled by Saffron Whisp. It had presumably been possible to maintain contact with her despite the telephone obstacles created by Sonia. She glanced at the accompanying picture of Jack and Saffron again. He looked grim and Saffron was clinging to his arm and wearing a skimpy T-shirt with TAKE ACTION! NOW! emblazoned across her emaciated bosom. Huh, talk about sucking up. Still, she'd do the same. Pandora sighed wistfully. Jack looked deliciously brutal in the picture; seeing it brought back all her old feelings about him. Lucky Saffron. She wondered if she was obsessed with Jack as well. Seeing the way she was draped all over him in the photo, it looked like it. Jack looked absolutely fed up, perhaps he was wondering why he attracted women like Atlanta and Sonia into his life. Maybe she ought to send him details about the Foreign Legion. Judging by his expression he looked as if he was about to do a runner any moment.

When she arrived home she took a deep breath and chucked the paper in the bin. OK, so Jack had provided the inspiration behind her novel, but it was over. And yet memories kept returning to haunt her, she couldn't quite forget the sight of him emerging from the shower, a clean white towel wrapped round his glistening brown body, the way he growled '*No!*' and the memory of his laughter. She couldn't resist retrieving the paper and squirrelling it away in a cupboard upstairs. 'Flakey or what?' she muttered to herself as she pulled down her suitcase and began to pack. Thank goodness she was leaving for Vienna in four days. An intensive German course would be enough to stop her thinking about anything else at all.

Pandora was kept very busy over the next few days saying goodbye to friends and packing. During the past few weeks she had had plenty of time to borrow from Emily's extensive collection of self-help books. Reading them had reinforced her belief that like most women she was only attracted to men she couldn't have and that she was confusing feelings of longing for feelings of love. 'That's it in a nutshell!' she had exclaimed one evening, flinging down the grippingly titled *Longing! The Truth*. Most of it had been psychobabble, but it had been interesting all the same. She was an intelligent woman, love was all very well, but at the end of the day it always led down the same road i.e. taking suits to the dry-cleaners and fighting for the remote control. Who needed it?

Thus empowered, she settled into her airline seat and opened her *Guide to Vienna*, feasting on glossy pages depicting cobbled streets and tiny cafes where women wearing hats sat all day eating cakes. But she found herself distracted by a heavenly whiff of aftershave coming from somewhere. Jack had used the same one and smelling it always set her pheromones racing. She shut her eyes and sniffed the air appreciatively. For a fleeting moment she imagined he might be sitting somewhere on the plane. Turning round to look, she caught the smiling eye of the distinguished looking man in the seat next to her. Pandora prayed he hadn't noticed her sniffing the air like a model in a daft aftershave advert and blushed furiously at the thought. She found herself blurting out stupidly, 'I was wondering what aftershave you were wearing, it smells divine.' She was still so overcome by the subtle pungency of the scent that she barely took in what he looked like. All her sensory perception seemed to have diverted itself to her nose.

'I'm afraid I haven't a clue. I am given it all the time and I rarely look at the labels.' He spoke perfect English with a slight German accent. 'I have what is known as an aftershave mountain at home. Perhaps I should donate it to the EC.'

They both laughed and the ice was broken. He had very piercing blue eyes, and though he was laughing she had the feeling he was assessing her in some way. His air of prosperity and quiet authority made her feel that his assessments were rarely wrong. Maybe her nose was ruling her head, but he was rather attractive. Definitely worth cultivating. Perhaps he might know where she could find an apartment. She had booked a hotel for a few nights but she wanted to find somewhere else as soon as possible.

They chatted casually and Pandora discovered that he was the president of Bruegler Electronics, a company so large even she had heard of it. She was very impressed and their conversation became much more animated.

'I don't know a soul in Vienna,' she confided. 'I'm staying at the Grand but I haven't a clue what it's like.'

'It's all right,' said Wolfgang in his flawless English, 'but you don't want to stay in a hotel for three months. I have many friends in Vienna who I am sure would be delighted to help you.'

'Gosh, do you?' Pandora looked up at him helplessly. 'I'd really appreciate it.'

'I am in Vienna for two nights,' Wolfgang went on smoothly. 'Perhaps you would permit me to take you out for dinner tomorrow night?'

'I'd love that,' said Pandora warmly. 'My diary is quite free at the moment.'

'I'm sure it won't be for long,' said Wolfgang, grimacing slightly as he retrieved her heavy vanity case from the overhead locker. 'What have you in here, a head?' he joked.

She smiled politely, noticing a wedding ring glistening on his left hand.

'My wife and I, we are living separate lives,' he informed her, noticing her noticing.

Goodness, thought Pandora, surely he didn't think she was interested in him in *that* way? What an alarming thought! He must be at least twenty years older than she was. Still, for an old bloke he was quite nice looking.

She was flattered when he rang early the next morning

to confirm dinner. Her course didn't start for a week so she had plenty of time to find a nice flat to rent. Perhaps Wolfgang would know where the best place was to start looking.

Later that evening Pandora sat, sipping champagne, bathed in candlelight and feeling very mellow. She kept catching delicious wafts of aftershave and Wolfgang, with his shrewd blue eyes, slipping confidently between German and English, was beginning to seem quite irresistible. The fact that he had a son who was nearly her age only served to make him seem more out of bounds and attractive. She was longing to say, 'If only I was twenty years older,' but thought it might be tactless in the circumstances. As she was about to crack into the caramel topping of a delicious looking crème brûlée, Wolfgang cleared his throat and looked at her intently.

'You don't have to look too far for somewhere to stay, Pandora. I would be delighted to lend you my flat in the centre of Vienna. It is in a good area and I think you would find it to your taste. I am hardly ever there, and it would bring me great pleasure to know that it was being used by such a charming girl as yourself.' He flinched slightly as a piece of caramel flew though the air and landed on his immaculate jacket.

Pandora's eyes widened. 'Oh, but I would have to pay you something if I stayed there.'

'Certainly not!' His Teutonic tones rang round the restaurant causing her knees to weaken.

'Oh, all right then.' Pandora capitulated gracefully.

'I am only in Vienna about twice a month, and when

I am here I would like to be permitted to take you out for dinner.'

'It sounds a wonderful arrangement to me,' said Pandora through a haze of champagne-induced bon-homie. Was she having an out-of-body experience? She couldn't quite believe that someone was actually asking her to be his mistress. Any moment now he would be offering her a flower allowance. But wasn't this what she was looking for? A nice no-strings relationship with a securely married tycoon? Someone who would pat her on the head during infrequent visits and mutter, 'Don't worry your pretty little head about that,' before making love to her and disappearing back to his wife who would get the dirty socks while she got the flowers and free accommodation?

'In that case,' purred Wolfgang smoothly, 'I shall arrange for my driver to come and pick you up tomorrow morning. He will take you to my apartment and if it meets with your approval he will give you a key so you can make yourself quite at home. There is just one thing I have to ask of you.'

'Yes?'

'I need to rely on your discretion. Although my wife and I lead separate lives, I hold a responsible position in the business world, my wife is the close friend of the Chancellor's wife and we mix with many influential people. While she is not a particularly jealous woman and she is prepared to turn a blind eye to my, um, *friendships*, I should hate to embarrass her publicly.' He reached over and took Pandora's hand. 'And you are so charming. I saw you checking in at the airport and I said to the hostess, "Please, I must sit next to that girl".'

Pandora was very flattered. 'Did you really?'

'Of course. And then I saw you again in the book-shop, buying very many magazines, and struggling on to the aeroplane clutching lots of heavy bags. It made me smile.'

She had a quick pang, remembering how Jack had laughed at her when she had struggled on to the plane carrying bags full of Swiss yogurt. But that was a lifetime ago. Meanwhile Wolfgang was carrying on as if he was smitten. It was rather nice, she was beginning to take quite a shine to him. As long as he wore a condom, what could be the harm in it?

To Pandora's surprise, Wolfgang didn't suggest that she spend the night at his flat but simply dropped her off at her hotel, kissed her hand and promised to ring her the following evening.

Pandora giggled as she let herself into her room. What had she agreed to? She must be mad, she would never do this if she was in London. But finishing her novel and arriving in Vienna had loosened something in her. When she was ninety she wanted to look back on her life and feel she had tried *everything*. Besides, being a mistress would be marvellous material for her next novel.

She glanced at her watch; it wasn't too late to ring Beatrice. She would know if she was being completely amoral to consider this extraordinary offer. And as a Swiss banker her discretion was assured. Wolfgang wasn't the only one who wanted to keep this little arrangement secret.

Beatrice burst out laughing when Pandora outlined the situation. '"I love your aftershave"! I can't believe you said that, it's so deliciously corny!'

'It's a great line though, it worked a treat.'

'Obviously. I think you're doing this just so you'll have something to write about.'

'Yes, I suppose I do see it as a sort of career move. Being a mistress will help me understand the nuances of human behaviour more thoroughly.'

'Bullshit. You just want free accommodation and occasional sex,' said Beatrice succinctly.

'Well, the flat does sound rather super, and Wolfgang is actually quite fanciable if you like the older man. He's very tall and distinguished looking, and he's very well read. And he sounds deliciously authoritarian when he's speaking German.'

'What was the name of the company he's President of?'

'Bruegler Electronics.'

'Wolfgang Bruegler? God, I know him. Well, I know *of* him. Bruegler Electronics is a huge company. I'd make sure you get a huge flower allowance if I were you.'

'But I feel a bit guilty about his wife really.'

'I wouldn't. She's probably relieved to have the prestige without the sex. Not all women like being *bothered*,' explained Beatrice with Euro-pragmatism. 'Though I wish someone would bother me occasionally.'

'Me too,' agreed Pandora. 'Wolfgang could be perfect.

It's sort of a business arrangement really, everyone knows where they stand. Besides, he's very attractive. I'd want to go out with him whether he was offering me free accommodation or not. But tell me honestly, would you do something like this if you were in my shoes?'

'Probably not. I've had one affair with a married man and it was enough to put me off for life. He kept saying he was going to leave his wife but he never did.'

'God, I remember. Still, you wouldn't have wanted to be lumbered with a shit like that anyway.' Pandora remembered that Beatrice had been cut up for weeks, it had been so unlike her. 'Perhaps this sort of thing only really works if no one falls in love with anybody,' she continued. 'The last thing I want is to pinch someone else's husband, it was bad enough having one of my own. Besides, lest we forget, I'm here to learn German.'

'And the best way to learn German is to find a—'

'German lover!'

'I'll wangle a nuisance trip to Vienna before you leave,' said Beatrice. 'I want to check out your apartment and give you a German exam to find out how hard you've been working.'

'You can come and stay with me.'

'It's a done deal. Ring me tomorrow from the apartment and let me know what it's like. I'm very intrigued.'

'*Vita lurga.*'

'*Vita lurga.*'

Pandora felt immensely reassured. She was longing for excitement and adventure. Like a snake, she had cast off a skin and now she was alone with her sparkling vanity case in Vienna, with its new sights, sounds and experiences, free to reinvent herself in which ever way she chose.

Wolfgang's chauffeur appeared at ten the following morning. Pandora felt a little sheepish as he impassively put her suitcases into the boot of the capacious Mercedes and drove the short distance to Wolfgang's flat. Parking the car, he handed her a key, explaining in immaculate English that she was to check the apartment, and if it met with her approval he would bring up her luggage. Pandora was grateful that she could snoop around and get a feel for the place without anyone watching. If it wasn't fabulous she would turn round and check into the hotel again.

It was fabulous. Taking up the entire top floor of the building, it had highly polished parquet floors, Biedermeier furniture and fabulous pictures. She took a deep breath and wandered over to the huge picture windows which revealed Vienna in all its glory. Even the bathroom was perfect, it looked as if someone had hollowed it out of an enormous piece of creamy white marble. It, too, had a large window with extensive views over the city and beyond. Talk about good *feng shui*, thought Pandora, wandering from room to room in a daze. It was the sort of flat one saw in exclusive magazines. She had hardly believed they existed, let alone imagined staying in one. She raced downstairs and asked the chauffeur to help her bring up her things.

Six weeks later Pandora arrived at the patisserie where she was meeting Beatrice. It was the first time Beatrice had had the chance to get to Vienna and Pandora was longing to see her. It was very cold outside and it was a relief to escape into the warm cafe. As she sat down a sumptuous tea trolley was wheeled past, releasing a delicious aroma of coffee, warm cinnamon and steaming chocolate but Pandora gazed past it indifferently. She'd been feeling a bit low and hadn't had much of an appetite recently. She glanced at her day-old copy of the *Daily Mail* and kept an eye on the door. It wasn't long before Beatrice appeared and Pandora waved her paper excitedly at her. 'Beatrice! I'm over here! Hey, your hair looks great.' Beatrice's glossy chestnut hair had grown since they had last met and now fell halfway down her back, while the subtle use of brown eye shadow enhanced the colour of her striking green eyes. Heads turned as she slipped off her coat and sat down next to Pandora.

'Thanks. I had a make-up lesson when I was on a business trip to Paris last week, it's made quite a difference. You're looking great too – have you lost weight?' Privately Beatrice thought Pandora was much too thin, her tailored tweed jacket was hanging off her slim frame and her face was pale and gaunt.

Pandora smiled wanly. 'A bit. I think I'm about to be reincarnated as a coat hanger any day now.'

'So how's it all going with Wolfgang?' asked Beatrice curiously.

'It's OK, I mean he's terribly kind and generous, but he is *around* rather more than I thought he might be. The original arrangement was that he'd stay three nights a month.'

'Which is about perfect,' agreed Beatrice, trying to

avoid looking at the mouthwatering display of sachertorte on the tea trolley as it perambulated past.

'But now he's here three times a *week*. It's a bit time-consuming because it means I can't study or go out with the other people on my course when he's here. And he hardly needs any sleep. Sometimes we make love until about two in the morning which is fabulous – but then he gets up and starts doing paperwork and ringing Japan and America. It's totally knackering. Still, there are compensations. When we're in bed he talks to me in German so I'm picking up all sorts of useful phrases, and he's very generous. He took me shopping last week.' She flashed a stunning gold Cartier watch at Beatrice and smiled.

'I think I'd better tell my clients to sell their shares in Bruegler Electronics. Old Wolfgang is obviously getting a bit distracted,' laughed Beatrice.

'And how's life in lovely, romantic Zurich?' asked Pandora.

'You're the only person who thinks Zurich is remotely romantic. I guess it's because you have fond memories of that man – I've forgotten his name – the one who took you to the Dolder Hotel. Now *that* is a romantic hotel. A client took me to dinner there last week.'

'Anyone interesting?'

'Well, yes, but he's married. I'm not like you, I want someone who's free so I can get married myself. Another dead-end affair wouldn't suit me at all.' She stirred her coffee wistfully.

'You're still not really over that married man, are you?' asked Pandora gently.

'Some days I think I am and others – well, I'm not so sure. I get asked out and I'm meeting lots of people, so who knows? And I love my work, I really do. It keeps me sane.'

'Thank God for that. At least we have some control over our careers, unlike our love lives. By the way, I'm loving the course, I can speak quite a bit of German now.'

'Obviously you can say, "Darling, would you buy me a diamond-encrusted Cartier watch?"'

'Funnily enough that was the first thing I learnt. Next week I learn how to say "Now I'd like a more expensive one, please, and while we're at it, can I have matching earrings, a necklace and a bracelet too". I am joking, by the way. God, I'm so dreadful. Talking to you like this makes me feel terribly guilty. Oh well, I'll be back in London in a month and then I shall devote myself to writing for *Action!* and other worthy causes.'

Beatrice glanced at her watch. 'I must just have a quick look at your flat and then I'll have to shoot back to the airport. I wish I could stay longer but I shouldn't really be here at all.'

The girls quickly gathered up their things and dashed across the street to Wolfgang's apartment. Beatrice was as thrilled with it as Pandora. 'It's simply gorgeous.' She stroked the marble in the bathroom. 'How clever of you to find it!'

'And I owe it all to my nose. If Wolfgang hadn't been wearing that delicious aftershave, I might never have started talking to him. I definitely wasn't in the mood for conversation.' She fiddled absently with one of the gold taps and stared bleakly out of the window. She suddenly felt terribly unhappy. 'He had this marble shipped over from Italy,' she added in a choked voice.

Beatrice touched her arm. 'Darling, what's wrong? You can't hide anything from me, you know.'

Pandora sat down on the edge of the bath and burst into tears. 'Since I came here I've been so busy pretending to be someone else that I've forgotten who I am. Seeing you has made me realize how sleazy it all is. Wolfgang is the first man I've slept with that I didn't at least *think* I was in love with. If he hadn't smelt so nice and I hadn't drunk so much and he hadn't had this flat I'd never have given him another thought. And now he rings up all the time, he's always here, I've got this awful feeling that he might have fallen in love with me. He's even started talking about leaving his wife. It's not a game any more and it's all so dreadfully serious.'

'Yes, but married men hardly ever do leave their wives. Maybe he's just saying it because he thinks that's what you want to hear.'

'God, I hope so. I don't want to *marry* him, for God's sake! His wife sounds really nice, she raises tons of money for charity and they have loads of children. I just feel so guilty about it all. If I really loved him it wouldn't be so bad. But as it is, I feel no better than a prostitute.' She blew her nose loudly. 'He left his wallet here last week and there was a picture of me in it. Imagine if his wife had found it!' She dried her eyes and got up. 'You coming here has helped me make up my mind. I'm going to pack up my things and clear off. I should never have stayed this long.'

'You can't stay here if you feel like this, but where will you go?'

'That's easy enough, a hotel. It'll be such a *relief* not being anyone's beck and call girl any more.' Pandora was starting to feel much better now that she had come to a firm decision. She had thought that Wolfgang would help erase all memories of Jack from her mind, but he hadn't. Last week she had been in a crowded bar and heard Jack's laughter coming from somewhere but when she'd turned round it had disappeared like a mirage. Instead of missing him less she found she missed him more. Wolfgang's adoration and constant presence just made her feel worse.

It took longer to write Wolfgang a note explaining her sudden disappearance than it did to pack her suitcases and walk out of the door. Once outside in the street, she raised her arm confidently and summoned a taxi, asking him to take her to the Sacher Hotel in flawless German. She was free again! She wasn't sorry to leave the flat. It signified the end of a chapter. One day she would have a place just as stunning; the difference was that it would be her very own.

Chapter Twenty-two

A month later Pandora returned home. Thankfully the flight was very quiet and she had a row to herself. She had made up her mind not to talk to any more strange men and to avoid all emotional complications until the book came out and she could afford to look haggard again. Till then she wanted to stock up on early nights, go to the Ritzy Marina club and have facials before she officially burst on to the London scene looking lithe and rejuvenated, ready to publicize her novel bigtime.

As soon as she let herself into her flat she dumped her suitcases and rushed to the telephone.

'Hi, Poppy. It's me, Pandora. I'm back from Vienna and ready to do anything really – *Desert Island Discs*, *Playboy*, the front cover of *GQ Magazine* . . .' God, she'd give *anything* to appear on *Desert Island Discs* and be asked probing yet delicate questions about her sex life.

'Hello, Pandora,' said Poppy cheerfully with a sinking heart. God, now Pandora was back on the scene she wouldn't get a moment's peace. 'I love the novel, it's hilarious. I've sent it to *Harpers & Queen* and *Tatler* for them to review. They'll get back to me by next week if they want to interview you.'

'Or take a picture?' asked Pandora hopefully.

'Yes, you never know. It's very much their sort of thing. I'm glad you liked the cover, by the way.'

The cover design had been finalized and sent to Pandora while she was in Vienna. Her request to appear on it with Annabel had been politely but firmly refused, and instead a drop-dead gorgeous model was skiing down a mountain wearing a black see-through chiffon dress and a tiara. The Milk Tray man was hot on her tail and balancing a tray of champagne and a box of chocolates on a ski pole.

'Yes, it was great fun. It sums up the novel perfectly.'

'Well, it was lovely to talk to you, Pandora. I'll be in touch with you about any interviews as soon as I hear anything.'

But what about *Desert Island Discs*? thought Pandora glumly, replacing the receiver. Had anyone sent a copy of her novel to Sue Lawley? Oh well, Emily said Poppy was the best in the business. She would just have to leave everything in her capable hands.

Pandora had begun making notes on her next novel. She was thinking about writing about a girl who has an affair with a man she doesn't particularly fancy just because he uses the same aftershave as the man of her dreams, but Emily said the story was unrealistic and no reader would empathize with such a stupid heroine. But various ideas

476

were starting to emerge from somewhere, and often a chat with a friend or an overheard conversation on the bus would trigger off an idea which she would quickly scribble down in a notebook.

One morning Poppy rang. Pandora thought she must be dreaming, Poppy *never* rang. But then again, she telephoned Poppy so often she probably didn't need to.

'I'm sorry to bother you, Pandora.'

'Oh, it's no bother!' said Pandora enthusiastically.

'*Harpers & Queen* rang this morning, they absolutely adore the book and want to include you in a feature about up-and-coming frothbuster authorettes. Would you be interested in taking part?'

'Of course! I'm there already!'

'Great. Five of you are to meet next Thursday at ten o'clock in the morning at a studio in Covent Garden. They asked if you would bring a pair of skis, a cocktail dress and a Balaclava. Apparently they're thinking of photographing each girl in the context of her novel.'

Pandora put down the telephone feeling slightly confused. She could understand the skis and the cocktail dress, but the Balaclava? Were they confusing her with Salman Rushdie? It was all very peculiar.

Next Thursday she struggled into the photographic studio weighed down with ski boots but feeling deliciously *sportive* because of her skis which she had nonchalantly balanced on one shoulder. She had sensibly decided to leave her Balaclava at home. Party girls did not wear Balaclavas in public.

She glanced around eagerly, looking forward to making

contact with other frothbuster authorettes. The place was a hive of industry. A chandelier had been set up in the corner and a girl about her age was being helped up a stepladder. Presumably she was going to be photographed swinging from it. How exciting! An enormous paper cake had been set up in another part of the room and an authorette wearing a bunny girl costume was practising popping out of it. Another area had been turned into a sort of rustic scene with bales of hay. A grumpy authorette was trying on a misshapen Jane Austen-style bonnet and being told to cheer up. 'I'll *kill* my agent,' she was muttering in between cigarettes. A fashionably emaciated fashion victim wearing black leggings and a pair of Doc Martens dashed over to Pandora.

'You must be Pandora, judging by the skis. Ay'm Tamarind Whisp, ay'm helping set up the shoot. Let's go into the changing room and get your clothes sorted out. We've been sent a whole lot of stuff from Gucci and Armani so pick out anything you like.'

The day was getting better and better, thought Pandora as she waded through the piles of skimpy silk dresses and impossibly high stilettos that filled the room. She eventually settled on a flimsy pink baby doll dress with a matching pair of diamond-encrusted fluffy mules. She placed a tiara on her head and glanced at herself in the mirror. It was the perfect ensemble. Tamarind wafted back in and did a double take. 'Darling, it's to *die* for. But can you ski in it?'

'Of course!' said Pandora cheerfully, gazing at her

fluffy mules hopefully. 'By the way, are you related to Saffron Whisp, the model?'

'Yah. She's may sister, ectually.'

'Gosh, I met her once in a restaurant. Isn't she going out with someone called, um, Jack Dudley?'

'Oh, that finished ages ago. She was madly in love with him but he was such a shit to her.'

'So what did this, um, Jack Dudley chap do to her then?' asked Pandora cosily.

'He never rang when he said he would and he cancelled dates at short notice. All he ever did was work, it used to drive her mad. And she suspected that he was still hung up on some old girlfriend who had disappeared somewhere. God, I don't blame her.'

'Yes, he sounds like a complete nightmare,' agreed Pandora thoughtfully, trying to balance on her skis without much success.

'The mules will have to go, darling,' observed a fey photographer. 'What about these little flatties?' He pointed to a pair of pink ballet shoes.

'Yah! Right!' agreed Tamarind. 'We can decorate them with pompoms and bits of fur, for an *après ski* sort of look, yah?'

'Yah, why not?' agreed Pandora happily, as a make-up artist began covering her face with a thick layer of unguent.

Eight hours later Pandora staggered out of the studio and into a taxi. She was absolutely shattered. The photographer had decided to place her skis at an angle which meant her feet had had to be strapped on to them.

Two assistants had stood out of sight holding up an invisible safety harness which she had hung onto for dear life. Her tiara had kept dropping off because the wind machine had been so strong, and she'd completely lost track of her cleavage. In fact, the whole thing had been a bit of a nightmare. She hadn't even had time to fraternize properly with the other up-and-coming frothbuster authorettes as they'd had their own personal obstacle courses to contend with. No wonder models were such an odd shape! She was starting to sympathize with Saffron. If she had to do this every day she'd have a personality problem too. She had fixed a bright inane grin on her face and thought about Jack solidly for eight hours. Could the mysterious disappearing ex-girlfriend that he was still hung up on be her? It was a dreamy thought, but probably totally implausible. She wondered what had really happened the weekend he was supposed to take her to Cliveden.

A few days later Poppy rang *again*. Life really was becoming exciting!

'Darling, the shoot was a great success. They *love* the pictures. We love the pictures. You look gorgeous. Very, um,' she paused, 'fecund.' Pandora's heart sank, she knew she should have tried to control her cleavage.

Poppy went on, 'On the strength of the pictures I'm getting lots of interest from the glossies. I suggest we milk it for what it's worth. You're going to be hot property, Pandora. Can you face it?'

'Yes, I can face it,' said Pandora bravely. God, she might become famous! Journalists might start asking her for beauty tips and for her views on world peace. She could plug *Action!*. That would please Sven.

'That's the spirit. Can you come in this afternoon so we can go through everything?'

'Of course,' Pandora agreed eagerly.

The Red Duck offices were housed in a glossy modern building in the City. Pandora always felt proud and excited every time she visited. She loved the shiny brass plaque outside which stated 'Red Duck Publishing', and the notice inside that said, 'Authorized Persons Only Beyond This Point'. She was an authorized person! Making her way up to the nineteenth floor she felt purposeful and confident. She had created a product and now she was going to sell it. She thought of all the people who were also involved, whose jobs depended on the success of books like hers. While she had been working away in solitude, it had been hard to remember that all these other people were part of the process too.

Poppy welcomed her warmly. 'Hi there. Have a look at the prints while I fetch us a coffee.' Pandora sat down happily. She had never been offered a cup of coffee at Red Duck before, things were really looking up. She glanced at the pictures and hardly recognized herself. The photographer had done a brilliant job. Clouds of blonde hair were billowing around her face and the baby doll dress appeared to be floating in the breeze. Unfortunately her cleavage was the only thing that hadn't defied gravity and her boobs looked as if they were about to part company from the dress at any second. But overall she was very happy with the pictures. She really looked as if she was skiing.

'Great fun, aren't they?' said Poppy, returning with two cups of instant coffee. 'You look very, um . . .'

'*Sportive?*' supplied Pandora hopefully.

'Well, the chaps in the print room used a different word, but yes, you do look quite sporty. Because there is so much interest, we'd like to help you arrange the book launch to maximize the publicity. Have you thought at all about venues?'

'Well, I did make a provisional booking at the London Dungeon.'

'Funnily enough, we had a launch there last year for a thriller, it was a great success. I don't know how suitable it would be for a frothbuster romance though.'

'Oh, it would be perfect. Just think of all the trysting possibilities in Dr Crippen's sitting room. Where else could you say to a man you fancied, "Meet me in five minutes in the Spanish Inquisition torture chamber"? It would be terribly sinister and romantic at the same time.'

'Hm,' said Poppy thoughtfully. 'It *might* work . . .'

'And the magazines would be able to get some great photos of celebs cavorting behind cauldrons of boiling heads.' Pandora was starting to get quite carried away.

'Why not?' agreed Poppy suddenly. 'It would certainly be lots of fun. I'll get on to them and fix things up. Now, are you free next week?'

'Oh yes. Completely.'

'Good. Because *GQ* would like to do an interview and take some pictures on Monday, the *Daily Mail* want to photograph you at the ski show skiing in a selection of cocktail dresses for their Femail section, the *Sunday Times* Style section wants to talk to you as well. Shall I go ahead and plan everything and get back to you later?'

'Yes, do. It all sounds terribly exciting.'

'I think you'll love it and it'll help get sales off to a really good start. I can sense we're on a roll so let's just go with it.'

Pandora spun downstairs and into the street with stars in her eyes, oblivious of the grey skies and congested streets around her. Red Duck had agreed to make all the arrangements, all she had to do was produce the guests. Poppy was right, they were on a roll!

To Pandora's delight everyone was enthusiastic about having the party at the London Dungeon. She raked through her address book, taking the opportunity to renew contact with friends she hadn't seen since before her retreat to Switzerland. Annabel was coming into her own, suggesting various mouthwatering micro celebs with which to tempt the hordes of photographers who would hopefully appear. They spent an evening drawing up the final guest list which Annabel promptly faxed to various suitably up-market magazines and newspapers. Every facet of the *beau monde* was represented – celebrity aristocrats, deposed royals, pop stars, supermodels and television presenters. Annabel had started a cunning rumour that Pierce Brosnan was going to show up dressed as the Milk Tray man, but Pandora suspected that this was probably gilding the lily.

'Shall we ask Jack?' asked Annabel hopefully. 'I've been reading about him quite a lot recently. He seems to be doing awfully well.'

Pandora had had the foresight to buy shares in Dudley Enterprises a year ago and checked the price every day. It was so important to keep up with one's investments. She knew that shares in Dudley Enterprises had doubled in six months. It was certainly doing a lot better than Pandora's Mines which appeared to have stabilized at one pence a share.

'No fear. I'd rather be strung up naked from an electricity pylon for three weeks without food or water than even have to *glimpse* that man again.'

'Oh, all right then,' said Annabel. It was unlike Pandora to be so vitriolic but maybe she was just feeling nervous about the book launch.

'By the way, Möet and Chandon have agreed to provide free champagne if they get a mention in all the magazines. It's going to be a tremendous party, Pandora. You are lucky, when the book comes out you'll become quite famous. You'll be able to give up writing and spend the rest of your life opening supermarkets and being written about by Nigel Dempster.'

'How dreadful,' lied Pandora. 'Actually, I thought I'd quite like to help with *Action!*'s dolphin rescue campaign. I have nightmares about those poor dolphins in Hawaii swimming around in bathtubs. Sven's still working on a campaign with the *Daily Mail* to establish a huge dolphin and whale sanctuary out there. Maybe I could help out with that. Then I'd have an excuse to live in

Hawaii.' Pandora gazed mistily out of the window. She could almost hear the roar of the ocean and the sound of wind chimes shivering in the sea breeze . . .

'Wake up, Pandora,' said Annabel briskly; she would rather roast in the fires of hell for evermore than live somewhere *Hello!* did not cover. 'Let's get this party sorted out then you can dream away to your heart's content.'

Pandora dragged herself reluctantly back to the present and glanced at the guest list again. 'D'you think all these celebs will turn up?'

'Of course,' laughed Annabel. 'They'll love to be associated with something intellectual like a book. Most of them can't read and if they're photographed holding a copy of your novel it'll do wonders for their intellectual credibility.'

'So we're doing them a favour by inviting them really, aren't we?'

'Exactly,' said Annabel crisply.

Pandora spent the next three weeks taking part in a flurry of publicity events organized by Red Duck and fielding telephone calls about her prospective book launch. She'd had a brainwave while talking to Sven about the dolphin article she'd sent him and offered to give all her royalties to the *Action!–Daily Mail* Dial a Dolphin Campaign. Sven had been thrilled and offered to plug her book in the magazine and feature her on the front cover. She didn't know why she hadn't thought of it before. Once Poppy had ascertained that Red Duck's profits wouldn't be impaired, she too had been enthusiastic.

'It'll be so good for sales. We can say on the cover that for every book sold, a proportion will go towards saving sweet little dolphins. It's a great idea! You might even start a new trend amongst authors!' she finished doubtfully.

Davina and Pandora spent two days combing the whole of Knightsbridge for a suitably glamorous outfit, finally settling on a gold sheath dress that clung to Pandora like a second skin. If one couldn't go over the top at one's own book launch, when could one? Davina was planning to wear her favourite dress that she had had for thirty years. 'It's the one I wore the night I first met your father.'

'Of course, the slinky blue one,' said Pandora over a deliciously creamy cappuccino at Prêt à Manger. 'Remind me of the story again.'

'Darling, I must have told you a thousand times!' exclaimed Davina.

'Just tell me one more time, please,' wheedled Pandora.

'It was the night of my twenty-first party, my parents had hired the ballroom of the Hyde Park Hotel which they could only afford because they'd sold a Canaletto – can you imagine! I still have nightmares, it was *such* a beautiful picture. Still, it was a lovely party. Anyway, I was dancing with George, we had just got engaged which was rather fun, and then I caught sight of your father standing at the bar just looking at me. Someone must have brought him along, we were always short of men . . .' She sipped her coffee thoughtfully.

'And then what happened?' asked Pandora, gripped by the romance and drama of the story.

'Darling, you know what happened. He started making

his way over, to ask me to dance presumably, but my mother suddenly appeared from nowhere and insisted I go and cut my birthday cake. Then I was busy dancing and having a lovely time and when I next saw James he was busy chatting up your mother. And the rest, as they say, is history.'

'Gosh, that's so romantic. I'm thrilled that you and Dad are coming. You won't feel awkward about seeing Mummy again, will you?' Davina and Georgina hadn't met since Pandora's wedding.

'Of course not. I rang her last week and we had a lovely chat, it was just like old times. We're looking forward to meeting up again at your party. I know I haven't said this before, but not a day goes by when I don't thank you for doing what you did. Your father and I are so happy together. My one dream is that now you've had this great success you'll find someone who can make you as happy.' Davina's eyes misted over with tears and Pandora was so choked she couldn't speak for a moment.

'I quite liked someone a lot once, but it didn't really come to anything. I guess I'm not really cut out for a great romance. I'll just have to resign myself to writing about other people's. It's easier that way.'

'That someone you mentioned, it's Jack Dudley, isn't it?'

'Yup. He was pretty special, but it kind of fizzled out. I guess he wasn't that keen on me at the end of the day.'

'To be fair, you did just disappear to Switzerland with no forwarding address.'

'I'm sure he could have found it if he'd wanted to

enough. Where there's a will there's a way. I mean, the man is running a company valued at over two hundred million pounds. Tracking me down wouldn't have been impossible. Put it this way, he should think twice about applying to work for MI5.' They both laughed. 'I do still think about him sometimes though. There's some song about him being the only one who can make me laugh and cry at the same time. Whenever I hear that it always reminds me of when we . . . Oh, I'm being ridiculous. Please don't repeat this to anyone, it's just me being stupid. I'm perfectly happy as I am, life is so frantic at the moment I haven't got time even to think about having a boyfriend, let alone actually have one. Heaven knows who I'm going to write about in my next novel.'

Later, as Davina sat in a taxi taking her back to the exquisite Belgravia *pied-à-terre* that James had bought her last year, she smiled a small, secret smile. She tapped a number into her mobile telephone. 'Darling, it's me. I'm going to spend an extra night in town. Could you get me a number from your Institute of Directors directory, d'you think? I've got an idea . . .'

Chapter Twenty-three

The morning of the party Pandora woke early and leapt out of bed, feeling sick with nerves. She only had ten hours to get ready for the party which was due to start at six that evening. Annabel and Red Duck were taking care of all the arrangements between them. When she had asked what she could do to help, she had been told firmly to keep out of the way and just concentrate on being as glamorous as possible. This suited Pandora very well and she was planning to spend the whole day in Harrods' hair and beauty salon being massaged, exfoliated, plucked and *coiffed*.

Several hours later she emerged from the beauty salon feeling relaxed and energized. She would need all her strength to cope with the evening's excitements, which promised to be massive. After rushing home to slip into her slinky dress, she flung on an ankle-length mac for anonymity as the dress was far too flashy to wear safely on the streets, and hailed a cab to the London Dungeon.

Annabel and Poppy were already there, supervising

last-minute arrangements. The dungeons looked superb; masses of black candles had been lit and there were glorious displays of flowers everywhere which made the place look more mysterious than sinister. There were also three life-size posters taken at the *Daily Mail* ski show of Pandora skiing down an artificial ski slope wearing a negligée which revealed embarrassing amounts of touched-up cleavage. Pandora cringed. *GQ Magazine* had just featured her in an article, wittily entitled 'Bimbos With Brains, A New Pheromone?' and used the same picture.

'The star has arrived!' cried Annabel, throwing her arms round Pandora. 'Guess what? Red Duck have asked me to do their celebrity PR. Poppy says they'll *pay* me to take famous authors to parties and drive them around London. Can you imagine? Talk about a job made in heaven.'

'That's great!' said Pandora, touching her friend lightly on the arm. 'Annabel, I'm so grateful for your help in arranging all this and I'm thrilled that something nice has come out of it. You really deserve it. It just goes to show that what goes round comes round.' She was shivering with nerves. 'Shit, I'm nervous. Shall we have some champagne?'

'Of course, there's loads of it.' They flagged down a passing waiter and helped themselves. 'Congratulations. Here's to your fame and fortune. We won't get much of a chance to talk later so just remember to enjoy yourself and to get in as many photographs as possible holding your book and revealing as much cleavage as you can stand. Shouldn't be too difficult in that dress. Oh, look! It's Beatrice!'

They all greeted one another excitedly. 'I just flew in and got a taxi straight from Heathrow,' said Beatrice, shrugging off her cashmere coat to reveal a little black dress. 'Look, it has no back.' She pirouetted, revealing a large expanse of smooth brown skin.

'Oh, it's so good to see you, Beatrice,' said Pandora, her eyes welling up with tears. 'I can't remember the last time we were all together like this, it must have been at my wedding.' She shuddered. 'I'd like to propose a toast. Please raise your glasses. To friendship, and let us remain unscathed by the ravages of love for as long as possible.'

'Hey, steady on, speak for yourself. I'd welcome a little ravaging if it's all the same to you,' said Annabel. 'Straighten up, girls, the punters are starting to pour in.'

'I hope I know some of them,' whispered Pandora, watching the door nervously before smiling in relief as Emily appeared, closely followed by Davina and her father.

'Darling, you look fabulous!' said Davina, greeting her stepdaughter warmly.

'Where is it?' asked James.

'Where's what?'

'The book. I thought you said you'd finished it.'

'I have.' She dug into her handbag. 'I've got one copy but I can't give it away because I'm to be photographed with it. I think they decided not to give any copies away so that people buy their own. It's better for sales.'

'That's a mean trick. I was hoping to fill the car boot.'

'Anyone interesting appeared yet?' asked Davina, doubtfully fingering a spiky black flower arrangement.

Pandora glanced around. The place was beginning to fill up now, and to her great pleasure she realized she knew most of the guests. She waved at several enthusiastically. Several sinister looking Israelis clutching mobile phones and wearing dark glasses were stumbling around, unable to see very much in the gloom. 'Oh good,' said Pandora, 'all the General's cronies have turned up, which must mean the General is lurking somewhere.' Photographers were busy taking pictures and everyone appeared to be enjoying themselves.

'Miss Black? I'm from *Vogue*, can I take a picture of you and your parents?'

'Is Georgie here? She should really be in this picture,' said Davina, glancing round. 'There she is. Come on, Pandora, let's go and fetch her.' James rolled his eyes heavenward as Davina and Pandora hurried over to Georgie, the two older women hugging one another and talking nineteen to the dozen.

'Darling, we're all so proud of you,' said Georgie emotionally in between photo opportunities. 'It's such an achievement.'

Davina was looking around anxiously.

'Are you looking for someone?' asked Pandora.

'Oh no. Just admiring this extraordinary place. Look, you go and join the young people. Georgie and I have lots of catching up to do.'

Georgie smiled, and Pandora noticed there were tears in her eyes. 'I think I've seen this dress somewhere before,' said Georgie, and both women laughed.

'You should remember it,' said Davina. 'You borrowed it enough times.'

James was engrossed in a realistic enactment of a sixteenth-century hanging next to them. 'It says here that criminals could avoid going to the gallows if they found someone who would marry them. Interestingly enough, most people opted for the hanging.' He glanced at Georgie and Davina who were shrieking with laughter about something. 'Can't say I blame them really.'

'C'mon, Dad, you don't mean that. Let's go along to the Jack the Ripper Experience. That'll cheer you up.'

On the way, Pandora dumped him on a glamorous girlfriend who had a thing for older men and shot off to the Meet Dr Crippen Experience. She was intercepted by Annabel who was being chatted up enthusiastically by Sven. 'He's gorgeous, I can't believe you haven't introduced us before. You know I have a penchant for the Nordic type.'

'Your charming friend was just telling me about her love of animals,' said Sven smoothly.

'Especially the dead ones she gets to wear on her back,' said Pandora.

Annabel kicked her in the shin and smiled sweetly, before being distracted by a woman wearing a ghoulish mask locked within one of the cages. She read the accompanying inscription out loud. '"The Scold's Bridle was used to muzzle women who misused their tongues to the scandal and abuse of their neighbours." What a terrifying thought.'

'Ugh, creepy,' agreed Pandora, peering sombrely into the cage. 'I was just on my way to the Meet Dr Crippen Experience. D'you fancy coming along?'

'I'm more of a Jack the Ripper girl I think,' said Annabel, peering at her programme. 'Hang on, we mustn't miss the Divorce in the Middle Ages exhibition, it's been sponsored by *Divorce! Magazine* so it's bound to be pretty gory. It's starting next door in a few minutes, come on.' Pandora and Sven followed her into the next room where groups of savage women appeared to be brutalizing men with *unspeakable* instruments. Beneath a crack in the floorboards Pandora could just make out a frighteningly realistic wax dummy being torn apart by rats in what looked like a coal hole.

The gruesome atmosphere was having an oddly lascivious effect on her guests, who were taking advantage of the unusual atmosphere to indulge in all sorts of *louche* behaviour. It was so dark that Pandora couldn't recognize the entwined couples trysting in corners. 'I'm glad everyone seems to be getting along,' she said to Annabel. 'Having the party here has really broken the ice.'

'That's one way of looking at it,' said Annabel, drooling at Sven who was engrossed in a display of a man slowly being pulled apart on a rack. 'I can't resist him. I'm going to ask him to a secret tryst.' She sidled up to Sven and whispered in his ear and then sidled back to Pandora.

'What did you ask him?'

'To meet me at the stake in two minutes. Isn't there anyone here you want to tryst with, Pandora?'

'No fear,' said Pandora firmly. 'I'll leave you to it. Good luck.'

She turned round and was grabbed by a cluster of old school friends who dragged her off to the Jack the Ripper Experience. She was momentarily distracted by the sight of a woman sawing a man's head off and when she turned round her school friends had been sucked up in the stampede towards the Joan of Arc Out-Of-Body Experience. Looking around, she wondered if she wasn't having an out-of-body experience herself. Her mouth was dry from talking so much and she was more than a little drunk. She put her hand out for a moment, steadying herself on an axe which was sticking conveniently out of the floor. She had done it, she had actually written a book! People no longer thought of her as daffy little Pandora, a failed housewife, living off the proceeds of an unearned income, but as a success in her own right. Though her throat was sore from talking and her mouth ached from smiling she felt proud, strong and happy.

Taking a deep breath to give her strength, she caught a delicious whiff of familiar aftershave . . . She smiled to herself, she wasn't going to fall for *that* old trick again. Glancing round, she caught sight of a tall figure with his back towards her. He was wearing a white shirt and had rolled the sleeves up. In the gloom she could make out a pair of strong forearms on which a flashy gold Rolex glittered. It looked like Jack. She pinched herself. That wasn't possible, he hadn't been invited. He turned round and their eyes met.

'Oh, hi, Pandora. Just thought I'd drop by and offer you my congratulations. Great party.' He glanced at the severed heads bobbing around the cauldron of boiling fat next to them. 'Christ, man,' he put on a thick Afrikaans accent, 'I thought I'd seen everything after Angola but you Brits are even worse.'

All her repressed feelings flooded back and her knees weakened with longing. He was bigger than she remembered and there were flecks of grey in his dark hair. All her senses were overwhelmed, the sight, sound and smell of him made her feel quite faint. She edged slightly closer, taking a deep breath. Umm, it was the same. She'd leap over a bridge of ice to smell that same smell.

They didn't say anything for a moment and just looked at one another. And then, before she knew what was happening, he had wrapped her in his arms and kissed her with a passion that took her breath away.

'How did you know about the party?' she asked quietly.

'Aah, I never reveal my sources.'

'I'm afraid I have to insist. If you don't I might have to threaten—'

'Well, in that case . . . I had a visit from a certain Countess of Rashleigh last week.'

'Davina? What did she want?'

'She told me that I was the hero in your novel and that you were the perfect woman for me. Despite all your peculiar habits.'

'She didn't!'

'She did. Besides, I had nothing better to do tonight so I thought I'd come along. By the way, I brought you a little something.'

He handed her a small box. She opened it. Inside lay an envelope. She glanced at him with smiling eyes and ripped it open. It contained a first-class ticket to Hawaii in her name, leaving London on the twentieth of December. She gasped with delight.

'Thought you could probably do with some sun,' said Jack blandly.

'I don't know what to say.'

'I liked your article in *Action!* about the dolphins. I thought you could take me up Diamond Head and show me them for yourself.'

'I'd love to. Jack, we must do something about Ocean Zoo, it's so cruel.'

'Um, well, I have done something.'

'What?'

'I've bought it. I'm going out on the twentieth to supervise the preliminary release. We've penned some of the ocean off and the keepers are going to start teaching the dolphins how to fend for themselves in the wild. It'll take quite a while. We're still deciding what to do about Sunny the killer whale.' He frowned to himself. 'I don't know if he'll ever be able to fend for himself, he's got sores all over his body and he's pretty sick.'

'Oh, that's dreadful.'

'Anyway, if you're free on the twentieth we'll check it out for ourselves. There's a sea horse farm out there which is doing some interesting medical research that I'd like to take a look at too. Besides, I could do with some sun, I haven't had a holiday for a year.'

Pandora squeezed his hand.

At that moment Davina rushed up to them. Her eyes were sparkling. 'Jack, I'm so glad you could make it.'

'I wouldn't have missed this,' said Jack, gesturing at some of the cauldrons that were cooking various bits of body. Every now and then there was an ear-piercing scream and a severed limb would be ejected into the air only to be swallowed up once more. 'Nice place for a party.'

'I'm from *How're Ya Doin'?* magazine,' a little man had crept up to them, 'and I'd just like to take a couple of photos of the glamorous authorette and her beau next to Anne Boleyn being executed, if you don't mind.'

'Davina, I want you, Georgie and Dad in it too. Dad, come on, it's time for another photo opportunity.'

James staggered over, groaning.

'Cheer up, Dad. This is Jack, the chap who runs Dudley Enterprises. He owns one of those beautiful houses on the beach in Hawaii next to the hotel that you and Davina like to walk past every day.'

James shook Jack's hand warmly. 'I read about your takeover of Palm Industries in the *FT*. Well done, you got it for a good price. They used to be one of my competitors before I sold my business. Bunch of complete sharks, good to see them shafted.' Both men laughed. 'Talking of Hawaii,' James continued to Pandora, 'are you all set to fly out on the eighteenth?'

'Um, actually, Dad, I've kind of had another offer. Jack's asked me to stay with him. He's just bought Ocean Zoo and he wants me to write an article about it.' She glanced at Jack who was laughing about something with Davina. 'Of course, if you'd rather I stayed with you and Davina considering it's Christmas, I'll tell him I can't go.'

'No, don't do that,' said James hurriedly. 'It'll save me a fortune!' But he looked a little sad.

'Well, you always said you thought it was about time someone else forked out for my holidays.'

'True. You're serious about him then?'

'I guess so. But I'm not going to rush off and elope with him or anything ridiculous.' She gave a strange, high-pitched laugh. 'Besides, after Christmas I'm going to Israel for four months to research my next novel.'

'Are you? Well, just be careful, I'd hang on to him. He's obviously worth a few bob.'

Annabel rushed over, handcuffed to Sven. 'Ooh, look, we've been clamped, isn't it heavenly!' she whispered to Pandora, glancing around. 'Hey, there's Jack! Right next to you. Did you know?' She turned back but Pandora had disappeared. 'Pandora? Pandora!' She caught Davina's eye. 'Where on earth has she gone? She was here a minute ago.' But Davina who had eyes in the back of her head looked vague and gave a small sphinx-like smile.

'No, I can't!' Pandora was saying to Jack in one of the trysting places out of sight of her guests. 'I'm going to Israel for four months, it's all planned. I'm going to write an epic love story set in the Negev Desert. I can't just drop everything and spend six months in Hawaii with you!'

'What's it going to be about? A couple of rocks that fall in love? Gives new meaning to the phrase "getting your rocks off", I suppose.' Pandora smiled, stroking his wrist with a light finger. 'Stay with me in Hawaii, Pandora. I need you to give me a hand with Ocean World,' Jack continued persuasively. 'And dolphins and sea horses are a hell of a lot more interesting to write about than rocks.' But Pandora had darted off into the darkness.

'Pandora,' called Jack. 'If you don't come back this minute I'll—'

'Do what?' replied Pandora, reappearing just out of his reach.

'Give you a good thrashing!'

'You'll have to catch me first,' and she scooted off, a bright smile illuminating the darkness, careering straight into Davina who had come looking for her.

'Darling, there you are! Your father is taking us all to Annabel's. Would you and Jack like to come along?'

Jack reappeared, resting his hand proprietorially on Pandora's neck. She shivered blissfully, melting into his heavy grip. 'Um, that's up to Jack . . .'

Going Too Far

Catherine Alliott

*From the bestselling author of The Old Girl Network;
'[An] addictive cocktail of wit, frivolity and madcap
romance' Time Out*

*'You've gone all fat and complacent because you've got
your man, haven't you?'*

There are some things only your best friend can tell
you but this outrageous suggestion is met with indig-
nation from Polly Penhalligan, who is recently
married, trying for a baby and blissfully happy in her
beautiful manor farmhouse in Cornwall. At least, she
was, until Pippa's unfortunate remark forces her to
realise that her idyllic life of gorging on chocolate
biscuits, counting her seemingly endless blessings
and not getting dressed until lunchtime could be
having a few unwelcome side-effects.

So Polly decides to razz things up a bit – and agrees
to allow her home to be used as a location for a commercial. Having a glamorous film crew around
should certainly put something of a bomb under rural
life, shouldn't it? But even before the cameras are set
up and the stars released from their kennels, Polly's
life and marriage have been turned upside down.
This time, it seems, she's gone too far . . .

0 7472 4607 6

HEADLINE

Splash

Val Corbett, Joyce Hopkirk, Eve Pollard

'Bold, bubbly and deliciously bitchy. From three women who have seen and probably done it all'
Michael Dobbs, author of *House of Cards*

Katya, Liz and Joanna have been friends for years; closer even than sisters, they have always shared everything – except men. They have always supported each other on their way to the best jobs in a world dominated by men, acquiring the trappings and luxuries of authority that are the envy of other women. Nothing could drive them apart – or could it?

Now they're coping with new pressures. Katya is breaking all her own rules, for her new lover is married and she won't tell even her closest friends who it is. As the Television News Personality of the Year, Katya is a front page story waiting to happen – and the news, much more sensational than mere adultery, is beginning to break. It's just the story Liz needs for Page One to clinch her appointment as first woman editor of a British national daily newspaper. Their friend Joanna, editor of a glossy women's magazine, argues no story is worth destroying a friendship for – but how can Liz resist the splash of the year?

SPLASH is the story of power struggles between men and women, of unexpected love and the hurt of betrayal. Above all, it is the story of a friendship. No woman who has ever had – or been – a friend should miss it.

0 7472 4889 3

HEADLINE

A selection of bestsellers from Headline

LIVERPOOL LAMPLIGHT	Lyn Andrews	£5.99	☐
A MERSEY DUET	Anne Baker	£5.99	☐
THE SATURDAY GIRL	Tessa Barclay	£5.99	☐
DOWN MILLDYKE WAY	Harry Bowling	£5.99	☐
PORTHELLIS	Gloria Cook	£5.99	☐
A TIME FOR US	Josephine Cox	£5.99	☐
YESTERDAY'S FRIENDS	Pamela Evans	£5.99	☐
RETURN TO MOONDANCE	Anne Goring	£5.99	☐
SWEET ROSIE O'GRADY	Joan Jonker	£5.99	☐
THE SILENT WAR	Victor Pemberton	£5.99	☐
KITTY RAINBOW	Wendy Robertson	£5.99	☐
ELLIE OF ELMLEIGH SQUARE	Dee Williams	£5.99	☐

All Headline books are available at your local bookshop or newsagent, or can be ordered direct from the publisher. Just tick the titles you want and fill in the form below. Prices and availability subject to change without notice.

Headline Book Publishing, Cash Sales Department, Bookpoint, 39 Milton Park, Abingdon, OXON, OX14 4TD, UK. If you have a credit card you may order by telephone – 01235 400400.

Please enclose a cheque or postal order made payable to Bookpoint Ltd to the value of the cover price and allow the following for postage and packing:

UK & BFPO: £1.00 for the first book, 50p for the second book and 30p for each additional book ordered up to a maximum charge of £3.00.
OVERSEAS & EIRE: £2.00 for the first book, £1.00 for the second book and 50p for each additional book.

Name ....

Address ....

....

....

If you would prefer to pay by credit card, please complete:
Please debit my Visa/Access/Diner's Card/American Express (delete as applicable) card no:

Signature .... Expiry Date ....